the

QUEEN

and the

CURE

New York Times Bestselling Author

AMY HARMON

Copyright © 2017 by Amy Harmon
Editing by Karey White
Cover Design by Hang Le
Map Design by Maxime Plasse

Library of Congress Cataloging-in-Publication Data

Harmon, Amy
The Queen and the Cure (The Bird and the Sword Chronicles) — 1st edition
ISBN-13: 978-1545391778 | ISBN-10: 1545391777

PRONUNCIATION GUIDE

Aren – AIR uhn

Ariel – AH ree el

Bin Dar – BIN Dahr

Brisson – BRI suhn

Caarn – CAHRN

Corvar – COHR vahr

Corvyn – COHR vin

Degn – dayn

Dendar – DEN dahr

Enoch – EE nuhk

Firi – FEAR ee

Isak – EYE zuk

Janda – JAHN duh

Jeru – JEH roo

Jerick – JEH rik

Jedah – JAY duh

Jeruvian – jeh ROO vee un

Jyraen – jeh RAE un

Kjell – Kel

Kilmorda – Kil MOHR duh

Koorah – KOOR uh

Lark – Lahrk

Lucian – LOO shun

Meshara – Meh SHAH ruh

Padrig – PA drig

Quondoon – qwahn DOON

Saoirse – SEER shuh

Solemn – SAW lem

Sasha – SAW shuh

Tiras – TEER us

Volgar – VOLH gahr

Zoltev – ZOHL tehv

In that day shall he swear, saying,

I will not be a healer.

Make me not a ruler of the people.

Isaiah 3:7

PROLOGUE

Light glanced off of the empty throne and streaked across the wide room, peeking around corners and climbing the walls. Silence was the only occupant. Something fluttered overhead, breaking the stillness. Vines with leaves so emerald they appeared black in the shadows, wrapped their way around the rocks and past the windows, filtering the light and casting the interior in a wash of green. The castle was holding her breath. She'd been holding her breath for so long.

There were no animals inside the castle walls—maybe a small mouse or a bird in the forest of trees—but no grazing cattle or galloping horses. No dogs barked, no lazy cats sunned themselves on the rock walls. No pigs in the sty or chickens in the coops. Nothing that required care, nothing that needed tending to. But the spiders had been busy. Webs clung and quivered, draped over the portraits and the sconces on the walls, swinging from the chandeliers and tapestries, creating an illusion of lace on every surface. Goblets and silver saucers were set upon the long banquet table, the platters and bowls filled with empty expectations making a long, neat row down the center.

Beyond the castle yard, rows of trees, one beside the other, the branches intertwining and their trunks pressed together like lovers in the dark, stretched in an impenetrable ring around the castle, a forest of silent watchers, living but lost in timelessness. Trees of every kind, interspersed and interwoven, created a dense wall encircling the castle. Some trees grew only as high as a tall man while others soared into the sky, their trunks wider than a circle of six maidens with their hands joined in a May Day dance. Upon closer inspection, some of the trees had faces, a series of hollows and rises that gave each one personality and character. One had the look of a dozing giant, one the appearance of a child at play.

The trees were not aware of the passing of days or the turn of the seasons. They simply slept, locked inside where nothing could touch them or take them away. No one had thought to wake them and tell them the terror had passed.

ONE

"Everything has an origin story. Every place. Every person. We come from the womb of a woman, who came from the womb of a woman, who came from the womb of a woman. We inherit gifts and weakness, we are born in triumph and strife, we are swaddled in kindness or indifference, and we are made to learn and walk among others who have their own origin stories, their own burdens, and their own history."

Sasha's voice was low and lilting as she bathed the feverish head of her aging master, telling her stories that calmed and comforted, distracting the old woman from her pain and her fear. Death hovered around the small stone house, scratching at the door, peeping through the windows, impatient to make its claim.

"What is your origin story, Sasha?" the old woman pleaded, a question she'd asked a hundred times.

"I don't know mine, Mistress Mina," Sasha soothed.

"You must go and find it," the old woman insisted weakly.

"Go where?" Sasha asked patiently. The conversation had become almost a ritual.

"Your gift will lead you."

"Why do you insist on calling it a gift?" Sasha pressed.

Mina sighed heavily. "You know why. You know the legend. Tell me the story again."

Sasha did not sigh, though the story that filled her head was one she'd told so many times it seemed rote and tired, devoid of magic or truth, though her mistress insisted it was the origin story of all mankind, even Sasha.

"With words, God created worlds," Sasha began, and the old woman relaxed, her eyeballs quivering, seeing the story behind her lids. Sasha spoke softly, soothingly, but felt little solace herself. "With words, He created light and dark, water and air, plants and trees, birds and beasts, and from the dust and the dirt of those worlds, He created children, two sons and two daughters, forming them in his image and breathing life into their bodies of clay," she recited obediently.

"That's right," Mina murmured, nodding. "You tell the story so well. Tell me more."

"In the beginning, the Creator gave each child a word, a powerful word, which called down a special ability, a precious gift to guide them in their journey through their world. One son was given the word *change,* which gifted him the ability to transform himself into the beasts of the forest or the creatures of the air. One daughter was given the word *spin*, for she could spin all manner of things into gold. The grass, the leaves, a strand of her hair. The word *heal* was given to another son, to cure illness and injury among his brothers and sisters. Another daughter was given the word *tell*, and she could predict what was to come. Some said she could even shape the future with the power of her words.

"The Spinner, the Changer, the Healer, and the Teller lived long and had many children of their own, but even with blessed words and magnificent abilities, life in the world was dangerous and difficult. Oftentimes, grass was more useful than gold. Man was more desirable than a beast. Chance was more seductive than knowledge, and eternal life was completely meaningless without love."

"Completely meaningless." the old woman repeated, and began to weep, as if the ancient account underscored her own life. But instead of urging the younger woman to continue with the retelling, she picked up the story on her own, weakly tiptoeing through the tale, touching on the parts that meant the most to her.

When the old one's voice finally trailed off, her tears drying on her cheeks, Sasha rose and emptied the basin of lukewarm water outside of the earthen hut, pulling the thick flaps over the opening and leaving the ties loose so she could return quickly if the old woman cried out.

But the origin story continued on in her head—the Changer, the Spinner, the Healer, and the Teller, and the children that came after them. Hundreds of years. Generation upon generation, gifts celebrated and revered, then squandered and abused, and finally buried and denied as the only Gifted who remained became hated and hissed at. One by one, the Tellers, the Healers, the Changers, and the Spinners were destroyed. The forces of the king cut off the Spinners' hands. They burned the Tellers at the stake. They hunted the Changers like the animals they resembled and stoned the Healers in the village squares, until those with special gifts—any gift—were afraid of their abilities and hid their talents from each other.

The village of Solemn was quiet, the air scorched of light or life, the heat of the day slumbering with the stricken hamlet. A sob suddenly pierced the air, and Sasha braced herself for the name that rose on the scream. It came, the identification making her lips tremble and her eyes smart. Another child had died. Edwin. The little boy with the bent leg.

The weakest were being taken first.

Sasha moved away from the rows of huts and the more state-ly structures of the elders, working her way on weary legs toward the water that flowed through the canyons. It wasn't as close as the river that came from the east, but she didn't think it would make her sick the way the water from the east had made Mina sick. When Mina had started to decline, Sasha had gone to the kindest of the elders, Mina's brother, and told him to warn the people not to drink the water, that the water carried something dark. He counseled with the other elders. None of them were ill, and they'd been drinking from the eastern river for a long time. They said she was mad and she would frighten the people. They told her to hold her tongue or she would lose it.

Not long ago, there had been a great battle in the land of Je-ru. Wrongs righted. Oppression lifted. But little had changed in the villages of Quondoon. The merchants came to Solemn from Jeru City bearing wares and tales, and Sasha's master had sat with the elders, hearing the stories of the powerful King Tiras who could fly like a bird and who had done away with the old laws. Now the Gifted were free to roam and do their worst, the elders said, though no one had ever seen a Spinner or a Healer in Solemn. There were Changers in Doha, the village nearest them —an old man and a child, though they could only partially change, sprouting wings or powerful haunches at will, but unable to completely transform. Sasha had never seen them, but the elders were dismissive, laughing at the oddity, claiming it more a curse than a gift. The merchants brought more talk from Bin Dar —the land to the north—of great birdmen who made nests and ate human flesh, but no one from Solemn had seen them either. Sasha was not a Changer, a Spinner, a Healer, or a Teller. She was something else entirely. No one talked about Sasha, but their silence did not equate to safety, and Sasha had no confidence in a king so far away or laws that were supposed to protect everyone. Even slaves.

He had a face that she wouldn't forget and one she couldn't remember. She shouldn't have been able to see him so clearly. It was night and he hovered above her, shadowed beneath a half-eaten moon. His eyes were like the sea, blue but not untroubled, and his mouth was her anchor, making promises that kept her from floating away. His hands were gentle, his words were rough, and when he asked her to come with him, she did, rising from her body and becoming someone new.

But they still found her.

Figures moved in and out of the mist, shifting and searching. People screamed and shadows flew through the air, diving and swooping. She hid, flattened against the ground, her face in the dirt. She tried to draw breath but choked and coughed as she breathed in bits of earth. She covered her face with her scarf to strain the air and crawled forward. There was no sound. She tried to shout and felt the shape of his name on her lips, a word she couldn't hear. A word she didn't know.

Whop, whop, whop.

The sound echoed in her head and her chest, and the world of hidden figures and flying death whirled away as the beating grew louder.

She'd fallen asleep too close to the fire.

Again.

Her hair and face would be streaked with soot, and she'd drawn ash into her lungs. The house was too hot for a fire, but she hadn't been able to keep Mina warm, and the coals were slower to die than the old woman had been. Her heart was pounding and her throat was raw. The slapping sound became sharper, heavier, and it left her head and shook the air with the sound of a thousand wings.

"Sasha! Let me in. Untie the flaps."

7

Sasha rubbed at her eyes and rose unsteadily to her feet, drunk on the old dream. She was weary and her cheeks burned. She'd been too many days at her master's bedside, tending the old woman until, like the dream, Mina had drifted away. She'd mourned alone, setting up a call into the night that had been met with moans and little more. Mina's brother had come with the elders only hours before. They had taken the body of her master away and left her behind.

"Sasha! Let me in!"

"Maeve! You'll wake the whole village," she warned, stumbling to the door and unknotting the ties with weary hands. The girl, small and dark like many of the people of Quondoon, tumbled through the opening and fell into Sasha's arms.

"Sasha. Run. Go now! They're coming for you," Maeve gasped. "Mina can't protect you anymore. They're coming. I heard them. They're scared, and they blame you."

"For what?" Sasha cried. But she knew. Maeve knew too, and didn't waste time with unnecessary words, grabbing at her hand and pulling her forward.

"Where will I go?

"You're free. Go wherever you wish."

"But this is my home."

"Not anymore. Mina is dead. And you soon will be if you don't leave now!"

"I'm not properly dressed." Sasha reached frantically for her head covering, needing to shield her pale skin and her bright hair. Her shoes were outside the door.

"You've no time!"

Then Sasha heard it. Felt it. And she recognized it. She'd seen this moment. The sensation of loss and . . . relief washed over her. It had come. There was always relief when visions became truth. She didn't know why.

From far off there were shouts and cries, as if the village was under attack. But there were no pillagers on the borders, seeking entry. There were no dragons in the air, breaching the borders of the city of Solemn. The enemy was within the gates.

The crescent moon, gloating and glowing in its safety above them, made their night travels across the plain a cold pleasure. The sky was devoid of clouds and littered with shards of stars. The cliffs rose up like marooned ships, their ragged stone masts pointing at the star-filled heavens, and their horses began to descend, winding their way downward into Solemn on the far edges of Quondoon. Kjell of Jeru, Captain of the King's Guard, had only been there once before, but he remembered the simple attire of the desert dwellers, their covered heads and their quiet ways.

They'd seen no sign of the Volgar—the monstrous birdmen —in the last few days, no nests or carcasses, no stench or even stray feathers, and he wondered again at the hysterical reports in the villages on the border of Bin Dar about devastation in Solemn. But there was something in the air, and his horse, Lucian, was restless, chuffing and flighty, resisting the descent and the press forward.

It would be so much easier if he had Queen Lark's ability to command and destroy. Instead, he and an elite group of warriors had traveled through the provinces of Jeru, north to Firi and west to Bin Dar, east to Bilwick and back to Jeru City, hunting the Volgar the hard way, at the end of a blade. He'd spent the last two years on the back of his horse, destroying what was left of the winged creatures that had once laid waste to vast provinces and almost decimated an entire kingdom.

When he'd received word that there were flocks of the birdmen in the cliffs of Quondoon, he'd left Jeru City again, oddly grateful there was something to do. Tiras, his half-brother and the king of Jeru, ruled ably, finally freed from the affliction that had kept Kjell so close for so long. They'd rarely been apart since the day Tiras ascended the throne in their father's place, young and Gifted, with no one else to turn to but his illegitimate older brother. But Tiras didn't need Kjell anymore. Not in the same way.

Kjell didn't desire riches. He didn't want power or position. He'd never longed for possessions or even a place to call his own. Though he was older than his brother, he'd never wanted to be king, and he'd never envied Tiras—legitimate son and heir to the throne—who shouldered the weight of his responsibility with a calm acceptance Kjell had never mastered. Kjell had always been happiest watching his brother's back or lost in the heat of battle, and he'd always known who he was.

He hadn't been especially proud of it, but he'd known.

He was the bastard son of the late King Zoltev and the servant woman, Koorah, who'd warmed His Majesty's bed for a time. A very short time. She'd died in childbirth, and Kjell had been named by the midwife, who thought his infant cry had sounded like the scream of a Kjell Owl before it attacks.

But there was more to a man than his parentage. More to a man than his blade, or his size, or his skills, and all that Kjell had once known had shifted and changed in the last year. He'd been forced to accept parts of himself that he'd always denied. He was Gifted. One of *them*. One of the people he'd feared and forsaken. And it had not been an easy adjustment. It was as if he'd battled the sea all his life only to discover he had scales and gills and belonged beneath the depths instead of casting nets. He no longer knew who he was or what his purpose might be. Or maybe he knew and just didn't like it.

It had grown cooler as night fell. It would be hot—too hot—when the sun rose again, but Quondoon enjoyed extremes. Heat in the day and cold at night, towering peaks and flat plains, brief, punishing rains followed by long, dry spells where the rain refused to fall for months on end. The people of Quondoon were shepherds and scavengers, weavers and potters, but they didn't grow much. They couldn't. Kjell wondered again at the Volgar sightings. The Volgar preferred the swamp-lands. If the Volgar were nesting near the villages of Quondoon, they had truly grown desperate.

An eerie howling rose up suddenly from the precipice above them, and Lucian started in fright.

"Halt!" Kjell commanded, and his men obeyed immediately, hands on their swords, eyes on the canyon walls to their right, looking for the source of the sound. As they watched, figures materialized on the bluff that rose and plateaued to the right. The city of Solemn lay beyond. But these weren't suspicious sentries. These were wolves who resented the interruption of their evening's activities, and the baying rose again, making the horses shudder.

"There's something there, Captain. Something wounded—or dead. The wolves want it," a soldier spoke up, his eyes glued to the darkness that clung to the base of the tallest cliff.

"If it's Volgar, it's alone. The wolves wouldn't go anywhere near a flock," Jerick, his lieutenant, spoke up.

"It isn't Volgar," Kjell answered, but he dismounted and drew his sword. "Isak, Peter, and Gibbous, stay with the horses, the rest of you, fall in behind me."

His men obeyed immediately, creeping through the brush and dry grass toward the base of the sheer wall that jutted from the earth. The shadows obscured whatever lay crumpled—for there was indeed something there—among the pale rocks. Something rippled—a dark billowing—like a Volgar wing, and Kjell paused, bidding his men to do the same.

Oddly, the wolves felt no compunction toward silence, and a lone howl rose above them before the others joined in the chorus. The baying did not cause the shadows to shift or the rippling to halt, and Kjell moved forward again, eyes on the shuddering darkness.

With several more steps, the moon unveiled her secret. The movement they'd seen was not a Volgar wing but the billowing dress of a woman, lying in a lifeless heap. Her hair was crimson, even in the shadows, blending with the red of her blood and the warmth of the earth. She lay on her back, her eyes closed, the oval of her face as pale and still as the rocks around her. Her arms were thrown wide like she'd embraced the wind as she fell.

Her back was oddly bent and one leg twisted beneath her, but she bore no teeth or claw-marks, and her clothes weren't in tatters. It was not a Volgar attack; she'd fallen from the ledge above. Jerick was the first to close the distance and kneel at her side, touching the white skin of her throat with the impudence he usually reserved for Kjell.

"She is warm, Captain, and her heart still beats."

Kjell wasn't the only one who gasped, and the shocked intake of air echoed around him like a den of snakes, hissing through the huddled soldiers. She was so broken.

"What do you want to do?" Jerick raised his gaze to his leader, and the question was clear, though he didn't voice it. Jerick knew Kjell was a Healer. They all knew, and his men both feared and worshipped him, watching in awe as he restored the fallen and the dying with nothing more than his hands. But he'd only healed those he had affection for, those he served and who served him. And he hadn't done it often. He'd healed a few of his men. He'd healed his brother. His queen. But he'd been unable to find the power when there was no . . . love. He laughed bitterly, making the men around him shift awkwardly, and he realized the mocking chortle had escaped his lips.

"Go," he commanded abruptly. "Take Lucian and the rest of the horses and find a place nearby to wait."

No one moved, their eyes on the crumpled woman and the pool of blood that called to the wolves outlined on the cliffs above. The wolves were waiting for the soldiers to retreat and leave the girl.

"Go!" Kjell barked, sinking to his knees, knowing he'd wasted time when there was none. The soldiers rushed to withdraw, wary as the wolves, obeying their captain, but unhappy about doing so. Jerick didn't leave, but Kjell had known he wouldn't.

"I can't do this while you watch," Kjell admitted brusquely. "It makes me too aware of myself."

"I've seen you heal before, Captain."

"Yes. But not like this. I don't know her." Kjell placed his hands on the woman's chest and felt the warmth of her heart, willful even as her body begged to be released from its torment. He listened for her song. For the single, clear note that would aid him. Her spirit, her force, her *self.*

"Imagine that you do," Jerick urged softly. "Imagine her . . . full of life. Running. Smiling. Mating."

Kjell's eyes shot to Jerick's, and his lieutenant stared back unapologetically, as if imagination was something that came easily to him and should therefore come easily to Kjell.

"*Imagine* that you love her," Jerick repeated.

Kjell scoffed, resisting the sentiment, and bowed his head. He closed his eyes against Jerick's gaze. His hands curled against the woman's breast, urging her heart to obey, and an image rose, unbidden, in his mind. A woman who smiled at him with eyes that kept no secrets and told no lies. A woman with fiery hair like the one who lay before him, alone and dying. He lashed out again, demanding that Jerick depart. She was dying and he was listening to the mutterings of a foolish knight who'd clearly been too long without a woman. *Running, smiling, mating.* Bloody fool.

"Leave me, Jerick. Now." If Jerick remained, Kjell would flog him. Jerick must have realized his captain would give no more quarter, for he turned away, and Kjell heard him depart through the brush, his stride dejected.

Kjell ran his hands over the slim ribs of the woman, feeling the jagged pieces of broken bones, and he bade them mend. He didn't pray as his hands roved. The Creator had given him this curse and this cure, and he wouldn't beg for an increase.

The woman resisted him, her slim frame stubborn in its death throes.

Kjell started to hum, purely on instinct, matching his timbre to the intermittent baying of the wolves above him. After a moment, he felt the tell-tale tingling in his hands, and his pulse surged in triumph. He commanded his body to share its light, and the shattered cage of her ribs righted beneath his touch, lifting her chest and curving outward into his broad palms. And still, he couldn't hear her song.

"Where are you, woman?" he asked her. "I feel your heart and the seeping of your blood. Sing to me so I can bring you back."

He moved his hands to her thighs, feeling the shape of her body return, the bones of her legs knitting together and notching into the curve of her hips. When her spine became a long, straight line, he rolled her to her side to run his hands over the back of her skull. It was wet with blood and soft in his hands. He swallowed back bile, surprised at his squeamishness. He had gutted men and beasts and never winced or even hesitated.

"I am a man with little imagination," he whispered, smoothing her hair. "I cannot pretend to love you. But I can heal you if you help me."

He strained, still listening for that one note that would save her life. He'd been in this position once, years before, straining to hear something he'd never heard, hardly knowing what he sought, but listening all the same. At the time it was his brother, and his wounds had been just as grievous as this woman's. Kjell had saved him. He'd healed him. But he'd also *loved* him.

Fear trembled in his belly, and the heat in his hands instantly lessened. He forced his thoughts back to his brother, to his affection, his respect, his devotion. The thought became strength, and the heat in his hands became light.

He leaned down and whispered in her ear, sing-song and coaxing.

"Can you hear me, woman? Come sing with me." The only songs he knew were bawdy and lewd, simple tunes about lifting skirts and brandishing swords.

"Come to me, and I will try to heal you. I will try to heal you, if you but come back," he chanted softly, the melody monotone, the lyrics weak, but it was a song of sorts, and it fell from his lips in a husky plea.

"Come to me, and I will give you shelter, I will give you shelter, if you but come back." His lips brushed the lobe of her ear, and he felt an odd shudder that passed from his mouth and lifted her hair. Her heartbeat strengthened as if she heard. He continued to chant, allowing hope to make him a liar.

"Come to me, and I will try to love you. I will try to love you, if you but come back."

He heard a single, solitary peal, almost inaudible. Almost imaginary. Almost gone. A bell ringing once.

But it was enough.

Kjell lifted his voice, grasping the pitch and pulling the tone from the winking stars. Suddenly the death knell became a merry tolling, clear and bright. It grew and grew, and still he hummed, until the sound resonated in his skin, in his skull, behind his eyes, and deep in his belly. He was euphoric, vibrating with sound and triumph, his hands smoothing back the matted hair from blood-stained cheeks and staring down into eyes so dark they appeared infinite. Their gazes locked and for a moment, there was only reverberation between them.

"I saw you," she whispered, the bell becoming words, and Kjell drew back, releasing his grip on her hair, the song in his throat becoming shocked silence. He clenched his hands and felt her blood on his palms.

"I saw you," she said again. "You're here. You finally came."

TWO

er words were senseless. He'd healed her body but her mind was something he couldn't touch. Kjell sat back on his haunches, putting a few feet between them.

"Are you . . . all right?" he asked. He wanted to ask if she was whole—healed—but didn't want to draw any more attention to what he'd just done. His gift frightened people. It frightened him. She began to raise herself up gingerly, and he extended his hand to assist her. She didn't take it, but paused, sitting silently as if listening to her body. He needed to stand. His knees were numb, and his hips screamed from kneeling so long at her side. His head felt light and disconnected from the rest of his body, as if it floated above him like a cloud, thick and weightless, his thoughts muddled with fatigue.

His hands trembling, he pushed himself up, demanding that his cramped legs hold him. The healing had left him bled out, depleted, and he didn't want his men—or the woman who watched him with hollow eyes—to see the after-effects of using his gift. They couldn't know. Such knowledge was noted and tucked away, a secret to be traded among warring tribes and plotting men. He was not loved like his brother and had never inspired a similar loyalty. But he was feared like his father, and that suited him well enough.

The woman rose with him, defying the blood that still soaked the earth where she had lain. She was taller than he expected—long and slim—saving him from getting a crick in his neck to look into her face. Her hair was unbound and fell in matted disarray past the swell of her hips. Her thin dress, little more than a gown for sleeping, stuck to her skin in gory splotches. Her feet were shod in the short leather boots of a desert dweller, as if she'd left her home in a hurry, prioritizing shoes over her clothing.

"What is your name?" he asked. She hesitated, and he suspected that she was going to lie to him. He was well-accustomed to women who lied, and immediately braced himself not to believe her.

"I am called Sasha," she supplied reluctantly, and his brows rose in disbelief.

It was hardly a name. It was a command used on horses or cattle—often accompanied by a kick to the flanks or a slap to the rump—to get them to move. He hissed the word several times a day, and wondered who had given the poor woman her moniker.

"And where is your home, Sasha?" He winced as he addressed her.

She turned toward the cliff that loomed above them, steep walls and jagged teeth, unwelcoming in the flickering torch-light.

"I live in Solemn, but it was never my home." There was grief in the simple revelation, and he braced himself against it. He did not want to know her pain. He'd done what he could for her. Some pain was not within his power to ease. She said no more, but continued staring at the cliffs, as if her life had truly ended there, and she didn't know what came next. She took a few steps toward the cliff wall, and he stepped aside, following her with his eyes. His gaze caught on a white cloth caught by the brush that grew in the cracks and crags about twenty feet from the base of the cliff. The woman—Sasha—moved toward it as if it belonged to her and scrambled up several feet before he realized she had every intention of scaling the wall to reach it.

"Come down. I won't heal you twice."

She bowed her head briefly, as if she knew she should listen, but then continued, scurrying upward several more feet and untangling the pale fabric from the branch while clinging to the wall with curled toes and one hand.

"It is mine," she informed him—slightly breathless—when she stood in front of him once more. She wrapped the cloth carefully over her blood soaked hair and secured the edges around her waist. She was calm and composed, and her serenity made him wary. He'd healed her body, but a physical healing didn't erase her memory or alter her experience. She had fallen. She had teetered between life and death. Yet she did not cry or tremble. She didn't ask him questions or seek to understand—or explain—what had happened.

"There is a stream in the crevice between the cliffs. I will show you and your men," she said.

"How did you know I was not alone?" he asked.

"I saw you," she replied, repeating the first words she'd said, and his stomach shivered uncomfortably at her insistence. She'd been unconscious when they found her.

He whistled sharply, the sound piercing the darkness, sending a signal to his men. He waited, his eyes on the strange woman, until Jerick and several other men stepped out from the shadows and halted with stunned curses. A lance clattered against the ground.

"The woman knows where there is water. We'll stay here for the night," Kjell directed. "Gather the others and bring me my horse."

"And Solemn?" Jerick asked, recovering quickly, as if he'd never doubted his captain's ability.

The woman jerked like the word was a whip against her flesh.

"Tomorrow," Kjell answered, and her eyes shot to his. "We'll go tomorrow. When it's light."

Sasha was curled nearby, Kjell's cloak tucked around her, the length of cloth she'd reclaimed from the cliff folded beneath her fiery hair. He could now see that the cloth was the palest blue, shot with streaks of white, like the sun had bleached it unevenly. When he'd fallen asleep, she was still huddled near the fire in his cloak, her simple, dark blue gown spread out to dry nearby. She'd clearly found him in the dark and lain beside him. She was closer to his feet than his face, but near enough that he would have stumbled over her had he risen before dawn. He didn't know what to make of her proximity beyond the obvious: If he'd healed her, she had value to him. If he valued her, she was safer with him than with anyone else.

In the gathering light, the copper flecks on her skin were bolder, reflecting the warmth of her hair. The blood had left her dress stained in darker patches, but she was relatively clean, her hair free of gore and glorious in the yawning rays that stole across the plains from the east and collided with the crags. She'd been right about the water—a stream tumbled from a crevice and collected in a gulley between two jagged walls—and she'd lead them through a narrow canyon only minutes from where they'd found her. She'd waited until the men had filled their bellies and their carafes before kneeling beside the pool and rinsing her matted hair and soot-streaked skin. Her blood-soaked gown was another matter, and Kjell had left her with his cloak and a wedge of soap, withdrawing to a small clearing nearby with his men.

He found himself hoping she would slip away, back to the life she'd almost lost. But she didn't. When she approached him, wrapped in his cloak, her hair dripping, holding her wet dress, he'd given her food and directed her to sit. He'd asked Isak—a soldier with a gift for fire—to start a blaze, and she huddled beside it, her head resting on her drawn-up knees. His men moved around her cautiously, keeping their distance and their own company, their wonder making them reticent, but he found them staring at him as often as they stared at her.

There was awe and more than a little fear in the looks they cast his way. They knew what he'd done, but they still couldn't believe it. They'd seen him mend a bloody gash or a broken bone, but they'd also watched soldiers die in his care—gone before he could do anything for them but return their bodies to their families or bury them on a battlefield. All of his men had withstood the attack on Jeru City—though few had witnessed his singular part in it. But they'd all witnessed this woman—bloodied and lifeless—made whole once again.

Their awe made Kjell grind his teeth and snap at anyone who looked at him for too long. His head ached dully and the tips of his fingers were numb from holding on to his temper. He ate with purpose and no pleasure, attempting to restore his energy and plug the slow drip of patience from his chest. Unable to do either, he immediately retired far from the fire and his men's itchy reverence, barking at Jerick when he tried to follow.

"Make sure the woman is given what she needs and none of what she doesn't, and leave me alone."

"Yes, Captain," Jerick agreed, falling back instantly.

Kjell tossed his pallet to the ground and, without even removing his boots, fell onto it and into a sleep as deep and dark as Sasha's eyes.

Now morning had come, and he watched her, wondering if those eyes were as dark as he remembered. When she opened them suddenly, coming awake like she was accustomed to fearful slumber, he saw they were exactly that dark. They disturbed him, the pupils indistinguishable from the surrounding hue. He'd seen skin like hers—pale and speckled like a sparrow's egg, but never in combination with eyes so black. She stretched, shuddering a little as she did, her body shaking off the vestiges of sleep.

She'd caught him looking at her—staring—and it embarrassed him. He was not accustomed to feeling uncomfortable, especially not in the presence of someone who meant nothing to him, and he rose to his feet, shaking the dust from his clothes and rolling his pallet tightly, securing it with twine. After a moment, she rose as well, shrugging off his cloak and handing it to him. He took it without comment. The sun was already heating the earth and would be relentless before long. He watched from the corner of his eye as she wrapped the pale blue cloth over her hair, creating a cowl that shaded her face. She crossed the long ends of the cloth over her chest and tied them at her waist to keep them from catching the breeze.

"There is sickness in Solemn," she murmured—startling him further—her voice oddly sweet yet still rough with sleep. "There is sickness there and you are a Healer."

"What kind of sickness?" he asked.

"Fever. Delirium. The hair falls from the heads of the very young and the very old. The children aren't growing. Some are malformed."

"Is that why you fell? Were you sick?"

"No," she murmured, and he realized he didn't know which question she answered. "I was not sick, but my master was."

"Your master?"

"I was a . . . slave."

"Why were you a slave?" he asked. She frowned and her brows furrowed slightly. He wanted to know the circumstances of her servitude, but she didn't seem to understand.

"Why are you a Healer?" she retorted, as if healing and slavery were similar. He snorted, struck by the comparison, but she did not explain herself further. Instead, she took several hesitant steps toward him, her hands folded demurely. Without warning, she dropped to her knees, her eyes on the ground. Then she leaned forward and touched her forehead to the dirt, inches from his feet. Her hair pooled around her like a shroud. "My master is dead. You healed me. I belong to you now."

He drew her to her feet, his hands wrapped around her thin arms, and set her away from him adamantly, shaking his head.

"No. You do not. I healed you of my own free will. I lay no claim."

"I will stay with you."

"No! You will not." His voice was harsh and far too loud, and he noted with chagrin the interest of the men around them who were no longer sleeping. One of them laughed, though he smothered it. Kjell glowered, and they were immediately busy with their boots and bedrolls.

Sasha kept her head bowed, her veil hiding her face. Satisfied that she had heard him and that she would obey, Kjell stepped away.

She followed.

He climbed to the water between the rocks, and she moved silently behind him, far enough that she wouldn't bump into him if he stopped suddenly, but close enough to make him bristle with annoyance. His bladder was full and his temper was short, and he needed her to give him some solitude. She seemed attuned to this, and moved away from him suddenly, behind an outcropping, and he did the same, finding a moment's privacy before she rejoined him at the waterfall.

He cleaned his teeth and washed his face, his arms, and his neck, scraping the beard from his cheeks with his blade, growling at her when she offered to do it for him. He gave her his soap and his tooth powder, and she thanked him humbly, making quick work of her own ablutions, weaving her long hair into a rope and rewrapping the cloth over it again.

"Will you go to Solemn?" she asked as they made their way back to the men and the horses.

"That is why we came."

"You came . . . for Solemn? You are the forces of the king. I thought the forces of the king hunted the Gifted."

"The king *is* Gifted." Not to mention the king's brother. "I am hunting Volgar."

"The birdmen?" she asked, clearly surprised. "There are no Volgar here."

"None?" He stopped and stared down at her, disbelieving. "There are rumors of great devastation in Solemn."

"The only devastation in Solemn is sickness." She stared up at him soberly.

Kjell groaned. The Creator save him from his gift. He wanted to kill birdmen. Not play nursemaid. If there was illness in Solemn, he would put his men at risk. If he exposed them to sickness, they would only take the disease to other parts of the kingdom, to other lands in Jeru. He could not raise the dead, and he could not heal an entire village. The very thought made his heart cease and his knees tremble.

"You cannot heal them all," she said quietly, divining his thoughts. "But you could heal some."

He doubted he could heal even one. "I cannot bring my men to a village stricken with disease."

She nodded hesitantly, but she did not drop her gaze. "I . . . understand . . . but I do not believe they would become sick."

"Why?"

"Because the sickness is not in the air."

He waited, his hands on his hips, wanting to mount his horse and ride away, but his guilt compelled him to listen.

"I believe the disease is in the water that comes into the village from the east. If your men will fill their carafes here, wash themselves here, and stay away from the water from the eastern stream, they should be fine. Some people seem resistant to it. The strong and those in their middle years are less affected. Or maybe it is just slower to grow in them. But many people are sick."

"So if I heal them . . . they will grow sick again," he surmised. "Because they have to drink to live, and this little brook is not enough to support a village." He tossed his hand toward the stream that wasn't much more than a steady trickle collecting in a shallow pool before it continued on its way between the rocks.

"If you heal enough of them, maybe they will be well enough to leave."

Kjell cursed, running his hand through the hair that brushed at his shoulders. Images of traveling back to Jeru with a thousand refugees straggling behind him made him grind his palms into his eyes to obliterate the thought.

"Why haven't they left already? The villages to the north bear no signs of sickness. I've come through every village between here and Bin Dar."

"The people don't believe me. They don't believe there is sickness in the water. I need to convince them. But I cannot go back to Solemn alone," she said, her voice low.

"Why is that?"

"They drove me from them."

"Drove you . . . from them," he repeated flatly.

"Over the cliff," she explained.

"They forced you over the cliff?" Anger lit his voice, though it was not directed at her. Still, there would be a reason for such actions, even if it sickened him. "Why?"

"I saw it. I saw them drinking the water. And I saw them growing sick. I told the elders." Her words from the night before took on new meaning.

"You *saw* it?"

"I see many things."

"Are you Gifted?" he asked quietly.

"I cannot heal." She shook her head as if his was the only true gift. It was not an answer, and his mouth hardened at the evasion.

"Are you Gifted?" he repeated more forcefully.

"I cannot heal . . . but sometimes I can save," she amended. "I have learned that if I remain silent about what I see, it always comes to pass. Sometimes, even when I'm *not* silent, what I see comes to pass, and I can only brace myself. But there have been times when I've been able to . . . move people from the path of the storm."

"You couldn't save yourself from being run over a cliff?"

"No," she whispered, and her eyes grew bright, black pools that shimmered with tears. She blinked rapidly. Then her gaze became distant, and she lifted her chin, letting the light caress her cheeks and the breeze tug at the tendrils of hair peeking out beneath her veil. He watched as several emotions flitted over her face before her features relaxed and her gaze sharpened on his once more.

"They know you are here."

"Who?" he asked, bewildered. He was still caught in the memory of her broken body beneath the cliffs, struck by the changing expressions on her face, and distracted by the fire of her hair.

"They are coming. The elders of Solemn. They want to trade with you."

"Trade? We are soldiers. Not peddlers. We have little beyond our weapons and horses, and those are not for sale."

"Not trade," she shook her head, modifying her statement, speaking slowly as if trying to unravel something she didn't completely understand. "They have . . . offerings. The night watch must have reported your presence."

"Why do they bring gifts?"

"I cannot see everything." She shook her head again. "Intentions are especially difficult. Maybe they know you are the King's Guard, and want to bring you presents in exchange for your favor. Perhaps they are afraid you know of the sickness, and that you will take advantage while they are weak."

A whistle pierced the air, signaling to Kjell, verifying Sasha's prediction. Kjell abandoned his questions and started down the hill to the clearing, but Sasha descended more slowly, tucking herself behind the soldiers scrambling to ready themselves before the visitors arrived. Kjell mounted Lucian, desirous to be in a position of authority, even if there was no threat. In the near distance, winding down the mountainous pass, six men approached, not on horses, but on great, lumbering camels with lashes that curled above their enormous nostrils. The elders were dressed in pale robes and, like Sasha, their heads were covered, protected from the sun. They came to a stop with a wide gulf still dividing them from Kjell and his men.

"I am Kjell of Jeru," Kjell greeted, his voice raised to be heard. "Captain of the King's Guard. We are here in search of Volgar. We are here only to serve. Not to condemn or . . . collect." There'd been a time when the King's Guard had accompanied the tax collectors as well. Thankfully, those days were a thing of the past. The provinces sent money to the kingdom of

Jeru for the support of the guard and the protection of the realm. Collecting it was now a duty of the lord of each province.

The bearded man in the center of the group, his face as thin and dark as the trees that grew in the Drue Forest, responded, "We have heard of you, Kjell of Jeru. You are the king's brother."

Kjell would not deny his relationship, but he also refused to feel any pride in his status. The blood that connected him to the king was not blood he was proud of. He also wasn't certain being notorious was a good thing. His past was not especially pristine. He simply waited without confirmation for the man to continue.

"Greetings to you and your men. I am Syed. We've brought gifts for His Majesty and ask that you extend our fealty to him when you return to Jeru City." The suggestion was veiled, but Kjell did not miss it. The elders had ridden out of the village to head them off. It would be greatly appreciated if the King's Guard would continue on, never entering Solemn.

It was entirely the wrong move. Kjell hated to be told what to do.

"That is very gracious, Syed. But we don't need gifts. A meal, a bath, and maybe a day's rest is all we require. Our horses could stand the rest and food as well. Then we will be on our way. Can your village accommodate us?" Kjell's voice was mild but his eyes were shrewd, testing his audience. So far, everything Sasha had said was proving true.

The bearded man stiffened, and the men around him squirmed, exchanging weighted glances.

"There is . . . trouble in our village," Syed hedged. "Some of our people are sick. It would be wise for you to pass by."

"Our captain is a skilled Healer," Jerick spoke up. "He healed one of your women last night. She'd fallen and was near death. Perhaps he can bring relief to your village." Jerick's voice rang with a sincerity few would sense was false. Kjell would have silenced him—violently—had it not served his purposes. Clearly Sasha had confessed something of her story to Jerick the night before.

"Sasha!" Kjell called to the woman who hid herself behind his men. "Come forward, woman. Show them you are well. They must have been concerned when you didn't return last night. The wolves were out." He felt his men shift and part, but didn't turn his head. He heard Sasha come forward and saw her presence noted on the faces of the elders of Solemn before him.

One of the six, a white-haired man with great jowls, drooping eyes, and a sorrowful air, spotted Sasha and gasped visibly, his chest lifting beneath his yellow robe, his hands tightening on his reins. The animal he rode felt his tension and backed up obediently. The man wanted to bolt, and he wasn't the only one.

"She is a witch," a fat elder jeered. "She has lived among us for three summers. She brought evil with her. Fires and floods. Pestilence and disease. We ran her out at the end of our spears, but she flew from us."

Kjell regarded him darkly, seeing the crumpled body of the woman in his mind's eye, her body broken and bleeding. She had not *flown*. If she could have flown, Kjell would not have had to heal her bones and sing her spirit back to her flesh.

"It is against the laws of Jeru to harm the Gifted," he rebuked.

"She made our people sick. She will make your men sick too. Your horses will die, and your bones will turn white on the plains of Quondoon. Now she sits among you, and you will suffer like we did." This from Syed, his eyes dancing between Kjell and Sasha, who stood before the elders, inexplicably alive and well. She said nothing to defend herself—she didn't speak at all —and Kjell followed her lead. He'd learned there was little that could be said to change a mind. Especially the minds of those so convinced of a woman's guilt they would run her off a cliff as punishment for her crimes. He would let her decide the fate of those who had condemned her. It was something King Tiras would have done.

"What should we do, woman? Do the people of Solemn deserve healing?" he asked, his hand on his sword, his eyes on the men who wished him gone. So be it. He *wanted* to go. He would leave the village in their misery.

"All people deserve healing," Sasha answered immediately, and Kjell's heart sank in his chest. The man on the right, the man with the sagging jowls, retreated farther.

The leader of the elders raised a trembling finger and pointed it at Sasha. "You are not welcome in Solemn," he hissed.

"Prepare your people, Syed," Kjell said, dismissing him. "We're coming to Solemn." He waved the elders off, and his men closed ranks around him, swallowing him up protectively, herding the elders backward at the end of their lowered spears, quartering no further argument or conversation. Kjell waited until the elders had turned, spurring their camels back toward Solemn, their gifts rejected, their fears realized.

"Jerick, take a dozen men. Go to Solemn. Make sure the elders don't stir up trouble. I will not be far behind. And Jerick?"

"Yes, Captain?"

"You do not speak for me. Ever. I choose to heal whom I will. You volunteer that information far too freely. Do not do it again, or I will send you back to Jeru City."

"Yes, sir." Jerick's shoulders tightened defensively, but Kjell wasn't finished. "Do not drink the water in Solemn. Any of you. Drink only what is in your flasks. And wait for my arrival." Jerick's brows rose in surprise, but he nodded, turning his horse and yelling orders to the soldiers already mounted around him.

When Jerick and the first group of soldiers had departed, Kjell instructed the men who remained to fill their carafes, break camp, and prepare their horses. When they rushed to do his bidding, he dismounted and turned to the silent Sasha. She did not look at him. Her gaze was blank and fixed in the direction the elders had gone.

"You do not have to go into Solemn. I want only to see what is happening there so I can ascertain the risk. Then I will be taking my men and moving on. I have no wish to remain in Quondoon any longer than necessary. I want to fight beasts . . . not small minds."

"I do not draw evil to me," Sasha whispered, as if she hadn't heard him at all. "I do not bring pestilence or fire. I do not cause suffering. But sometimes I know when it is coming."

Kjell grimaced but didn't silence her.

"I only tried to warn. But warnings unheeded often become . . . tragedies. And I was easy to blame. My master—Mina—told her brother, Byron, an elder who is well-respected among the people, about my visions. He told the other elders, and they started to blame me for causing the things I saw. When Mina grew ill and Byron came to see her, I told him what I'd seen . . . about the water."

"This Byron—he didn't believe you?"

"He acted as though he did. He told the elders. But he didn't warn the village. Or if he did, they didn't believe him either."

"And he did not try to stop the villagers last night?"

"No. Maybe he didn't know. But he was with the elders here, though he didn't speak." Her throat worked against the emotion lodged there, her betrayal evident, and Kjell guessed the "well-respected" Byron was the elder with the trembling hands and drooping skin.

"I don't see everything. I don't see most things. And I rarely see good things. I see pain. Fear. Death. Anger. Maybe because love isn't as . . . dark, it's harder to see. The terrible things put off a scent. A signal. Or maybe they send ripples through time."

"Ripples?"

"Like ripples in a pond. You throw a stone into the water, and the impact sends waves outward in every direction. It is like I am on the shore, yet the ripples still find me, far as I might be from where—or when—it all occurs. I cannot control it. Most of the time, I can't change it. I can only see it and do my best to warn of its arrival. Some ripples are just that . . . ripples, but some are huge waves. Sometimes we can catch the wave and ride the current. Sometimes we can dive beneath the churning, but we cannot keep the wave from coming. Sometimes it only brushes my feet, and sometimes I only observe, but the wave still comes."

"And you saw me?"

"Yes. Many times. More times than I can count. I saw you, and I saw death."

"Your own?" he asked. She saw him, and she saw death, yet she wasn't afraid of him.

"Yes. And no. I saw the moments that came before. I felt the anger of the villagers. I saw my fear . . . and falling. I knew I would fall."

"And you want me to *help* these people?"

"Some of them," she whispered, and she tried to smile. "Maybe not all."

"They will still hate you," he replied grimly.

"Some of them. Maybe not all," she repeated, nodding. "But *not* asking you to help them . . . when I know you can, would be like knowing the water is bad and not telling anyone. It isn't about me. It's about responsibility. The Gifts we are given are not given for our benefit but for the benefit of mankind."

Kjell groaned inwardly, his dread growing by the second. This slave woman, this red-haired paragon of virtue and long-suffering, would be his undoing, and it would not be a sweet unraveling.

THREE

S he followed him, her gait brisk, keeping pace with the
guard as they entered Solemn on horseback. The village
was an assortment of clay and stone structures, one blending into the next, rising out of the dust and butting against the
cliff walls. Quondoon was a desert bedecked with the occasional
rich oasis, and Solemn, sitting at an elevation that grew rocks
and little else, was not one of them.

Kjell slowed and demanded that his men circle their horses
around Sasha, shielding her from the eyes of those who might
wish her harm. She was the reason he was here. He didn't want
her dragged off.

As they made their way along the main thoroughfare—the
only street bigger than a mountain path—the villagers watched
from their doorways and the sides of the street, their animus obvious, their eyes watchful and wary. Some of them even fell in
behind the soldiers, their fear not as great as their curiosity, and
by the time they reached their destination, a small parade had
assembled behind them.

Jerick and the first group of soldiers, as well as the elders of Solemn, were gathered in front of an establishment hung with a sign that declared it an inn. Kjell didn't suppose there were many travelers on the road to Solemn, but apparently there were a few. The building boasted three stories, forming a rectangular edifice complete with rows of perfectly square windows and topped with a flat roof. Some sort of garden was built on the roof, the trees and plants giving the establishment the appearance of hair. On both sides of the street, similarly styled clay structures stood in solidarity—a forge, a church, a stable, a tavern, and an apothecary. The apothecary was the largest building, and Kjell wondered if the owner had grown rich selling herbs and tonics to the sick people of Solemn.

"We have begun preparing a feast," Syed said, raising his voice to be heard. The people grew quiet, their resentment palpable. "You can take your horses to the stable." He indicated the structure and the enclosure across the way. "You are our guests. We will have our women prepare baths for your men, though it will take us some time to arrange quarters for so many."

"I've decided we will not need baths or food. We are told the water is unclean," Kjell said, projecting so his words reached the edges of the crowd. A murmur rose through the assembly.

"It's making your people sick," Kjell insisted.

"You may be the King's Guard, but you know nothing of Solemn," Syed protested.

Kjell shrugged. "It matters not to me whether you believe me. We will not be staying in Solemn. And we will not be drinking the water." They would not even be dismounting from their horses if he had his way.

"The woman lies," an elder hissed, pointing toward Sasha, laying the blame, and Kjell shrugged once more, though his ambivalence was feigned.

"Why would she do that?" Kjell demanded.

"To frighten the people," Syed warned.

"To frighten them so much they would kill her?" Kjell scoffed. A guilty muttering rose again.

"She is clearly unharmed," another elder said. "She lies to you too. It is she who makes the people sick."

The villagers pressed and surged, closing around Kjell's men, emboldened or simply curious, he couldn't tell, and the horses shimmied and stomped, feeling the energy and the emotion gathering. They were armed soldiers on horseback, protected by their prowess and recognized as emissaries of the king. He was the king's own brother, yet he knew that if the elders of Solemn could incite the crowd, the sheer numbers would overwhelm them.

Someone threw a stone, and then another. Rocks began to rain, striking the horses and the occasional guard, but they were aimed at the woman who had been accused of causing all the suffering. Sasha cried out in pain, and Kjell drew his sword. His men, following his lead, immediately unsheathed their own.

"By order of the crown, there will be no harming or casting out of the Gifted. They are bound by the same protections and laws every citizen of Jeru enjoys. If you stone, you will be stoned. If you harm, you will be harmed. If you cast someone out without cause, you will share the same fate."

The people began to step back, and his men moved their horses forward, their swords extended, their intentions clear. Some of the villagers began to run, some covered their heads, and the elders threatened wildly, demanding the soldiers leave the village at once.

He felt a hand on his leg, tugging at him, demanding his attention, and he looked down into Sasha's frightened face. Her veil had fallen and her hair was in tumbled disarray.

"They are suffering. Will you help them?"

"There has to be some justice," he argued incredulously, staring down into her bottomless eyes.

"There *was* justice. *You* are my justice. You saved me. Now you will redeem them," she implored.

"I will not!"

"You are a Healer, not an executioner."

"I am both!" he roared, his indignation toward her almost as great as his outrage over what had been done to her.

"You can't be both," she rebuked gently. A knot was already forming on her cheek, and a thin line of blood welled up in the abrasion. His anger swelled again, so great it enlarged his chest and pounded in his temples. He pressed his fingertips to the wound and wiped the blood away, leaving flat, unbroken skin in its wake.

"Kjell of Jeru is a Healer," Sasha shouted, her eyes locked on his, pleading. The murmur became a new kind of rumbling. "He healed me, and he can heal your sick," she cried, lifting her voice to the crowd. "Bring your sick to him, and you will see."

A hush grew over the riotous crowd, and for a moment every breath was drawn in wonder. It rippled through the gathering, the possibility of her assertion, the prospect of hope. His men were motionless, their blades level, listening for his command. The people were frozen in anticipation, silenced by the seduction of a chance. And Sasha clung to his leg, beseeching, waiting for him to bend to her will. He eyed the villagers, their cautious faces, their veiled optimism, the scorn of their leaders. And bend he did.

"If they want to be healed, let them come," he acquiesced. "Let the innocent come. But I will not heal *them*." He tipped his blade toward the elders, condemning them. "I can't heal men's hearts," he added, and immediately felt the weight of his own guilt.

Sasha nodded, withdrawing her hand from his leg. She turned without another word and began to push through the crowd that only minutes before had been trying to stone her.

They parted for her immediately.

Kjell didn't know where she was going or what she intended, but he drew in behind her and his men followed, a procession of soldiers being led by a servant girl. The wake became wider, the stones forgotten, and the people watched them go.

Kjell wondered if anyone would follow, if anyone would have the faith to bring their dying to him. There was a time when he wouldn't have followed a Healer. Not for himself. But maybe for Tiras. For Tiras he would have done anything. He would have risked the derision and ostracization of the non-believers. He would have taken a chance and faced the disappointment of false hope. He'd done it over and over again. But their faith was not Kjell's problem. If they wanted to be healed, let them follow. He would not make it easy for them.

Sasha led Kjell and his men to the empty house of her deceased master, a small home of rock and clay with heavy rugs over the doors and windows. She seemed convinced the people would come and pushed the rug over the door wide to welcome them when they did. Kjell climbed down from his horse, handed his reins to Jerick, and commanded him to post half the guard around the house and the other half back at the clearing where they'd camped the night before.

"I can't stop you or your horses from getting sick if you drink the water. I may be able to heal you once you are, but I can't be easing your bowels every time you take a swallow. We will take shifts. Use your swords to keep order if you have to. We will be vigilant, and we will leave as soon as possible."

Sasha was right. The people came. The first to arrive was a man who was lame, not ill. He hung back, waiting for someone else to go first. He was soon joined by others, some curious, some cautious, many accompanied by people who were obviously ill. Children were carried, men and women were assisted, and some villagers came alone to see what the Healer could do before raising the hopes of their sick. A large crowd gathered, talking amongst themselves, eyeing the home of Sasha's master, whispering about the servant who had "risen from the dead." They all knew Sasha had been chased over the cliff, and Kjell's fury rose inside him again. Their knowledge made them guilty, yet here they all were, in search of a blessing.

He watched them from a window, the covering pushed aside just enough for him to see the growing numbers. Sasha had straightened the small home and changed her gown into something equally plain but not nearly as stained. She tidied her hair and washed herself in water he could only guess she'd fetched from the pool between the cliffs. She poured him a glass of tepid wine and drew some dried meat and hard bread from a cupboard in the small galley, placing it on the table and bidding him eat.

He did as she asked, demanding that she eat as well, and refused to partake until she obeyed him.

"They are afraid," she said quietly, eating daintily, her eyes in her lap.

"Courage is a small price. If they want healing they can pay it," he grumbled, but his stomach twisted as he spoke. He was afraid too. He hoped the people would leave.

"Peace of Jeru," someone spoke shyly from the door, and Sasha rose so quickly her small stool toppled. She didn't stop to right it, but walked quickly to the shadowed entry, her hands stretched toward the woman who stood just beyond, her head covered, her posture timorous. Great circles hung below her eyes and her dress could not disguise the frailty of her body.

"Kimala," Sasha greeted, as if the woman was a welcome friend. "Come." The woman name Kimala allowed herself to be drawn into the house, and from outside, voices cried out, accusing her of foolishness.

"The captain can help you." Sasha said with certainty.

Oh, gods. He didn't think he could. He stood, battling the need to run, knowing he couldn't, knowing he shouldn't. He moved away from the table, toward the woman who was clearly as frightened as he was. She couldn't run. He could see she was barely walking.

"Lie down." He pointed at the low bed Sasha had covered in fresh linens, and Sasha assisted the woman, helping her recline until she lay looking at Kjell with fear and fascination. He knelt beside her, and placed his soldier's hands upon her chest. Her heart practically vibrated, her rapid inhalations fluttering over her lips like tiny wings. The hope in the room took on its own heartbeat, pounding in time with her hummingbird heart.

He couldn't hear a melody. Not a single, solitary note. He couldn't hear anything but her echoing expectation, and the realization made him desperate. He yanked his hands away. He was not equipped to wield his gift. His heart began to pound, and his anger—at himself, at Sasha, at his father, at the Creator, at the very world he was born into—bubbled inside him. He was a warrior. He was not a man who loved or nurtured. He'd been given a gift that was so at odds with who he was that he wanted to howl in frustration and sink his sword into something lethal.

The walls of the hut seemed to swell and retreat, making him sway dizzily and close his eyes. He realized he hadn't taken a breath for a very long time. Suddenly he felt a palm, calloused and slight, pressing into his.

"Kimala is a mother," Sasha said softly. "She lost her first child, and her second. But last winter she gave birth to a beautiful little boy. He was strong and his cry was so powerful that all of Solemn heard it. Now she is sick, and she worries that she won't be able to take care of her son." Sasha's soft voice brushed against his closed eyes, and her hand stayed pressed against his as she continued talking, telling him about the mother who longed to see her child grow. Kjell's anger retreated, and something else took its place.

Compassion. He felt compassion.

He opened his eyes and noted the gathering despair in the woman's gaze. Sasha was holding her hand the way she held his, linking them together. Without letting go of Sasha, he placed his palm on Kimala's chest once more and listened harder.

The note was so faint he hardly trusted it, a whisper of air that could have been nothing more than an indrawn breath, but he exhaled, matching the sound, so different from the soul-deep, healing melodies he'd felt before. The volume increased, until the breath resembled a sigh and the sigh became a shudder. He made the sound with his teeth and tongue, his hand still in Sasha's, her hand still clasped around the woman who had begun to stare at him in wonder. Her color warmed, the darkness beneath her eyes and the pallor around her lips disappearing as he pulled the disease from her skin and coaxed it from her bones, setting it free with a final gust of air.

"Bring me another," he demanded, turning to Sasha. She nodded once and released his hand. She drew the woman he'd just healed to her feet. Kimala moved as though she were in a stupor, her lips trembling with what could only be described as joy.

"Thank you," Kimala cried, reaching her hand toward him, and he rejected her thanks with a swift shake of his head. "Go and do no harm," he said awkwardly. "Sasha. Quickly," he urged, afraid of losing the thread of connection he'd established with his finicky gift. Sasha obeyed, running from the house and returning with a child who was so weak she had to be carried, lying limply against Sasha's chest, her dark eyes huge and pain-filled.

"This is Tora. Tora loves birds. She can mimic all their calls." The little girl squeaked softly, the cry like no bird Kjell had ever heard, but Sasha smiled. "See? I know that one." She pursed her lips and whistled gently, copying the sound the child made.

Sasha laid the girl down on the bed in front of Kjell, and the child closed her eyes as if the bird call had been her last. Without waiting to see if he needed her, Sasha slipped her hand in his, then grasped the child's hand, connecting them. He laid his palm on the little girl's tiny chest and strained to hear something that would guide him. He thought he heard whistling and opened his eyes to bid Sasha to cease. She was watching him soundlessly, her lips soft and silent.

He realized the whistling wasn't in his ears but in his chest and in his hands. The child's song was very like the timid chirping of a small bird. He focused on the sound and struggled to rec-reate it, his throat constricting, resisting the pitch.

His grip tightened on Sasha's. "The bird call. Do it again," he demanded. She obeyed instantly, trilling softly, and he grasped the sound, magnifying it until his head and hands were ringing with the ear-shattering vibrations. Then he focused on the inky illness that coated the child's every breath and infused it with the piercing shrill. It disintegrated with an audible pop, and the child's lips parted in a soft snore. He'd put her to sleep. He fell back, releasing the pulse and removing his hands.

"It's gone. She's well," he gasped. "Take her away and bring me someone else."

Sasha scooped the child up and was out the door before he could ask her twice. With each person she brought before him, she told him something about them, something small but signifi-cant, something that allowed him to find the kernel of human connection that made healing possible. And she always took his hand.

He healed one after another, each healing song a different timbre, a different cadence, a different tone. Some songs sounded more like a series of clicks, some were high and shrill, some the sighing shape of the wind, like the mother who'd brought forth a child, only to grow ill shortly after. An old man had a song like a deep bass drum, and Kjell's spirit thrummed with the strain of matching it. But match it he did, and the old man's sickness fell away, leaving him free to leave Kjell's presence by his own strength.

There were some he could not heal. A girl of twenty summers stared at him glassily. Sasha smoothed her hair and told Kjell how the girl loved the wildflowers in the rocks. But Kjell couldn't hear anything but Sasha's kindness. If the girl had a song, it was locked away somewhere he couldn't reach. She was still breathing, her heart was beating, but she was gone. Another child, carried into the house in his mother's arms, was also beyond healing. His mother insisted he was still alive—she screamed at Kjell when he shook his head—but the little boy's limbs were limp and his eyes were cloudy. He'd been gone for hours.

One man, not much older than Kjell and riddled with pain, sat gingerly on the bed in front of him, but when Kjell asked him to lie back, he shook his head as if he weren't ready.

"This is Gar. He's very sick," Sasha said softly, her eyes troubled, her lips tight. "His wife died last month," she explained. "He misses her."

Kjell placed one hand over the man's heart and one on his back, easing him down gently. He didn't have the time or empathy for indecision. The man began to weep, and Kjell ignored him, searching and finding the mellow strains of the man's healing song easily. But when he tried to capture it, it changed, becoming a dissonant chord. Kjell didn't know which note to sing. He hesitated, unsure, and the chord rose from the man's skin, fluttered through Kjell's fingers, and drifted—a tendril of smoke —higher and higher, until Kjell could no longer hear it.

When Kjell opened his eyes, he found Gar's gaze fixed on the ceiling, his face smooth with peace.

"He didn't want you to heal him," Sasha whispered. "He wanted to go."

"His song was so strong. I could have eased his pain," Kjell argued, his sense of loss surprising.

"You did ease his pain," Sasha replied simply. She closed Gar's eyes and covered him with the pale blue cloth she wore over her hair.

"That's yours," Kjell protested. He didn't know why it bothered him. She'd climbed the cliff to retrieve it and now she was giving it away.

"His wife was kind to me," she explained. She left the room and immediately returned with three villagers. They carried Gar out, their eyes full of questions, and the process continued.

At one point, the sounds and songs began to run together, and Sasha refused to bring Kjell another citizen of Solemn. Instead, she pushed him down on the low bed he'd knelt beside for countless hours, placing a cushion beneath his head. Unable to summon a sound, he succumbed to her soft hands on his hair and her whisper of, "Well done, Captain. Well done."

He awoke to sunlight and the scrape of a knife against his face.

"You are not my servant," he murmured, opening his bleary eyes to the tickle of her unbound hair against his folded hands. She set her blade aside and scooted quickly away, pouring him a goblet of wine and helping him to sit. His body ached like he'd spent a week in battle or been dropped from the sky by a bird-man. He downed the wine, and she promptly refilled it. It was mild and weak and far warmer than he liked, but it quenched his thirst. He fell back against the cushion, and she returned to his side, pulling his head into her lap.

"I will finish this. Then I will go. You've been asleep for two days," she said demurely. "You're turning into a bear."

He snorted and her lips quirked, the corners lifting prettily before pursing in concentration once again. She used an oil that smelled of sage and made his skin tingle, and he closed his eyes and let her have her way. Her silence didn't speak of secrets but of peace, and he let it wash over him. She was odd in her strange confidence, in her complete lack of pretense, and he felt an easing in his chest and a release in his head, like she'd loosened the past and tightened the present, making him more aware of the moment and less concerned with what had come before. He liked her.

"They will let you stay in Solemn. I will see to it. This home will be yours, and you will not be a slave. You will have nothing to fear," he promised, needing to give her something.

"There is always something to fear," she replied, her eyes on the blade she wielded. She said no more, and he was too drowsy to press the issue. He forced himself to remember the cool breezes of Jeru City, the shade of the trees, the sound of his brother's voice, the clash of blades in the yard, the smell of fresh hay in the stables. He made himself think of home, yet he felt no pull toward it. Instead, it was his head in the lap of a slave, the silk of her breath on his face, and the tenderness in her hands that soothed him.

"You don't look like the people of Quondoon," he said simply, resisting the lethargy that wanted to pull him under again.

"No. Mina said I am ugly. My hair is not black and straight, my skin is not brown. I'm freckled and pale. My hair is the color of fire and it curls and tangles no matter how much I try to keep it smooth," she said ruefully. "But it is the only home I know."

"You are not ugly."

Her back stiffened in surprise, and the blade paused on his skin for a heartbeat. He cursed inwardly, but when he avoided her gaze and offered no further comment, she turned the conversation away from herself.

"Do all the people in Jeru City look like you?" she asked.

"No. But there are many more people in Jeru City than in Solemn. There are more people in Jeru City than in all of Quondoon."

"You are the brother of the king?"

"Yes."

"So are you . . . a prince?"

"My brother is a king, and I am a soldier. That is all."

"You look like a king," she protested softly.

He was a big man—bulky even—layered with muscle and sinew hardened down by years of combat and grueling physical labor. He'd grown up in the jousting yard, dragging a sword before he could wield one, shielding himself from blows before he learned to land them. He looked like a soldier.

But he also looked like his father. And his father had been a king.

Kjell's hair was just as dark and his eyes were the same pale blue. Cold. Flat. Cruel. His father had never claimed him, but it had never mattered. When people saw Kjell they always knew.

"You were born in Quondoon? Where is your family?" he asked, pushing his own paternity out of his thoughts.

"I am of Kilmorda. But Mina says I was born a slave, and I will always be a slave."

"Kilmorda was destroyed by Volgar."

"I am told I was the daughter of a servant in Lord Kilmorda's household."

"Lord Kilmorda and his family are dead." The whole valley was a wasteland of Volgar nests and human remains. The villages were desolate, homes and fields were empty, and the carcasses of cattle and sheep were strewn across the country.

"Yes. That is what I am told."

"You don't remember?"

"My first memories are of fleeing to Firi with other refugees. I knew no one. I had nothing to eat. No clothes. No family. In Firi, I was indentured and sold and brought to Quondoon."

"Solemn is a long way from Kilmorda."

"Yes," she agreed quietly, "but I do not miss what I cannot remember."

"Why don't you remember?"

"I don't know. Mina said it was because I am . . . simple." Sasha's voice changed, and he couldn't resist looking at her. "But I can read. I can read *and* I can write. The slaves here in Solemn do not read or write. I learned how . . . somewhere."

"But you're a Seer . . . surely you must have visions of your family."

"I don't see what has already been. I can only see what is to come, and even then, it's like the breeze. I don't call the breeze, it finds me. The things I see are like that. I don't call them to me. They come. Or they don't."

She'd had no visions of her family. He wondered why. He could choose whether or not to wield his gift. She didn't seem quite so lucky, though he supposed her choice lay in whether she kept the visions to herself.

"There was a man who walked with me from Kilmorda to Firi. When my feet bled, he helped me bind them. When my mouth was dry he gave me water. And he told me stories. I was afraid, and he told me stories. I came to Quondoon with a head full of tales and no memories. No sense of myself. It was as though the Creator formed me from the clay, fully grown, like the Changer, the Spinner, the Healer, and the Teller. But even they knew from whence they came. They knew to whom they belonged."

They knew to whom they belonged.

His brother had always had that sense of belonging. Tiras was arrogant in the way all kings were arrogant, but that was merely survival. Tiras's opinion of himself guided the opinion others formed about him. A king had to act as if he belonged on the throne. Kjell would have never been able to convince anyone he belonged.

"But now I belong to you," Sasha said firmly, and she dried his face with a cloth, indicating she had finished.

He sat up abruptly, startling her, distancing himself.

"No. You don't." He stood, and a wave of dizziness flooded him. She reached out to steady him, but he shrugged her away.

"You must eat. Sit. I'll bring you food and more wine," she insisted, rising beside him. Her hands were folded in front of her, her eyes cast down.

"Sasha." He waited for her to lift her eyes to his. She was very composed, but her eyes shimmered with disappointment.

"You don't belong to me. The people I healed, the people you helped me heal . . . they don't belong to me either. That is not the way it works. I do not want a servant, and I don't need a woman." He spoke slowly as if he spoke to a child, and she nodded once, indicating she heard him.

"Mina said I was simple. She said I must obey her and I would be safe. But I am not simple. I am not stupid." Sasha's voice was almost musical in its tranquility, but beneath the surface there was steel, and the gleaming in her eyes had changed. He'd made her angry. Good. Some fury was in order.

"You are not stupid. But you are too forgiving and too trusting. You are a Seer, yet you don't see the obvious," he said.

"Most of the time the obvious blinds us to the hidden."

Kjell sighed heavily, pressing his palms to his eyes. The woman had powerful opinions for someone so defenseless. He pulled on his boots and ran fingers through his hair, determined to dismiss her. She stood quietly by, waiting for his direction.

"Where are my men?"

"Jerick is outside. The others have been taking shifts, as you instructed. They are helping bring water from the mountain stream."

He tried to thank her, but the words felt false, so he simply shook his head and left the house. He had business to attend to, and then he was getting on his horse and leaving Solemn and all her people behind.

FOUR

The village had come alive. There was new life, and people scurried and scuttled. Children were underfoot, and an outdoor market, not all that different from the market in Jeru City's square, lined the main thoroughfare. People were selling their wares and talking excitedly among themselves. A new well was being dug. A man from Doha was coming to Solemn. He was said to have the Gift to call water. He would walk without shoes, his toes curling into the dirt, and he could feel the water beneath the surface, no matter how deep. For the time being, the village had assigned all the able men to carry water from the stream near the cliffs.

Kjell was greeted with awe and tears. It made his stomach clench and his hands sweat. His name was called out, and food was pressed into his hands, presents laid at his feet. He tried to give it back, to refuse, but the people backed away, leaving their offerings and shaking their heads. One woman brought him a goat, tugging it behind her with a determination not to be outgifted.

"No!" he roared. "I am a soldier. I can't take your goat." The animal bleated piteously, and the woman looked as though he'd struck her. She wore a pale green scarf over her hair. The material was soft and fine, and the color would not draw the heat.

Sasha had given her veil away.

"I will take your head covering. Give me that instead. You keep the goat."

"But the goat is a better gift!"

"I don't want it. I want the scarf. I need two more like it, in different colors. And three dresses. About your size. And boots. For a lady." He reached for his coin pouch, but the people around him, enlivened by his requests, ran to fulfill them.

The woman smiled, nodding happily, and shyly withdrew her scarf. Her hair was as black as Sasha's eyes, and Kjell's mind immediately returned to the things he'd learned that morning. Sasha did not belong in Quondoon.

He brushed the niggling aside, immediately distracted by tradesmen and women, presenting him with veils and gowns and jewelry and shoes, sized to fit a tall, slim woman.

He pushed the ridiculous away—the jewelry and the slippers that would tear with any use—and barked his preferences with little fanfare, choosing colors that wouldn't compete with Sasha's hair or absorb the sunlight, and fabrics that wouldn't abrade her skin or be difficult to wash. He'd never selected clothes for a female, and he spent more coin than he made in a month, just to be done with it. He paid two young boys to trail him with his purchases, but had hardly made it out of the market when he was hailed by the elder named Byron, the brother of the deceased Mina, Sasha's master.

"Captain!" Byron called, his girth making him struggle to catch Kjell. Kjell stopped abruptly and turned, directing the boys to Sasha's house and asking them to deliver the purchases to the woman who lived there. They seemed to know who she was—

one of them called her the red witch—and trotted off, eager to do his bidding, his money in their pockets.

"We are grateful, Highness," Byron said, bowing slightly as he reached him. "The people of Solemn will never forget you."

"If it were left to me, I would have let you all rot. Your gratitude is misplaced." He ignored the title. "You owe the woman a great debt."

"I will give her to you," Byron rushed, spreading his hands magnanimously.

"You will . . . give her to me?" Kjell asked, his voice flat.

"She may be of use to you," the elder continued eagerly. "And she is no longer of use to my sister."

"The elder said she'd been among you three years. How did she get here?"

"I was in Firi, in the employ of the Lord of Quondoon." Byron puffed his chest proudly. "The refugees flooding Firi were numerous. You know that. She was with a group of people, many of them from Kilmorda, looking for work. I saw her on the blocks with a dozen other women. She was blank. Like a wall. I found it useful. The other women were crying. Traumatized. She wasn't. I didn't want trouble. I wanted a companion for my sister."

Even the name Firi made his stomach knot and tighten. "I have no use for a slave," Kjell said. "You will give Sasha her freedom. You will give her your sister's home. And you will provide money for her welfare."

"She is not safe here," Byron protested, and he had the conscience to look embarrassed by the admission.

"You are a powerful man. You will see to it that she is."

Byron swallowed, nodding.

Sasha thanked him with a smile for the packages he'd had delivered, but her smile slipped away when he told her he was leaving.

"This is your house. You will serve only yourself from now on." He placed a small purse filled with gold coin on the table. "This is yours. There will be more. I've seen to it."

Her eyes rose to his, dark and knowing, and his confusion and frustration writhed within him. She didn't argue or count the money. She watched him walk from the house without asking him to take her with him, but he condemned himself with every step.

His horse had been readied, his men assembled, and within minutes they were riding back through the streets of Solemn, the farewell far different than the welcome had been. Children ran, people called out, and once again, a procession formed behind them, throwing bits of rice and wishing them Godspeed, as though they were off to wage war, instead of leaving the battle behind them. On the outskirts of the town the other half of the King's Guard waited, watching their approach, unsmiling, unimpressed by the change in the villagers.

Kjell wanted to turn his head to see if Sasha was among them. He wanted to look at her once more, to see if she had joined the farewell procession, but he resisted. He had restored her health, made arrangements for her welfare, and he did not owe her anything else. And she owed *him* nothing. She was free to go wherever she wished. He rode with his back stiff, his eyes forward, and he left the crowd behind, the well-wishes and cries fading into silence.

"She follows, Captain," Jerick murmured beside him.

Kjell jerked around, finding the lone figure trailing them a short ways off. She appeared to be running. It was hot, and the temperature would make the travel slow. The horses would not be able to carry the soldiers far if they pushed them, but Sasha would hurt herself if she tried to keep pace on foot.

"Blast. Bloody hell!" Kjell swore softly.

"We grow farther away every moment. She will go back," Jerick said mildly.

"No, she won't," Kjell stewed. He closed his eyes against his guilt and his strange elation. She followed. And he was glad.

"I can't leave her. She was driven out of Solemn. If she doesn't want to remain there, we need to take her somewhere else," he said.

"I agree, Captain."

"But where?" Kjell barked, wishing Jerick hadn't capitulated so readily.

"Take her to Jeru City. She can work in the palace."

"She cannot remain with a group of soldiers until we return to the city. It could be a month before we return."

"You don't trust your men to behave themselves? Or you do not trust yourself not to soften toward her?" Jerick asked, a small smirk around his lips.

"Stop speaking, Jerick."

"She reminds me of our Lady Queen," Jerick mused, ignoring him.

"She looks nothing like the queen." Queen Lark was diminutive, a waif of a woman with silver eyes, soft brown hair, and an iron will.

"No . . . still. There is something," Jerick argued.

There *was* something. It was in the stillness of their bodies and the stiffness of their spines, even when they bowed their heads. The woman—Sasha—was oddly regal for a slave. Queen Lark shared the same bearing.

Kjell wheeled his horse around, his men drawing to an immediate halt, their hands on their reins, their brows furrowed.

"Wait for me here," he commanded. He felt their eyes on his back as he crossed the distance to the figure who trailed them, but he felt her eyes most distinctly. She watched as he approached, the veil he'd given her fluttering like pale wings in the breeze. She held a small bundle, most likely her few possessions. The bundle made his throat catch, and he wondered if she'd included the things he bought for her.

He didn't know what to say. Words had never been his weapons or his way. He tripped over them and spoke in anger when he spoke at all. Anger was comfortable for him. She lifted a hand as if she knew why he'd returned, and he closed the gap between them. Leaning down, he ignored her upraised arm and instead, encircled her waist and drew her up in front of him. He felt her gasp and the shudder of relief that ended on a soft, "Thank you, Captain."

"I am not your master. I am not a savior or a saint. I am Kjell. You can call me Kjell or call me nothing at all. I will take you where you can find work."

"I will stay with you."

"You will not."

She didn't protest further, but he felt her resistance, and he quietly reveled in it.

They rode for two days, riding east toward Enoch. Sasha didn't complain, though she slept so deeply at night he knew she was taxed. Still she rose before him each day, determined to make herself useful. She was quiet, as if waiting for him to give her permission to speak, and though he was accustomed to solitude, her silence rankled.

She seemed comfortable with him physically, allowing herself to relax within the cradle of his body. It would have been excruciating for both of them otherwise. He had tried to remove his breastplate, making it more comfortable for her, but she shook her head adamantly. "There will be fighting."

"When?" Her gift—like all gifts—made him uncomfortable. But he wasn't fool enough to doubt her. In his experience, very few people wanted to be Gifted, so when they said they were, they were owed belief. He'd learned that the hard way.

"I don't know when," she answered. "But there will be a battle. And you will need to protect your heart."

"You can see that?"

"I don't see things exactly as they are or as they will be. My visions are more like glimpses. Pieces and images, pictures and suggestions. Sometimes it is easy to put the pieces together. I'll see water. I'll see sickness. I draw conclusions." She shrugged. "Other times, I see things I don't understand at all, and it isn't until they are happening that I recognize the signs."

He kept his armor on and directed his men to do the same, though the heat was sweltering and there were no signs of the Volgar. Now he baked in his breastplate and stewed in her silence.

"Speak, woman," he insisted on the second day, her hushed expectancy wearing him raw. She jerked and strained to see his face though her head was beneath his chin.

"What would you like me to say?" she asked, clearly surprised.

He racked his brain, angry that he had to ask her to converse with him, and grasped at the first thing that entered his mind. "You said you awoke with no memories, but there were stories in your head."

"You want me to tell you a story?" she asked hopefully, and he felt like a child. But if he was a child, he was a desperate one.

"Yes. Tell me one of your stories."

"I can tell you the origin story. It was Mina's favorite."

"Changers and Tellers and Spinners," he muttered. He didn't want to talk about the Gifted.

"And Healers," she added.

"And Healers," he acknowledged. He definitely didn't want to talk about Healers. But Sasha did.

"Have you always known you could heal?" she asked cautiously. It served him right. He'd asked her to speak, now he had to answer.

"An old woman—a diviner of gifts—once told me that the gift of a Healer is the easiest to deny. Especially among those who are comfortable with war and suspicious of love." He had never forgotten the words. They'd seared themselves on his heart the moment he heard them. "I spent a long time denying."

"Are you still denying?" she asked.

"Still resisting. The woman told me that for every life I save, I give up a day of my own. Though how that could be proven is a mystery to me."

Sasha jerked, and he wondered what he'd said. "You healed two hundred people," she whispered. "I *asked* you to heal them."

"I have never been able to heal like that before. I am not particularly skilled."

"But . . . you healed *me*." She seemed stricken by the realization, and fell back into silence. He tried again.

"I don't want to hear the origin story. I know it too well. Tell me a story you don't think I know."

She didn't respond immediately, and Kjell waited impatiently, tempted to prod her.

"Once, in a place where the rocks and the grass grew together, a king reigned over a people who could shift into trees," she started hesitantly, as though forcing her thoughts from where they'd been to where he wanted them to be. "When conquering armies would come to enslave them, the king's people would encircle his kingdom and spin themselves into a forest wall, tall and stately, bending with the wind but not breaking, protecting the kingdom from those who would do her harm. But there was a girl among them, a princess who could not shift, and there were conquerors who could fly."

Something niggled. "I've heard of this place."

She tipped her head quizzically. "You know that one? Should I tell you a different story?"

"No. Continue."

"The girl who could not spin climbed up into the largest tree to hide, sheltered by the leaves, but the invaders could smell her blood. They could hear her heartbeat. The king knew that she would not be able to hide forever, no matter how great the forest or how tall the branches, so he sent her away, far from the land of Tree Spinners."

"Did she ever go back?"

"No. But the kingdom waits, unchanged, for her return. If you walk through the forest and look at the trunks, each one has a face hidden in the bark, a shifter waiting to become human again, sleeping inside the tree."

He noticed the men traveling closest to them were listening, their heads bent to hear her story, and he bristled at the intrusion. When one story ended, they asked for another, and another, until they were all traveling at a snail's pace, ears peeled, listening to her spin tales. Her voice was pleasing—low and gentle—and she told the stories as if they were as much a part of her as the palms of her hands or the red of her hair. When they stopped for the night, they'd traveled only half as far as they should have, and the men begged her for more stories around the fire.

Each night was a different tale. She described the creatures in the Drue Forest and the trolls from the mountains of Corvyn— Kjell told her of the queen's valued friend, Boojohni. She knew stories of the Changer who became a dragon, of the king who built an army, of the lark who became a queen. Some of the stories she told were true—recent history—and the men loved those stories even more, nodding as she polished their own memories with the burnished glow of retelling. Sasha claimed those stories had spread all over the land, traveling from one mouth to another until they found her in Solemn. When his men asked her if she knew about King Tiras slaying the Volgar Liege only to be mortally wounded himself, she nodded and looked at Kjell.

"I've heard that tale. And I've heard the tale of a mighty Healer, saving the king and restoring balance to the kingdom," she said.

Kjell grunted and stood, embarrassed. His men cleared their throats and shared weighted looks. He sent them all to bed, kicking dirt on the fire Isak started, just to make them disperse. They had no rabbits to cook, no water to spare for tea, no reason for a fire. The men rose reluctantly and, with beseeching looks, thanked Sasha for the entertainment. In only a few days, armed with a string of tales, she'd turned his battalion into a herd of sheep, following at her heels without a thought in their head but the next morsel.

She mothered them. She mothered him.

He hated it and loved it. He wished her quiet and prayed she would never stop talking. She made him both jubilant and miserable, and he found himself waiting with irritation and anticipation each night for the moment the men gathered and looked at her with pleading eyes and she acquiesced, telling them stories like they were children around her knees.

Each morning he awoke to boots that had been shined, clothes that had been shaken and aired, and a horse that had been brushed. She always woke before him, no matter how hard he tried to beat her to it. It was as if she *knew* when he would rise. His men smirked at her devotion, but she was so genuinely easy to be around, so cheerful and meek, that it was hard to tease her.

She just smiled and played along, unconcerned with jest, indifferent to anyone's opinion but his.

He could tell his disapproval bothered her.

He didn't ignore her. But he didn't dote on her either. He never asked her for a thing, yet he never thanked her for anything she did. She rode with him each day, never complaining, saving her best stories for him, and he listened, rarely contributing, pretending he was ambivalent toward her.

She'd grown quiet after a particularly interesting story about sea creatures in the Jeruvian Sea, and he was strategizing ways to make her speak without actually asking for her to do so.

"There's a storm." Sasha tugged on his arm. She turned her face, making sure he was listening. She wasn't panicked, but her pulse thrummed at the base of her throat, and her eyes grew so wide they frightened him. It was just a smear on the horizon, a writhing in the distance that portended the arrival—or departure—of something that would never reach them. But Sasha saw something else.

"There's a storm coming," she repeated, and pointed toward the dark smudge, her finger outlined against a sky so impossibly blue, he should have laughed. He didn't.

She began looking this way and that, searching for shelter. "There will be sand everywhere. We won't be able to breathe." Her chest started to rise and fall, as if oxygen deprivation had already begun. Then she shuddered, shrugging it off and keeping herself grounded in the present.

Kjell cursed, his eyes scanning the way hers had done moments before. The terrain from Quondoon to Enoch was rolling and relentlessly unvaried. Red dunes and dust littered with the occasional sandstone outcropping surrounded them in every direction. They needed a gully, something to create a barrier between them and what was coming.

He grasped Sasha's chin and drew her gaze.

"Do you see shelter? Where should we go?"

She shook her head helplessly, and he could see the growing panic in her black gaze. Warning them of a tempest was of little help if there was no way to escape it. Then her eyes fell to Kjell's lips and something shifted in her face, like she'd seen something entirely different than a looming storm.

"A cave. We are in a cave," she murmured.

He released her chin and looked again, scouring the landscape for a hiding place large enough for two dozen men and an equal number of horses.

"There!" To his far right a rocky protrusion jabbed the sky like the remains of an ancient temple. It was far enough off that it could be bigger than it seemed or prove completely insufficient. But Sasha was starting to tremble, and her eyes had strayed once more to the innocuous dark cloud in the distance.

His men were still unaware, and he roared instructions, pointing toward the ridge and demanding they follow him. They didn't hesitate, veering to the right, pushing to keep up with him. He heard Jerick cry out and turned to see that the darkness at their backs had grown, spreading, gobbling up the sky.

"Sandstorm!" his men shouted, and the rest of their words were lost in the wind. They spurred their horses toward the stony shelf, flying across the sand, racing the tempest.

Beneath the jutting overhang, as wide as three horses end to end, and as tall as two men were high, was an enormous cavern. The depth was obscured by darkness, causing a moment's hesitation, but they had no choice. The horses balked, but the growing roar at their backs urged them forward.

"Lead them in!" Kjell shouted and slid from his horse, pulling Sasha with him.

"Isak, we need light."

The fire starter rubbed his palms together, spinning a flame between them, widening his hands as his orb grew, lighting the immediate recesses, and making the walls around them jump into instant relief. Kjell led the way, one hand on his horse's mane, the other on his sword. He wasn't especially fond of serpents, and he had little doubt there were snakes in the cave. Snakes and bats.

"Deeper!" Jerick yelled, and Kjell pressed still farther into the darkness.

"We're all in Captain," Jerick called a moment later, and they halted, one woman, two dozen men, and their mounts, bathed temporarily in the warm light of Isak's blaze. Seconds later, Isak released the flame with an apology. The ball of fire was too hot for the people huddled around him, too flammable for the clothes he wore, and with no torch to light and no way to shelter the flame, he had to extinguish it.

"There was once a Spinner who could turn memories into stars the way Isak pulls fire from the air," Sasha spoke into the gloom. "I will tell you the story when the storm passes. Don't worry. It *will* pass."

She was trying to comfort them, a lone woman among soldiers who were well accustomed to supreme discomfort and fear.

A rush of tenderness gripped Kjell, followed by a glimmer of fear. Her voice had sounded odd in the chamber, like she floated above them. He reached for her, suddenly afraid that he would lose her into the black space pressing around them. In the darkness, free from judgment and the awareness of his men, he tucked her body into his, wrapping his arms around her, returning the reassurance she so easily offered.

For a moment they could all hear each other—the chuff of the horses, the changing of positions, the rustle of clothes, the scrape of shoes upon the rocks. Then the storm brought deep night with it, a black so complete, no light shone from the mouth of the cave and all sound was swallowed up in its fury.

Kjell was rendered blind and deaf, but he could feel her heartbeat against his belly, her face pressed to his chest, and the weight of her hair spilling over his arms. Fingertips brushed his face, and for a moment he stood motionless as she traced his eyes and his nose, his lips and his ears, seeing him in the dark. He thought about her mouth and the way she'd looked at him when she saw the cave in her mind.

He could kiss her. He could taste her lips and swallow her sighs and wait out the tempest exploring her mouth.

The desire wailed within him like the squall around him, but he resisted, unwilling to do what was expected, even if it was what he wanted. Her hands fell to his shoulders and she stood unmoving in his arms, her cheek on his chest, and he spent the storm in equal parts agony and bliss.

FIVE

The landscape had changed when they exited the cave, and for a moment, none of them spoke, but stretched their legs and tried to adjust to the light and disorientation. Somehow, even though they'd escaped the brunt of it, grit stuck to their skin and coated their brows and eyelashes, and Sasha shook out her hair and her scarf, beating her hands against her dress and shaking out her shoes.

Kjell found the highest point, little more than a mound of sand, and took out his spyglass, eager for Enoch and a bath. A haze hung in the air, obscuring the view in every direction. The sun was invisible, the light filtered and red. There was no horizon, no east, west, north or south. No matter the direction, the outlook was the same. Enoch would have to wait another day.

Eventually, Sasha joined him on the rise, bearing good news. "Some of the men are exploring. Isak made a torch out of horse hair and a strip of cloth. There's water farther back in the cave! Not a lot, but enough to wash our faces and fill our flasks."

"Then we'll stay here tonight. We can camp in and around the cave. It does us no good to travel if we're going in the wrong direction. We'll just become more lost, and no one will find us out here."

"We're lost?" Sasha asked. She didn't seem especially concerned.

"For the moment," he replied, still futilely searching. He snapped his glass closed, and scrubbed at his skin. For a man who spent the majority of his time on horseback, he despised being filthy. Sasha handed him her scarf, and with a sigh, he accepted it. He'd pulled her close in the darkness, and he didn't have the energy or desire to push her away again.

Without her veil he could see an angry strip of red, blistered flesh on the side of her neck where the relentless sun had found exposed skin.

"You're burned," he said, returning her scarf. It had helped to remove the sand from his eyelashes, if little else.

She nodded, shaking the veil once and recovering her head. He drew it aside and pressed his palm to her sore skin, making her flinch. When he moved his hand the blisters were gone, leaving a line of large, golden freckles in their wake. The freckles bothered him. He ran his thumb across them, wanting to wipe them away, puzzled. When he'd healed Tiras, he'd left no scars. He'd restored him completely.

"Don't do that," Sasha said, her voice sharp. It surprised him. Sasha's voice was never sharp. He dropped his hand, raising his eyes from her skin and stepping away, confused. She'd welcomed his proximity in the cave.

"It is a burn, Captain. It will heal on its own." She pressed her fingers to her neck, hiding it.

"It is done."

Her shoulders slumped. "You can't keep doing that."

"I can. And I will," he retorted, covering his confusion with ire.

"I didn't know your healing came with a cost," she murmured. "I don't want you to heal when you don't have to."

Realization flooded him. She didn't want him to heal her because she thought it cost him. *For every life he saved, he gave a day of his own.* He didn't know if soothing blisters constituted saving a life, but she was clearly upset by it.

"For all I know, I will live to be a very old man with more years on this land than I know what to do with. That is the one thing about my gift that has never bothered me, the possibility that I might be trading my days away."

"You are kind," she said softly.

"I am not kind," Kjell scoffed.

"And you are good," she added.

"I am *not* good!" he laughed.

"I have never known a man like you."

"You were a *slave* in Quondoon! The men you *knew* were not trying to impress you."

"Neither are you, Captain. Yet I am still impressed."

"Then you have a lot to learn."

She nodded slowly, and he was immediately remorseful. Her old master had told her she was simple. She was *not* simple. She was wise . . . and infuriating.

"Why do I make you so angry?" she asked.

"You don't make me angry," he argued, frustration making his hands curl.

"I do," she insisted, looking at him steadily.

"You do not know me. You have no idea who I am. You think I'm a Healer, but I have slain more men than I have healed."

She was silent for a moment, absorbing his confession. He began walking back toward the cave, expecting her to follow.

"You are wrong, Captain," she called after him. "I do know you. I knew your face before I met you. I saw you more times than I can count. You have always given me hope."

His heart tripped and his feet followed, and he stopped walking to avoid falling on his face in the shifting sand. He didn't look back at her, but she had to know he heard her. With a lusty exhale, he resumed walking, minding his step.

There were serpents in the cave. Coiled in the dank corners, unaccustomed to being prey, and blinded by the fire starter, they were little match for lances and swords, and the men ate well for the first time since leaving Bin Dar a fortnight before. Sasha didn't help them kill the snakes, but she didn't balk at skinning them, and she ate the meat with the same relish as the men. It didn't take long for someone to remind her that she'd promised them a story when the storm passed, and she nodded amiably and settled in for her tale.

"When Isak held the fire in his hands today, it reminded me of a story I once knew. In the beginning, there were only four gifts. Telling, Spinning, Changing and Healing. But as the years passed and the people multiplied over the land, the gifts grew and changed, and new gifts emerged. Power grew and evolved. In some of the Gifted, telling became seeing and healing became transforming. Some of the Changers began to shift into more than one animal, and spinning became more and more diverse. Some Spinners could turn air into fire, like Isak. Some turned objects into illusions. Some could even spin themselves into trees."

"—but not animals," someone inserted, and Sasha nodded.

"No. That would make them Changers."

"But there was one Spinner who was so powerful he could spin thoughts into stars. They called him the Star Maker." She was quiet for a moment, and the men all raised their faces to the stars, looking for the brightest light. The sky had begun to clear and the moon lurked behind the haze, glowing dully. Kjell raised his hand and moved his thumb across the muted swath, remembering Sasha's golden freckles.

"When someone grew old and was close to death, the Star Maker would draw their memories into his hands and shape them into orbs of light, releasing them into the heavens, so they could live forever."

Isak cupped his hand and created a flame, showing off for Sasha, and she smiled as he released it, tossing it as if he too were a Star Maker.

"Sometimes, he would call the star back, pulling it down from the heavens, so those still living could hold the memories of the ones they lost."

The men chimed in then, naming the people they missed, the people they'd lost, and the oldest soldier, a man named Gibbous who had been in the King's Guard for as long as Kjell could remember, called out the name of a woman, his eyes glued to the heavens.

Jerick hooted, surprised, and the mood was broken. Isak, determined to keep Sasha talking, asked her if she'd lost someone close to her.

"I am the one who is lost," Sasha said. "And I don't think anyone is looking for me." The corners of her mouth lifted wryly, and Isak looked momentarily stricken. Kjell glowered at him. His men had become too familiar with the servant woman. It wasn't good.

They unrolled their pallets in the mouth of the cave, leaving the horses hobbled outside. Kjell volunteered for the first watch, needing solitude.

He didn't get it.

Sasha found him when the camp quieted, and she perched beside him, casting her eyes out at the empty expanse, mimicking his posture.

"You are angry again," she stated softly.

He didn't deny it, though anger was too strong a word. He was weary. Restless. Distracted. Intrigued.

"Having a woman traveling with a group of warriors is dangerous," he said.

"Why?" The question was quietly distressed.

"Because if they care for you—and they all do—they will stop looking out for each other and they will all start looking out for you. It's not your fault. It's not theirs. It's simply the way we are."

"I see," she whispered, and he ceased speaking, knowing that she did.

She stayed with him as the moon rose higher in the sky, sloughing off the haze and lighting the dunes around them. Before long, Sasha was curled on the sand beside him, her head on her scarf, her legs and arms drawn into her chest, and he sighed, knowing his men would think they dallied.

But he didn't wake her. Not yet. He would let her stay a while longer.

The horses slept, his men dreamed, and he kept watch.

They entered Enoch ten days after leaving Solemn, dusty and dirty, longing for baths, wine, and beds that didn't encourage sand spiders and stiff backs. There'd been no battles, despite Sasha's warning, and their armor was dingy, their skin chafed, and their horses in need of grain and grooming.

The land of Enoch boasted the River Bale, the largest river in all of Jeru. It extended for one hundred miles, just below Jeru City all the way to the borders at the south of Enoch, and because of that, the province enjoyed trade with the kingdom and the Northern provinces, unlike its poorer neighbor, Quondoon.

Along one side of the River Bale, fine homes and respectable businesses lined the streets. Sheltered women and cherished children moved freely, and a cathedral erected for the first Lord Enoch overlooked the river and cast a disapproving shadow upon the opposite bank. Across from the safe and the acceptable—with only the width of the mighty river to separate the two—all manner of decadence and depravity had become well-entrenched.

The wealth was just as evident on the far bank of the Bale, if not even more so, the free flow of money and vice drawing the respectable and disreputable alike. Gaming and gambling drew the greedy and the bored. Taverns and teahouses enticed the hungry and the hiding. Elaborate public bathhouses, where washwomen would draw a man's bath, clean his clothes, and keep him content while he waited for them, attracted the soiled and the lonely, and kept them coming back again. Luxurious inns boasted rooms that were fully stocked with food and fair company, and the drinks never stopped flowing.

It all bore the purifying sheen of money, but the women were still concubines and the spirits still made men foolish. Kjell's men were eager to be impetuous and imprudent for several days, and when they boarded their horses and secured lodging, they dispersed along the streets of Enoch with firm orders to be prepared to ride out in two days' time. Kjell was among them, Sasha deposited in a room of her own with a maid at her beck and call and the benign instruction to do whatever she wished.

Yet Kjell worried.

And he fretted.

Then he grew angry that he worried and frustrated that he fretted. Finally, after spending hours doing the things that usually brought him pleasure and relief, he stormed back to the inn where he'd left her. He stomped up the stairs to her room and pounded upon the door of her chamber until she opened it with weary eyes, the wafting scent of rose petals, and freshly-washed hair. He grunted his relief that all was well, repeated his edict that she go wherever she pleased, and turned and stomped to his own quarters, directly across the wide corridor.

Then he stood inside his room and listened at his door, straining his ears to see if she left. She didn't. Where would she go? Did he think she'd followed him from Solemn only to leave him in Enoch? He threw himself across the massive bed and fell into restless sleep, wishing she was curled nearby and hating himself for it.

He would take her to Jeru City. He would find a place for her in the queen's service, and he would be free of her.

He returned to the bathhouse the next day, determined to lose himself in his old ways, to soothe himself in water and steam and scent and skin. But the woman who attended him looked like Ariel of Firi—it was the look he thought he preferred—with dusky skin and full lips, round hips and heavy breasts. Her thick, black hair was arranged in fat ropes down her back, and he found himself wishing it was unbound, the curls untamed. When she looked up at him, her eyes carefully lined in kohl and heavy-lidded with pretended ardor, he felt nothing but self-loathing. He immediately sent her away.

He washed himself and donned fresh clothes, eager to be on his way though he had no destination. He walked aimlessly, his eyes empty and his mind full, when he thought he saw the washwoman again. He recoiled, wondering why she would trail him, and realized it wasn't her at all.

The woman passed by, eyeing him with blatant appreciation and he realized his mistake. She didn't resemble the washwoman from the bathhouse. Not really. She resembled Ariel of Firi. Did every woman have her face, or did he see her treachery in every woman? He looked for her wherever he went. He'd never spoken her name again, never told Tiras that he searched, but he had never stopped.

She would be difficult to find. She'd beguiled him for many years, feigning devotion and fealty, swearing her loyalty to the crown while plotting to undermine it. She was a woman who could change from one animal to another, flying from place to place, shifting as her climate and surroundings required. She would blend in until it was safe to be seen. Then she would take what she wanted and hurt whom she must.

She had never been satisfied with being the daughter of a lord or an ambassador of a province. She'd wanted more, circling Tiras and using Kjell, plotting to make him king so she could take her place beside him. But Kjell had never wanted to be king and suddenly another woman had been named queen—a little bird with powers even greater than her own. Unmasked, Ariel of Firi had disappeared.

He had no doubt she would surface again. When she did, he would not be a Healer. He would be an executioner, and there would be justice.

He walked until dusk and returned to the inn, lurking outside of Sasha's chamber, famished and dissatisfied. He could hear her inside and wanted to see her, even for a moment, but spent the evening in his chamber, eating his supper alone, and wishing the morning would come. As the hour grew late, he found himself outside her room again—telling himself he was only seeing how she fared—and discovered that the door was unlatched. He pushed it wide, alarmed, and stepped inside. No candles were lit, no supper had been consumed, and her bed was neatly made.

Sasha stood by the window, and she'd pushed the drapes wide to let in the moonlight. It appeared she was waiting, though for what he couldn't guess. He pushed the door closed behind him, making her jump and making him scowl.

"Your door was ajar. We aren't in the middle of Quondoon, Sasha. We're on the banks of Enoch, and there are plenty here who would like nothing better than to drag you off."

Her hair was loose around her body, and her eyes were on the moon, but when he spoke she turned from the window and met his gaze. She was breathing rapidly like she was afraid, and her eyes were so wide he thought he must be too late, that something or someone had already harmed her.

"Sasha?"

With a deep inhale and little warning, she pulled her new dress over her head and stood naked in the moonlight—bare skin and rosy-tipped breasts, gently flared hips and long limbs—all of her softness exposed to the night. He could have closed the distance between them, if only to shield her from his eyes and cover her with his body, but he stepped back instead. He saw her hands flex at her sides, resisting the urge to cover what she'd revealed, and he knew she was frightened.

"What are you doing?" he moaned, simultaneously horrified and transfixed. He *knew* what she was doing. He was not an innocent and a woman's body was always something to be appreciated. But the setting was all wrong. Her pale skin and vivid hair looked garish in the darkness, a sacrificial offering to an idol she'd created—an idol he knew did not exist—and he took no pleasure in the sight of her, even as he acknowledged her beauty.

"I am yours," she said simply, but there was a tremor in her voice—just the smallest hint of distress—that made Kjell's legs feel weak even as his head swam with the vision of her. "I am not a child. I have lain with men. Twice Mina arranged it. She told me it would keep us safe. Now I belong to you. I will lie with you if that is what you wish."

Outside a bird shrieked, and the sounds in the street beyond and the establishment below seemed to swell all around them, in chorus with the pounding of blood in his head. Sasha started to sink to her knees, supplicating and subservient, and Kjell raised a warning hand.

"Don't you dare kneel!" he roared, and she froze, her chin snapping up. Her eyes—deep and sad—reminded him of the well in the Jeru City square where Jeruvians shouted their wishes, only to leave, disappointed and hoarse. He would not make the same mistake. He would not yell, and he would not make foolish wishes.

He stalked toward her, pinning her in place with his gaze. Bending, he grabbed her gown from the ground and offered it insistently. When she made no move to take it, he tossed it at her. It collided with her chest and slid down her body, pooling at her feet once again. His eyes followed the descent but he forced them to stay at her feet.

"I know why you are doing this," he said, moderating his voice.

"Because it is expected?" she offered, though it was more a question than an explanation.

"You want to bind us together. But lying with you will not bind me to you. It will only further bind *you* to me. Do you understand?"

Sasha was silent, as if she didn't understand at all.

"Men like me don't—" he paused midsentence and rephrased. "Men don't lie with women because they . . . love them. Men find pleasure in the act. That is all. It is women who find something else."

He picked up her dress once more, finding the opening and forcing it over her head, keeping his eyes averted as best he could. It bunched around her neck and her arms weren't in the sleeves, but it covered most of her salient parts. His fingers brushed the place where her shoulder met her throat, and he felt her jerk. She might want to please him, but she was afraid of him too. She began to right her clothing, shoving her arms back into the sleeves and securing the ties at her breasts.

"You and your men, you went to the washwomen yesterday." It was said without accusation, but Sasha clearly knew that the washwomen offered a variety of services. "You gave one of the women your body, Captain, and you took hers. Why will you not do the same with me?"

"How do you know this?" he gasped.

"When you left me here, I saw it, as if it had already happened."

His stomach roiled, and he stumbled back.

"You are far more trouble than you are worth," he whispered, mortified that she had seen him, and worse, that she'd admitted it to him.

"That is what Mina used to say," she whispered, bowing her head. "I'm sorry if I've made you angry. I cannot help what I see." Her voice broke, and he knew he'd wounded her. "I am trying . . . so hard . . . to understand you."

"If you want to understand something . . . then ask." He knew as soon as he said the words, he would regret them.

"And you will tell me?" Her voice was so wistful he could only nod.

"We will be on the back of that horse for another fortnight. I will tell you." She nodded and he inclined his head as well, indicating a bargain agreed upon. He had to get out of her chamber. His hands were shaking and his lungs burned. He turned and strode toward the door.

"Kjell?"

It was the first time she'd ever said his name. She usually called him captain or master, though he'd put an end to the latter very quickly. He froze.

"Yes?"

"You said if I came back . . . you would try to love me."

He turned his head, caught in the familiarity of the words.

"What?"

"Come to me and I will try to love you, I will try to love you, if you but come back," she chanted softly. "I heard you . . . and I came back."

"I lied," he said, breathless. He made himself look at her again, so she would believe him. She was covered from head to toe, and yet he could still see her unclothed.

"Who were you lying to?" she asked.

"To you," he whispered, lying again. He looked for his anger. Where was his bloody anger? *Come to me and I will try to love you. I will try to love you, if you but come back.*

She made him want to try. She made him want to lie again.

"It didn't feel like a lie," she said, and he could only stare at her silently, willing her to let it go. But she persisted, relentless in her undressing.

"You didn't kiss the wash woman. Why? Do men not find pleasure in kissing?"

His body tightened and he turned away, reaching blindly for the door.

"You said if I didn't understand something I should ask."

"Yes. Men find pleasure in kissing," he ground out.

"Will you kiss me?" she asked, and he cursed, slamming his hand against the heavy wood, making it tremble and his resentment soar. He turned on her with his weapons drawn.

"Why?" he made his voice cold, but he didn't wait for her to answer. "If I do not kiss you . . . are you going to take off your clothes and offer yourself to one of my men?"

She flinched and he cursed.

"Why would I do that?" she whispered.

"You are trying to survive. I understand that." He *did* understand it, and he wouldn't hold it against her, even if it bothered him. Survival was ugly, and she'd survived terrible circumstances. Still, such behavior would cause problems among his men.

"You are wrong. That is not who I am." Her voice shook, and for the first time, he saw fury in her face.

"It is who we *all* are, Sasha. Every man and every woman. We are all just trying to survive."

"Why do you hate me so much?" she asked, her voice level but her face flushed. Her eyes were molten, and he wondered how he had ever thought them blank. They snapped and sparked, radiating heat and life and emotion.

He closed the space between them and sank his hands into her heavy hair, lifting her chin to his so he could drive his words home. The angle parted her rosy lips, and he scowled down at them, their very color suspicious to him.

"I don't hate you," he choked out. "I don't *trust* you. I don't want to feel *anything* for you. And you are determined to make me your fool."

She answered him with clawed hands, pulling at his hair the way he pulled at hers, her arms bracketing his face, her body crowding him. Her sudden aggression surprised him. For once, her anger rivaled his own.

"Do you feel this?" she asked, her hands tightening in his hair, making his scalp burn. "What about this?" She stood on tiptoe and sank her teeth into his lower lip, hanging on like a rabid wolf as he hissed and gripped her face between his palms to make her stop.

They were nose to nose, chest to chest, his lip caught between her teeth when he realized that her breasts were soft and her thighs firm, her temper hot and her mouth wet. Her face was delicate beneath his hands, the line of her jaw smooth and silky, her eyes as liquid as the blood that roared in his head. She released his lip from her teeth, but her hands didn't loosen in his hair, and she didn't retreat.

"Do you feel me now?" she asked, but her voice cracked, her anger melding into uncertainty.

It was something Lady Firi would have said—bold and imperious—but Ariel of Firi wouldn't have released his lip, and she wouldn't have watched him with the same mixture of expectation and vulnerability. Lady Firi would not have waited for him to kiss her with lips that trembled or eyes that begged. She would have bit him and scratched him and wrapped herself around him, taking what she wanted.

"No," he lied, harsh. Hell-bent. But his heart betrayed him, quaking, terrified that Sasha would believe him—finally—and release him, shamed, as he intended her to be. Shame was a wonderful weapon. But she didn't step back, didn't pull away from him. Instead, she continued to lay herself open, an emotional obeisance that was unfathomable to him.

"How can I feel so much when you feel so little?" she cried, her breath moving against his lips, the mere inches between them a contradiction to the lies he told. He couldn't answer her. He would give himself away. So he stared stonily, unflinching in his deceit. Her lids closed, as if his glaring refusal hurt her eyes. Her lashes, as black as her eyes, lay against her freckled cheeks and, freed from her gaze, he shuddered. She was precious to him. Precious and so . . . lovely.

She was *so* impossibly lovely.

Men who made their living with a sword were large and strong, or they didn't last for long. Women who made their living serving others were lithe and lean, with very little left over for themselves. Kjell was a warrior, Sasha was a slave.

But he felt her.

She must have sensed his tremor, for her mouth returned. No anger this time, no teeth. She simply placed her lips on his, connecting them, as if by doing so she would see inside him, hear his thoughts, and know for certain that he was immune to her.

If she had lain with men, those men had only taken, not given, because she did not seem to understand the art of the act or the steps typically followed to create pleasure. She did not curl her tongue against his or even part her lips to invite him in. Hers was not so much a kiss as a need to get closer—to know—and her mouth was completely still against his. Soft. But still.

Then her lips parted slightly and she inhaled, drawing his heart from his chest, out his captive lips, and into her lungs. It was in that moment that he lost his grip on denial and plummeted into the warm abyss of acceptance.

The hands he'd never withdrawn from her face shifted, his fingers curling against her skull, holding her to him, and his lips began a frenzied game of seek and find, his tongue following the path of his soul, the soul she'd extracted with her indrawn breath. She welcomed him with thoughtless ardor, matching the press of his lips and the heat of his mouth with jubilance, arms clinging to his back, her body vibrating like a bow string.

Wrapped around each other, their mouths melded and mated, only to retreat and reclaim, colliding over and over again. He would not be able to let her go, he thought. He would *never* be free of her. The knowledge flitted past the black of his closed lids, a shooting star fierce and fleeting, only to be absorbed into his wonderment.

SIX

He kissed her like a starving man only to push her away like he'd had his fill. He hadn't. He was still ravenous, still empty. She gazed at him with swollen lips and a million questions, and he felt the wildness in his eyes, in his heart, and in his head.

He strode to the door, changed his mind, and marched back toward her, deciding hunger was preferable to thirst. Being near her quenched something in him, and his chamber was a desert. "I don't want to leave." He folded his arms defensively, as if she would demand that he go. "I will stay . . . but I won't . . . partake. I won't touch you. And you won't touch me."

She nodded eagerly, clearly not as famished as he, and immediately pulled a thick fur from the bed and made herself a place on the floor.

"Sasha," he barked. "You are not my servant. You are not my slave. That is *your* bed. You will sleep there."

She instantly obeyed, but a smile played around her lips. She was laughing at him. He was a bloody fool. But still . . . he could not make himself leave.

He stayed with her, but he kept his word. He didn't touch her again. Instead he stretched out on the floor, a pillow beneath his head, waiting for her to go to sleep so he wouldn't be tempted to keep her awake.

"Do you want me to tell you a tale?" she whispered into the darkness.

"No," he rasped. Her voice would destroy him. Shred him. He could only lay in silence, listening to her breathe.

"Will you ever kiss me again, Kjell?"

"No, Sasha," he bit out, his palms pressing into his eyes.

"Never?" Her voice was so doubtful he wanted to laugh—damned fool—and he wondered if she saw kisses in their future. The thought drew him up short.

"Not tonight, Sasha," he amended, and he knew he'd already begun to slip.

"Why?" she asked, and the word twisted in his belly like a sword. He thought he might bleed to death on her floor, confused and wounded, desperate to understand himself and be understood.

"Because I have loved and hated all the wrong people," he admitted.

"And you don't know whether to love or hate me?" she asked, her voice almost tender.

"No," he confessed.

"I have been hated before. But I don't know if I've been loved. I think . . . once . . . I must have been, because I know how to love."

"Do you know how to hate?" he asked, his voice sharp, ricocheting through the chamber. "If you don't know how to hate, how could you possibly know how to love?"

"I don't have to know how to die to know how to live,' she said simply, and he found he had no response.

"Tell me who it was that you were so wrong about," she pressed.

He considered feigning sleep, but felt like a coward.

"I hated Queen Lark. Despised her. And I was cruel to her," he answered.

"Why?"

"Because I loved my brother, and I was afraid she would betray him."

"But she didn't?"

"No. She . . . saved him." Sasha waited silently for him to continue. "I hated Lark—who deserved none of my dislike. But I loved my father." The sword kept turning.

"Of course you did. I love mine, and I can't even remember him."

Kjell half laughed, half moaned, grateful for her sweetness even as he raged against it, but her next words had him writhing again.

"And you loved a woman who loved herself above all else."

He didn't answer. He couldn't. And then her voice grew faint, as if she'd suddenly become drowsy but wanted to finish her thought.

"She was very beautiful. But she didn't want to be just a woman. She wanted to be everything. She changed into a silky black cat and wrapped herself around your legs. You tried to pick her up, but she rent your clothes with her claws and made you bleed. She turned into a bird, and you tried to stay with her, but she flew too high and too fast. When you were about to give up, she called to you, and lured you closer, and you joined her on the edge of the sea. She walked into the water and became a creature from the deep, a shark with layers of teeth, and you followed her across the waters, begging her to change. She became a beautiful white horse and swam to the shores. She convinced you to climb upon her back. She said she'd carry you. But instead she changed beneath you and you were thrown to the ground."

"I thought you didn't see the past." He wondered which of his men had seen fit to share their captain's history.

"Maybe she is *not* the past," she suggested, so softly he barely heard the words.

The humiliation and rage that always filled him when he thought of Ariel of Firi scalded his throat and made his heart race like he was being pursued.

"I do not love her anymore," he whispered.

Sasha was quiet so long he thought she must have fallen asleep. He closed his eyes as well, knowing he should leave, knowing he wouldn't. He'd spent too many nights sleeping close to her; now he didn't want to sleep apart.

"I have seen her, Kjell," she sighed.

He gasped and rose from the floor, approaching the bed so he could stare down at her. Her hands were curled beneath her chin, the covers pulled around her shoulders. Fiery hair spilled across the pillows and brushed her face. Her eyes were closed and she breathed deeply, lost in sleep or in visions, he couldn't be sure.

"Where, Sasha?" he asked.

But she didn't answer.

They left Enoch before the sun was high. Kjell's men were bright-eyed and straight in their saddles, faking good spirits, a full night's sleep, and strict abstinence. They knew if they wanted a repeat of the kind of freedom they'd experienced during the last two days, they would need to be convincing. Still, Kjell caught more than one man looking back at the bustling city; no one was especially eager to leave her behind.

Between the city of Enoch—named after the larger province —and the borders of Janda, there was little to see and less to do. Kjell had acquired another horse where he boarded his stallion, a pretty, brown mare with a strong back and a pleasant disposition. The horse had nuzzled his neck and eaten from his hand, and when he'd saddled and mounted her, she'd accepted his weight and direction with a docile patience he was sure would suit Sasha.

Sasha needed her own mount if he was to survive her company.

The mare didn't cost him much—the stable master seemed eager to be rid of her—and he haggled with the stable master's wife to fetch two riding gowns for him as part of the deal. She procured three, and he'd returned to the inn, shoved them at Sasha, and demanded that she change.

For once, he'd risen before her—he'd never actually slept— and left her chamber so he wouldn't have to greet her when she woke.

"I cannot pay you, Captain," she'd said, running her hands over the buttery cloth and marveling at the voluminous folds which disguised the breeches beneath.

She had resumed her subservient ways, making it easier for him to retreat behind his previous persona, the one who hadn't seen her unclothed. Neither of them mentioned fevered kisses or his sojourn on her floor.

"I don't demand payment," he barked, and she left it alone.

Now she rode beside him, her eyes forward, posture erect, handling the horse with an ease that belied her history.

Jerick was unusually quiet throughout the morning as they followed the dusty road that would continue in a long, straight path toward Janda. When the way narrowed at a deep ravine, they fell into a single-file line, and Kjell sent Sasha ahead, holding back until everyone else had crossed. Jerick waited beside him, watching the others proceed.

"I thought you might find work for her in Enoch," Jerick commented softly, his eyes on Sasha's slim back.

"I am taking her to Jeru City. Wasn't that your suggestion, Lieutenant?" Kjell answered darkly.

"Yes . . . but I saw you leave her chamber this morning, Captain."

"You will do well to control your thoughts and your tongue, Jerick."

"If you don't mean to keep her, you cannot use her," Jerick snapped.

Without warning, Kjell snatched his blade from his boot, striking out with a glancing swipe and nicking Jerick's left cheek.

"You were warned, Lieutenant."

Jerick reared back, his hand on his sword, his face bleeding, his ego clipped. The wound was shallow, but a soldier's pride was deep, and Kjell waited, tensed for the young lieutenant to make another challenge. Jerick had never been able to hold his tongue. It was the thing Kjell both loved and loathed about him.

Jerick's eyes flickered to the woman in question and back to his captain. Sasha's presence among them was already wreaking havoc. Kjell was not a Seer, but he'd seen this moment coming. He would have to claim the woman for the good of his men, or he would have to let her go. Sooner rather than later.

"She is mine."

Jerick's eyebrows rose, and his hand fell from the hilt of his sword. His horse shimmied, mirroring his surprise, and Jerick wiped at his cheek, smearing the blood across his nose.

"She is yours?" Jerick asked, his venom notably absent. "What does that mean, Captain?"

Bloody hell if he knew what it meant. But he'd said it, and his stomach flipped once and then again before it settled.

"It means you will never again question my motives where Sasha is concerned."

"Yes, Captain. I will tell the men."

"Damnation, Jerick." Kjell wanted to shove the man from his horse.

"It is better that they understand, Captain," Jerick said gravely. Kjell cursed again, snarling at Jerick's false solemnity.

Jerick mopped at his bleeding cheek again, and Kjell groaned, noting that Sasha and the rest of his guard now waited on the opposite side of the ravine, observing the exchange. He was fairly confident the conversation hadn't been overheard, but the animosity—and the blood—was hard to miss. Raising a hand to his mouth, Kjell pulled his glove free with his teeth and placed his bare palm on Jerick's cheek. With a humming sigh, Kjell healed the wound he'd inflicted, leaving nothing behind but smeared blood and a smirk on his lieutenant's face.

"Thank you, Captain."

"Cease speaking, Jerick."

"You cut Jerick. And then you healed him," Sasha said, after riding silently beside him for an interminable hour.

"Yes." Kjell knew the question was coming.

"You giveth and you taketh away?" Her voice was troubled. He wanted to ask her what bothered her most . . . his anger toward Jerick or his casual use of his gift. But he didn't.

"I chastised him . . . then I forgave him," he said.

"Why?"

"Because everyone deserves healing." He meant to mock her, but his delivery was weak and his target unfazed.

"Hopefully everyone won't *require* healing." Sasha's brow furrowed, drawing her freckles together in unanimous disapproval.

She didn't press the issue or needle him further about his quarrel with Jerick, but she had not forgotten his promise to answer her questions. Over the next week she peppered him with inanities, and he always answered, even when he would rather listen to her talk. His men kept a wide berth while they traveled, affording them an odd privacy that Kjell liked too much. Jerick had clearly informed them of their captain's claim.

Fine. Just as long as he didn't inform Sasha.

Whenever Kjell could manage it, he would turn her questions back around, saving himself from closer examination, and she answered him without artifice, without hesitation, and he found he wanted to know everything about her. Every miniscule, paltry crumb.

The terrain from Enoch to Janda was a continuous, slow climb that leveled out only to drop again, terrace after terrace, until reaching sea level in the center of the province. Kjell had planned to curve through Janda, assess any Volgar presence with a visit to the lord, skirt the hills on the border of Degn and the lower regions, and cut through the corner of Gaul before heading northwest back to the City of Jeru.

Along Janda's southern rim, the terraces fell off suddenly, creating sheer drops to the sea five hundred feet below. The sea was named Takei, and the salt levels were so great a man could practically walk on its surface. The province of Janda had profited from the extraction of salt from the Takei Sea for a thousand years. The Bale River emptied into the Takei, which stretched east and west on the extreme edge of Enoch all the way to the middle of Janda. Kjell had considered that the Volgar might be nesting on the cliffs and on the beaches, but few creatures could survive on the salty water. The briny Takei was more suited to sea creatures than birdmen.

They could smell the salt on the breeze as they crossed the wide, Jandarian grassland, sitting high above the body of water, and Sasha was inspired with another round of questions.

"Land or sea?" she mused.

"Land. The sea is too elusive," he replied easily.

"I love the sea," she sighed.

"You remember the sea?" It surprised him. Quondoon was nowhere near the sea.

"Yes." She nodded. "I do. I suppose I remember the sea the way I remember how to read or how to walk or how to breathe."

"The seashore was beautiful in Kilmorda."

"But not anymore?" she asked sadly.

"It will take some time for Kilmorda to be beautiful again."

"Someday," she murmured, and Kjell didn't know if it was something she saw or merely wished for.

"Darkness or light?" she asked after a moment.

"Light."

When he didn't elucidate, she chided him. "It is not enough to choose, Captain. You must explain your choice."

He sighed, but he didn't mind terribly. "In the light everything is obvious. There are no secrets. You simply have to look in order to see."

"What was your mother's name?" she parried, keeping him off balance. It was an effective technique. He hadn't lied once.

"Her name was Koorah. She was a servant in my father's castle. She died at my birth." In three simple sentences he'd told her everything he knew about his mother. Name, occupation, death. Nothing more.

She tipped her head at that, regarding him thoughtfully. He did his best not to squirm in the saddle.

"Bird or beast?" she asked, pivoting again.

"My brother is a Changer. He would tell you there is nothing like being a bird. But I have no desire to fly. I don't have any desire to *change* at all. I struggle enough with who I am without shifting from one form to the next."

"Song or tale?"

"I sing to heal, but I take great pleasure in hearing you speak, in hearing your stories," he admitted gruffly.

She beamed, her smile lighting her face with such pleasure that he wondered why he hadn't been trying harder to make her happy. She was so beautiful when she smiled.

"What gives you joy?" he asked abruptly, wanting to uncover ways to make her smile again. He immediately felt ridiculous, as if he were trying to woo her, and his hands tightened on the reins, making his horse whinny in protest and Sasha search his eyes.

She looked away rapidly, her cheeks growing ruddy, as if his question embarrassed her. Or maybe it was the answer that embarrassed her.

A gentleman would have apologized for making her uncomfortable, but Kjell was not—nor had he ever been—a *gentle* man. He was not educated in the art of flowery words, false sympathies, or fake sentiments.

She spoke quickly, quietly, as if she wanted him to listen but wasn't brave enough to make sure he heard. "When you kissed me, I felt . . . joyful. In fact, I've never felt joy like that in my whole life. I've never felt *anything* like that. If I had . . . my lips would remember. My heart would remember. I want very much to feel that way again."

Kjell's heart swelled, filling his chest with a sensation that resembled floating. He drew Lucian to a stop. Sasha halted beside him, confused. Jerick tossed a puzzled look toward them.

"Take the men. Go on ahead. Sasha needs to rest for a moment. We'll catch up shortly," he instructed. Jerick immediately signaled the men to keep moving, assuming, as Kjell wanted him to, that Sasha required privacy for personal reasons.

Sasha didn't dispute his claim, but her brows were drawn, her lower lip tucked between her teeth, biting back her words. He waited until the last man had rounded the crop of umbrella thorn trees ahead and slid from Lucian's back, no hesitation, no second thoughts. His pulse roared in his ears and tickled the back of his throat, and he reached for Sasha, pulling her from the saddle of the docile, brown mare.

She squeaked, and he felt her surprise against his lips as he lowered his head and pressed his mouth to hers.

He didn't close his eyes as he tasted her, not in the beginning. He didn't want to look away. He wanted to see her pleasure, to witness her joy. The horses at their backs made a V behind them, the lemongrass brushed at their legs, and the cooing mutter of sandgrouse nearby registered only distantly, part of the flavor of the experience, a dash of sound and texture.

But Kjell heard only her sigh, felt only the silk of her mouth, and saw only the spikey tips of her lashes as they fluttered in surrender. Or maybe it wasn't her surrender but his, for his legs trembled and his eyes closed, his lips moved in adoring supplication, his heart broke and bowed down before her, and his chest burned in elation.

Her fingers brushed his face, and her mouth sought his, even when he withdrew slightly so he wouldn't fall down. Their breath mingled in frenzied dancing, tumbling over and teasing their sensitive lips. He pressed his forehead to hers, resisting the desire to make her sigh again. He'd let himself forget for a moment that he didn't want her. He circled her waist with his hands and put her back on her horse so he wouldn't pull her down into the grass.

"That is . . . joy," Sasha whispered, looking down at him. "It has to be."

"No. That is pleasure," he replied curtly, stepping away from her horse. She stared down at him, her gaze knowing, absorbing his terse dismissal.

"Maybe pleasure feels like joy. But pleasure can be satisfied, and joy never needs to be. It is a glory all its own," she said.

He turned away, almost ashamed of himself, and prepared to mount Lucian.

Suddenly, with no reason or provocation, the mare Sasha was seated on shot forward.

Sasha cried out and teetered, but managed to hang on. She pressed herself against the horse's neck, grasping frantically for the lost reins. Kjell lunged for the mare, but was too slow. He shouted, alerting his men, and mounted Lucian, pursuing the spooked mare now racing toward the cliffs, bolting like she'd seen a rattler. Sasha could only cling to the horse's mane, her veil whipping free, the panels of her yellow dress streaming behind her. Kjell spurred Lucian forward, covering the space between the galloping mare and his stallion. Lucian's superior size and strength made the smaller horse easy to catch, but the mare was undeterred. They flew across the plateau, the drop looming closer, the mare heading straight for the ledge at full speed. Kjell attempted to turn the fleeing horse, to cut her off and change her course, but the mare simply charged ahead, dropping her head and, if anything, increasing her speed.

"Sasha!" he shouted, needing her to look at him, to know what he was about to attempt. She turned her head slowly, her face pressed to the mare's neck, her eyes wide with horror. If she let go she would, at the very least, be badly hurt. If she didn't let go, she would go over the edge with the crazed horse.

Kjell drew abreast of the mare, matching her pace. With the experience born of warfare on horseback, of wielding a shield and swinging a sword, of holding on with nothing but powerful legs and sheer terror, he lunged to the side and snaked his right arm around Sasha's waist. With absolute faith, Sasha released the mare's mane and hurled herself toward him as he dragged her free. Pulling her across his saddle, his thighs anchoring them both to the stallion beneath him, he bore down on Lucian's reins, turning him to the left and demanding he halt.

"Whoa, Lucian! Whoa!"

The stallion drew up immediately, slowing until he could safely stop. Pawing and tossing his head, he whinnied desperately as Kjell and Sasha watched the brown mare, without ever slowing or altering direction, careen over the edge and disappear. There was no equine shriek of terror, no smattering of rocks marking her descent, no fading sounds of alarm. She was just . . . gone.

Kjell's men had joined in the pursuit, fanning into a circle to corral the crazed animal, and they drew up around them, breathing hard, faces shocked. A gull, flapping wildly, feathers fluttering, rose up from beyond the cliff's edge like it had been startled by the falling horse.

"We've disturbed their nests," Sasha gasped, her face pressed into Kjell's neck where she clutched him tightly.

She was breathless, panting, and Kjell was still lost in the horror of the narrowly-avoided tragedy. Then Sasha was pushing herself upright, her hands braced against his chest, trying to catch her breath and communicate simultaneously.

"Captain, the Volgar! We've disturbed their nests."

SEVEN

From beyond the cliffs, in the space where the horse had disappeared, the sound of beating wings filled the air, a hundred times greater than a flock of gulls, rising over the edge and making the horses shudder and scream.

"Get back!" Kjell shouted, knowing a battle near the drop would favor the Volgar, not the King's Guard. They raced back toward the hard-packed path that cut the savannah, back across the distance they'd just traveled, chasing and being chased, exchanging one horror for another. But the Volgar didn't swoop and drop.

They were thin, their skins papery and yellow, their wings shredded like a spider's web. These weren't the Volgar who grew large and fat in the valley of Kilmorda. These were Volgar who were becoming extinct. Their eyes glittered desperately, and their beaks snapped and clicked, beating at the air high above the soldiers, frantic for blood but too weak to take it. They circled like vultures, looking for an opportunity—a smaller victim, an exhausted horse, a space between soldiers.

"Dismount and draw together!" Kjell roared. The horses were accustomed to battle, to the shriek of the winged beasts, to carrying a warrior while he wielded a sword, but Kjell couldn't fight with Sasha in front of him. He slid from the saddle, dragging her with him, his arm around her waist, not even waiting for Lucian to come to a complete stop.

The horses shuddered but didn't bolt, and the soldiers clustered quickly, drawing the horses down, creating a formation with their backs facing inward and their lances bristling outward. The soldiers on the outer edges knelt, the next row crouched, the inner rows stood, and the soldiers in the center held their lances at near vertical, protecting the formation from directly overhead, making a sphere of sharp edges around both man and beast with Sasha pushed to the center and told to crouch and cover her head.

They watched the birdmen swarm and circle, waiting for an opening.

Kjell saw it before it began, the horror of bloodlust, of hunger and desperation. The Volgar had no sense of self-preservation. Or maybe they had lost all instinct in their desire to eat. They started falling from the sky, several birdmen sacrificed themselves upon the upraised spears. The impact impaled them but also dislodged the lances, creating an opening for the beasts behind them and breaking the formation. One birdman hit the ground and immediately lost a wing on Kjell's sword. Another bird plunged, then another, their wings folded to increase their speed.

"Scatter!" Kjell roared, commanding his men to change the formation. His men immediately widened the circle and released the horses, slapping their rumps to make them run, creating chaos and distraction.

"Brace!" Kjell ordered, and his men dropped to their knees, still back to back, their lances butted against the ground. Kjell remained standing, giving himself greater mobility, awaiting the

AMY HARMON

next bird's arrival, his sword black with blood, his stance wide. One birdman drew up mid-dive, distracted by the galloping horses, and the Volgar in his wake catapulted past him. The Guard let them fall, expanding their circle and contracting it, keeping Sasha in the center, protecting her even as the birds pounced.

One minute Kjell was brandishing his sword, separating a birdman's body from his head, the next he was on his back, looking at the sky. Sasha pressed him into the grass, her eyes pupilless in her face, her skin leached of color, her hair tumbling around them.

Then she was lifted straight up off the ground, dangling over him from the talons of a birdman, her eyes still strangely blank, her arms reaching for him as she was propelled upward.

The birdman stuttered mid-flight, as if the weight of the woman proved too much for him in his weakened state. The other Volgar began lifting off, eager to share the birdman's catch and escape the weapons that had already decimated more than half of their flock.

"Sasha!" Kjell was on his feet hurling his lance before he could think about missing, before he could even consider the blood that was growing in an ever-widening stain on her pale dress.

The point of his spear sank into the birdman's throat, reverberating with the force of impact, and Sasha swung her arms and tossed her head, kicking to free herself. The birdman sank, choking on the green-black blood that poured from his mouth, but he refused to release his prize. The other Volgar swarmed around him, talons extended, hearts visibly pounding in their emaciated chests, eager to take her from him. Another lance pierced the captor's left wing—Jerick's aim was true—and the mortally wounded birdman, hovering about ten feet above the earth, released Sasha too late to save himself. Sasha didn't stay down, but shot to her feet, racing toward Kjell, arms pumping, hair streaming, and Kjell brought down two birdmen before he could push her back to the ground with a furious order to "stay the hell down!" His men closed around her again, swords out, faces lifted toward the sky, waiting for the next rush.

There wasn't one.

Three birdmen lived to fly away, their shredded wings and bony bodies disappearing beyond the cliffs from whence they came.

"God damn you, woman!" Kjell moaned, sinking to his knees beside Sasha. She pushed herself up gingerly, her face tight with pain, one armed wrapped around her middle, her hand pressed to her side, trying to cover the blood that soaked her dress.

"You aren't wearing your breastplate," she said softly, her eyes forgiving him even as she scolded. "You didn't protect your heart, so I had to."

"The horses are scattered, Captain. But we need to walk. We can't stay here. The Volgar carcasses will draw other predators," Gibbous urged. The Jandarian savannah was known for its lions, and though the men had not seen any sign of the packs since crossing from Enoch, they didn't want to attract their attention. Volgar bled the wrong color and they stank like hyenas, but somehow Kjell thought the lions might not care.

But Sasha's blood was red, and she was bleeding a great deal. Kjell scooped her into his arms, and his men fell in behind him, loping across the dry grass to the cluster of trees where Kjell had kissed Sasha an eternity before.

"I have to heal her, or the lions will follow her scent, no matter how far we go," he barked, calling a halt to their progress. He didn't think about how much blood Sasha had already lost or that his shirt was soaked through where he held her tightly against him. "Stop just beyond the trees. Half of you stay with me, the others fan out. We need to find the horses," Kjell ordered. He shot out orders—a blade to cut away the back of her dress, a flask to make her drink—and then demanded his men give him enough space and privacy to make her well.

Long grooves scored her back, so deep he could see the white of bone beneath the bubbling blood. He pressed his palms to the wounds and willed them closed. Her blood warmed his hands and stained his fingers, but the wounds did not mend. He turned her on her side, pressing a hand between her breasts and finding her heartbeat. She watched him with calm acceptance and faith-filled eyes, but her face was so pale he couldn't see the gold in her skin.

"Sasha—sing with me," he pled, the first waves of doubt making him desperate. Her song was all around him, crystal clear, a chiming he now recognized, a peal of bells that had healed injuries far more grievous than the ones he now struggled to close. Yet he couldn't close them.

"Come with me and I will try to love you," she whispered, smiling gently, her eyes growing heavy.

"That's right," he nodded. He closed his eyes, letting the pealing pulse beneath his skin, but the gashes down her back mocked him, becoming garish grins that laughed at his failure.

He buried his face in her neck and wrapped her in his arms, magnifying the clangor of her healing song until he shook with it. His head was a gong, his heart the beat that kept it ringing. And ringing. And ringing.

"Kjell," someone said.

"Captain," he heard again, and the knell in his skull became an echo. His muscles were locked and he couldn't open his eyes.

He could feel Jerick above him and sensed that time had passed while he rang the alarm. The sky was dark, and small pit fires ringed the encampment, keeping the creatures at bay. Kjell concentrated on loosening his fingers one at a time, peeling them from Sasha's skin, releasing her so he could roll away. He fell to his back with a groan, the blood rushing back into his limbs, his body coming awake.

"We need you. There's something wrong with Peter. He's throwing up blood," Jerick said.

"Sasha?" Kjell moaned.

"She sleeps, Captain. You've healed her wounds. She's fine." Jerick sounded confused, irritated even.

"I need to see them."

"Who, Captain?"

"Her wounds. I need to see her back," he hissed, gritting his teeth against the pins and needles in his arms, the burning in his back, and the stabbing in his calves and feet. Jerick turned the sleeping Sasha toward him, coaxing her onto her belly and moving the tattered edges of her dress away from her injuries.

Even in the orange glow of the firelight, Kjell could see that the gashes were closed, but thick, purple lines extended from Sasha's shoulder blades to her waist. There was no infection, and the pain had seemingly gone. But the marks remained.

He struggled to his knees and Jerick was there, slinging one of his arms over his shoulder to help him stand.

"Are you ill, Captain?" Jerick asked, realization making his voice rise in panic. Kjell could heal his men, but none of his men could heal him.

"Stop talking, Jerick."

He didn't allow himself to think at all, to wonder if his Gift was waning. He stumbled through the rows of sleeping soldiers, Jerick supporting him like a drunk being led to the next round of debauchery.

When they reached the ailing soldier, Kjell fell to his knees beside him.

"Get me something to drink, Lieutenant," Kjell ordered. His throat was so dry he couldn't swallow and, as usual, he didn't need an audience. Jerick hesitated but turned to leave.

97

"We need you, Captain," he said softly. "Don't give what you don't have."

"What I don't have is something to drink," he muttered, and Jerick sighed and left to do his bidding. Kjell flexed his hands and laid them on Peter's chest. The young man's song was low and mellow, and Kjell strummed it carefully like a loose lute string.

"There you are, Peter," he urged. "Make it easy on your Captain, will you? I'm a little spent."

He thought of the first time he'd seen the boy, light on his feet and impossibly quick with a sword. He'd grown into a powerful man and a trusted soldier of Jeru. The fondness in Kjell's heart became instant warmth in his hands.

Peter moaned softly, and his breathing began to ease. Kjell tightened the metaphorical string, the tone becoming more strident, and marveled at the impossible ease of the task.

Peter was sitting up asking for water before Jerick even returned.

When Kjell, hydrated and somewhat revived, eased back down beside Sasha, she stirred and opened her eyes.

"Sleep. All is well," he soothed, covering her with a blanket and moving his rolled cloak beneath her head.

She sat up gingerly, as if she weren't sure of her body, and he worried again at his difficulty in healing her.

"Sleep, Sasha."

"You are covered in blood," she murmured.

"Yes. But it isn't mine."

"I will wash you," she insisted. He clearly hadn't healed her need to coddle him.

"No. You will sleep."

"But I am healed. You healed me *again*." Her voice was almost a wail, and it made him smile, in spite of himself.

"Your dress is in tatters. If you rise it will fall off."

She frowned. "It was my favorite one."

"I will buy you a new one," he reassured her. "Please . . . I need you to sleep." She laid back down reluctantly, but she didn't sleep.

"I have seen the Volgar before. They were in Kilmorda," she said.

"Yes. You remember?"

"I don't know if it's a memory . . . or a story someone told me. They don't look the same."

"They are dying."

"I feel no sadness for their suffering," she admitted as though she thought she should.

"Compassion is wasted on the compassionless. There are some things not meant for this world. A man has the right to survive. And Volgar and man cannot exist together. I don't want to eat him. He wants to eat me. Do you see the dilemma? There are some beasts that should not exist." He thought about his father, about the animal he'd become, the monsters he'd made, and the creatures he'd harmed. The only sorrow Kjell felt was that he hadn't been the one to stop him.

"I should tell you a tale," Sasha mused, refusing to quiet down. "Something about a mighty Healer who is *lucky* to exist, considering he refuses to protect himself." He heard teasing but sensed pique. It made him smile again.

"If you will rest I will tell you a story," he offered.

"You will tell *me* one?"

"Yes. I will tell you one. Now hush," he said.

She smacked her lips closed and widened her eyes, indicating she was ready.

"When I was a child, there was a hound that used to sleep in the king's stables. He was ugly. Someone had burned his fur off in huge patches. He was missing an eye, and he always limped. But he was sweet and docile. He didn't snap or bite. He didn't act as if he'd been abused.

"No one knew where he came from, but the servants didn't run him off because he had a calming effect on the king's horses, particularly one stallion—a gift from a lord—that would not be tamed. The horse was violent but his blood lines were impeccable, and King Zoltev wanted to get at least a couple of foals out of him. The hound would sleep at the stallion's feet. The horse would stomp and whinny and thrash for a few minutes, but the dog would not be cowed, and the horse would settle, covering the mares without hurting them.

"No one bothered to give the dog a name. No one showed him any affection. They called him dog. But he was allowed to stay. He never barked, and he was always glad to see me, so when no one was around, I would pet him and call him by the name I'd given him."

When he didn't offer the name, Sasha looked up at him expectantly.

"Tell me what you called him," she demanded.

"Maximus of Jeru."

He'd never told a single soul about Maximus of Jeru. He expected her to laugh and felt his own lips twitch at the memory. But Sasha looked at him steadily, absorbing his words as if they revealed something terribly important.

"Why?" she asked.

"Because he deserved a noble name. He had a noble heart."

She nodded once, accepting that.

"His limp improved, and his coat began to grow lush and shiny around his scars. Maybe I healed him, though I didn't know it then. I thought my affection was healing him. He started following me around wherever I went."

"What happened to Maximus?" There was trepidation in her voice, and Kjell answered immediately, not allowing himself to feel pain over old wounds.

"King Zoltev, in a fit of anger, killed him. Kicked him until he was dead and threw his body into the moat. But the king paid for his anger when his stallion went berserk and killed his prized mare."

"Is that what Gibbous meant . . . when he referred to me as the stable dog? He was talking about Maximus?"

"Gibbous called you a dog?" His voice was flat, but he was instantly seething. He would sentence Gibbous to a dozen lashes.

"He meant no harm. He said he liked dogs more than people, so I should be flattered. Gibbous is not especially . . . tactful."

No. He wasn't, but he had always been a good soldier, and Kjell's temperature cooled slightly. He would still have words with the imbecile.

"So tell me . . . how am I like Maximus?" she pressed, not seeming to care that she'd been insulted. Kjell was not eager to further the comparison, but he knew instantly what Gibbous meant.

"You follow me around because I healed you. You don't get angry when you should. You are kind to those who are cruel. You have a noble heart."

"And a noble name," she added without inflection.

He laughed and she laughed too, softly.

"Your name is growing on me," he admitted. She sighed, a happy sound that made him pull her closer, letting his body more fully shelter her.

"Sasha?"

"Yes?" she answered, her voice drowsy.

"You must never do that again."

"Do what, Captain?"

"Try to protect me."

She was silent, considering, and he waited to see if she would argue or acquiesce.

"I saw you die. I saw talons pierce your heart. And I could not let that happen," she whispered.

She said no more, but he felt her distress at the memory and wished he'd waited until morning to chastise her. Eventually, her breathing eased and her muscles loosened, and he closed his eyes, drifting off to sleep, tucked beside her on the Jandarian plain.

The rains began to fall just after dawn, waking them and soaking their clothes. It wasn't cold—the rain or the air—and they stood out under the sodden sky and let the torrents wash them, cleaning their skin and rinsing their clothes. The horses had been gathered while they slept, and Kjell even retrieved his soap, using the opportunity to get as clean as modesty would allow. He shrugged off his shirt and soaped his chest, reveling in the natural shower and the woman who held her tattered dress around her shoulders and let the rain comb her hair. Laden and dripping, it reached the tops of her thighs, covering the scars on her back and sparing him the pangs of doubt that rose in him when he thought about them.

His men acted like children, scampering in the downpour with bare feet and wrestling in the long grass, and when the rain ceased as suddenly as it had begun, they built a makeshift tent to allow Sasha the privacy to peel off her ruined dress and don a new one. Traveling with a group of men in a landscape that afforded minimal natural cover was its own hardship, but they'd all managed, and she'd never complained. Kjell and his men did their best to get dry themselves, eating a breakfast of dried meat and hard bread, while they waited for the sun to dry the prairie so they could continue on their way.

Isak, the fire starter, approached him when he was checking Lucian's hooves for rocks and thorns, the memory of the bolting mare still fresh in his mind.

"Captain, can I have a word?"

"Speak," Kjell agreed, running his hands down Lucian's legs, over his sides, and inspecting his teeth. The stallion let him, accustomed to his master's attentions, but the fire starter waited for him to finish, as if he needed his captain's eyes. Kjell released Lucian's head and met the younger man's gaze. A thin line of sweat broke out on Isak's lip, and he cleared his throat once before proceeding.

"Captain, last night I drew second watch. I was weary, but I'd had no spirits." His eyes shot to Kjell's. "I know the rules. I saw . . . a woman. She . . . she was unclothed. At first I thought it was Mistress Sasha. And I looked away. I thought . . . I thought maybe . . . she . . . you . . ." he rubbed his hands over his face. Kjell waited, unable to tell where the story was leading and unwilling to steer it, even if it meant steering it away from himself.

"I looked again, Captain. I'm sorry. I couldn't help myself. But it wasn't Sasha. The woman's hair was dark and she was . . . fuller . . . than Mistress Sasha." His hands created the outline of a voluptuous body, and he blushed furiously before scrubbing his hands over his face again. "My apologies, Captain. I have no opinions on whether Mistress Sasha is . . . full . . . or . . . flat." He winced and Kjell ground his teeth. Damn Jerick.

"Focus, Isak."

"There are no tribes here on the plain, are there Captain? Could she have been a tribal woman? She was there, naked, standing just beyond that fire." He pointed to the fire pit nearest the tree beneath which Kjell and Sasha had slept. Kjell's blood ran cold.

"Then she was gone. She just disappeared into thin air. I searched the area, walking the perimeter over and over. I almost stepped on a snake—a big, spitting adder that scared me half to death. I looked for prints this morning, but the rain has washed everything away."

"What happened to the snake?" Kjell asked, eyes narrowed on the young man.

"I left it alone, Captain. That snake took off through the grass, away from the camp. I let it go."

Kjell nodded, his lips pursed and his eyes grim.

"Do you believe me, Captain?"

"Yes, Isak. I do." He believed him, and the possibilities made his mind reel. He turned away from the man, his eyes finding Sasha, the melon color of her fresh dress giving her the appearance of an exotic flower. She'd worked her hair into a fat braid that hung over her shoulder like a red boa constrictor. The comparison made his heart catch.

"We're leaving," he shouted to his men. "Mount up. And keep your eyes out for snakes."

EIGHT

hey traveled for two days without incident—no Volgar, no
snakes, no naked women appearing on the edge of camp.
But it was not unclothed phantoms or birdmen that concerned Kjell. He tripled the nightly watch and put a guard near
Sasha while she slept. His men didn't question him—Isak had
shared his account of the black adder and his sighting of the tribal woman, carefully omitting any mention of Sasha and mistaken
identity in his retelling.

"This was not like the snakes in the cave. This snake was
aggressive. It spit like a cat and rose straight up into the air," Isak
marveled.

"They don't like the herds. They shake the ground and make
the snakes nervous. They don't want to be trampled. Our horses
are probably to blame for the adder's irritability," Jerick mused.

"Adders are deadly, but the captain could have healed you,"
Peter chimed in, still awed by his own curing at the captain's
hands.

"Yes, but who will heal the captain?" Sasha rebuked gently.

Kjell's men shifted in their saddles, chagrined, and Kjell sighed, wrapping Sasha's thick braid in his hand and tweaking it gently. "You will cease trying to protect me, Sasha," he murmured, speaking directly into her ear so he wouldn't have to chastise her in front of his men.

"I will not," she whispered, but raised her voice to include the guard, evading him and turning their thoughts from their captain's vulnerabilities. "I know a tale about a snake . . . would you like to hear it?"

The men agreed heartily, but Kjell did not release her braid.

"There was a place, a land of great beauty, where the flowers grew endlessly and the air was soft and mild. Where the seas were fat with fish and the people flush with happiness. There was a good king and a young queen who ruled over the land. The king built his wife a beautiful garden and filled it with every kind of tree. But there was one tree whose fruit was more desirable than all the others. The fruit was white and sweet, but the man told his wife she could not eat that fruit. He told her she could eat the bounty from every tree in the garden, but not that one. She was forbidden to even go near it. Every day the woman would look at the tree, longing for a piece of the fruit, because it was the one fruit she could not have.

"The king knew that the queen desired the fruit from the forbidden tree, but instead he brought her grapes from the vines, firm and dripping with juice. He brought her apples and pears of every color. He peeled oranges and fed them to her with his fingers, trying to distract her from the fruit of the one tree she wanted.

"But one day, the young queen went to the garden alone, and she found herself drawn to the tree again, hungry for the fruit. She got closer than she had ever been, so close that she could see a snake, glittering and gilded with gold, wrapped around one of the branches. To her surprise, the snake began to talk to her. He hissed a promise to the woman, 'If you eat this fruit, you will see all things. The king doesn't want you to eat it, because you will be all-knowing and all-powerful, and you will leave him.'

"The queen scoffed at the snake. She would never leave the king. She just wanted to taste a perfect, white pear. She moved closer to the tree. Too close. She reached out her hand to pluck a piece of the fruit, and the snake struck, sinking his fangs into her arm.

"When the king found the queen, she lay next to the tree, dying, a piece of the white fruit still clutched in her hand. She never even got to taste it. The king realized that he'd forbidden her to eat the fruit but he'd never warned her about the snake."

"The snake tricked her," Gibbous whispered, shocked. Some of the men shared smirks at his outrage.

"Yes. But he hadn't lied about everything. The queen *did* leave the king. She died," Sasha said, her gaze solemn. The smirks disappeared, and the men grew reflective. Kjell stared at the landscape ahead, wishing he'd never heard that particular story.

In the days that followed no one shirked his duty or fell asleep on his watch. No one wanted to be the cause of the captain leaving them.

They did not continue in a straight line along the Jandarian Plain, paralleling the cliffs that dropped into the Takei Sea. Kjell had intended to travel to the city of Janda, just east of the sea, to confer with the lord of the province. But every step toward Janda took them further from the City of Jeru, and Kjell was eager—for the first time in his life—for the cover and safety of the castle walls. He saw danger around every rock, trouble around every bend, and an attack from every direction.

He kept his concerns to himself, driving his men hard, their horses harder, and veering north instead of east, heading for the mountainous pass that cut through the hills that bordered the southern edge of Degn. It would have been less strenuous to go around, but foregoing the journey to Janda and cutting through the mountains of Degn shortened their journey by two weeks.

Sasha showed no signs of fear or fatigue. She seemed to enjoy the journey, perched before him on Lucian, taking in the scenery and keeping them all from wearing too badly on each other's nerves. In the evenings, surrounded by the King's Guard, she told stories, in the day she made conversation, and each night she slipped her hand into Kjell's as she fell asleep. He didn't kiss her again, didn't look for moments to steal her away and take what his body increasingly yearned for, but each day, she sectioned off another piece of his heart, and his impatience for Jeru became anticipation for something he hardly dared hope for. He could only pray his growing obsession with having the fruit would not blind him to the snakes.

The sun was just beginning to lower over the ancient seabed beyond Nivea when Kjell, Sasha, and the guard began to descend into the city of Jeru. Light dappled the ground and pinked the sky, and the walls of Jeru gleamed with black brilliance in the distance.

"She is the most beautiful city in the world," Kjell said softly, and Sasha could only stare. Green flags beat the rosy sky and sentries sounded their horns. Even a mile off, the sound carried on the wind. They'd been seen.

"Are you sure you aren't a prince?"

"I am a brother," Kjell said. "And that is infinitely better."

The people of Jeru gathered and tossed greetings and glad tidings, waving and running alongside the small contingent of the King's Guard as they made their way through the city gates, down the wide streets, and climbed the hill to the castle itself. The battle with the Volgar within the castle walls had made Kjell a bit of a legend, but few Jeruvians had actually seen what he'd done. He'd made himself scarce in the years since Zoltev and the birdmen had been defeated, since Tiras had escaped the curse that had bound him, and since Jeru City had begun the long road of integration and tolerance toward the Gifted among them.

But people loved to talk—as evidenced by the fact that Kjell's story had traveled to the villages of outer Quondoon, to a dusty hamlet like Solemn, and to the knowledge of a fire-haired female with a love of tales. Sasha's face was wreathed in smiles, and she waved back at the children and clapped at the excitement of the citizens, welcoming the king's brother home.

"They love you, Kjell!" she cried, her eyes wide and her face flushed.

"They do not love me. They love King Tiras. They love his queen. They love Princess Wren. It has nothing to do with me."

The guard was trained to allow no separations between each horse as they moved in formation through a crowd, but as they neared the base of the hill leading up to the castle and the cathedral beyond, a man pushed his way through the throng that lined the thoroughfare and broke out into the street just ahead of the mounted procession.

The man was heavily bearded—the growth covering what little Kjell could see of his face. His forehead and eyes were shrouded by the deep cowl of the cloth he wore banded around his head. His clothes were dusty, his feet sandaled, his back bent over a staff, but he stood in the path of the horses and made no move to get out of the road. He reached out a hand as if to bid them halt.

"Move aside, sir," Jerick called, inching forward to clear the path. But the man side-stepped him, his eyes on Sasha, his hand still raised.

"Saoirse?"

The word that hissed from his lips sounded like Sasha's name, but not. It curled around the man's tongue, hooking on the *r* before he released it with a sigh. It felt ominous, like the man had spoken a curse in a different language. Sasha stared at him, eyebrows drawn low over her ebony eyes. Then she raised her face to Kjell's, confusion coloring her expression. The guard had come to a complete stop, the man causing a bottleneck in the narrowing street. Kjell lowered his lance, wary of the stooped stranger who had obviously mistaken Sasha for someone else.

"Step aside, man," Kjell demanded, startling him. The man looked around, clearly unaware of the attention he was drawing.

"Forgive me, Captain," he said, bowing so low his head was level with his knees. Then he stepped out of the way, sending a furtive glance over his shoulder as he melded into the crowd.

Sasha sat frozen in front of Kjell, her head tipped to the side, listening the way she was prone to do, seeing something no one else could see.

"Saoirse," she murmured, drawing the sound out slowly—*Seer-sha*—and Kjell found that his mind was repeating the word as well. He resisted saying it aloud, ever cautious, ever suspicious.

"Did you recognize that man?" he asked.

"No," she said slowly, shaking her head. "No. But he seemed to know me."

"Jerick!" Kjell called, straightening his lance. "Follow him. I want to know who he is."

Jerick nodded once, needing no further instruction. He took Isak and Gibbous and peeled off the main procession in pursuit of the man who had already disappeared into the well-wishers.

Maybe the man had simply been curious. He wasn't the only one ogling the red-haired woman seated in front of the captain of the King's Guard. Kjell groaned. He'd been foolish to enter the city this way. He was drawing too much attention and speculation. The last time the guard had brought a woman home from a Volgar crusade, she had become Queen of Jeru.

Three years before, King Tiras had returned from the first battle in Kilmorda with a female captive from Corvyn. He'd locked Lady Lark in a tower room—a means to control her treacherous father—and proceeded to become her prisoner. Now all of Jeru bowed at her feet.

Kjell had no desire to deposit Sasha in a room and put her under armed guard. But he wanted to keep her, and he had no idea how to go about doing so. Now the whole city would be making assumptions about the woman in the company of the captain. Before long, he would have to make his claim, just like he'd done with Jerick, and he instantly resented the entire, inquisitive, meddlesome population.

They didn't proceed to the courtyard, like they would have done if they accompanied the king. Instead, they crossed the wide drawbridge, entered beneath the enormous portcullis, and turned left toward the king's stables. Lucian's ears were pinned forward, his gait quickening for grain and the end of his journey.

It was hearing day, Kjell realized belatedly, the line from the Great Hall spilled out from the east entrance and blocked the way to the stables.

"What's going on?" Sasha asked, her eyes dancing from the carefully manicured shrubs to the waiting subjects, who eyed her as curiously as she eyed them. As they'd approached, she'd removed her veil to gaze at the parapets and the domed fortress of Jeru castle, and her hair rippled around her shoulders, blazing in the pink glow of the setting sun.

"Once a week the King and Queen see their subjects, resolve disputes, and give rulings on complaints brought before them. It is incredibly tedious, and they've been at it since dawn. Judging from the length of the line, it's been an espccially long day." As Kjell spoke, a trumpet sounded, indicating the end of the day, and the people still waiting for a hearing began to disperse, grumbling as they were turned away, forced to come back the following week.

"Beckett," Kjell called to the groom who was ushering the guard into the stables, a grin across his weathered cheeks.

"Welcome home, Captain!" Beckett cried, hands outstretched, his eyes immediately drawn to the horse. "Hello, Lucian. We've missed you, boy."

Kjell stepped down from the stallion and raised his hands to Sasha, lifting her from Lucian's back and letting her legs adjust before he dropped his hands from her waist. They'd been riding since dawn with very few breaks.

Beckett had suddenly forgotten the horse entirely, his eyes on the pretty maid, his mouth hanging open.

He bobbed and ducked, smiling shyly, and Kjell dismissed him with more patience than he felt.

"Take Lucian and make sure he is well-rewarded, Beckett. Check his right flank. He's been favoring it since our last run in with the Volgar."

"Yes, Captain," Beckett said, bowing to Sasha again, tipping a hat he wasn't wearing, before awkwardly turning and leading the stallion toward the stables.

"Come, Sasha." There was no time like the present. Now that he was home, Sasha in tow, he didn't know what to do with her. He could present her to Mistress Lorena, the housekeeper, and demand that she be given a room and a hot meal . . . and then what? He didn't give orders to the royal staff. He would have to present her to his brother before long, and knowing Sasha, she would demand to be given work. He would present her now, corner his brother and the queen in the Great Hall, and be done with it.

He took Sasha's hand and marched toward the gardens, pulling her behind him without any explanation, bypassing the wide eastern entrance for the private entrance, feeling self-conscious and oddly anxious. His nerves made him angry, and when Sasha pled with him to tell her where they were going, he barked at her and walked faster.

He strode into the Great Hall and veered toward the dais where King Tiras and Queen Lark sat conferring with the King's Council.

Kjell, you are dragging the poor woman like she has committed a crime and you are bringing her before the court.

Kjell winced and slowed, hearing Lark's voice in his head, her ability to communicate through thoughts still as jarring as it had ever been. He continued toward the throne, though he moderated his pace. Sasha was a reluctant weight pulling against him as he blazed ahead.

"I'm home, brother," he thundered, his voice unnecessarily loud, his heartbeat unpleasantly fast. He hated the Great Hall, the throne that had once belonged to his father, the traditions it housed, and the tapestries interwoven with a history that excluded him.

Tiras rose—sleek black hair and dark skin, lean height and long muscles—cutting off his council without a word. Where Tiras was dark-skinned and finely chiseled, Kjell was pale-eyed and roughly hewn. Where Tiras was restrained power, Kjell was brute force, and where Tiras was wise, Kjell was merely shrewd.

Kjell would rather be like Tiras—wise and powerful—but wisdom and power were not things a man could simply choose. Kjell didn't mind their differences—he was incredibly proud of his younger brother—he just recognized that he was the lesser man and wished it weren't true.

Tiras stepped down from the dais with the grace of a jungle cat, and greeted Kjell with outstretched arms and unabashed relief that his brother had returned. Tiras was the person Kjell had always loved most in the world, and he let go of Sasha's hand and let Tiras embrace him, enduring the affection, though he struggled to return it with the King's Council looking on.

Beside him, Sasha dropped into a curtsy so deep and demure, her head nearly kissed her knees.

"Majesties," she breathed, her long tresses falling around her, brushing the marble floors. Tiras extended a hand, helping her rise, and he smiled at her with obvious speculation.

Kjell rushed to explain before Tiras drew his own conclusions.

"Tiras, Queen Lark, this is Sasha. Of Quondoon. Of . . . Kilmorda." Kjell bit back a curse at his clumsy introduction and continued with more care. "I have promised her a position here in the castle. I would view it as a personal favor if she could remain here. For the time being. For the near future." He ceased talking.

"We have been traveling for a long time, Highness. Forgive me for my appearance," Sasha stammered, blushing.

Kjell thought she looked beautiful and didn't understand the wide, incredulous look she tossed his way before curtseying again.

"You will forgive my brother," Tiras said. "Kjell has so few friends. We welcome you." Tiras grinned wickedly, his eyes calculating, his words smooth.

Lark rose from her throne and joined her husband, extending a hand to Sasha as she summoned her lady in waiting, who hovered nearby. "I will have Pia escort you to Mistress Lorena," she said. "She will take good care of you. If employment is what you seek, we will see to that as well. But for now you will rest. It was not so very long ago I was dragged from Corvyn by one of Kjell's *closest* friends. I had to be carried from the horse. I am impressed by your stamina."

The king's eyes gleamed at his queen's tart reference, but this was not what Kjell had intended. He had not planned for Sasha to be taken away and "seen to." He watched Pia escort her from the room, quelling the urge to keep her in his sights. She'd barely left his side since Solemn. Four weeks and three days since he'd found her near death at the base of a cliff. Since then she'd ridden in his arms, slept by his side, and crept inside his walls.

The King's Council observed with craning necks and prying eyes, and Kjell sneered at them, jutting his chin and tossing his head toward the wide doors.

"Go and do no harm," Tiras dismissed them, and waited until they gathered their scrolls and scuttled from the hall, bowing repeatedly to him and the queen before taking themselves away.

"You look good, brother," Lark said to Kjell, her eyes affectionate, her voice kind. "We've missed you."

"He looks like a great, dusty, bristling bear," Tiras laughed "And yes, we've missed you. Now tell us about the girl."

"She was a slave in Solemn, in the province of Quondoon. The people tried to kill her because she was Gifted. They ran her from the town and forced her off a cliff at the end of their spears. I healed her," Kjell offered awkwardly.

The queen blanched and Tiras hissed. He held himself responsible for every injustice, and Kjell had no doubt there would be emissaries sent to Quondoon in the near future.

"What is her gift?" Tiras asked, eyes flat, hands clenched.

"She is a Seer. She tried to warn the people when she saw harm. They harmed her instead."

"You called her Sasha," Lark said, her brows raised in question.

"Yes. That is what she's called. I feel like I'm insulting her every time I say her name," Kjell admitted.

"She doesn't comport herself like a slave," Tiras mused, his jaw still tight. He'd abandoned his teasing grin and his cutting remarks.

"She was sold in Firi and indentured by an elder of Solemn and a delegate of Lord Quondoon. It is believed she was once a servant in the house of Lord Kilmorda before the province fell. I wonder if perhaps she was something more."

"It is believed?" Tiras asked, incredulous.

"She doesn't remember." Kjell shrugged.

"She is familiar to me," Lark said, her brows furrowed above luminous eyes, her small pointed chin cradled in her palm.

"It is the hair," Tiras remarked, his eyes trained beyond Kjell where Sasha had been, turning pages in his head, trying to find something he'd once seen.

"I've never seen hair like hers," Kjell interjected, and felt a wash of embarrassment at the awe in his voice.

"No. Not as deep a red," Tiras said. His eyes were troubled.

"Lady Sareca of Kilmorda had hair like that. She was a friend of my mother's. She came once to Corvyn before my mother's death and several times after. My father considered Lord Kilmorda an ally. Surely there is someone from Kilmorda who would remember a girl like Sasha in the lord's house," Lark ruminated.

"Zoltev was convinced the lordship in Kilmorda gave refuge to the Gifted, and he put a great deal of pressure on the lord of the province to continually prove his innocence," Tiras said.

"Or maybe he wanted to control the ports and the wealth in Kilmorda," Kjell said. "I was old enough to accompany the guard to and from Kilmorda several times before Zoltev disappeared and you became king, Tiras. Kilmorda was the richest province in Jeru, even richer than Degn. Lord Kilmorda had close relationships with the lands to the north, conducting trade that did not involve the oversight of the kingdom. Zoltev didn't like that."

"It was no coincidence that Kilmorda was the land he most completely destroyed," Tiras agreed.

"And no coincidence that the lord of the province and his family did not survive the attacks," Kjell added.

For a moment the conversation lulled, the king, the queen, and Kjell all lost in their own memories of what Kilmorda had endured.

"Sasha will be our guest, and she will be safe here," Lark promised. "We will see to it, and we will do our best to find someone who might be able to identify her."

NINE

S asha was not terribly comfortable being a guest.

Mistress Lorena, under the queen's direction, put her in a room in the same wing as the family, assigning a lady's maid to dress her hair and assist her in her daily toilette. Dresses were commissioned, and all manner of bits and baubles, underthings and overskirts, slippers and shoes, and handkerchiefs and head scarfs were brought in for her use. Sasha accepted it all with gracious wonder but promptly donned one of the dresses Kjell bought her in Solemn and braided her own hair.

When Lark discovered Sasha could read and write, she asked her to act as her personal assistant, though Lark's abilities made assistance feel more like providing company rather than work, and Sasha was accustomed to work. Kjell overheard her needling Mistress Lorena for a bucket of water and a stiff brush to scrub the cobblestones in the courtyard.

The first morning after their arrival, he found her wrapped in a fur, asleep on the floor outside his door. The next night he left his door unlatched for the first time in his life and lay with his ears straining for her arrival. When he heard a slight scuffling and a small bump against the corridor wall, he rose and led her into his chamber. He patted the side of the bed farthest from him, and she promptly climbed in and fell asleep. Every morning after that, he found her curled beside him, and every morning he woke her before sunrise so she could return to her own room to avoid alerting the very curious staff of their arrangement. He never denied her. In fact, they never even spoke of their odd need to continue what they'd started weeks before.

During the days he hardly saw her. And he missed her. He ached with it. In the pit of his stomach and the back of his throat, in the balls of his feet and the palms of his hands, he missed her. It horrified him, and he made himself volunteer for patrol, staying away two days longer than needed just to prove he could. Then he practically ran through the halls of the castle, through the kitchens, into the cellar, and out in the gardens looking for her.

He found the queen instead, sitting among the roses, a book in her hand and Wren in her arms. The book floated in front of her, the pages turning at her command.

"Are you abusing your power, Lady Queen?" he asked.

"I am *using* my power, brother. I don't want Wren to tear at the pages."

"Wren is sleeping."

"Yes. And I want to hold her and read. The book is heavy," she protested, but humor danced in her large, grey eyes. "Are you looking for Sasha?" she asked.

"Yes," he said, sheepish.

"You look as though you are desperate to find her," she remarked, commanding the book to lower and close. She was teasing him, but it was the absolute truth, and he was certain she knew it.

He *was* desperate to find her.

"You feel something for her," Lark said. She didn't ask, didn't over-exaggerate. Lark was incredibly careful with her words, as they could curse men and control beasts. She approached every interaction with the fear that she would harm unintentionally, and listened far more than she spoke.

"Yes. I feel something for her," he admitted quietly, grateful he didn't have to admit more, and sank down on a garden bench at an angle to his brother's wife.

"And you don't want to?" the queen asked.

"I have tried not to."

"But feelings don't always obey."

"No." He shook his head. "They don't. But I don't trust . . . my feelings. Especially because I healed her. The healing has created a . . . bond. A strong one. An unnatural one."

"I see." She was silent for a moment, as if examining his confession for holes.

"Do you have feelings for me?" she asked suddenly.

Kjell's eyes shot to hers, and he knew she saw the curse he swallowed.

"No," he clipped.

The queen laughed, the sound light and silvery, like the woman herself.

"I admire you," he amended. "I would die for you, gladly. I even . . . love you. But . . ." he struggled to explain something he didn't understand himself.

"But you healed me too, Kjell. Remember?"

He hadn't considered that.

"Yet the bond is very different than what you are feeling for Sasha, isn't it?"

Even her name hurt him, piercing him sweetly, and he hung his head in submission.

"I have loved badly before," he grunted. He could barely say the words, and they were mostly unintelligible. The queen, however, did not miss them.

"I see," she sighed. She didn't argue with him, didn't question his feelings or his misgivings. She just let the statement be, accepting the truth of it. He *had* loved badly, and the kingdom had suffered. *He* had suffered. Terribly.

After a time, the queen spoke again, returning to the matter at hand.

"Sasha is devoted to you."

"Yes." He agreed without equivocation. He knew that she was.

"But you don't trust *her* devotion either?" the queen asked.

"It is born of gratitude and servitude. I don't want either of those things from her."

"What do you want?"

When Kjell failed to respond, Lark answered for him. "You want her to love you. It is an entirely different thing, isn't it?"

"I think so, yes," he confessed, and felt both relief and pain at the admission. "I am not easy to love."

Lark laughed again, and he winced. "That, my dear Kjell, is a good thing. The very best things in life are born of difficulty. Whatever comes too easily is easily abandoned."

"It is the height of irony. I am forced to care in order to heal. I've spent my whole life not giving a damn."

"You are such a fool, brother." Lark smiled to soften her words, but they still stung, and his eyes shot up and his jaw cracked. Lark was his queen, but he didn't have to like what she said.

"Kjell," she soothed. "You care too much. And when you commit, both you and Tiras are just like your father. No half measures. All in, to the death. But Zoltev committed himself to power. You commit yourself to people. It is significantly more painful."

His shoulders slumped, and he rose from the bench. He *was* a fool. And he had a sneaking suspicion the queen was right. She was often right.

"Tiras will be back soon. You should speak with him, Kjell."

"Where is he?"

"Somewhere abusing his power." Her smile was rueful, and she commanded the book to rise and open.

"Flying?"

"Flying. I will tell him you seek his counsel," she murmured, allowing him to continue on in his search. He took a few steps before he spoke again, tossing the question over his shoulder.

"Is she well?" he asked.

"What?" Lark replied, clearly confused.

"Wren. Is she well?"

"Ah," Lark sighed, and her voice smiled. "Yes. She is perfect."

"She has grown since I last saw her. She is beautiful," he admitted, surprising himself with his sincerity.

"Thank you, brother."

He was almost through the garden when Lark called out to him.

"She is in the library, Kjell." He quickened his step and heard her answering laugh. Curse his obviousness.

Kjell had never liked the library. Endless knowledge and obedient words, everything in its proper place, everything with a beginning and an ending. Tiras loved the rows of shelves. Kjell just wanted to knock them down.

Sasha was perched on a ladder, one arm clutching the top, one arm stretched high, wielding a duster made of goose feathers, her tongue caught between her lips in concentration. Either she didn't hear him coming, or she was too intent on her precarious position to spare him a glance.

He reached up, wrapped his arms around her legs, and toppled her into his arms.

Her small squeal became a smile, and she sighed his name as he stepped behind the tallest of the shelves, hiding them from the wide, double doors and from anyone who might come to check on the new maid. Sasha twined her arms around him, looking at him like he was the sun and she'd been lost in the dark. She pressed her lips to his cheek so sweetly that he moaned and let her feet find the floor. Then his fingers were in her hair and on her face, touching her nose and her chin, touching the freckles he saw when he closed his eyes.

"What are you doing?" she asked, her voice catching, her body pressing into his.

"I'm counting your freckles to make sure you haven't lost any." He felt her teeth on his shoulder, as if she wanted to get closer, to consume him. He bundled her hair in his hands, nipping at her chin and her throat, following the path where his fingers had been.

Then he was kissing her, telling her all the things that he couldn't say, listening for all the things he needed to hear. His hands cradled her hips and slid up her slim back, tracing and retracing, reveling in the feel of her and in the knowledge that she welcomed him.

"Thank you," she sighed into his mouth. He withdrew slightly, just enough to glower down at her.

"You are thanking me for kissing you?"

"Yes. Every time you do it, I'm afraid you will never do it again."

"Why?" he asked, incredulous.

"I can't explain it," she whispered. "It isn't something I see. It's something I feel."

"How can I make that feeling go away?"

"You must promise to never stop kissing me," she said, her face solemn. "You must kiss me relentlessly and never cease."

He nodded, every bit as solemn, and immediately obeyed.

"Sasha!"

She was trembling, her eyes open, but something about her gaze and the sounds in her throat convinced him she wasn't awake.

He shook her gently, kneading her arms and stroking her hair.

"Sasha, wake."

One moment she was somewhere else and the next, with him. He saw the light come back in her eyes, the awareness, but her trembling continued and her mouth struggled to form words, still caught in the place where the mind was a contortionist and the body was paralyzed.

"I s-saw you," she stuttered.

"And do you see me now?" he asked quietly, making sure she was with him in the present.

"Yes." Her eyes closed briefly, but there was no relief in her face. He released her, moving away. When she slept near him, he kept his distance. He had to.

"I saw her."

He didn't have to ask who she meant.

"She will not hurt you. I will not let her," he promised.

"It is not me I am afraid for," she murmured.

"If she wanted to harm me, she could have done so many, many times. Yet she hasn't."

She nodded, agreeing with him, her eyes darker than the night outside his window. But he knew she hadn't shared all she'd seen, hadn't told him all she feared. Sasha told stories, but she never told lies. Maybe her dreams felt like lies. Or maybe she simply didn't dare speculate on what she didn't completely understand. Lark would tell her that was wise, that words could be spoken into reality.

He didn't kiss her or pull her close to comfort her, and she didn't seek it. Alone this way, with nothing to stop them, the only thing keeping them apart was never coming together in the first place. He did not touch her and she did not touch him, not in the dark, not in that way. Not yet. And pleasure did not belong in the same bed as fear.

She didn't return to sleep but lay quietly beside him until dawn, as if staying awake would allow her to see the threat before it came to pass. Just before daybreak, she crept from his bed, and he let her go, feigning sleep so she wouldn't worry that she'd disturbed him.

Before she slipped out the door he thought he heard her whisper. "I will not let her hurt you."

TEN

Kjell was not the only Healer in Jeru. Healers who had kept the secret of their abilities for longer than he, who could wield and heal with little thought, lived among the people of Jeru. Spinners, Changers, and Tellers too. They had congregated in Nivea, near the ancient seabed, among artisans and craftsmen, just beyond the Jeru City walls. When Tiras passed the edict protecting all people, even the Gifted, they had not seen fit to venture out. Change was difficult, even for those who could change at will. Instead, Jeru came to them.

At Lark's urging, Kjell brought Sasha to Nivea to see if the old Teller and diviner of Gifts, Gwyn, could unravel the mystery of Sasha's past. Like before, his presence was noted immediately and looked on with some trepidation. His past had not been forgotten in Nivea, and his gift did not greatly impress.

He found Gwyn in the garden of the small home of Shenna the Healer, sitting with her face tipped to the sun, drinking in the rays as if they sang to her. And maybe they did.

"The Healer returns," she greeted, not opening her eyes. "I knew you would."

"You're a Seer. I'm not especially impressed. And Shenna told you I was coming."

"Still so prickly. In a world of Changers, it is good that some things stay the same."

Kjell sat across from the woman, knowing what she expected. The stool had been placed there for him, he had no doubt.

"She is lovely, the woman you brought home from Quondoon. Where is she?"

"The gods save me from Seers," he sighed, only half-serious. "She is with Shenna, in the cottage. I wanted a moment with you alone," Kjell retorted.

"And why is that, Healer?"

"Don't you know?" Kjell replied dourly.

"I am not all-knowing, Captain. My eyes see what they will, and I've never been able to choose."

"That's what Sasha says."

"She is a Seer," Gwyn said. "And she was punished for it."

"Yes, and I healed her. She was near death. It was the first healing I have performed on a stranger."

"The most difficult healing of all, sharing your gift with someone you've never met," Gwyn remarked.

"I almost doubted it could be done." He was comforted by the knowledge that she understood.

"Even the queen—as powerful as she is, as magnificent as her ability—is bound by certain constraints. Imagine how terrible the world would be if men were all-powerful," Gwyn murmured. Neither of them spoke of the king who had been very powerful indeed.

"I tried to heal her twice. The first time, she was near death. The second, seriously wounded. The second time, I almost failed. It took hours and every ounce of strength I had to close her wounds."

"You were successful?" She sounded shocked.

"Yes . . . but she still bears the scars."

"You are a powerful Healer, indeed," she marveled.

"I will not be able to heal her again," he mourned. "I can feel it."

"No. Probably not. Every gift has its limitations. We are delicate creatures, aren't we? But our fragility makes us better people. It is good that the gift we want most is the one we aren't given." She paused. "A Healer cannot heal himself."

He nodded. "Yes. I know."

"When you heal, you give your very self away," she explained.

"Shenna told me for every life I restore, I lose a day of my own," he said.

"But Healers live longer than most," she reassured. "Still . . . I'm not talking about shortening years upon the land, Healer. When you heal, especially great wounds, your life force merges with the life you save. And that person becomes *part* of you. A Healer cannot heal himself," she repeated slowly. "Thus he cannot heal twice. Or very rarely."

She smiled, her face wrinkling into a thousand lines, and Kjell resisted the urge to smooth them, simply to see if he could.

She brought his hand to her face, as if she knew he wanted to touch her and was too reticent to do so. Her skin was warm from the sun, and he held his palm there, pressed against her cheek, soothed by her presence.

"In Solemn, I healed two hundred people, most of them very ill."

"A wonderful gift. And depending on the severity of the illness and the depth of the healing, you will not be able to give it to them again."

"What use am I to those I love if I can't heal them whenever they need it?" he whispered.

"The people who love you do not love you for your power, Kjell. That is their gift to you." Gwyn patted his hand and brought it to her lap, palm up, looking at the lines there. They sat in contemplative silence for several moments.

"But that is not the only reason you've come, is it?" she needled.

"No." Kjell guessed she already knew exactly why he was there.

"Then bring her to me, lad." Gwyn grinned, swatting at his hand, a twinkle in her eye.

Kjell turned to fetch the women, but saw they were already approaching. Gwyn tipped her head toward them, as though her ears worked better than her eyes.

Sasha greeted the old Teller as she had greeted the queen, with a deep curtsy and a bowed head.

"Come, girl. I'm just an old woman. No need for that," Gwyn protested, but Kjell could see that the greeting pleased her. "Sit beside me."

Sasha obeyed immediately, tucking herself beside the Teller, who took her hand the way she'd taken Kjell's.

"You've already seen Bartol—what can I possibly tell you that you don't know?" Gwyn's voice was wry.

Bartol was an entertainer, one of the Gifted who'd been a court jester before the laws had made having a gift a boon instead of a curse.

Bartol made Tiras laugh with his antics, but Kjell had mocked the man more than once for his inane talents. In his opinion, Bartol's gift was a useless one—a weak variation of seeing that served no purpose. Bartol took great pride in telling people what they already knew, things like, "You ate lamb last Tuesday. You fear heights because you fell from a tree when you were a child. Your best mate is Garvin. Your mother was Janetta. The day of your birth there was a terrible blizzard. You've a mark on your arse shaped like a ship." All of it ridiculous, all of it unhelpful.

The man had been taken a bit more seriously since the king's edict, and Lark had asked him what he could tell them about Sasha. Bartol had immediately proclaimed Sasha the daughter of Pierce and Sareca of Kilmorda, and the queen said he spoke truth. But Bartol had known nothing beyond Sasha's parentage, and had proceeded to rattle off a string of things Sasha could have told them herself, as well as a few things—like the color of the king's drawers and that Princess Wren had cut a new tooth—that no one cared to know. Bartol had made Tiras laugh, and the queen had declared it a miracle, but Sasha had still insisted on dusting books and scrubbing floors. She might be the daughter of a lord, but there was nothing and no one to return to in Kilmorda. And Sasha still couldn't remember them.

"We thought you might be able to see who Sasha is," Kjell said.

"Who she is?" Gwyn asked frowning. "She already knows. Better than most, I would say. Who do *you* think you are, girl?"

"I am his," Sasha said without hesitation, her gaze level and unflinching.

Gwyn crowed softly, as if the answer pleased her even more than the greeting, and Kjell felt his belly and his face get hot.

"No, child. He is yours," Gwyn said, and Kjell grimaced. Gwyn ignored him, her gaze still on Sasha. "You have come a long way," she mused.

"Yes," Sasha answered.

"And there is a journey yet to come. Do you see it?" Gwyn pressed.

"To my home?" Sasha asked as if she already knew.

"To your home," Gwyn confirmed.

Kjell wanted to interrupt, to protest. This was not what they'd come for. Kilmorda was in ruins. There would be no journey to the province if he could help it. But he held his tongue.

"You have the eyes of a Seer, Sasha," Shenna said softly, inserting herself into the conversation.

"Yes. I'm not a terribly good one. It is a frustrating gift. It is a talent that rarely heals and usually frightens. It frightens me."

"It frightens me too," Gwyn said. "Our gifts are often burdens, aren't they?"

Sasha wilted, her eyes on her feet, and Gwyn was silent for a long time.

"You are a Seer, but that is not your dominant gift," Gwyn said thoughtfully.

Sasha looked surprised, even hopeful, and she waited expectantly, lifting her eyes back to the old woman.

"You magnify the gifts of others. You make them stronger. You have strengthened our Kjell many times," Gwyn said.

"I don't know if that is a gift, Mother Gwyn," Sasha said slowly. "Or if that is simply . . . love."

Kjell froze.

"But that is the best gift of all," Gwyn said.

Kjell wanted to bolt, overwhelmed with the need to be alone and to never be alone again. He stood abruptly, and Sasha stood as well, ever his faithful shadow, gently releasing the old woman's hand.

"We've made the Healer uncomfortable." Gwyn sighed, irritated. "Go on ahead, Captain. I want to say goodbye to this girl."

He needed no urging and turned and strode from the garden.

"Captain?" he heard Shenna call behind him. He counted the Healer as one of his friends, though she might not know it. She'd taught him a great deal about his gift. He trusted her, and he thought she'd come to trust him. Or at least respect him. He paused and waited for her to catch up to him, but he kept his back to her. She was too intuitive, and he was too disturbed.

"I offered to heal her scars. The ones on her back. She wouldn't let me," Shenna said, her voice troubled.

That sounded like Sasha. Still, he didn't turn around. He needed a moment, and it didn't seem like he was going to get one.

"How did you know about her scars?" he asked.

"They are still tender. I sensed them."

He flinched.

"She said they are a reminder," Shenna continued.

"Of what?" His tone was plaintive.

"That she may not be able to heal, but she can save."

"Bloody hell," he cursed.

"It does no good to fight what she sees. Or to fight her," she added softly. "Mother Gwyn is the same way. It's like throwing yourself against the rocks."

He nodded, suddenly resigned, and stepped out of the garden gate, waiting for Sasha.

If there was to be a journey to Kilmorda, he would need to talk to his brother.

He was reminded of the days when Tiras locked himself away in dungeon rooms or sequestered himself to his chambers. Kjell had become his eyes and ears and feet and hands, keeping the kingdom afloat while continually covering for his brother, who was losing himself a little more each day. He'd dragged Lark through the halls at all hours of the night to help him, desperate for assistance, yet distrustful and derisive, convinced she was his brother's worst mistake.

And she had saved them all.

Now he found himself walking through the halls of the castle again, seeking Sasha, wanting redemption yet unable to trust himself. He'd loved a woman once. Or thought he did. A woman who understood him well enough to play him like a harp. A woman who had brought Jeru to its knees. He'd been wrong before. He'd been foolish and afraid. Fear makes hate, and he'd hated all the wrong people. He would not be used again.

She met him at the door of her chamber, flinging it wide as if she'd watched him approach. Her color was high, her eyes bright, her lips parted like she was struggling for breath.

"You saw me coming?" he murmured, stopping in the entry, wanting her desperately while wishing he'd never come.

"I don't see everything," she began, and he said the words with her, matching her tone and pitch even as he added, "Yes. I know."

"You're creating ripples with your stony heart," she said softly, and he wanted to smile at her word play, at the memory of her explanation of the ripples in the pond and how they often managed to reach her on the shore eventually.

She turned and walked into her room, and he followed, shutting the chamber door behind them. She perched on the edge of her bed, her hair pooling around her, reminding him of the day she stood in the rain, battered and bedraggled, clinging to her clothes while he clung to his resistance.

He loved her then. He loved her now.

He'd loved her from the moment she'd opened her eyes beneath a moonlit sky in Quondoon and greeted him like she'd been waiting forever. And he needed to tell her.

He sank to his knees before her, abandoning his resistance completely, and she drew him to her, cradling his head in her lap, and stroking his hair.

"Did you see . . . us?" he whispered, needing reassurance.

"When I see you, I rarely see myself," she whispered. "But I hoped."

Still kneeling in front of her, he wrapped his arms around her hips and drew her from the bed and into him, connecting them from their knees to their noses, his arms supporting her weight. For a moment she hovered slightly above him, her hands braced on his shoulders, eyes searching, wanting but waiting, until the exquisite became the excruciating, and he wound one hand in her hair, lifted his chin, and pulled her to him, mouth to mouth.

He kissed her, taking her to the floor because he was too overcome to stand, clinging to her body because he was too undone to go slow. The storm pounding in his limbs and in his belly began to build in his heart, seeping through his skin and gathering in the corners of his eyes. He wanted to weep. It was the strangest sensation, the most puzzling reaction he'd ever experienced. He wanted to lay his head on Sasha's chest and weep.

Instead he breathed against her lips, withdrawing enough to move his mouth along the delicate bones of her collar, over the swell of her breasts, before he paused, his eyes closed, his forehead pressed to her abdomen.

He was happy. The feeling surged through him, an echo of the swelling he'd felt when Sasha had told him his kisses made her joyful. He was . . . happy. And he wasn't killing anything. There wasn't a sword in sight or a birdman in the sky. He was lying on a stone floor with Sasha in his arms, her hair twined around them, her hands on his face, her heart pounding beneath his cheek, and he was perfectly and completely happy.

"There once was a man named Kjell of Jeru who could pull trees from the ground with his bare hands," he began, not even knowing exactly what he was going to say.

"So he was a very strong man?" Sasha asked, not missing a beat.

"Yes. The strongest."

She laughed softly, the tremor making her body move against his.

"He could wrestle lions and toss bears and once killed ten birdmen with his bare hands. But the man was lonely. And his heart was dark."

"Not *so* dark," she murmured.

"Shh. It is my story."

She pinched him and he rose up to kiss her again, punishing her mouth with his lips and his tongue, unable to help himself.

After a breathless moment he withdrew, panting, his eyes still on her mouth, even as he tried to refocus his thoughts. Sasha's eyes pleaded and her lips begged, and he knew if he didn't continue with his story now, there would be no more conversation.

"One day he found a beautiful girl with hair like the sunrise and skin dappled with light," he continued softly. Sasha grew still and her hands ceased caressing his back. "The girl was kind to Kjell of Jeru, even though he was cold. She was patient with him, even though he was angry. She was soft, even though he was hard."

Kjell made himself look at her, made himself meet her gaze. She was listening intently, her eyes so wet and deep he wanted to sink into them. Then he *couldn't* look away.

"She followed him around and held his hand in the dark. She helped him find his way home and tried to slay birdmen for him. She wasn't very good at it. But she tried."

Ah. A smile. Good. His chest expanded again, nearly exploding, and he couldn't breathe.

"The mighty warrior, mightiest in all the land—" He paused, unable to tell her he loved her. The words were too flimsy and too formal, too misused and too overused. So he gave her another truth. "The mighty warrior was . . . happy. And he wasn't lonely anymore."

Moisture trickled from the corners of her eyes and hid in her hair, and he rushed to finish, unable to bear her tears, even if they were happy ones.

"Sasha of Kilmorda, of Solemn, of Enoch, of the plains of Janda, of every place in between, will you be Sasha of Jeru?"

"Sasha of Kjell?" she asked.

"Sasha of Kjell," he answered.

"I am yours, remember?" she reminded him, as if she'd already said yes a thousand times.

"And I am yours," he whispered. She beamed through her tears, making his chest burn all over again. "The bans will be read. Tiras has given his blessing. And if you must go to Kilmorda, I will go with you."

"Soon?" she asked, her lips still wet from his kisses.

"Very soon," he agreed.

She surged up, and her lips found his again, frantic and clinging, and he answered with a desperation of his own. But he would not love her on the floor. Not the first time. He would be a good man. A wise man. A gentleman. For the first time in his life, he would be a *gentle* man. He would ask her to take him, but not before he gave himself away.

He pushed back to his haunches and rose to his feet, lifting her in his arms. When he laid her across the bed, she watched his hands loosen the ties of her gown, watched him remove her clothes, and when he was through, she watched him touch her. She didn't close her eyes or drift away in sightless pleasure. She didn't turn her head into the pillow or gaze blindly into the flickering light. With her eyes she followed his fingers and trailed his palms, observing the path he took and the reverence he administered.

Her thumbs caressed the corners of his mouth, feeling his kisses with her fingers as he pressed them onto her lips and into her skin. She didn't look away when he shed his own clothes and wrapped her body around him. She didn't shy from his ministrations or tremble from his weight, but pulled him close, eyes wide, lips parted, breathing him in as he sank inside her.

There were no secrets, no sorrows, nothing hidden, nothing lost. They saw not what would be or what had been, but only what was.

She saw him.

He saw her.

And they saw nothing else.

ELEVEN

S asha's hair was uncovered, spilling in endless curls, an eruption of fire. She wore a dress of pale gold that moved with her body and accented her skin, and Kjell knew the queen had played a part in procuring the gown. Lark didn't wear gold—it would have looked odd with her silvery eyes and ash-brown hair, her spiked crown, and her tiny, bird-like figure—but the precious metal suited Sasha perfectly. The queen wore mid-night blue, and together the women were fire and ice, sunlight and moonshine, and Tiras laughed at Kjell when his steps fal-tered upon entering the ballroom.

It was a masquerade, an ancient Jeruvian tradition, where a man would remove the mask of his betrothed, revealing her iden-tity, and claiming her. With the unveiling, the announcement would be made, both to those in attendance at the masquerade and also to those outside the walls. Tiras had made it a royal event—demanded it even—and the hall dripped with candlelight and spun with color, the masked ladies and well-groomed men filling every nook and crowding every cranny, celebrating the engagement of the king's brother.

"The mask does little good when you wear a crown," Tiras observed, his eyes on his small wife, her bejeweled mask more a decoration than a disguise.

"Or when your hair is the color of fall leaves," Kjell added, unable to look away from the fiery tresses and the smiling mouth of his intended.

Tiras snorted, his hand moving to his older brother's shoulder and squeezing gently.

"You are a poet, Kjell," Tiras grinned.

"No. I have just lost all desire to pretend," he confessed.

"The announcement will be made, and tonight the royal crier will read the bans from the tower wall," Tiras said, "and you won't be able to turn back."

"I don't want to," Kjell replied. "But I do wish we could quietly make our vows and be done with it. We are not royalty. We do not want or need the traditional service or the pomp and circumstance that goes with it."

"You are my brother and the captain of the King's Guard, and she is Lady Kilmorda. You will not skulk or hasten the arrangement. It is another victory for Jeru that an heir of Kilmorda has been found and mighty Kjell has been tamed," Tiras teased.

Kjell endured his brother's banter and accepted his duty without further argument. If the king insisted on ceremony, he would conform, but the Jeruvian marriage rites would change nothing. He had already pledged himself.

Tiras wasted no time. The announcement was made at sunset. Bells rang from one end of Jeru City to the other, and the royal crier stood on the wall and read the bans over and over again, repeating himself as subjects gathered and listened, then ran to share, eager to spread the news.

"Kjell of Jeru, captain of the King's Guard, son of the late Zoltev, and brother of the noble King Tiras, will wed Lady Sasha of Kilmorda, daughter of the late Lord Pierce and the late Lady

Sareca, may the Creator keep their souls. So it is written, so it will be done on the fourth day of Antipas, the month of constancy. May the God of Words and Creation seal their union for the good of Jeru," the crier announced, shouting the words into the setting sun and flinging them at the stars.

In response, the cry went up again and again, "Hail, Kjell of Jeru, brother of the king. Hail Lady Sasha, daughter of Kilmorda."

The dancing began as the bells ceased ringing, and Kjell endured that too. He played his part and knew the steps, treating it like swordplay, just to get through the sequences duty demanded. Sasha was drawn into one dance after the other, and she stumbled a bit, twirled a little too often and too early, but caught on quickly. Before long she was swaying in time, weaving through the lines, making him forget he hated dancing. She was a golden candlestick, slightly taller than the other women, and he was drawn to her light, again and again. When they were apart, she watched him as he watched her, unable to look away.

When the evening waned and the tower bells tolled midnight, he joined his brother and his queen on the dais, Sasha at his side, and bowed his farewell to the departing guests. As the last of the attendees made their way past the dais and exited the great hall, Jerick entered quickly through the king's private entrance and approached Tiras, bowing deeply and apologizing profusely.

"Majesty, forgive me. There is a visitor at the drawbridge. He seeks entry."

"What is his business?" Tiras sighed, clearly ready for the night to end. The clock had struck, the dancing was done, and the celebration had all but concluded. Only a few drunken noblemen, the musicians, and the king's staff remained. Sasha yawned deeply and tried to disguise it, and the queen's crown was slightly askew.

"He insists he knows the lady from Kilmorda," Jerick explained, apologetic, his eyes glancing off Kjell and Sasha before returning to the king. "I would have sent him away and made him return on the morrow, but the captain has had us looking for this man."

Kjell's heart momentarily lost its rhythm and Sasha straightened beside him. Tiras raised his brows in question, but when Kjell affirmed the claim with a brisk nod, Tiras consented to give the man a hearing.

Moments later, Jerick and another guard returned, accompanied by a shrouded visitor. They stopped ten feet in front of the throne, as tradition demanded, and commanded the man to state his name.

"King Tiras, Queen Lark," the visitor intoned, his voice low and unremarkable. "I am Padrigus of Dendar. Thank you for receiving me at this hour."

"Bring him closer," Tiras said to the guards, inclining his head. "Then leave us and remain outside the doors."

Kjell appreciated the king's request. If this was a man who knew Sasha, who bore knowledge of her past, Kjell did not want an audience listening in, not even one comprised of men he would trust with his life. The two guards escorted the man forward and, releasing him, withdrew from the hall. When the great doors closed, Kjell stepped down from the dais and stopped directly in front of the man.

"You are the man we saw in the street the day we arrived in Jeru," Kjell said, not interested in pleasantries with a stranger. The man had removed his beard, greatly altering his appearance, but Kjell recognized the slope of his shoulders and the slant of his head. He was gaunt and stooped as if he'd grown accustomed to carrying a great weight upon his back, and just like the day in the street, he wore robes instead of a tunic and breeches, the wide cowl making him look like a prophet instead of a pauper. When he pushed it back, revealing his face, Sasha gasped.

"Padrig?" Sasha cried, taking a step forward and extending a hand to the old man. Kjell stepped in front of her, barring her path.

"You know him," Kjell asserted. It wasn't a question but a statement. She clearly recognized the man.

"Yes." Sasha nodded emphatically. "He is the man who helped me. He walked with me from Kilmorda to Firi," she exclaimed, her eyes shining with recognition.

"Milady, I've been looking for you for so long," Padrig whispered. His legs buckled, as though the burden on his shoulders had suddenly been lifted and he'd lost his balance. He was old, but his age was more worry than years, more grey hair than deep lines. Kjell moved to help him stand, and the man gripped his arms to steady himself.

"Why have you just come forward? We have been in Jeru City for a fortnight. My men searched for you, but you had fled," Kjell demanded.

"Forgive me, Captain," Padrig murmured, bowing his head. "There were many things to consider."

"Yet you came forward tonight?" Tiras asked, his brow furrowing.

"I heard the bans, Majesty. They confirmed her identity," Padrig explained.

"Please, Padrig. Sit. You look so worn," Sasha implored, welcoming his presence the way she did most things, with joy and instant acceptance.

Kjell eased him toward a chair but the man refused, finding his strength and releasing Kjell's arm. He braced his legs as if preparing for a storm, and Sasha ducked around Kjell and took Padrig's hand, a luminous smile curving her lips.

"You are the only thing I remember from my life," she marveled. "You were kind to me. And I never got to thank you."

"She is Lady Sasha of Kilmorda, isn't she?" The queen asked Padrig gently, and Kjell wanted to yell, to tell everyone to cease talking for a moment. But the conversation gained momentum around him.

"Yes," he nodded emphatically. "Sometimes . . . we called her Sasha. But her given name is Saoirse." There it was again, the word he'd said in the street. Seer-sha. He'd known who she was, even then.

"We?" Kjell interrupted.

"Her family. Those who love her." Padrig could hardly speak, though it was clear there was a great deal more to say.

"Why can't she remember, Padrig?" Kjell asked, suspicion making his voice sharp.

Padrig didn't answer, but he gripped Sasha's hands desperately, his throat working, his lips muttering, and Kjell's dread mushroomed into fear. Kjell placed his hand on Padrig's thin chest and pushed him back. He drew Sasha behind him, standing between her and the trembling man. Slowly, his eyes on Padrig, he withdrew his sword and leveled it at the man's throat.

"Kjell," Sasha reproved, putting a warning hand on his shoulder.

"Sasha, step back," he demanded, refusing to yield. Sasha dropped her hand, but she didn't retreat.

"Sasha was sold in Firi as a slave. She was brought to Quondoon. She was mistreated and abused. The people tried to kill her." Kjell pinned Padrig with his gaze, his voice deceptively calm. "Where were you?"

Padrig made no move to protect or defend himself, though his eyes beseeched, and he swallowed visibly.

"Kjell." This time it was Tiras who reprimanded him, but Kjell did not lower his blade. There was something terribly wrong, and Sasha had become very still at his back, her breathing shallow.

"You knew who Sasha was, yet you didn't tell her. And then you left her."

"I did not leave her, not the way you think," Padrig denied, shaking his head.

"Let him explain, Kjell," Sasha implored quietly.

Padrig took a deep breath, his eyes lingering briefly on the king, asking for permission to carry on. When Tiras inclined his head, urging him on, Padrig continued.

"I went to Lord Firi. I thought he would receive me. He knew Lord Pierce and Lady Sareca of Kilmorda, and he had a daughter of his own."

Padrig paused, and his mouth tightened with memory.

"Lord Firi was very ill. He could not see me, so I was given an audience with his daughter, Lady Ariel of Firi."

The name was like a gong in the great hall, echoing and ear-splitting, and Padrig seemed to expect this response, for he stopped and waited, allowing his announcement to sink in.

"I told Lady Firi that if his lordship would provide us sanctuary, I would give him something in return." Padrig hesitated once more, his gaze sweeping the women and men who gaped at him, their ears still ringing.

"What did you offer him?" the king pressed.

"I have a . . . *gift*, and I was willing to share it with him." He paused again, letting his meaning become clear.

"The Gifted have nothing to fear in my kingdom. What is your gift, Padrig?" Tiras asked, impatient.

"I am called the Star Maker," Padrig said carefully, his stare riveted on Sasha. She gasped and Kjell felt ill.

"You are a Spinner," Sasha said, delighted. "Just like the story."

"They weren't stories, Saoirse." Padrig shook his head. "I gave you the stories so you wouldn't be so afraid, and so when the time came, you would recognize the past."

"You took her memories," Kjell said, his realization dawning.

"Yes," Padrig admitted.

"You took them? Why?" Sasha asked, dazed.

"To keep you safe," Padrig pleaded. "Only to keep you safe. But I failed."

"Clearly," Kjell snarled. Padrig inclined his head in shameful acknowledgment, even as he continued his tale.

"Lord Firi needed a Healer. I could not give him that. But I told his daughter that I could give him a sort of immortality. I could take his memories, the very essence of who he was, and I could place his consciousness among the stars."

The group was silent, marveling at his claim, lost in his story.

"When Lady Firi realized what I could do, she demanded that I show her." Padrig shook his head regretfully. "So I did. I was trying to convince her to help. I was desperate. I told her about Saoirse. I thought she might know of her—both daughters of neighboring lords."

"What did she do?" Kjell asked, unable to even speak Ariel of Firi's name. His heart was a cauldron in his chest, spilling heat into his stomach and his limbs, scalding him.

"There is enormous power in memory," Padrig prefaced. "Memories provide great knowledge. I pointed out the stars of the great kings to Lady Firi. Then I called down Saoirse's memories, the newest star in the sky, and held it in my hands. I showed Lady Firi the smallest wisp of a memory so she would understand what I offered her father."

"She didn't want to help her father." Queen Lark's tone was flat, but her eyes gleamed.

"No," Padrig whispered. "She didn't. She wanted me to give her the stars. All of them. She wanted me to open them up, to let her see each one. She wanted the knowledge in the memories for herself."

"What did you show her? Which memory?" Kjell asked, a terrible knowing seeping into his skin.

"It was *you*, Healer. Saoirse has had dreams of you since she was a child. Because of that, her memories and her visions are intertwined, past and future, interconnected and indistinguishable. When I withdrew the strand of light, it was your face Lady Firi and I saw. You were kneeling over the king. The king appeared to be dead, and you were mourning."

The shock rippled through the gathering, and Kjell was not the only one who reached for something to hold onto.

"But I healed him!" Kjell protested.

"Yes," Padrig murmured. "Yes. But memories—and visions —are like that. They are pieces and parts. Lady Firi and I only saw that small glimpse."

"She thought Tiras would die," Kjell breathed.

"Lady Firi was certain you would be the next king. She demanded to see all of Saoirse's memories. But I refused." Padrig shuddered, reliving the decision. "I released Saoirse's star, sending it back to the heavens. Lady Firi was enraged. She put me in the dungeons, determined to break me."

"And Sasha was left alone, with no memory of who she was," Lark said, supplying the culminating piece.

"Yes," Padrig said, his expression tragic. "When Lady Firi went to Jeru City, the dungeons were emptied. I was released. But Saoirse was gone. I thought Lady Firi had her killed. But maybe she supposed she was of little threat—or consequence— without her memories."

"I want them back," Sasha demanded abruptly, her voice shaking, her eyes shimmering. She had listened in stunned silence, and her sudden demand drew the attention of the gathering. The Spinner stepped toward her, apology etched in every line of his face.

"And I will give them to you," Padrig said, bowing slightly before her.

"I want to see your gift," Tiras commanded, his voice still awestruck at the Spinner's revelations. "I want you to show us what you showed Ariel of Firi. And then you will return what you have taken from Lady Saoirse."

Padrig swallowed and nodded. "Yes, Majesty. But I will need to see the sky, and we will want to be unobserved." His eyes shifted briefly to Kjell, perhaps because he sensed Kjell's animosity and distrust, perhaps because he simply feared his size and his blade, but Kjell took note. And his apprehension grew.

King Tiras led them from the great hall and into the gardens, fragrant and quiet in the deepening night. Sasha moved as if she were walking to her own execution. Kjell escorted her like he wielded the axe. Queen Lark pressed soothing thoughts upon them, telling a rhyme that was more a blessing than a cure. Dismissing the guard to stand at each entrance to discourage someone happening upon the royal party, Tiras commanded Kjell and the women to stand back. Then he bade the Spinner to proceed.

Without warning, much the way Tiras changed or Kjell healed, Padrig simply exerted his will, calling on something inside of himself. Throwing back his head to better see his canvas, he lifted his hands toward the sky and, with the tips of his fingers, he began moving the stars.

"There she is," Padrig breathed, and he paused, pointing at a winking light. As if he drew water from a well, he began pulling the star toward him, hand over hand, until it began to fall on its own, gaining momentum. The light grew closer and closer, brighter and brighter, making the group wince and step back.

With hands outstretched to catch it, he drew the star to him without ever touching it at all. It hovered above his palms, a tiny universe of light, an irresistible globe of forbidden fruit.

"This is yours, Lady Saoirse," he said humbly, and his audience stared, awestruck. Such power and light would have been irresistible to a woman like Ariel of Firi. The Star Maker had condemned himself, and Sasha, the moment he had raised his hands to the heavens.

"Show us what Lady Firi saw," Kjell demanded.

"I can't. When I withdraw a strand of light, a memory, I don't know what it is. And once the memory is shared this way, unlike in our thoughts, it disappears. I cannot call it back."

"Then show us something else," Sasha urged. Kjell sensed her awe but also her trepidation. The orb belonged to her, but she had no way of knowing what it contained.

"As you wish."

Padrig turned his palm, cupping the glowing orb above his left hand. With his right, he pinched the surface of the light between his finger and his thumb and withdrew a tendril from the whole, pulling it free. With a little flick of his wrist, he released it into the air. The tendril shimmered and stretched, flattening out into a sheen so thin, the air rippled with it.

"Watch," Padrig breathed.

A woman appeared on the glassy surface, staring back at them as though she saw them too. Her hair was as scarlet as Sasha's, her skin as freckled and pale, but her eyes were blue and her mouth was pinched in worry.

"Lady Kilmorda," Queen Lark cried.

"My mother?" Sasha asked.

"Yes," Padrig verified, and then he was silent as the memory unfolded before them.

"They are just dreams, Saoirse," the woman said. *"Just stories. You love stories. You can tell me, but you can't tell anyone*

148

else, do you understand? The servants will talk. They will say you are Gifted. That you see things. And I won't be able to keep you safe."

"Like Lady Meshara?" a childish voice—disembodied and echoing like it came from inside a huge iron pot—inquired.

The woman nodded, her eyes terrified, and she reached out and smoothed the hair of the little girl whose eyes they saw through.

"I can almost feel her hand," Sasha whispered, touching a lock of her hair.

"The memory is gone, but the feeling remains in your heart." Padrig affirmed, and the memory winked away, finished.

"She knew what happened to my mother." Lark's mouth trembled, and she reached for the king's hand.

"Yes. That is why Lord Kilmorda sent Saoirse to Dendar, beyond the reaches of King Zoltev and his zealots," Padrig explained.

"They sent me away?" Sasha cried.

"You were a child when you came to Dendar. When Dendar became too dangerous, you were sent back to your family in Kilmorda. I went with you. We didn't know that eventually, Kilmorda, across the Jeruvian Sea would also be overrun. All I could do was get you out. I saved you in Kilmorda, but I failed in Firi."

"Please . . . show me more." Sasha's eyes were glued to the orb, hypnotized by its light, hungry for answers.

"You won't be able to keep these memories we watch. I need to put them back in your mind," Padrig warned.

"Just one more," Sasha begged. "Seeing them is its own memory."

Again Padrig extracted the thinnest thread of light and let it go. Instead of a mother's face and words of distress, the image they saw was of endless green grass in a field speckled with yellow blooms. In the distance, a strip of deep blue sat above the green and above that, an endless sky. Harmony limned the image, as if the memory was one of contentment. A tall man with shoulders so wide and hips so slim he resembled a cross, stood a ways off, his hands on a staff, his greying head tilted to the breeze.

"That is not Kilmorda," the queen said softly, her eyes riveted to the scene.

"No . . . it is the Valley of Caarn." Padrig exhaled, staring with great longing at the image that was already dissipating.

"Was that my father?" Sasha asked, her voice soft, her eyes troubled.

"No. That was King Aren of Dendar."

"I don't understand," Sasha said, shaking her head in confusion. Kjell didn't understand either, and the pulsing, impossible light in the Spinner's hands was beginning to blind him.

"What aren't you telling us?" Kjell's anger erupted, cauterizing his fear.

"I can tell you the story, everything that I know, every jot and tittle. Or Sasha can remember it for herself," Padrig urged quietly.

"She needs to know, Kjell," Tiras said gently. "Those memories belong to her. She deserves to have them back."

"It is up to you," Padrig said to Sasha, moving so he stood directly in front of her, hands outstretched, the ball of light between them.

"Do you *want* to remember?" Kjell asked Sasha, looking away from the orb and searching her eyes.

"She must," Padrig insisted. "It is the only way."

"She doesn't have to do a bloody thing," Kjell bellowed, and Padrig grew silent, cowed by Kjell's adamancy.

"Will who I *was* change who I am?" Sasha asked, though her eyes still held Kjell's.

"You will lose nothing," Padrig reassured. "There are memories that will hurt. There are memories you won't want in your head. But with the joy comes the sorrow, and I can't separate one from the other."

Sasha took Kjell's hand and he quaked, wishing he could scoop her up and take her away, the Sasha who loved him, who had accepted her lot with clear eyes and a compassionate heart.

"I am ready," she said, and Padrig wilted a little, his relief evident. He closed the space between them and gently, as though he placed a crown on her head, he brought the orb down over Sasha's hair. The light was absorbed into the crimson strands, soaking into her scalp, making her tresses glow like fire. Her eyes fluttered closed, and for a heartbeat she was a glimmering statue, completely still, immersed in all that had been taken from her.

Then her legs buckled and a keening tore from her throat. Kjell caught her up, his sword clattering to the cobblestones.

"What have you done?" Kjell cried. Sasha jerked in his arms, her hands pressed to her eyes, and the keening became a tortured scream.

"She is remembering," Padrig mourned. "She is remembering, and some memories are painful."

"May the Creator damn you," Kjell roared.

"There was no way around it, Healer." Padrig had begun to weep. "She is not just Saoirse of Kilmorda. She is not simply the daughter of a lord."

Padrig laid his hands on her head and pulled the memories from her mind, coaxing them upward, spinning them into a great, glowing orb. Then he released the sphere, and it floated up into the sky and joined the stars, bright and shimmering, safe from

discovery, shining down on the girl who no longer knew who she was.

Images melded one into the other, and the star that had risen into the sky returned again, settling upon her. Pictures flashing, flickering, upside down and inside out. They bounced and wavered, then shifted again. Womanly fears became childish dreams, girlish longing became survivor's pain. Kjell became a liberator, and a king became a tree, Sasha became a slave, and a girl became a queen.

Nothing fit and nothing matched. She shook her head and looked again, allowing the sediment of memory to sink into place, creating a path she could follow from beginning to end.

Her father's sightless eyes, her mother's broken body.

Running.

Padrig pulling on her hand and urging her forward.

She'd known the birdmen were coming, but her visions had become confusing bits of reoccurring history, and she'd stopped being able to tell what was Dendar and what was Kilmorda, what was long ago and what was recent past.

What was now and what was then?

"Then" was a white horse with blue eyes she wanted so badly to ride, a bed that was too big, and a world surrounded by people far too tall. Her mother's scent, her mother's hands, her mother's hair all reminded her of rose petals, fragrant, soft, and red.

"Then" was her mother's fear. Or maybe that was now. Had her mother always been afraid? "Then" was her father's stories and the books he helped her read.

"How does the story end, Saoirse?" he would say. Together they would spin visions into fairytales, complete with happy endings.

She believed in happy endings.

A woman named Meshara held her hand and asked her how many summers she had. "I have seven summers," she said, and the woman smiled. "You are so tall. But you are not so much older than my Lark. You will be great friends one day."

One day. But not then.

"Then" was the sands of Kilmorda, the blue of the sea, the ships that brought treasures from Porta, Dendar and Willa, places she promised herself she would one day go.

One day became that day.

A trip across the Jeruvian Sea, her belly tossing and her mind weak, wanting her mother and cursing the things she saw. She saw him, *the Healer with the dark hair and the sad, blue eyes. She saw him breathe life back into a child, small and dark, whistling like a bird, and she begged him to find her on the water and ease her heaving stomach and broken heart.*

Dendar. Then moved into later, and later creeped closer to now, yet still stayed so far away.

Dendar was rarely cold, but it rained the way she cried for home. It rained and rained, until finally . . . it stopped. She stopped. Home became a castle named Caarn in a valley that smelled of earth and grain and sky. The trees were sentries, safe and tall, monuments to a people who didn't cut them down but bade them move. And move they did, upending their giant roots, finding a new place to grow, and circling the valley while leaving room for those who would eventually join them.

In the castle, she befriended a king, a patient guardian and kind protector to a lonely girl. He loved the forests and named the trees, and he took her with him when he walked among them.

"This is my grandfather," he sighed, patting an old tree with sprawling roots. He wiggled his fingers and his nails became soft and green. They grew, twining up his arms in clinging vines.

"Someday I will come here too," he said to the forest.

"Will I?" she asked, wishing.

"No, Saoirse. You are not a Spinner. Your gift is to see."

The days passed, and then the years. What she saw became who she was.

"Will I ever go home?" she asked the king, her tears falling on his shoulder.

"I don't know. Will you?" She stared into his beloved face, confused and surprised.

"What do you see, Saoirse?"

"I see Dendar."

"Then you must stay."

Flowers and wreaths. The soft petals of her mother's hands had become petals in Saoirse's hair. Padrig stood before them, his arms raised to the stars, but he did not pull lights from the firmament. He drew vows from their mouths. He pronounced them man and wife, King Aren and Queen Saoirse, and the people crowed and clapped.

She saw her reflection in the glass and realized she had grown into her mother—tall and straight, a child no longer, a crown on her head and thorns in her heart.

She saw Dendar, but she saw more. She saw the Healer, his hands braced against a tree, wracked in lamentation.

Leaves changed, yellow and gold, orange and burgundy. Then they were gone, leaving Grandfather Tree and the rest of the forest bare and skeletal. But the green came again, clothing the trees and carpeting the fields in grass. Beyond Caarn, the king traveled, returning with terrible news and growing fears.

"Tell me, Saoirse, what do you see?"

Birdmen, winged dragons with the chest and legs of a man. Beasts that drank blood and ate flesh. She saw them over the trees and in the valley, above the hills and across the streams. She saw them everywhere.

"Whatever it is that your parents fear, it cannot be worse for you there than in Dendar."

Trees. Silent and waiting. Endless trees and empty fields, and a trip back to now, across the sea.

"We will wait for you, Saoirse, here in the valley of Caarn," they said. "Come back to us, Saoirse, here in the valley of Caarn."

Padrig pulled the memories from her head and, wrapping them in light, he let them go. Let her go.

"Sometimes our memories can hurt us, Sasha. So I will tell you a new story."

Knowledge merged and met the past, and the past became an avalanche, a flood, a tempest comprised of wind and sand.

She and Kjell had not escaped the storm after all.

She couldn't breathe, and she couldn't speak. Each grain of sand was a shard in her skin, a terrible truth that completely changed the landscape. All that was became all that is, churning and changing, rearranging, until Sasha was swept away and Saoirse took her place, no longer plagued by who she'd been, but completely destroyed by who she was.

TWELVE

Kjell climbed the broad staircase, Sasha in his arms, Lark on his heels. Tiras would see to the Spinner. He would see that justice was done. And if he didn't, Kjell would. But for now he could only whisk her away, his heart in his throat, fear in his veins, Sasha weeping against his chest. Lark commanded the door to his chamber to open before they even arrived, she ordered the covers to toss themselves aside before he crossed the room, and when he laid Sasha across his bed, the queen's mouth moved around words of comfort.

> *"What is past is done and gone,*
> *Ease the torment of this one,*
> *In her heart and in her mind,*
> *Let her rest and forget time."*

Lark couldn't heal and she didn't compel, but her powers of suggestion and her ability to command were unmatched. Regaining her speech had made her considerably more powerful, yet she wielded her words so carefully.

Sasha quieted, her trembling becoming an occasional shudder, her tears slowing. Her hands released the cloth of his shirt, her muscles relaxed, finding reprieve in sleep, and Kjell collapsed beside her.

"I will stay with her. The memories are with her now, and whether she sleeps or not, she is processing," Lark volunteered.

"I should not have allowed it," Kjell said.

"You sound like your brother," Lark said softly.

"No. He sounds like me," Kjell argued. But he sighed and rose from the bed, looking down at the woman curled in tormented slumber.

"Go, Kjell. Sasha will be here when you return. You need answers and at this moment, she can't give them to you."

When Kjell returned to the Great Hall, Tiras sat on his throne, surrounded by empty space and high, arching windows that framed the night and the silence in the room. His face was like stone, his hands gripping the arms, his feet braced wide like he was preparing to stand.

"Sit, brother," he said.

"Where is the Spinner?" Kjell asked, unwilling to comply.

Tiras leaned forward and clasped his hands in front of him, meeting his older brother's gaze.

"Sit," he asked again.

"Just speak, Tiras," Kjell shot back.

"Sasha is not Lady Saoirse of Kilmorda," Tiras stated, his eyes never leaving Kjell's.

"What?" Kjell asked, impatient, wishing Tiras would cease babbling and start beheading.

"She is Queen Saoirse of Dendar," Tiras said.

Kjell stared at his brother, dumbfounded, too many pieces of the story still unaccounted for. Tiras began to speak again, trying to explain.

"King Aren of Dendar is a powerful Spinner—his *people* are Spinners, but most of them don't spin objects into illusions or straw into gold. They make things grow. They are able to spin themselves into plants and trees and bushes and grass."

"Caarn means tree. *Tree*. They spin themselves into trees," Kjell whispered. He reached for something to hold on to, and collapsed to the dais of his brother's throne, obeying Tiras after all.

"Sasha's story. It wasn't a story. It was real," Kjell breathed. No. Not Sasha. *Seer-sha*. Queen Saoirse. The name rolled around on Kjell's tongue like burnt sugar, sweet and bitter, inviting and unwelcome.

"Dendar was overrun by Volgar. Porta and Willa were decimated first, then Dendar. Then Kilmorda. Padrig is a Spinner, but his gift is different from the other people of Caarn. Because of this, when the Volgar came, the king—Padrig's nephew—charged him with keeping Saoirse safe. She could not protect herself . . . nor could she hide," Tiras continued, tripping over the explanation like he hadn't had time to process it himself.

"She's a queen," Kjell said, lightheaded and tempted to laugh. He should have known. No wonder he wanted to worship at her feet.

"You don't understand, Kjell," Tiras interrupted softly. He moved down to the dais and sat next to his brother, his eyes on the floor. His compassion demanded it. "She is not the heir to the throne. She is not related to the king. She is the *wife* of the king. She is King Aren's . . . queen."

Kjell raged through the castle hallways, demanding access to the Spinner, Tiras following behind like he was a toddler in danger of falling.

"Where is he, Tiras?" he shouted.

"You will hurt him," Tiras said. "I can't allow that."

"I will kill him!" he confirmed, searching mindlessly, slamming doors and frightening the staff. Dawn had come, but the castle had just gone to bed.

"You cannot kill a man for telling painful truths, Kjell."

"I can kill him for letting me believe a lie!" he bellowed.

"There were no lies, Kjell." Tiras shook his head. "Nobody lied to you."

Kjell shoved past his brother, and Tiras finally let him go.

He paced the hallway outside her room, not able to sit at her bedside, not able to sit still at all. Lark kept a vigil, just like she'd said she would, but when Sasha finally woke, she refused to see him.

Lark stepped out into the corridor, her face drawn, her hands stretched out to him, ready to comfort, armed with excuses. But he would not be comforted or denied. He pushed into the room, and Lark didn't stop him. Sasha lay very still with her eyes closed.

He waited by her bed, sprawled in a chair like a drunken fool, muttering to himself and waiting for her to open her eyes and look at him. Lark had taken down Sasha's hair and helped her to remove the golden gown she'd spent the whole night tempting him in. She was awake behind her closed lids. He'd watched her sleeping often enough to know. Her chest rose and fell rapidly, and her hands were clenched.

She couldn't look at him. Only days before, he had made love to her and she couldn't look away.

She turned her head into the pillows and in a voice that barely resembled the Sasha he knew, she asked him to go.

"Please, Captain. I need you to leave."

And he could not deny her.

Days later, he was called into the library, summoned like a royal courtier, and he obeyed again, paying special attention to his appearance, combing his hair back from his face and carefully shaving the growth from his jaw. He had a maid press his tunic and a porter shine his boots. Then he strapped on his anger and his disdain and made sure he was late.

She was waiting alone, as carefully coiffed as he, no feather duster or ladder to climb. No sweet pleading for another kiss. There wouldn't be another one. She'd seen the truth all along.

And still she didn't look at him.

"You are Queen Saoirse of Dendar." It was the only thing he could think to say.

"Yes," she replied. He expected her to elaborate. To cry. To fall into his arms. But she sat primly, her hands in her lap, her back straight, her face forward, and her eyes focused beyond his head.

"Should I kneel? What is customary when speaking to a queen in Dendar?" he asked.

Her face remained immovable, but her throat convulsed briefly.

"You may stand," she whispered. "You owe me no fealty." She swallowed again, but her eyes stayed averted.

"I see. So tell me, how did Lady Saoirse of Kilmorda, a child, grow to be Queen Saoirse of Dendar?" He matched her tone, the unemotional delivery, the feigned boredom.

"I was Gifted, and my parents were afraid. They knew what happened to Lady Meshara of Corvyn. I was just a little girl, but I could see terrible things. I would tell them elaborate stories that always seemed to come true. I made their lives miserable." She paused, collected her thoughts, and proceeded without inflection.

"An arrangement was made between Kilmorda and Dendar. A betrothment. I was sent to Dendar along with three ships filled with gold, fine silk, and exotic spices. When I was twenty summers, I became Queen. A year later, King Aren sent me back to Kilmorda. He told me it was just for a while. Dendar was under attack, and unlike the rest of Caarn, I couldn't spin to protect myself."

She wrapped her story in concise sentences and careful words. She didn't embellish, didn't add drama or flair the way she usually did. The delivery was dry, flat, and colorless. Everything that Sasha wasn't.

"Why did Padrig take your memories?" he asked the question with just enough disdain to let her know he was no longer convinced that he had. It was theatrics. He knew Padrig had taken Sasha's memories as surely as Kjell had stolen her kisses.

"King Aren ordered him to. He told Padrig if Kilmorda fell, I would try to return. He knew if I could remember Dendar, I would try to go back, and I would be killed."

"And will you?" he pressed, nonchalant.

Finally, her eyes found his.

"Will I . . . what?" Ah. There she was. Sasha of Quondoon. Persecuted servant, looking to him.

"Will you go back?" he asked. And there *he* was. The Kjell of old, scathing and sharp.

She didn't explain herself or say, "It is expected," or "I must," or "I have no choice." She simply replied, "Yes."

Yes.

She would be going back.

"King Tiras and Queen Lark have agreed to arrange a small contingent of soldiers and supplies from Corvyn to Dendar," she expounded. "There was wealth recovered in my father's house. It is now . . . mine. Padrig has not been back since we fled. He doesn't know what we will find, but he is confident Caarn is waiting, and we will be welcomed home."

How kind of King Tiras and Queen Lark. How very considerate. They were arranging all the details. He wanted to kill his brother.

He bowed slowly, with great pomp, the way he used to bow before Lark, just to make her seethe. "I wish you safe travels, Your Highness. It has been a pleasure to have served you." He kept his gaze locked on hers as he straightened.

She didn't reply, but her eyes grew bright and her lips parted slightly, as if she wanted to speak but hadn't decided what to say. He stared at her a moment longer, waiting for words that didn't come, before turning on his heel and striding from the room.

For days he avoided all the chatter, all the glorious gossip of the long-lost Queen of Dendar who had miraculously been found alive and rescued by the valiant king and his good queen. He didn't want to know. Didn't want to hear. Didn't want to count the days until she was gone. But there were preparations he couldn't ignore and people he couldn't evade. Jerick cornered him—making everything decidedly worse with his effusive sympathy—only to run from his presence. Tiras summoned him several times, but Kjell defied his edicts.

He spent hours in the yard, taking his rage and impotence out on anyone who would come against him with a jousting stick, a sword, or a spear. When he realized his men were eyeing him with more pity than fear, he abandoned them too, leaving Jeru City for endless patrols with only Lucian and his sour thoughts for company. Still, avoiding a Seer indefinitely proved impossible.

Sasha found him four days later in the royal stables, mucking stalls that he'd already cleaned, feeding horses that were too full to eat, and oiling saddles that were already gleaming. Her hair was arranged in a crown of braids and loose curls that hung obediently down her back and past her breasts, as if each one had been carefully placed. Her gown was the same soft green as the scarf he'd bought her in Solemn, her lips pink, her nails buffed, her presentation perfect. But her dark eyes were bruised and weary, and her cheeks were pale beneath the smattering of copper. She didn't appear to have slept, and the starch he'd observed in the throne room was missing from her posture.

"We are leaving the day after tomorrow," she said softly.

"Go and do no harm," he shot back, the traditional Jeruvian parting sounding like a slap. She turned away from him and pressed her palms to her face, easing the sting.

"I remember. But I haven't forgotten," she said, her voice breaking slightly.

"I don't know what that means," he answered, but he abandoned the bales of hay that didn't need to be moved again and dropped down onto one of them.

"I remember. I remember everything. And everything has changed. But I have not forgotten how I feel about you."

His throat closed and his skin burned, and he fisted his hands in his hair so he wouldn't reach for her. He kept his eyes on the wooden slats of the stable floor, waiting for her to continue. But she didn't. Instead she began to cry. It was not the keening of the night when Padrig returned her memories. It was not the gentle sniffling of a tender moment, or the pretty cries of a manipulation. Her cries were so deep and raw, they ricocheted through his chest and reverberated in his head. She shook with them, her hands covering her eyes and her hair creating a shroud reminiscent of the day she sank to her knees and declared herself his.

"Tell me what you remember." Maybe it was foolish, but it was a story he wanted to hear, even if it killed him.

"They're gone. My mother and my father are gone," she cried. "I remember Kilmorda. I remember my life. I remember my . . . self. And I am gone too."

"No," he soothed. "You are not."

"I remember the king. I remember King Aren," she rushed, as if she had to tell him, had to get it all out.

He couldn't breathe.

"He was a good king. He was kind to me. I grew to love him, and I was happy."

How could relief and despair exist together? Yet they did, and his heart rejoiced even as he mourned the truth that sealed his fate.

"I am glad," he choked, and made himself say it once more. "I am glad."

She shook her head adamantly, her curls dancing around her, caressing her neck and her face, stroking her back, touching her arms when he could not.

"Please . . . don't . . . say that. Don't tell me you are glad. If you don't mourn with me, no one will." She turned toward him and extended her hand, pleading, asking for comfort. She'd held his hand so many times, taken it in support, in solidarity, in supplication.

He rose and took it, gripping the long, slim fingers, counting the freckles on her skin with his eyes so he wouldn't touch them with his lips. She clutched his just as tightly, but neither of them stepped closer, neither narrowed the space nor crossed the new divide. Clinging to his hand, she continued, her thoughts tumbling over each other, her words coming quickly, confiding and confessing.

"I remember Caarn. The castle. The people. The forests and the hills. The valley of Caarn in Dendar became my home. And I loved her even more than I loved Kilmorda."

"Caarn is not gone. She is waiting for you. You can go back," he reassured. He didn't know what she wanted to hear. He didn't know what she needed to hear. *Knowing* was not his gift. It had *never* been his gift. Compassion, empathy, self-sacrifice and self-denial—he was not equipped with any of them. Yet the moment Sasha fell into his life, he'd been asked to continually exercise them.

"You told me once you were lost. There is a whole world waiting for you. A whole life. You aren't lost anymore," he said.

"I am more lost than I have *ever* been. Padrig told me I would lose nothing when he restored my memories, but he knew that was not true." She stared at him, agonized. "I lost you," she whispered, and his heart grew sharp branches and roots that unfurled and pierced his chest.

"I remember, but I have not forgotten," she repeated.

"Please, Sasha," he panted, trying to breathe around the briars.

"I am Saoirse. But I am Sasha too. And Sasha loves Kjell."

The words reverberated between them, round and reverent, and Kjell could only marvel and mourn that they'd been uttered at all. He couldn't bear to hear them, yet he repeated them over and over in his mind, hearing Sasha say them, reveling in each syllable.

"And Kjell loves Sasha," he admitted in return, each word a tortured confession. He'd never told her, and now he could only speak as though he were someone else.

Sasha hung her head and wept, beyond speech, the tears so heavy and wet she was doubled over with their weight. He couldn't watch anymore. He swept her up, embracing her, pressing her cheek to his and burying his nose in her hair.

"I would heal you if I could." He pressed his hands over her heart, to her cheeks and her brow, trying to soothe the sting of remembrance, but it wasn't a pain he could ease even if he'd never touched her before.

"I have given Sasha to you, but she was not mine to give," she wept. "I am so sorry, Captain."

"I know," he said, nodding, forgiving her. "I know." And in that moment he wondered if he'd actually known all along. Maybe knowing *was* his Gift. Because he'd known, deep down, from the very first, that she didn't belong to him.

He fell back into the straw, holding her, letting her grieve, grieving with her. She cried for a long time, laying in his arms, his cheek resting on her head, but there was no more speaking, no more apologies. And when the shuddering ceased and her eyes closed, he settled her carefully on the straw and told the stable master to make sure she was not awakened or disturbed. He was quite certain she hadn't slept since Lark had cast her spell. He certainly hadn't. The sleep would have been a glorious reprieve, but waking up and remembering was too hard. He winced at his musings. Sasha had been caught in a cycle of constant remembrance for three days.

He would not sleep . . . but he would drink. And he would think.

"You're sending her off with ships and supplies," Kjell accused, holding his flask in one hand while he held his head in the other. He wasn't nearly drunk enough to endure Tiras's presence.

"Yes. I should have sent ships long ago," Tiras said, unapologetic. Someone had ratted Kjell out, he was certain of it. One of his men had seen him and told the king he was holed up in the tavern, and Tiras had come running. Tiras never drank in the hostelry. When Tiras needed to escape, he changed. Kjell could not escape himself, no matter how hard he tried.

Kjell stared at his brother stonily, and Tiras sighed.

"Four years ago, refugees started trickling into Jeru from the lands north. Men, women, and children who climbed aboard anything that would float just to escape the Volgar. Somehow some of them made it to Jeru only to find that we were in a hell of our own. But we've come out of it, Kjell. It is time to see what remains beyond the sea. It is long past time."

"How convenient then. Let's all celebrate this amazing opportunity to explore and settle new worlds," Kjell mocked.

"It is not a new world for Queen Saoirse. I couldn't stop her if I wanted to. She is a woman of means. All that her father owned—and he was a wealthy lord—is now hers. She brought a ship full of riches to pay for an army to go back to Dendar. But there was no army to spare, and we know what happened in Kilmorda. The treasure was brought here to Jeru after the first battle in the valley of Kilmorda—you remember, don't you? Ten chests marked with the emblem of the tree. She described them to me. They belong to Dendar, and she will be taking them back with her," Tiras explained.

Kjell flung his heavy flagon at the wall and watched it erupt, spewing ale in a half-moon spatter before hitting the floor. The tavern owner looked balefully at the mess and then addressed the king with a small bow.

"The captain's been talking to the dog, Highness. Calling her Maximus of Jeru and nursing that same pint for hours. It might be time for him to go home," he suggested cautiously, mopping up Kjell's temper and admirably controlling his own.

Leaning down, Kjell sank his fingers into the thick fur behind the mutt's ears, scratching briskly. The dog's eyes rolled back in ecstasy, and her tongue fell from her mouth and flopped against the floor. She'd been his companion since he'd arrived.

"Ah Gilly. Ye've traded your dignity for pleasure, haven't you, girl?" the tavern owner sighed, talking to his dog. "Be careful, Captain. The bitch will follow you now. Ye'll never get rid of her."

Kjell shot up from the floor with a roar, and with his brawny arms, cleared the adjacent table of its contents, spilling spirits and overturning platters.

Tiras stood, narrowly avoiding being struck by a flying dish. He set a small pouch, heavy with coin, in the tavern owner's hand, grabbed Kjell's arm, and dragged him from the establishment.

The sun was so blinding Kjell stumbled and almost fell. He closed his eyes, not even caring where they walked, and let Tiras lead him.

"Are you really that sloshed, or are you just using it as an excuse to wreak havoc and talk to dogs?"

"I told you I was past pretending, brother," Kjell reminded, repeating his sentiments from the night of the masquerade, the night of the unveiling, hers and his. But he hadn't yet donned a new disguise, and he didn't think he ever would.

They walked to the mews, the shadowy quiet welcoming them. Tiras loved the mews—he felt safe there—and Kjell didn't have the energy to tell him that the mews made him think of unhappy changes, of losing his brother to a curse neither of them could control.

Hashim, the Master Falconer, approached with a tidy bow and prayerful hands. He was a Changer like Tiras, and he trained the royal carrier birds to fly to all corners of the kingdom, delivering missives and communications from the king. Years before, Hashim had found Kjell and Tiras on the road to Firi, sent on a false errand, and turned them back. Without him, Zoltev would have toppled Jeru.

"Majesty," Hashim greeted. "I've just received a message from Corvyn. All will be in order for the voyage to Dendar when the caravan arrives."

Kjell dropped to the long bench that lined the far wall, waiting for the conversation to end. Tiras thanked Hashim and spoke with him quietly for a moment before the falconer bowed and retreated once more.

Kjell watched his brother walk among the shrouded birds, noting his broad shoulders, his calm presence, his hands clasped behind his back like folded wings, resembling the eagle he never completely shrugged off.

"She leaves the day after tomorrow. It will be easier for you then," Tiras offered after a weighty silence.

"No. It won't. Because I am going with her." Kjell had told the dog. He'd told his ale. He'd told his heart and his head. Now he had to tell the only person in the world who would truly mourn his absence.

"Kjell . . ." Tiras protested, his voice falling off in disapproval. "You are drunk, and that isn't wise."

"I have never claimed to be wise. That has always been you, Tiras. Not me. And you and I both know I'm not at all drunk."

"Half of the bloody guard has volunteered to go. She will be in good hands," Tiras said.

Kjell scoffed, the chortle not quite lifting his lips. "Of course they have. But they are my men. I will lead them."

"I need you here," Tiras demanded.

"Why, Tiras?" Kjell asked, incredulous.

"Because . . . you are the captain of my guard. You are Kjell of Jeru. You are protector of the city."

"And you are a powerful king. The Volgar has been obliterated. I have spent the last two years looking for something to kill just to justify my existence."

"There is nothing for you in Dendar, Kjell," Tiras argued.

"I am not convinced there is anything for me *anywhere*."

"That is not true," Tiras pleaded. "You are my brother. This is your home."

"No, Tiras. It isn't. This castle has *never* been my home. I have stayed out of loyalty to you. But this is not about me, Tiras. She told me—Sasha told me—that our gifts are about responsibility. She is now my responsibility."

"No, brother. She isn't!" Tiras cried.

"Did I tell you where I found her?" Kjell shot to his feet, and he didn't wait for Tiras to answer. "She was broken, laying in a heap at the base of a cliff. I didn't think I could heal her. I had never healed anyone but you and the queen, and my devotion to you both—"

"—can't be questioned," Tiras completed his sentence.

"No, it can't," Kjell agreed, gritting his teeth against his sudden emotion. "Since I healed you, I've healed a hundred small wounds, a hundred minor injuries. But nothing like what I did the day when I restored your life. Not until I healed Sasha." He winced and corrected himself, using her proper name. "*Saoirse*."

"I made a bargain with her as she lay dying on the ground. I told her that if she . . . came back . . . that I would try to love her. But I haven't even had to try. I've tried *not* to."

"Kjell," Tiras breathed, weakening.

"I love her more than I've ever loved anything—or anyone—before. It was never a choice."

"The gods save us," Tiras sighed, and he was contemplative for a moment, as if trying to puzzle out a solution. Then he shook his head and met Kjell's gaze with compassion. "But she is the wife of another, Kjell."

Kjell nodded, accepting the verdict, his pain so great he was swimming in it, gulping it in in giant mouthfuls. But it was like trying to swallow an ocean, and he stopped fighting it, letting it take him. "The day I healed her, I gave myself to her. And I made her a promise. Just ten days ago, before all of Jeru, I pledged myself to her. Everything has changed. But nothing has changed for me. And I am going with her."

"I don't know what you'll find in Dendar, Kjell. Do you remember what Kilmorda looked like?" Tiras argued, changing his tactics.

"Yes. All the more reason to go. I will go with her, and I will put her back on the throne."

"Just as you put me back on the throne," Tiras said. "Caught in an eternal round of fixing what is broken and never finding what you seek."

"I have no ambition in myself," Kjell whispered.

"No. You don't. You never have." Tiras shook his head and pulled at his dark hair, vexed. "But perhaps fate has other plans, Kjell," Tiras warned. "I understand falling in love with a woman you don't think you can have. But you *cannot* . . . have her. Whether or not you go to Dendar . . . she is not yours," Tiras implored.

Kjell winced, remembering all the times he'd insisted just that.

I am yours.

You are not.

In his heart she had become his—her flesh, her breath, the weight of her hair and the devotion of her black gaze. That much could not be changed by a Star Maker's revelations.

"I will not shame you, brother," Kjell insisted, his eyes hard, his voice shaking.

"And I would not *blame* you, Kjell. But if you go to Dendar, and the kingdom of Caarn still exists, if King Aren lives, you will be putting yourself in the service of another king. And you must give him your loyalty."

"I am used to being in the service of kings," Kjell retorted. "If he is a good king—and Sasha says that he is—then I can serve him. And when I am certain that Caarn is restored and that she is safe . . . I will return to Jeru."

"And leave her behind?" Tiras challenged.

"Yes," Kjell whispered. "And leave her behind."

THIRTEEN

The journey to Corvyn would be nothing like the journey from Quondoon. When Kilmorda had been decimated and her people destroyed and scattered, her ships had remained in her harbors, empty, of no use or interest to the scourge of conquering birdmen. In recent years, King Tiras had attempted to rebuild the industry, sending teams of tradesmen and sailors to repair the ships docked at Kilmorda's ports and sail them to the ports in Corvyn and Firi. But with the destruction in Porta, Dendar and Willa, and no one to resume trade on the other side of the Jyraen Sea, those ships had gone from the Bay of Brisson, tucked between Kilmorda and Corvyn, to the harbors in Firi and back again, following the Jeruvian coast, never venturing to the lands across the Jyraen Sea.

The Bay of Brisson lay directly north of Lord Corvyn's fortress in the Corvar Mountains and word had already been sent to him that two ships should be readied, sailors gathered, and supplies loaded. One of the two ships en route to Dendar would carry an envoy to send east into Willa, and negotiations were already underway to send another expedition from Firi to explore what remained of Porta.

There was no love or familial feeling between Lord Corvyn and his daughter, the queen, and no loyalty or allegiance to King Tiras. The history between the provinces was long and painful, riddled with fear and injustice, political maneuvering and personal undermining. But Lord Corvyn was not a stupid man. Tiras was eager to resume old trade routes and reestablish connections lost to the Volgar blight. If the king wanted to commission two ships and the labor to sail them, Lord Corvyn would oblige, and happily. He would also make an obscene profit, Kjell had no doubt. If the ships were lost, they had never been Lord Corvyn's ships to begin with, and if they returned with good news and the possibility of new trade, all the better.

The ships were to sail from the Bay of Brisson across the Jyraen Sea, heading northwest toward Dendar. When they arrived in the Bay of Dendar, Kjell, Queen Saoirse, and one contingent would continue to the Valley of Caarn while the other would head east to the realm once known as Willa. The journey across the waters would take them little more than a week, if all went well.

Tiras had put his steward over the cargo, the caravan, and the men who would travel to Corvyn, and from Corvyn, to Dendar. Kjell made a few minor adjustments and put himself in charge. The steward gratefully turned it over to him, and just after dawn on a midsummer Jeruvian morning, ten wagons, forty horses, and fifty people—members of the King's Guard, a Star Maker, a queen, two maids, a blacksmith, a cook, a carpenter, and a slew of the Gifted, claiming talents just obscure enough to make them more odd than awe-inducing—left for Corvyn. Thirty sailors and two ships' captains would meet them at the Bay of Brisson in Corvyn, ready to sail.

He hadn't told Sasha he was coming, hadn't seen her at all since he left her asleep in the straw. Telling her his intentions implied he needed a response or permission from her. He didn't need either. So he didn't tell her.

When she saw him, mounted on Lucian, making the rounds through the assembled men and wagons, she had stopped abruptly, Padrig beside her. The Spinner said something to her and touched her arm, but her gaze never left Kjell's face, and she approached him with careful eyes and clenched hands, Padrig trailing her with disapproval and despair.

"I didn't think I would see you again," she said, her face a brittle mask, her voice strained. "Did you come to say goodbye?" she whispered, the word catching in her throat.

"No," Kjell clipped, and her mask wobbled and cracked. He looked away, searching the horizon and finding his strength. "I'm coming with you," he said.

The mask shattered and her eyes shone. For a moment neither of them breathed, the pain was so sharp and sweet. Then she reached for his hand. He took it, unable to bear her gaze for more than a heartbeat, but she didn't make him wait that long.

"Thank you, Captain," she whispered, transporting them both to the outskirts of Solemn, to the moment he turned and went back for her. But this time, he would follow.

She didn't linger or say more, but released his hand and moved away, not giving either of them more than that moment. A member of his guard escorted her to the stable master, who held the reins of a grey Kjell had chosen himself, a horse he'd watched grow from a foal, a mount that had never nipped or spooked and had never thrown a rider. But Padrig held back, his eyes on Kjell, his expression bleak.

"Captain," Padrig warned softly. "You will only cause her more pain."

"The pain she feels is not my doing, Spinner," Kjell shot back.

"Will you tell King Aren that you are in love with her?" Padrig pressed, his voice pitched low, his eyes lower.

"I betrayed no one, Spinner. She betrayed no one. You and your king betrayed her. And if King Aren sits on his throne waiting for his queen to return to him after all this time, *that* is what I will tell him," Kjell answered.

Lucian whinnied and tossed his head, agreeing, and Kjell found Jerick who had mounted his horse and signaled to the trumpeters on the wall. Kjell had only one more thing to say to the man.

"You do not get to make decisions for her anymore, Spinner. She will not be at your mercy. You will be at mine. Do you understand?"

Kjell waited until Padrig lifted his gaze, signaling he had heard. Then he urged Lucian to the front of the caravan, his eyes touching briefly on the green flags of Jeru, on her gleaming black walls, on her peaks and vales. He would miss her. But he would rather miss Jeru than long for Sasha, though he knew he would do both. Neither belonged to him, and he doubted either would ever let him go.

He found his brother standing on the ramparts, Lark beside him, and Kjell raised his sword in fealty and farewell as the horns began to wail, dancing from pitch to pitch and ending on a prolonged cry that echoed in his chest. Tiras raised a hand, keeping it lifted as if he would call him back, and Lark sent him a prayer across the distance, her words soft and sweet in his mind.

"Jeru needs Kjell," Tiras repeated, standing in the northernmost rampart with Lark, watching the caravan leave for Corvyn, and beyond that, for a destination no one was certain still existed.

"Jeru has you. And me. Maybe . . . Dendar needs Kjell," Lark said.

"It will end badly," Tiras worried.

"Be careful with your words, husband," Lark warned. "Maybe it will not end at all."

"You are speaking in riddles, Lark."

"He can't remain here. The moment he saved Saoirse's life, his path was set. Just as mine was set the moment I saved yours."

"He deserves happiness," Tiras said.

"Then those are the words we will say."

Tiras could not watch as the wagons, loaded with supplies, disappeared. He couldn't bear it. With uncharacteristic impatience he changed, leaving his clothes in a pool where he'd stood, becoming an instantaneous extension of wings and flight, taking to the sky to follow his brother for just a little longer.

Lark watched him go and spoke a prayer into the breeze, asking the Creator for his blessing.

In the lands we cannot see,
In the hearts we do not know,
In the kingdom of the trees,
Where my brother now must go.

Give him hope amid the pain,
Love amid the hate.
May safety guide his footsteps.
May mercy be his fate.

Northern Degn was temperate and grassy, with endless grazing and plenty of open space, but Corvyn was mountainous and cool with towering pines and winding ascents and descents. They wouldn't go to the lord's keep in Corvyn, but would cut across Degn and enter Corvyn where the Nehru River clipped the border. From there they would follow the river along the Corvar Mountains which extended into the southwest corner of Kilmorda. At the northern tip of the Corvars they would veer east to the Bay of Brisson which was shared by the two provinces.

It was the shortest course, a route with easy access to water and plenty of vegetation for the animals, but water meant the possibility of pockets of Volgar. Volgar mated, but they didn't reproduce. It was an instinctual exercise that bore no fruit. They built nests that never sheltered eggs, and they'd lost their Creator. They had no way to regenerate, a dwindling food supply, and continual decimation had winnowed their numbers drastically. But Kjell knew it would be foolish to think the threat had been completely extinguished.

The women that had been brought on the journey to assist Sasha were put to work attending other things. The queen kept her own company and had no desire or need to be waited on. That much had not changed. She rode the plodding grey with gentle eyes and steady feet, and Kjell checked the horse's saddle, his bindings, and his hooves continually, determined to avoid calamity. He would have felt better if Sasha was riding with him on Lucian. But that was not possible.

Sasha was different, her back straighter, like she stood guard over a past that demanded her protection. Or maybe her memories carried with them walls that she was forced to erect. She was more subdued, more introspective, as if consumed by the images of her old life, and Kjell wished he could see her memories too, just to feel close to her again.

His men seemed to understand that she was not the same Sasha anymore, not the girl who slept at his feet and followed him wherever he went. It was odd really. Sasha had discovered she was a queen instead of a slave, and it seemed a weight instead of a buoy, a burden instead of a blessing. She kept to herself when she slept, staring up at the firmament like her star was still embedded there, winking down at her. Padrig stayed at her side, but Kjell could not trust the man, nor could he imagine he would be much protection against the night. So Kjell stationed a guard to watch the camp and one to watch the queen, and though it hurt to be near her, Kjell was never very far.

One night she woke him, her hand on his shoulder, and he forgot for a moment that they were not on the Jandarian plain. Freed by sleep, he sat up instantly and pulled her into his arms. She let him hold her for a heartbeat, her body soft against him, her lips on his temple before she withdrew. Her eyes bore the echoes of premonition, and he smoothed back her hair, meeting her gaze, trying to tighten his thoughts and narrow his focus.

"We need to break camp, Captain," she urged.

"What did you see?"

"The rocks are falling," she said numbly, as if they were at that very moment, tumbling all around them. But the night was silent, the precipices peaceful.

She closed her eyes, and he waited for her to sort through the pieces of her dream. When she opened her eyes again, her face inches from his own, her gaze was clearer, her voice strong.

"I don't know when. The moon is lower when they fall." She looked up and tracked the distance across the sky before staring back at the looming wall of quiet stone. "I think there is time. But those are the rocks I saw." She pointed at the crags that rose directly above them, overlooking the quiet clearing ringed with trees and the rushing sounds of the Nehru River beyond.

Kjell rose immediately and with haste and few explanations, they woke the camp, hitched the horses to the wagons, and began to ease the weary caravan through the clearing and away from the Corvar cliffs, their eyes continually rising to the formation they left behind, a crouching rock creature waiting to leap from the ledge and bury them beneath his bulk.

It began as a smattering of gravel, dusting their heads and bouncing off the rocks. Then the ground rumbled beneath their feet and a mighty crack split the air. The horses shrieked and pulled against their reins, and the travelers picked up their pace, tired mutterings and doubtful glances converted to incredulous belief and surging adrenaline.

A woman's scream pierced the night, and the caravan froze, ears perked, faces lifted, wagons halted. The sound ricocheted around them, behind them, above them, beneath them, beyond them. The women in the caravan eyed each other in wonder. None of them had uttered a sound. The scream came again, more horror than pain, and the rumbling turned into a roar.

"Keep going toward the river!" Kjell bellowed, fear sharpening his instincts. He held back, pushing everyone forward, the wagon wheels bouncing and groaning over the uneven ground, forced to travel at a speed they weren't equipped to withstand. Behind him, in the clearing they'd just vacated, the trees began to sway and crack, branches bending beneath the weight of falling rock.

"Kjell!" Sasha screamed, and he turned his back on the snapping limbs and crashing boulders.

She was waiting for him, the little grey beneath her dancing and tossing his head in fear.

"Go!" he yelled.

But she held her position, letting the others rush past her toward the river before moving into the rear beside him. The first wagon had reached the banks of the Nehru, but the water was too deep, the river too wide, and the wagons wouldn't float. Kjell just hoped they were far enough from the slide to escape being caught in it. He pulled her from her horse, bringing her to the ground beneath him, sheltering her as best he could. Lucian bolted, the grey fell, and Sasha clung to him. The time for fleeing had ended.

For a moment he thought they would be overcome or tossed aside, the heaving and crashing behind them was so great, but the roaring ceased as suddenly as it had begun. They lay unmoving, waiting, listening. The forest continued to groan and quake, branches falling and leaves shaking, the shift and slide of unstable earth sending clattering sprays over the path they'd recently abandoned.

When silence finally ensued, Kjell drew back, his eyes on the woman beneath him, running his hands over her hair and down her body, making sure she was whole. She did the same, her hands searching.

"Are you all right?" she murmured.

"Yes. But Lucian is gone and the grey's leg is broken."

The grey tried to rise and fell back to the ground, its left hind leg bent oddly below the knee. Kjell shifted, easing himself away from Sasha and crawling to the injured horse. It whinnied piteously and tried to rise once more.

"Shh," he soothed, stroking her head, listening for a note to cling to but hearing only the horse's pounding heart.

Kjell didn't know if the grey would lay still long enough to let him heal its leg. He'd never tried to heal an injured animal before, but Sasha moved beside him with perfect faith and placed her hands over his. The horse shuddered but allowed Kjell to shift his hands down its flanks, bringing Sasha's hands with him as he searched for a song. He heard the grey's heartbeat, scared and strong, and filled his head with the rhythm, not knowing what else to do. Immediately his palms grew unbearably hot, then impossibly cold. Minutes later the horse straightened its leg, panting in relief, and Kjell withdrew his hands, the blood rushing from his head and making him sway, almost euphoric beside the quivering horse. The healing had been different, but a new threshold had been crossed.

"Kjell," Sasha said, her voice hushed in warning. "Look."

From the crater of broken branches and severed trees crept a lone wolf, moving toward them, head lowered, tail down. The wolf stopped, watching them, eyes yellow, teeth bared as if they had caused the destruction in the woods it called home. The wolf didn't draw closer, but stared as Kjell and Sasha rose and urged the grey to its feet beside them. Gingerly they began moving toward the river and the sounds of the caravan, their hands on the grey's mane, reassuring him while keeping their distance from the lurking wolf.

"She's gone," Sasha murmured.

"She?"

"The wolf."

"Maybe the rock slide separated it from its pack."

Sasha didn't reply, but turned her head again, her eyes scanning the woods.

"She will be back," she murmured.

They spent the remainder of the night on the banks of the Nehru, huddled around a fire Isak started, too shaken to sleep but unable to travel in the dark. Two wagons had bent wheels, Jerick's stallion sustained a jagged cut to his foreleg, and the blacksmith had dislocated his shoulder trying to restrain the horses hitched to his wagon. Kjell let others worry about the wagons and the wheels and saw to the injuries, pressing his hands against the bloodied gash on the stallion's lower leg—earning a knot on his forehead for his trouble—and resetting the dangling arm of the black-smith, who was considerably more grateful than the horse.

"It's better than new, Captain," the smithy marveled, cir-cling his arm and rolling his shoulders. "I will build you some-thing in my forge when we get to Dendar. I will repay you, Cap-tain. I'm not Gifted, but I have skills."

"Skills are better than gifts because you have to earn them," Kjell said quietly, uncomfortable as always with the attention.

"We suffer for our gifts, Captain. And in suffering, we earn them too," Sasha said softly, not looking away from the fire, and Kjell had no response.

"What is Dendar like, Majesty?" a maid asked, her eyes peeling back the forest where the rocks had nearly put them all in an untimely grave. The journey had suddenly become very real for the young woman.

"Yes, Milady. Tell us," Peter begged. He was young and less aware. The other men had kept a wider berth, a more re-spectable tone, and Sasha had seemed to regret the distance. "Mistress Sasha tells the best stories," Peter added.

"You will address her majesty as Queen Saoirse," the Star Maker demanded, and Sasha immediately interceded.

"I am simply Sasha to these men, Padrig. They may call me what they wish."

"They will call you Queen Saoirse," Kjell said, standing watch near the forest, his back to the group, and the travelers fell silent, cowed by his terse order. It was Jerick who dared speak up, as usual, making a new request.

"Tell us *your* story, Majesty," Jerick prodded softly. "Tell us about Caarn."

Sasha began reluctantly, clearly feeling an obligation to soothe the feelings Kjell had injured, and Kjell stepped deeper into the woods, leaving the banks behind. But her voice still found him.

"The people are kind," she said, "and the hills and trees are vast. I've been to Porta and Willa and to all corners of Dendar, but Caarn is where the king lives, where all kings of Dendar have lived, and where we will go." Her voice faltered, as if trying to find something to share that wouldn't hurt, and she rattled off a list of inconsequential details Kjell cared nothing about.

"The flag of Dendar is white and red, but the flag of Caarn is a tree on a sea of blue. The castle is not made of Jeruvian ore like King Tiras's castle, but from the rock that is almost as plentiful as the trees.

"When I was a girl, I would lose myself in the palace. In each wing there are ten rooms for sleeping. In the main house there is a grand entrance, two libraries, a great hall for feasts, a ballroom for dancing, a throne room to govern, and a hall for the king to welcome the lords from all of Dendar, Porta and Willa. An enormous kitchen sits on the back of the house overlooking the gardens with a place to breakfast in the mornings, a dining hall for the servants and a private hall for the king. There are three sitting rooms, one chamber for music, one for painting, and another for sewing and weaving where the light is especially good. The halls of Castle Caarn are hung with beautiful tapestries."

"Do you paint or weave, Highness?" the little maid asked again.

"No. I'm not . . . particularly good . . . at anything. My tutors were terribly frustrated with me most of the time."

"You're a Seer, Majesty," Padrig huffed, as if that was gift enough.

She was quiet then, and Peter rushed to encourage her, posing questions better left unasked.

"Is Dendar like Jeru? Is the king Gifted like King Tiras?"

Kjell winced and Peter yelped as if someone had swatted him.

"We are not warriors in Caarn," Sasha said diplomatically, covering the awkward question with a calm reply. "The people of Caarn are growers. Planters. Their gifts are of the earth, not of the body. But when I left, the castle was preparing for an attack."

"Why did you leave, Majesty?" someone asked, and Padrig rushed to her defense.

"Queen Saoirse didn't want to leave. But the king wanted her safe across the sea, far away from the birdmen."

"I wanted to go to Kilmorda and plead for an army to come against the Volgar, but King Aren was convinced that if the birdmen had no prey, they would move on, and lives would be spared. I saw the battle, and I knew he was right. If we tried to fight the birdmen, many would die and Caarn would fall," Sasha explained, her voice hollow and helpless.

Kjell realized his muscles were tensed, his eyes fixed on a forest he wasn't seeing, listening to the story he didn't want to hear. He understood duty and hopelessness. He understood trying to hold a kingdom together when it was falling apart. He understood having no solutions and no answers and charging forward anyway.

"We thought the water would be enough to keep the birdmen from Jeru's shores. But there are islands in the Jeruvian seas, and the Volgar Liege continued to create new monsters," Padrig added.

"I told myself I would return with help," Sasha said. "But I never did."

"You are returning now, Highness," Jerick reassured, and Kjell could picture him patting Sasha's hand with the familiarity that came so easily for him. "We will help you. There is no greater warrior in all the world than Kjell of Jeru."

"What if there are still Volgar in Dendar?" someone asked, and Kjell pushed away from the tree he stood beneath, stepping deeper into the forest, suddenly desperate for distance.

If there were Volgar in Dendar, the party from Jeru wouldn't even get off the ships. Kjell would throw Padrigus overboard, bodily restrain the queen, sail back to Jeru, and never look back. Kilmorda needed a lady as badly as Dendar needed a queen, and Kjell would gladly spend the rest of his days rebuilding the province if he had to. In the blackest part of his soul, he hoped there were Volgar in Caarn, and he knew that made him a bad man.

He whistled, calling to Lucian.

The horse had bolted during the rockslide and had not returned. Kjell picked his way through the trees, whistling and listening. There were wolves in the woods, and if Lucian was injured, the wolves would find him.

He heard a snapping and a whinny and followed the sound, knowing he should bring two of his men, knowing he wouldn't go back to the skittish gathering to get them. The darkness lay heavy in the trees, the forest licking its wounds beneath the cover, waiting for dawn to expose her injuries. The moon had sought shelter on the horizon, and the stars had all retreated to a safe distance.

He whistled again and listened.

Then, to his left, a shadow became a shape, and he breathed in relief, distinguishing the drooping head of his longtime companion amid the trees. But the horse moved and disappeared again, lost in the dense copse, and Kjell whistled once more, confused by the horse's refusal to come.

He changed course, his eyes peeled, his steps careful.

It wasn't Lucian.

The horse moving in and out of the trees was dark like Lucian, sooty-maned and chocolate-haired, but Lucian's flanks were dappled in white, his feet rimmed in the same color. Lucian was huge, bred to carry a man in full armor into battle, but the horse shifting through the shadows was much smaller, almost dainty, and she moved away from him, coaxing him to follow.

He didn't.

He held his ground, drawing his blade from his boot, waiting.

The horse paused as well, turning toward him, partially hidden, partially revealed.

It nickered—the sound almost a laugh—and suddenly the dark horse dissipated, drawing Kjell's eyes downward as the mane became fur and the long equine nose retreated into a narrow snout. The change was soundless, seamless—a momentary unfurling accompanied by a sense of arrival—and Kjell recognized the fleeting vulnerability that always accompanied Tiras's change.

But it was only fleeting.

An instant later, a wolf crouched where the horse had just stood, transformed and wholly aware. The wolf stretched spasmodically and lifted its head, its gaze challenging, and Kjell realized it was the same wolf Sasha had predicted would return. It yipped, a mocking come-hither, and turned, darting away into the undergrowth, leaving Kjell behind.

He froze in indecision, not foolish enough to follow yet needing to understand. Then his gaze narrowed on the shadowed undergrowth just beyond where the horse had become a wolf. The Changer had wanted him to see what was there.

A horse of Lucian's size wasn't easy to hide, but a dead horse was silent.

Lucian's reins were caught in the brambles as if he'd run helter-skelter through the brush, and in his fright, become ensnared. But there was too much blood for a mere entanglement. His throat was ripped out.

Kjell fell to his knees beside him, pressing his hands to the gaping wound, moaning in distress.

"No, no, no," Kjell begged. "No. Please, no." But Lucian, faithful in life, could not obey him now. His body was cold, his eyes wide and staring, and Kjell could not cure death.

When Kjell straightened the wolf was there, sitting quietly by, eyes gleaming, watching him. The hair stood on Kjell's neck as he rose to face it. One moment the wolf was looking at him, the next instant the wolf fell away, contorting and convulsing into something entirely new. Limbs unfolded, shoulders widened, a torso elongated, and a woman straightened from her hands and knees, the long coils of her hair undulating around her naked body. She was far enough away to shift before he could reach her, but close enough not to be mistaken. He could only stare, his hand on his sword, his lifeless horse at his feet.

Her hair was not the elaborate spill of gemstones and waves it had once been. It was wild and tangled as if she'd morphed from one beast to the next, never remaining human long enough to tend to it. She was beautiful in the way freshly-turned soil was beautiful. Dark and supple, uncultivated and cold. But he had no desire to bury himself within her. The earth would claim him soon enough, and when it did, she would not be the one he returned to.

"You have become very powerful, Kjell of Jeru. But even you can't bring back the dead," Ariel of Firi said, her voice echoing oddly in the silent wood.

"Yet the dead still follow me," he answered, not trusting his eyes.

"I am very much alive and very much in control," she murmured, and without warning, changed again, her naked limbs becoming wings, her flesh dissolving into feathers. With a scream that sounded eerily like a haunted child, she lifted up and above the trees, a Kjell Owl, mocking him with her power and her presence.

Without hesitation, Kjell turned and began to lope through the forest toward the river where he'd left the group, not attending to the horse he had loved, not removing the saddle or the bags, not burying the carcass so the forest could not continue to feed on Lucian's flesh.

Lucian was dead. Ariel of Firi was here, and no one was safe, least of all Queen Saoirse of Dendar.

FOURTEEN

Kjell went back after daylight to retrieve his saddle and his bags from Lucian's body. He brought Isak, Jerick and Sasha with him—unwilling to let her out of his sight—leaving the rest of his men with strict instructions to prepare the party to depart. They would need to maneuver the wagons along the river banks until they could cut back through the woods that separated them from the road through Corvyn.

His bags had been rifled through, his possessions scattered, the extra gold he carried missing.

He cared more about his horse.

The act was more defiance and disdain than theft, and as Kjell loosened the bridle and pulled the saddle from Lucian's body, he was consumed by an outrage that muted his grief.

Sasha gathered his strewn belongings with tragic eyes, filling the bags that Jerick slung over his shoulders, and then they stood back as Isak turned Lucian's remains into ash. The stink of singed hair and scorched flesh tinged the air and made their eyes tear and their throats ache, but Kjell couldn't bear to simply walk away without disposing of his friend. He didn't speak of the

Changer, of the threat that he didn't completely understand, and he let the others believe Lucian had been a victim of his own fright and a forest filled with hungry creatures.

In the days that followed, Kjell hovered near Sasha, sleeping on his sword, ignoring Padrig's pointed attempts to act as chaperone. Kjell had commandeered another soldier's horse and assigned the man to ride shotgun in the blacksmith's wagon. Sasha rode the grey beside him—as silent as she'd been in the first days out of Solemn—as they hugged the mountains that dipped down into Kilmorda. From a distance, the green stretch of land and rolling hills, dotted by villages too far away to examine, looked serene and promised peace. But the peace was hollow, the space stripped, and had they traveled inland, deeper into the valleys that lined the sea, they would have seen the piled bones and the empty villages, the scattered nests and the scars of war that left Kilmorda a verdant wasteland.

Eight days after leaving Jeru City, they smelled the sea and descended into the town sitting on the bay that shared its name, a place that had escaped the Volgar wave but had absorbed thousands of fleeing Kilmordians. As a result, Brisson had grown, spreading to the east—away from Kilmorda—and to the south, climbing into the foothills of the vast Corvar range.

After the cargo was loaded and the horses corralled, waiting to be loaded in the bowels of the ship for the week-long journey, the wagons were broken down into pieces that would be reassembled on the shores of Dendar. Ten chests of Dendar treasure had been loaded aboard the two ships as well, and Kjell knew better than to entrust the bounty with a group of sailors or a ship's captain hired by Lord Corvyn. Kjell's men took shifts on the docks, and the rest of the travelers made use of the marketplace and the public baths, making final preparations for the journey to a land that might offer few comforts and fewer guarantees.

Lord Corvyn, under Tiras's instructions, had arranged lodging for the queen, Padrig, and members of the King's Guard at an inn overlooking the docks and the two ships bound for Dendar. The lodgings were clean, the innkeeper gracious, and the food plentiful, if plain. But Kjell had no desire to stay at the inn. He wanted to spend the night on the docks with his men, free of the memories of an inn in Enoch and the first time he'd kissed Sasha, but he slept on Sasha's floor, though the two maids sleeping in the small adjoining chamber gave him some reassurance in numbers.

A sense of desperate celebration broke out, and as the night wore on the atmosphere in the inn's tavern grew more and more merry. The men coming in from the docks were loudly appreciative of a pretty wench with a lovely voice and bountiful breasts. She sang sad songs about brave knights and dragons, and Kjell, certain that no one could possibly sleep in the din—though Sasha hadn't so much as sighed—crept from the room, stationing a guard at the door with instructions not to allow anyone—or anything—inside. He walked to the moored ships, checked on the rotation of the guard, walked by the animal enclosures, and tried not to think about Lucian or the Changer who had killed him.

When a shape broke from the shadows, shrouded and slim, he half expected it, even welcomed it, and drew his blade, eager to put an end to the chase. But the shadow paused and said his name.

"Sasha," he hissed. "What are you doing?" He strode toward her and pulled her into an alcove. The inn wasn't far—singing and laughter were as potent as brine in the breeze—but Sasha was alone and it was dark, and danger crept around every corner and lurked in a thousand possibilities. He gripped her shoulders harder than he should, but she simply stared up at him, waiting for his anger to pass, as if she understood the fear that limned it and the sentiment that motivated it.

"Your instructions to the guard at my door were to not let anyone in. You said nothing about letting me out. And unfortunately, Captain, I outrank you."

Her words weren't defiant but resigned, and though he dropped his hands from her shoulders, he didn't step away. Slowly, like he was a wild creature and she didn't want to frighten him, she took a small step and leaned into him, resting her cheek against his chest. For several seconds they breathed together, connected only where her sighs warmed his heart.

"I see no trouble here tonight, and I wanted to be with you," she confessed.

"But you don't see everything," he whispered, repentant, and his arms moved of their own accord, enfolding her, his lips finding her hair.

"No. I see just enough to make everything I don't see more confusing."

He waited for her to expound, but she pressed her face harder into his chest, hiding her thoughts.

"Tomorrow will come, and I will have to be Queen Saoirse again and for every day after that," she said.

"And now?" he asked, hating the hope he had no cause to feel.

"Now I am just Sasha who loves Kjell."

He heard the surrender in her voice, and as she raised her face, his lips sought hers. She opened beneath him, welcoming his arrival. Their mouths melded and clung, tasting and torturing, jubilation flavored with loss. They withdrew only to come together again, to take just one more, and Kjell kissed her until his body raged and his lips begged for mercy.

It was Sasha who finally bowed her head, pressing her lips to his heart so they wouldn't return to his mouth. Their bodies quaked and thrummed, denied and despairing, until short breaths became longsuffering and pounding blood became quiet questions.

"She follows—Ariel of Firi," Sasha said.

"Yes," he rasped. Her hands curled in his cloak.

"Why?" she asked.

"I don't know." He shook his head helplessly and tightened his arms. "There is something she wants."

"She wants you," Sasha reasoned, as though it were the most logical thing in the world.

"She has *never* wanted me," Kjell argued. "I have nothing to give her. I have never had anything to give her. Once she thought I was going to be king. Now she knows I will never be."

"I have nothing to give you either."

"I never wanted you for what you could give me. Lady Firi wants to hurt me. Lucian's death proved that. There is only one way she can destroy me, Sasha. You must remember that and not put yourself in danger. Not for a moment's peace or a stolen kiss."

She nodded, agreeing, her face set, her mouth tight, and he wondered at her easy acquiescence.

"You must go back, Kjell," she said softly.

"Where?" he asked, befuddled.

"To Jeru City."

"I can't," he whispered, incredulous. "I won't."

"You cannot come with me to Dendar," she insisted.

"You cannot go without me," he shot back, undeterred.

"Beneath every ripple that finds me, behind everything I see, lies the fear that I will set into motion the very thing I am trying to prevent. When I was a child, I was so afraid of the things I saw, they would paralyze me. I would rock in the corner and press my face in my mother's lap. But hiding and fearing changed nothing. Then my father helped me turn my visions into stories. And we always gave them happy endings. He told me the worst thing I could do was doubt myself. He told me when I see something, I should act every time, immediately. So far, faith has always been the best choice."

"And what choice do you think you are making for me now?" he asked, dread pooling in his gut. Determination rang in her voice, and a resolute Sasha was a dangerous Sasha.

"When we left Jeru City, all I could think was that I was so glad I wouldn't have to say goodbye—not yet—and that I wouldn't have to leave you."

He had felt the same way.

"But I was weak," she added. "And I was wrong. And I am so afraid." Her chin wobbled, but she clenched her jaw, forging ahead. "I'm afraid that all the things I've seen are leading us to Caarn, to this time, and the thing I fear most will come to pass."

"And if I don't go to Dendar, none of that will happen," he concluded.

"Yes."

"But how will I keep you safe?" he murmured, and their eyes clung. Her voice shook when she spoke again.

"When I sailed to Dendar for the first time, I was just ten summers. I was terribly seasick, and the fresh air was the only thing that helped. My caretakers, an older couple who had worked in my father's house, would let me sleep beneath the stars just to keep the worst of the sickness at bay. I dreamed of you on the deck, just the way you are now." Sasha touched his face, almost reverent, pleading eyes and gentle hands. "I've always seen you this way—big, strong, your hair dark, your face unlined. My visions have always been of you, the way you are right now. I've never seen you any other way, and now I'm afraid that I never will. I've seen you in Caarn, and that thrills and terrifies me, because as much as my heart aches to have you near me, I will never, ever recover, never forgive myself if you are lost. I will never be Sasha of Jeru or Sasha of Kjell. It is not how life unfolded. But you will never be Kjell of Dendar. Not if I can help it."

A clattering in the street and a figure looming near the alcove made Sasha pull away and Kjell move in front of her, hand on his blade.

Jerick stepped into the swath of orange light spilling from the torches that lined the harbor, a bottle of wine in his outstretched hand, apology in his posture. He slinked forward, the bottle in front of him, until Kjell snatched it impatiently, relief and irritation making him short with his lieutenant, as usual.

"I came to keep you company on watch, Captain. I didn't mean to startle you. I was worried about Sash—about Queen Saoirse. But I see she has found you," Jerick said.

"You were so worried that you let her walk out of the inn in the middle of the night?" Kjell replied, aghast, wishing Jerick would go, knowing it was best if he stayed.

"I was neither the guard at her door, Captain, nor the man she followed," Jerick replied easily.

"Will you think about what I've said, Captain?" Sasha interrupted, stepping around him and out of the alcove, widening the distance between them.

"I am going to Dendar, Majesty," Kjell responded, and she nodded slowly.

"Then I will bid you goodnight," she said, obedient and sadly resigned for all her impassioned pleading.

"Go with Queen Saoirse, Jerick, and stay with her. Please. I am going to remain on watch," Kjell commanded, his eyes on Sasha's unsmiling mouth.

"I would like that back, Captain, when you're done." Jerick inclined his head toward the wine he'd offered moments before.

"Go, Lieutenant," Kjell warned, taking a long pull from Jerick's bottle just to be contrary, and he turned his back to the street, going deeper into the alcove, dismissing them both.

The liquid was warm, but his throat was caked in frustration, and he drank deeply again. The flavor was sweet if a little cloying, but he needed to douse the fire in his belly and the tumult in his chest. It didn't help. If anything, his mouth became drier, his agony deeper.

He tried to drink again, to swallow another mouthful, but his vision throbbed, ebbing and widening, tilting and turning, and for a moment he couldn't remember if he'd just healed an entire village or if Lucian had simply thrown him from his back.

But Lucian had *never* thrown him. Lucian was dead. Lucian was dead and Jerick was beside him once more. What had Jerick done to him? Something was wrong with the wine. Something was wrong with *him*. He swayed and staggered, and someone helped him fall. Then Sasha was kneeling beside him, holding his head against her chest. Sasha was kissing his mouth, and her tears were stinging his eyes.

"Jerick promised me he would look after you," she whispered. "He loves you, you know. They all do. I begged them to help me. To help you. Don't be too hard on him."

He tried to say her name, and it hissed between his lips like the mythical snake in the tree. But unlike the snake, she had beguiled him, and Jerick had helped her.

"When you wake, I'll be gone. And you must remain in Jeru," she entreated.

He begged her to come with him—he promised he would love her if she would just come back—but the words never left his mouth, and she walked away, drawing her dark cloak over her hair. Then Jerick was helping him stand—Gibbous too—pulling his arms around their shoulders and supporting his weight.

"Come on, Captain." Jerick soothed. "We've got you now."

"He's going to kill us, Jerick. We're as good as dead," Gibbous warned.

"Better us than the captain, Gibbous," Jerick reasoned, and Kjell watched himself take steps he would never remember, watched his men struggle to get him to the inn, a plastered drunk with a lolling head, watched them lay him across the bed in his rented room, lifting his feet and removing his boots, setting his sword beside him, as if he could possibly wield it. He watched them close the door and leave him behind, and watched his world go dark.

He was floating, absent, unaware for too long. When he awoke, it was to pain and light, and he struggled to resurface, if only to annihilate the source.

"Wake up, Captain." Padrig was pleading with him, slapping his face. He'd been doused in water—repeatedly, it appeared, from the pool he lay in—and he wore nothing but a pair of breeches and a grimace.

"Why am I wet?" Kjell groaned.

"I've been trying to revive you for an hour. They're going to leave us, Captain. I've paid off the first mate and one of the ship's captains, but the queen is insisting we depart, and your men have worked themselves into a lather over recent events. When Jerick said you weren't coming, I knew there was something afoot."

"Can you help me? I seem to be lost." Jerick spoke up from somewhere nearby. Kjell attempted to turn his head, to find his lieutenant, but the bed was in the way.

"I know who you are," Padrig soothed. "Your name is Jerick. And I will help you, kind sir. But I need your assistance,"

"You know who I am?" Jerick cried.

"Yes. I do. But this captain needs to get to his ship, and he's ill. You are young and strong, and you can help us. Then I will tell you everything I know," Padrig haggled. "But we must hurry."

"What is wrong with Jerick?" Kjell whispered. Dust coated his mouth and whirled in his thoughts, but beneath the haze he was beginning to remember.

"He's currently sitting mindless in the corner. I don't have your strength or your size, but I have my own ways of debilitating my opponents. I am quite good at plucking thoughts right out of people's heads, Healer, remember?"

"Explain, Spinner. Slowly," he demanded, and he commanded his numb arms and liquid legs to obey him. The room tipped and tossed him back to his knees.

"Lieutenant Jerick's memories are currently the newest star in the sky. He was determined to keep you from Dendar, so I had to change his mind."

Padrig helped Kjell rise and eased him down on the bed, handing him his shirt before trying to shove his boots on his feet.

Kjell swatted him aside and, swaying, managed to do it himself.

"Why are you doing this?" Kjell hissed.

"Doing what?" Padrig said, retrieving the confused Jerick from where he huddled against the wall. Jerick looked blankly at Kjell, displaying no recollection whatsoever. Padrig handed the befuddled, young lieutenant Kjell's satchel of personal belongings and two other bags. "One of these is yours, Jerick. Can you carry them to the ship?"

Jerick accepted them hesitantly, clearly not knowing what else to do.

Kjell tried to sheath his sword, and Padrig rushed to his side, guiding the blade home before Kjell stabbed himself in the leg.

"Helping me." Kjell kept his eyes closed, his blurred vision compromising his ability to stay on his feet.

"I'm not helping you, Captain. I'm attempting to help Dendar," Padrig replied. "Now lean on me, and I'll do my best to keep us both standing." Padrig stepped under Kjell's shoulder and slipped a thin arm around his waist.

They tottered down the stairs, Kjell trusting the Spinner to keep him moving in the right direction, while he concentrated on using his legs and staying upright. Jerick followed behind with constant reassurance from Padrig that all would be well.

"How is helping me helping Dendar?' Kjell asked, reeling.

"You must take this journey with us."

"Why? You said I would only cause Sasha pain."

"There are worse things than Saoirse's pain," Padrig huffed, staggering under Kjell's considerable bulk. "I am more worried about what she has seen." Padrig shook his head as if dismissing one thought for another. "Dendar doesn't need a warrior, Dendar needs a Healer," he said, inexplicably.

"What aren't you telling me, Spinner?" Kjell pressed, trying to order his thoughts and summon his comprehension.

"I am telling you that there is a reason Saoirse has had visions of you since she was a child. Dendar needs you both, as painful and impossible as it might be," Padrig muttered. "And I don't dare leave you behind."

Kjell could see the ships still moored in the harbor, and he focused on the white sails, the draped rigging, and the bunk he could fall into once he locked the faithless Gibbous and the traitorous Jerick in the brig. He hadn't decided yet what to do about the stubborn Sasha.

"Praise the Creator," Padrig panted. "I thought she would insist on leaving us both, Captain. I don't think the queen is as fond of me as she once was."

A shout went up. They'd been seen. Suddenly, Isak and Peter were bearing him up, taking his weight from the breathless Padrig.

"Captain Kjell! What is the meaning of this?" the captain of one ship—a man named Lortimer—was striding down the gangplank toward him.

"Where is the queen?" Kjell muttered to his men.

"She's down below, Captain," Isak answered immediately. "In her quarters. Gibbous put a man outside her door and the two maids inside with her. We thought you weren't coming. Jerick told us you were ordered back to Jeru City."

"Jerick lets his heart make a fool of him." He wasn't the only one. "Go fetch Gibbous. Tell him his captain would like a word." Isak ran to obey, and Kjell addressed the Spinner. "Give Jerick back his head, Star Maker."

"I will return the lieutenant's memories." Padrig said, but he hastened to add, "But maybe it is better if we leave him in Brisson Bay. Can you trust him, Healer?"

"Padrig, I don't trust anyone—not you, not Jerick, not even myself. Do as I say." Kjell was on the verge of collapse, and he didn't need Padrig's wheedling or interference. He also didn't need a mindless Jerick. Seeing his lieutenant afraid and disoriented made him angry. It made him think of Sasha, robbed of everything—home, family, even her self—walking to Firi, to bondage, because she didn't know where else to go.

"Very well, Captain." Padrig shrugged. He flung his hands upward and a beam of light shot down from the sky, drawing gasps and cries from the crew and guard. Villagers on the docks gaped and a few screams were heard.

"Bloody hell, Padrig." Kjell groaned at the theatrics.

"I don't want that on my ship!" Lortimer cried, retreating up the gangplank. "I won't have the Gifted on this vessel."

"Then you won't see a single coin," Kjell roared, "And we will unload our cargo and our people now, and you will answer to my sword before you will answer to the king." His temper seared the fog from his head, but it didn't ease the ache behind his eyes. He'd had enough sniveling and second-guessing to last him a lifetime.

Padrig palmed the light and turned toward Jerick.

Jerick took one look at the pulsing orb, and stumbled back, dropping the bags he still carried.

"Jerick!" Kjell thundered, "We promised we would help you. Be still."

Jerick froze, his eyes on his captain, and he nodded, displaying the same trust that was as much a part of him as the color of his eyes or the impudence he'd never been able to suppress. Padrig lowered the light over his head and Jerick shuddered, his eyes rolling back and his legs buckling.

"It doesn't hurt, Captain," Padrig reassured.

"How would you know this, Padrig? You are awfully glib with other people's pain," Kjell said, watching his lieutenant straighten and awareness settle over his features. A guard reached for Jerick's arm, steadying him, and Jerick's eyes found Kjell, shock and wonder flitting across his features.

Isak had reached the main deck, Gibbous on his heels, and Kjell could already see the suffering on the older man's face. He waited to address Jerick until Gibbous stopped in front of him and dropped to one knee.

"Captain, forgive me," Gibbous moaned, bowing his head.

"Not a word, Gibbous. You and Jerick will billet on the other ship and spend your first night in the brig. We won't speak of this again." Kjell turned to include Jerick in his statement. "I know you acted to protect me, but in doing so, you lost my trust." From the corner of his eye he saw a flash of red and pale blue skirts. Sasha stood on the quarterdeck, her hands gripping the rail, tears streaming down her cheeks. He knew she'd heard him, knew his words had pierced her, and he let his rebellious gaze and traitorous heart acknowledge her, absolving her, before he addressed the ship's captain.

"Prepare to sail, Lortimer," Kjell ordered, and with as much dignity and strength as he could muster, he walked up the gangplank, trusting that his men would—this time—do exactly what he asked.

FIFTEEN

For two days, Sasha stayed in her quarters, never setting foot on deck, never seeking him out. The two maids who quartered with her reported that she was seasick, and Kjell consoled himself with the fact that her cabin was probably the safest place for her. She wasn't the only one who suffered. The seas were mild, remarkably so, but the motion of the ship and the endless movement was not something Kjell could even attempt to heal in any of the travelers. It would be futile. The sickness would simply rise again, brought on by the waves and the interminable rocking.

Kjell felt no ill effects from the sea. He'd recovered from his bout with fury, betrayal, and drugged wine by remaining above deck where there was little to do but stay out of the way, and he enjoyed the peace of having no one looking to him or depending on him, if just for a day or two. Instead of sleeping in the officers' quarters or bunking with his men, he slept on the quarter-deck, climbing up to the crow's nest on the second morning despite the warning jest from Pascal, the first mate, that he was so big he would tip the boat over if he climbed too high. Kjell was used to his size and had carried it around most of his life. It had never stopped him before. He ignored the first mate and scrambled up the rigging until he reached the lookout. Bracing his legs as wide as the little platform would allow, he spent an hour getting to know the sea through his spyglass.

The waters had grown steadily bluer as they'd traveled farther from land. Kjell had never seen a color like it and wondered if the creatures beneath the surface were as brilliantly hued. A pod of whales—so many he thought for a moment he was seeing an island comprised of great, glistening rocks—rose to the surface, and trailed the two ships at a benign distance. They were beautiful, nonthreatening, and peaceful, but his enjoyment of their simplistic existence was marred by his suspicion that every beast below them and every bird above them was a Changer with unpredictable intentions.

In the quiet of the second night, he was awakened by a hand on his sleeve and a timid voice in his ear. He shot to his feet, ready to do battle with a wolf who had morphed into a whale, but discovered a weary maid instead. She cowered below him, her hands raised to ward him off, and he scrubbed at his eyes and lowered his blade.

"I'm s-s-sorry for waking you, Captain," she squeaked. "But the queen is so sick. She can't keep anything down, and she's burning up. She's been burning up for two days. I'm afraid, and I don't know what to do. I saw you heal the blacksmith. Maybe you can help her?"

He helped the poor woman to her feet and followed her down the hatch into the belly of the ship. The passages were made for smaller men, but he bent his head and dismissed the guard outside the queen's cabin with directions to go to bed. He would take watch.

The two women traveling with the queen had kept Sasha clean and as comfortable as possible, but the stench of sickness clung to the air, and their fear was evident by the way they huddled and fussed. Sasha's skin was so hot and dry he cursed. When her eyes fluttered open, misery-filled and feverish, he swore again.

"I'm just seasick, Captain. It happens every time," she reassured weakly. "It will pass."

He swooped her up, bringing her blankets with her, and the maids scrambled to open the small door and clear the way, hurrying behind him as he maneuvered sideways through the corridors, lifting the trailing covers like bridesmaids smoothing a veil.

"She needs fresh air. Bring me water, another pillow, and then try to get some rest. I will see to her until morning," he instructed. The women wilted in relief and rushed to obey. He sat with his back against the rail, eschewing the barrels lining one side for the deck, sitting with his legs stretched out in front of him, Sasha in his lap, her head against his chest. The temperature of her skin and the new frailty in her body made his stomach knot anxiously, but the air was clean and the breeze soft, lifting tendrils of her hair and stroking her cheeks sympathetically.

Her vision, her balance, her whole being was turned inside out, as if the gift that gave her second sight made her more sensitive to motion. Over and over he helped her stand and braced her as she leaned out over the glossy water and retched, her belly convulsing uselessly. He urged her to drink, even if she couldn't keep the water down.

She begged him to go, humiliated by the endless roiling of her stomach, but Kjell held her as she quietly suffered, and searched his mind for a story to tell.

"I watched the whales today . . . so many of them . . . there were little ones and enormous ones . . . a family—families. It is like they haven't seen ships in a very long time, and they are curious." He spoke to distract her, to comfort her, and by doing so, comfort himself.

"Is the water just as blue?" she asked. The darkness made everything grey.

"The bluest I've ever seen."

"The color of the sea is the only thing—besides being ill—that I really remember from the journey to Dendar and back again to Kilmorda. I remember the color of the sea . . . and I remember dreaming of you." She grew quiet again, pensive, and Kjell knew she worried over him and her inability to keep him from Dendar.

"Can you drink a little more?" he pressed. He thought the air was helping. Her cramping had eased and she hadn't thrown up for nigh on an hour. She sipped from his carafe and he blotted her chin, noting the easing of her fever and the growing confidence with which she drank.

"I thought you were angry with me," she whispered.

"I am," he admitted.

"But you are kind," she whispered.

"I'm not kind."

"And you are good," she said, repeating the lines they'd exchanged once before.

"I am *not* good." He felt like weeping. He was not good. He was not generous. He was not courageous or compassionate. He simply loved her. And love made him a better man. That was all.

"I have never met anyone like you."

"You were a slave in Quondoon," he whispered, and stopped. He couldn't continue the banter or repeat the things he'd once said to her. The journey then was about discovery. The journey now was about delivery. He would deliver her to Dendar, to a king, another man, and he would go.

"I was a slave in Quondoon and a queen in Dendar," she said, altering the original conversation. "I have changed. And yet . . . you are still Kjell of Jeru, and you have not changed toward me."

"I made a promise."

"To whom?"

"To you. I told you at the base of a cliff near Solemn, that if you came back I would try to love you."

"You told me you lied," she whispered, grief whisking away her words.

"It was not a lie, it was a promise. I intend to keep it, even when you make me angry. Even when you convince my men to act like idiots. Even though you are not . . . mine."

She moaned, and he tried to help her stand, thinking her stomach was rebelling once more, but she buried her face and he realized it was not sickness but sadness, and he relaxed back against the rails.

"Sleep, Sasha."

After a while she succumbed, becoming limp in his arms, lost in relief, and he listened to the waves caress the hull and whispered all the things he hadn't told her and now wouldn't ever tell her.

"It was not your face I fell in love with. It was not your great, sad eyes or your soft mouth, or the gold flecks on your skin or the shape of your body." His heart quaked and his stomach tightened, acknowledging that he relished those things too. "I fell in love with you in pieces. Layer by layer, day by day, inch by inch.

"I love the part of you that shows compassion even though no compassion has been extended. I love the part of you that held my hand and helped me heal. I love the part of you that reassures others when you are afraid. The part that mourned for Maximus of Jeru and the boy who loved him. I love the pieces of the woman who was lost but never misplaced her dignity, who couldn't remember, but never really forgot. Who was a slave but behaved like a queen."

When dawn came, Kjell rigged the lowest sail to cast a shadow over Sasha, worried about her getting too warm but afraid to send her back below deck. She had slept deeply for three hours without vomiting, and Kjell began to relax, reassured that the worst had past.

When she woke she was thirsty and pale, but her fever had broken and her stomach was calm. He helped her to her quarters, hopeful that she could spend the next two days before reaching Dendar recovering her strength. But she returned two hours later, dressed in a new gown with her hair neatly braided around her head, creating a thick crown worthy of her title. She looked lovely, but she didn't look well, and in addition to her fresh clothing, she wore the haunted expression and sunken eyes of things better left unseen.

"Tie everything down, send everyone below, and close the distance with the other ship," she said, raising her voice to include Lortimer and his crew. They stared at her blankly. Just like the night of the rock slide and the sky before the sandstorm, the water was so peaceful it made her demands ridiculous, even comical.

"What do you see, Majesty?" Kjell asked, and her eyes found his, acknowledging his use of her title.

"I see the ships being tossed and men in the water—men drowning," she answered firmly. "I don't know why."

Captain Lortimer wanted to drop his cargo in Dendar and be done with the lot of them. He was being well paid and the journey had gone without incident despite his fear of Padrig, who treated him with haughty ambivalence. Lortimer could afford to "appease the whims of a royal," and he shrugged at Sasha's insistence and allowed Kjell to order his crew about. The sailors followed Kjell's instructions with suspicious industry, muttering among themselves, but they were dismissive of a mere woman telling sailors what to do. The King's Guard and the travelers from Jeru, having seen her abilities firsthand, were less inclined to ignore her warnings. The guard set about redistributing the supplies in the hold and securing the stores, and the rest of the voyagers retired to their rooms to pray for deliverance.

They lowered a longboat over the side and sent a messenger across to their sister vessel with a warning to be on the lookout for hurricanes and anything—everything—else. Sasha stood on the deck, her body rigid, her hands gripping the rail, thankfully steady on her feet, her sickness abated, her fear great. And they waited, on edge all day.

The sun was sinking, brushing a shimmer of pink paint across a darkening sea, when Pascal saw something about two hundred yards off the bow.

"Captain, just ahead." The first mate handed Lortimer his spyglass and pointed at the brilliant horizon.

The emerging dome was so big it created the effect of a large rock rising from the sea before it vanished beneath the surface once more.

"It's probably a whale," Lortimer reassured, but he held the glass to his eye a little too long. Something undulated, and the odd projection rose and fell again.

"The whales don't bother the ships. In these waters, whales are the least of our worries," Lortimer added.

"Oh yes? And what do you worry most about?" Sasha asked, her eyes glued to the place where the unidentified creature had disappeared.

"Storms. And so far, Majesty, we are doing just fine on that account. I've never seen a calmer sea. We could actually do with a little wind."

The ship rocked suddenly, violently, as if it had scraped its hull against an underwater mountain, barely clearing the highest peak. The boat righted itself and the sailors hugged the masts and rails, peering into the sea to ascertain the threat. Pascal shouted down into the hold for a damage check.

"What are we hitting?" Kjell shouted, dragging Sasha back from the rail. She'd tumbled to the deck and immediately risen again, clinging to the side, trying to see what they'd struck.

The sailor in the crow's nest, hanging on with one hand while he searched the water with his spyglass, peering through the innocuous lapping, yelled back at him. "Not a damnable thing! There's nothing there."

The ship across the way was perfectly upright one moment, and the next, sailors were screaming, the sails tipping. The stern came completely out of the water, sending a few men overboard, and two enormous tentacles   knotted and pocked and as thick as tree trunks—curled around the long bowsprit extending from the vessel's prow.

"Architeuthis!" Pascal bellowed just as the lookout from the crow's nest began shouting the same thing.

They watched in horror and helplessness as the giant squid, wrapped around the front of the other ship, began to draw it downward. Shouts and screams accompanied bodies tumbling across the decks and into the sea before the bowsprit snapped with a resounding crack, leaving a jagged spar and temporarily shaking the squid free.

"Bring us closer," Kjell roared to Lortimer.

Jerick, twined in the rigging of the foremast, dangled above the creature with his bow drawn, doing his best to fire arrows at the glistening head of the beast while being tossed from side to side. Gibbous was inching out on the figurehead, and Peter was clinging to the front of the forecastle deck, stabbing at the clinging tentacles with his spear, attempting to land a fatal blow. Architeuthis, angered and stung, slunk to the starboard side and rose again, entwining two tentacles around the forecastle deck rail. Gibbous was catapulted into the water, and Jerick slipped, losing his bow as he grasped at the knotted rigging, trying not to tumble into the sea. The tentacles seemed to grow as the beast came farther out of the water, its smaller, side tentacles embracing the hull as the larger, front tentacles extended, wrapping around the foremast where Jerick was suspended. Peter, the only warrior in a position to do any damage, jabbed valiantly before being swiped aside like he was nothing more than an irritant. The mast bowed and cracked, and Jerick fell to the quarterdeck and didn't rise.

Without thought or doubt, Kjell threw himself over the port side, his spear clutched in both hands. Before he hit the water, he heard Sasha scream his name.

Isak, the fire starter, was suddenly in the water beside him, swimming toward the beleaguered ship and the creature intent on bringing her down. Isak couldn't build a fire in the sea or toss flames from sodden hands, but he began to glow, his arms parting the water in long strokes, drawing the giant eye of the tentacled creature. It watched, almost sentient, and as Isak and Kjell neared, the squid snaked a tentacle around Isak's luminescent form, lifting him out of the water and toward its bulbous head as if to examine him—or eat him. Isak extended his arms, palms flat, not even fighting the beast as he was drawn inward, face to face. Reaching out, he pressed both of his hands against the massive eye, searing the orb, blinding the creature.

Isak was hurled free, tossed away, end over end, and Kjell filled his lungs and dove deep, for once not fighting his tendency to sink like a stone. He swam downward with his lance, kicking with all his strength and sinking beneath the enormous, flailing squid. Then he rose straight up, his spear vertical and extended, and buried his lance into the mouth located on the underbelly of the beast. It writhed, the spear so embedded a mere foot protruded from the narrow slit.

For a moment Kjell was imprisoned by tentacles, encircled by a rapidly retreating Architeuthis. Then Kjell was free, rising as the beast descended into the darkness of the deep, still blind, still impaled. Kjell kicked toward the surface and the light that glowed there, unsure which enemy had been bested—a massive squid or a ruthless Changer.

The passengers and crew were already climbing into the longboat preparing to descend into the water, and those already in the water were swimming toward the undamaged ship.

He saw Isak being pulled from the water, clinging to a line, conscious and relatively unharmed. The second ship was damaged, the railing broken, the bow split, the bowsprit and foremast snapped in two. There would be no saving it or repairing it on the open sea, and the stores were already taking on water.

Kjell heard Sasha calling his name, raised his head and a hand indicating he was unharmed, and clung to a floating section of the prow, resting momentarily and gasping for breath, before he paddled toward the broken vessel.

"The lieutenant's in bad shape, Captain. We can't move him," a sailor called to him as the longboat was released into the sea.

"Help me up!" Kjell cried, and the rope ladder was dropped, slapping the water. He ascended, his legs and arms shaking with the strain of battle and the fear of what he would find.

A jagged piece of the mast pinioned Jerick to the deck of the damaged ship.

"Everybody onto the other ship," Kjell instructed, pushing through the few members of the crew and the King's Guard who remained behind. "I'll see to the lieutenant."

"There's not much time, Captain," the coxswain implored. "And even if you free him, he'll bleed out before you can do anything but toss him overboard."

"Go," Kjell bellowed, and the man stumbled back, nodding. "Get everyone off."

He could hear the sea in his head, and his vision swam, but he lowered himself behind his lieutenant, listening and breathing, attempting to muster the strength he would need. Jerick regarded him, trying to smile, but pain bracketed his eyes and undermined his cocky smirk. Kjell laid his hands on Jerick's chest, avoiding the stake protruding from his body, but withdrew his hands immediately, dismayed. All he heard was a smattering of disconnected cries.

"Your song is like a bloody flock of birds, Jerick! I can't duplicate it," Kjell groaned, desperate.

"I've always loved your drinking songs, Captain. Why don't you sing me one of those?"

"Cease speaking, Jerick," Kjell commanded, but Jerick's impudence made him laugh, in spite of himself. He closed his eyes and curled his hands around the piece of the mast protruding from Jerick's belly. He couldn't make Jerick whole if there was a stick buried in him. Somehow he had to pull it free without killing the man.

Kjell ignored the groaning of the vessel, the cries of those urging him to abandon ship. He thought of the wound he'd carved on Jerick's face, a mark inflicted to put him in his place. Kjell had wasted his gift. He hoped the insignificance of the wound he'd healed wouldn't affect his ability to save Jerick's life now. Jerick—disobedient, defiant, dependable, and dying.

Briefly Kjell wished for Sasha's hand in his, but knew he didn't need Sasha to help him find compassion for Jerick. Kjell loved Jerick. He loved him, and he could heal him. With a bellow for courage, he yanked the shaft free and cupped his hands over the bubbling blood that rose from the hole.

"You bloody son-of-a-bitch, Jerick. You will listen to me, Lieutenant. You will listen and do exactly as I say," Kjell shouted.

Jerick had done as ordered and ceased speaking. His eyes were closed and his breaths shallow, no more energy for jest. Someone was shouting Kjell's name, but he ignored them, pushing his fury and his fervor out his hands and into Jerick's abdomen, commanding Jerick's body to heal itself, to knit the flesh and mend the damage to every vessel and every vein, to every organ and orifice. He ordered Jerick's body to remember and restore, to preserve and endure, and he sang a damned drinking song—Jerick's favorite—bellowing the melody as he begged the boy to remain.

"Heave ho, back we go, the ale is coming to ya. Heave ho, back it goes, ale is flowing through ya," Kjell sang, and imagined it was healing, not ale, flowing into his lieutenant, soaking him in life and light. The salt water stung Kjell's eyes so he closed them tightly, feeling the heat in his hands and the vibrations in his palms.

And he sang, and he sang.

"Never mind, Captain," Jerick breathed after the fifth chorus. Kjell's eyes snapped open. Jerick was staring up at him cheekily. "I don't really like your drinking songs. I'd rather hear about love and fair ladies."

Kjell eased back, noting the pinking of Jerick's skin and the genuine grin on his lips. His shredded tunic—gaping open where the mast had skewered his stomach—revealed new, unblemished skin streaked with gore and the bloody imprints of Kjell's hands.

"I knew you cared, Captain," Jerick muttered and inhaled deeply, as if celebrating the sensation. Kjell rolled to his back on the remains of the forecastle deck and began to laugh, weakly at first, then with lusty appreciation, howling gratefully until Jerick wobbled to his feet and extended his hand. Together, they stumbled to the rails and, with little finesse, tossed themselves over-board, trusting that their friends on the other ship would fish them out again.

SIXTEEN

When the final headcount was made, Peter, Gibbous, two sailors, and the second ship's captain—Egen Barnaby—were missing and believed drowned. Five men buried at sea. Kjell took their deaths hard. Sasha took them harder, assuming responsibility for things she hadn't seen or properly prepared them for, blaming herself for the voyage across the water and the perils of the unknown. Regardless of Kjell's insistence that she could not manipulate fate, and Padrig's reassurance that the voyage would help more people than it hurt, she held herself accountable.

The remaining ship, now carrying twice as many passengers as she had at the beginning of her journey, limped into the Bay of Dendar two days later. Unlike Jeru's coast with its tropical trees and soft, sand beaches, Dendar's shores were rocky with soaring cliffs and narrow inlets just wide enough to sail a ship down the corridor, a buffer from the sea.

Once past the corridor, the inlet widened again to a sprawling shoreline, revealing the signs of abandoned prosperity and the well-constructed docks that had once moored dozens of ships, big and small. Amid the staggering cliffs, the greenery was rich and resplendent, the trees creating a shadowy sentry above the rocks. Beyond the harbor, a spiked wall also attested to human settlement, though it wouldn't have kept a single birdman from breaching the height and finding its prey.

As the ship entered the silent harbor, the travelers stood at the rails and waited, watching for signs of life before they moved to disembark. Empty structures and a desolate dock, it was Kilmorda without the ships marooned in the bay. Sasha was mute at the helm, as if she had expected as much, as if she'd seen the abandoned seaport.

"There are no ships," Isak marveled.

"No. Those who could flee, did," Padrig answered.

"And those who couldn't?" Isak asked.

"They died. Or they hid. Or they spun themselves into something the Volgar wouldn't eat."

"There is no one here, Spinner," Kjell said.

"We will go to Caarn," Padrig soothed, as if that would rectify everything, but Sasha looked at the Spinner, her brow lowered, her eyes shuttered, and Padrig said no more.

Half of the sailors and the guard were lowered into the water on the longboats and rowed ashore, waiting on the docks for the ship to gently moor so lines could be tossed, the anchor dropped, and a gangplank lowered. Four years after Queen Saoirse had left Dendar, she returned, disembarking with the weary voyagers sent to escort her home. No one ran out to greet them, no citizens of Dendar showed themselves or stepped out from hiding places celebrating the arrival of the bedraggled delegation from Jeru or the return of their queen.

With the loss of one ship, everything had changed. Captain Lortimer and his crew would be forced to either wait in the harbor until the expeditioners returned, or they could join them. Captain Lortimer wasn't eager to return to a sea with a creature who could drag a ship beneath the surface, but he still complained about his choices.

"I'm a bloody ship's captain, not an explorer." Lortimer grimaced. But he threw his lot in with Kjell, indicating he'd just as soon stay close to the man who could heal and kill with equal prowess. His sailors were quick to agree.

Kjell promised to intercede with King Tiras and convinced the men charged with going to Willa to remain with the group going to Caarn. There was strength in numbers, and too much was unknown. Faced with the reality of the expedition, staying together seemed the best option, and the travelers—minus the men they'd lost and the supplies and horses that had gone down with the ship—prepared for another journey. Wagons were unloaded and reassembled; enough horses remained to pull the wagons and the remaining gear, but the travelers would be walking to Caarn. All of them. The group was solemn, their outlook diminished, and their anxiety increased.

"It will take two days to travel inland to the valley of Caarn. But we aren't going to have to climb cliffs and drag these wagons through the grass and trees," Padrig encouraged. "There is a fine road, laid with stones. There are roads connecting every corner of Dendar. Caarn is at the apex with roots and branches spanning into the countries of Willa and Porta. The king, and his father before him, and his father before that, commissioned the roads, connecting the people to their king and his kingdom. Everything in Dendar is beautiful," he boasted.

The silence wasn't beautiful. It was eerie. Signs of the Volgar—strewn nests, the rare feather, and picked bones—were evident but old. No fresh remains, bird droppings, or stench littered the corners or clung to the air. A human skull, still attached to its long backbone like a macabre club, lay on the main thoroughfare. Someone had stayed behind in Dendar Bay, unwilling to run, and had met his death in the street he'd refused to abandon.

A little farther down, the remains of several birdmen were piled, and Kjell hoped the skull they'd seen belonged to their slayer.

They split into groups and perused deserted alleys and peeked into abandoned cottages. A tavern with neatly stacked goblets and corked bottles coated in dust lured them with her grimy bounty. The sailors helped themselves—the guard too—yet celebration seemed wrong, and they walked, traipsing through the quiet harbor town sipping spirits and growing more morose as they searched.

Bags of grain, suspended from beams in the stable to keep them from the rats, remained untouched and unused. Volgar birdmen didn't eat grain. Kjell and Jerick lowered the bags and fed the horses, loading what remained in the reassembled wagons to bring to Caarn. Kjell left coin in an empty sack and nailed it to the wall, just in case the owner ever came back and found his grain gone, his livery gutted of supplies.

"They intended to come back. It is easy to see. They've left almost everything behind. They intended to come back," Sasha insisted. "The day I left, this village was teeming with people. There was fear, but there was also excitement, adventure."

"Were these people Spinners too?" Kjell asked.

"Many of them . . . yes," she replied.

"Where did they go? The ones who didn't leave?"

"Everyone was going to Caarn. The king—Aren," Sasha stumbled on the name, and Kjell sensed her discomfort, as if she betrayed the king with every word. "Aren wanted everyone together, just as you are urging us to do now."

"But they haven't come back. Surely . . . they would have come back, eventually," he said.

"Yes. Unless they felt safer remaining. Unless . . . there is still danger."

"But it isn't that far. The wine, the grain, the homes with furnishings and belongings. Someone would have come back."

Kjell stopped. Sasha knew all these things and didn't need the burden of his observations. He didn't ask her what would happen if Caarn was as empty as the Bay of Dendar.

They reunited back at the docks, arms laden with discoveries. Half of the travelers from Jeru had lost everything they owned when the ship had gone down. No one was using the clothing left behind or the blankets on the beds, but Kjell hoped they wouldn't arrive in Caarn and have a shopkeeper recognize his boots.

"Chickens," Isak gloated, holding the headless, plucked birds by their curled feet. "And Jedah has more. They were just running wild. Volgar will eat chickens. If there were Volgar here, there wouldn't be chickens. It's a good sign, right Captain?"

Kjell nodded slowly.

"Yes. A good sign, and an even better meal. The inn has a galley as big as a castle kitchen. Start a fire, Isak, and get the cook to help you. We'll eat there tonight, and we'll eat well. We'll leave for Caarn in the morning."

They found oil and tightly sealed barrels of flour in the inn's stores and carried pails of heated water to the iron tubs of the well-appointed chambers. They ate like kings, filling their bellies with another man's bread, washing themselves with another man's soap, but that night, no one remained on shore except a few guards in the stables with the horses. Although beds and rooms were plentiful, the travelers chose to sleep on the ship, stretched out on the deck in nervous reverence of a bay that felt more like a burial ground.

Sasha slept in the quarters she'd occupied for much of the journey, and Kjell guarded her door, stretched out in the narrow corridor on a pallet that barely fit in the space. Jerick would relieve him halfway through the night so he could get some sleep, but he wouldn't grow complacent simply because they'd made it to Dendar. He dreamed of the squid, his lance protruding from its soft underside, sinking into the depths and, at the last moment, changing into Ariel of Firi with dead eyes and lifeless limbs. But he couldn't be sure, and he couldn't make himself believe the threat was truly gone.

An hour after the ship grew quiet and the lapping of the water started to make him drowsy, Sasha's door opened and she stepped out, gently closing it behind her. He sat up as she sat down, facing him, drawing her knees to her chest, the only option in the constricted passage. Her nightgown was an ivory silk and modest in every way, but her toes peeked out beneath the hem, and his stomach clenched with longing. He stroked the soft skin of one dainty foot before he forced himself to withdraw his hand.

"When we reach Caarn, you cannot sleep outside my door," she said gently. Her hair smelled of roses, but violet darkened the hollows beneath her eyes, and he knew he was not the only one who worried.

"Everyone on this ship knows I'm in love with you," he answered. "They all heard the bans read in Jeru City, they all know what was between us and what was snatched away. Do you not see their pitying looks and their curious gazes? They all know. I would stay away to protect your honor. But I can't do that. I can't do that and protect *you*."

"I know. But it is one thing to unknowingly betray, it is another to willfully betray," Sasha said.

"Yes. It is," he agreed. "When we reach Caarn, you must tell King Aren everything. He can't be the only one who doesn't know."

"I will tell him," she whispered brokenly. "I betray him by loving you, and I betray you by returning to him."

"You owe me nothing. There is no betrayal if there is no treachery. I know why I am here, and it is not to challenge the king," he said.

"My conscience demands that I acknowledge you. My duty demands that I deny you," Sasha said. "That *feels* like betrayal. Of myself. Of you. Of King Aren. And I don't know how to rectify it."

He was quiet, letting her find her composure, seeking his own understanding. He answered with the first thing that came to his head.

"Some things cannot be healed. They must simply be endured," he whispered, and grimaced. It was the truth, but it sounded like something Tiras would say, something that the old Kjell would have raged against, simply because endurance signified an acceptance of pain. He wanted to defeat suffering. Not live with it.

Sasha didn't answer, as if she too had trouble accepting it, but she took his hand the way she used to do, helping him endure. She rested her head against the wall and closed her eyes, but she didn't let go. They stayed that way for a long time, leaning against opposing walls but facing each other, knees touching, hands clasped. He thought she was asleep, but she spoke again.

"He will want you to leave, Captain. Aren is a good man. A kind man. But he is still a man, and he will not want you in Caarn." She spoke so softly, he knew the words were difficult for her to say.

"Then I will go," he reassured. And he would. But he would slay Ariel of Firi first.

The road to Caarn was indeed paved with neatly placed rocks—mile after mile of them—and Kjell drove himself mad seeing trouble beneath each one.

On the second day they skirted a river, the water sweet and cold with a waterfall high enough to stand beneath, providing natural showers for the travelers to wash. The ladies, all three of them, went first, and the men withdrew, giving them the privacy necessary. He wanted to forbid Sasha, to insist she stay by his side, but instead walked, fully-clothed except for his boots, beneath the spray and averted his eyes from the three women, who laughed and talked, their teeth chattering, and their bathing brief.

When he couldn't see Sasha, he made sure he could hear her, and asked that she humor him by keeping a running commentary when his back was turned or she was out of his sight. He knew some of the travelers and even many of his own men thought him overzealous. He didn't care. They didn't know what he knew. Everything was a threat. A lizard, delicate and apple green, darted through the grass, and Kjell's heart seized. Without thought he threw his blade, skewering the little beast. He watched it die, waiting for the change that would occur at death if it wasn't in its true form. But it remained a lizard, its limbs growing brittle, its color fading as life fled. Kjell chopped it into pieces, ignoring the voice in his head that told him he was being obsessive. He'd watched Ariel of Firi play dead before, lying still and compliant, an eagle snared by a Jeruvian poacher. When the danger had passed, she had simply flown away.

He was going to have to kill her. He knew that. He couldn't live with the constant threat to those he loved and to the people around him. At some point, he was going to have to concoct a plan to rid the world of Ariel of Firi. But until they reached Caarn, until he knew what they faced and what steps could be taken, he could only be vigilant and pray that her purposes, whatever they were, were not focused on the queen . . . at least not yet.

When they began to descend into the valley on the afternoon of the second day, the travelers grew lively and Kjell courted a sense of doom. Sasha walked beside him, her eyes gobbling up the countryside, lingering on the trees, touching the sky, reminiscing and reconnecting as they approached the end of the road and the dawn of never again. But the road ended in a mass of brambles and a wall of trees so high and thick, the travelers stopped and gaped.

The forest had grown over the road.

Jerick withdrew his sword, and some of Kjell's men followed suit, preparing to cut an opening in the wooded obstruction.

"It will take more than swords to tunnel through that, Jerick," Kjell said.

"Put your swords away. We will ask them to move," the Spinner sniffed, placing his twitching fingers upon the tree in the center of the road. He smoothed the trunk like it was the hair of a beloved child and laid his grey head against it, beseeching.

"I am Padrig of Caarn. My nephew is King Aren. My blood is of Caarn, my heart and loyalty are to Caarn. Pray you, let us pass," he boomed.

The tree seemed to hear, even to awaken, but though it stretched its branches and shifted its weight, it remained directly in their path, blocking the road into the valley of Caarn. Padrig tried again, pleading with the trunk of the tree to do as he bade, but the tree continued to guard the way.

The group waited, breaths drawn, watching the shivering trees who in turn seemed to be watching them.

"Can anyone ask it to move?" Jerick asked. "Or just Padrig?"

"Anyone can *ask*. But most people don't. Most people just draw their swords and start hacking away," Padrig snapped, caressing the bark as if trying to woo compliance. He seemed stunned that he could not convince the wooded wall to open.

"Pardon me, leafy mistress. I would like to pass." Jerick bowed gallantly, drawing laughter from the travelers.

"It takes a bit more than a polite request, Padrig," Sasha corrected the Spinner. "Yes, Jerick, anyone can ask. But the trees will not answer or obey. It takes the blood of Caarn and pure intentions to command a tree to move. We all have the best of intentions . . . but Padrig is the only one here who has the blood of Caarn flowing in his veins."

Padrig moved to the next tree and to the next, coaxing and cajoling, and though the trees inched and quaked, listening to him plead, the road remained impassable.

"No one doubts your blood, Spinner. But maybe the problem lies with your intentions," Kjell observed and placed his hands against the tree, mocking Padrig's posture but not his tone. He would not beg, but it couldn't hurt to ask. They had not come all this way to be denied now.

"I am Kjell of Jeru. Bloody move so we can pass," he grumbled. The branches of the tree Kjell touched began to lift skyward, separating from the boughs of the tree next to it. Straightening and stretching, a narrow divide opened between the two center trunks.

Jerick hooted in amazement. "Even the trees are afraid of you, Captain!"

"Who *are* you, Healer?" Padrig gasped. "You . . . y-you . . . must carry the blood of Caarn."

"I am Kjell of Jeru, Spinner. And you are trying my patience." The others gaped at him, awestruck and open-mouthed. "I have never set foot in Dendar before, much less Caarn."

"Impossible. Do it again!" Padrig insisted.

Kjell, too dazed and curious to be contrary, repeated his request on another tree, though this time he didn't curse. "I am Kjell of Jeru. We need to see to the welfare of the people in this valley. Please let us pass."

The ground began to quake, and the cobbled road began to split and crack. The tree Kjell addressed started to withdraw its roots—great tentacles coated in dirt—and climb from the earth, dragging itself free from the broken road and widening the gap in the forest wall, clearing the way before them.

"Your father was Zoltev, Captain, but who was your mother?" Sasha asked, her shock as evident as Padrig's.

"My mother was a servant woman in my father's castle. She died at my birth."

"And where was she from?" Padrig asked, reasserting himself as interrogator.

"Nowhere. No one. I know nothing of her but her name."

"And what was her name?" Padrig pressed.

Kjell regarded the Spinner in exasperation. The man knew too much and thought he was entitled to know more.

"Her name is not your concern," Kjell answered.

"And you are certain she was not of Caarn?" Padrig pressed.

"I know only what I was told." Kjell barked, impatient and uncomfortable. The trees were gone, but the roots left huge holes in the road, and Kjell turned to the men listening attentively to the exchange.

"The way is open, but the wagons still cannot pass. Let's fill the holes and replace the rocks," Kjell commanded, changing the subject from his mother and her origins.

A man named Jedah stepped forward and touched his shoulder. He'd signed on for the journey to Dendar claiming he was Gifted, but Kjell had yet to see what he could do beyond catching chickens with Isak.

"Let me be of use, Captain," he offered. With fluttering fingers and the palms of his hands, he scooped the air as if scooping the ground, and the displaced dirt obeyed his summons, rushing to return to mother earth, the sound like pounding rain against the sand. "I can't command the rocks," he apologized. "But the holes are filled."

"Well done, Earth Mover. That is not a gift I've seen before," Kjell marveled.

"It is not a gift that has proven especially valuable." Jedah shrugged.

"In a land of growers, such a gift will be greatly appreciated," Sasha said. "It is a form of Telling. Don't command the rocks, tell the dirt to move them," she suggested.

Jedah looked doubtful, but scooped his hands through the air again, his brow furrowed, his gaze narrowed on one of the displaced cobbles. It rattled and flipped, and he smiled in triumph.

"Keep practicing, Jedah," Kjell said, but began to move the stones into place. There would be time for practice later. They worked quickly, replacing the rocks and leveling the way so the wagons could pass.

Once they'd crossed through the opening in the wall, the earth groaned, the roots crawled, the branches snapped, and the hedge of trees resumed their positions, blocking the road and displacing the dirt and rocks all over again.

Kjell's men eyed each other nervously, and the travelers began to murmur among themselves. Now they couldn't leave if they wanted to. Kjell couldn't decide if he was comforted by the barrier or unnerved by it. If the Changer followed, she need only become a bird to breech the trees. But if the trees had created a wall, there was something worth protecting in Caarn.

They kept moving forward, unable to do anything else, but more than a few glances were tossed back toward the barrier and up into the canopy that lined the road. The wind whispered through the leaves, but there was no bird-song or animal chatter. In Jeru City, the chickens cackled in the courtyard and the bull-frogs sang a chorus in the castle moat each night. Kjell had curs-ed the cacophony on more than one occasion, but he found he missed the reassurance that came with sound. Absolute silence could not be equated with peace. More often than not, it portend-ed terrible things. He found himself checking the skies, expect-ing a Volgar swarm. But none came, and the silence persisted.

Then, just around the next bend, the castle came into view, nestled in a sea of green so intense the white rock of the walls glowed in comparison. It didn't sit on a hill like the palace in Je-ru, but in the center of the valley, the hub of a wheel, just as Padrig had described. The village huddled around it, hundreds of pale toadstools on the forest floor, and the ribbon of the road they traveled angled down toward it, pointing to the end of their journey.

Kjell remembered the way the trumpets had sounded the day he returned to Jeru City, Sasha seated in front of him on Lucian, his heart ebullient. No trumpets sounded or flags waved welcom-ing them to Caarn. Maybe they hadn't been seen. Maybe they simply needed to draw closer. Or maybe no one was expecting the triumphant return of a long-absent queen. As they descended toward the village, no people rushed out into the street to greet—or gawk at—the wary parade of foreigners who peered through the trees at the quiet cottages, the empty gardens, and the un-tended orchards. It was the Bay of Dendar all over again, but as they neared the castle, the trees became so thick they could no longer see anything but the palace gate and a looming guard tower.

The drawbridge was down, the portcullis raised, and unlike the trees at the border that had made them ask for entry, no watchman at the gate demanded they identify themselves. The travelers walked into the palace courtyard, unabated and undeterred, and stood, searching for life and further instruction.

SEVENTEEN

"Where is everyone, Padrig?" Sasha asked, her eyes trained on the piles of leafy debris and the detritus of neglect in the castle courtyard. She began to walk, calling out a greeting that would never be answered.

"Where *is* everyone?" she repeated, her voice more strident, her horror evident.

"I'm not entirely . . . sure," Padrig answered, his face stricken, his brow drawn. But his gaze shifted the way it had when he'd promised Sasha she would lose nothing when he restored her memories. He was telling half-truths again.

Sasha began striding toward the wide castle doors, and Kjell rushed to pursue her, throwing instructions over his shoulder to his guard.

"Search the keep, but do so in groups, just like we did in the bay. And Jerick and Isak, stay with the Spinner."

The doors were not barred or barricaded. Kjell and Sasha raised the looped iron knockers and pulled them wide, walking inside as if they belonged, as if the silence longed to be filled. Sasha *did* belong, Kjell reminded himself. He could picture her there, walking down the corridors, sewing in the light of the huge glass windows, her tongue caught between her teeth, looking out at the trees and the hills, seeing a future she couldn't have dreamed.

She belonged at Caarn.

She had reigned in the Great Room hung with lacy cobwebs and walked the endless marble floors that now coated the hem of her gown with a pale powder, the color of the white rock that formed the castle walls. The table in the king's dining hall was set for a feast that had never happened, and Sasha approached it, fingering the coated silver and the pewter goblets. Sasha's chair would have been at the far end, the one inset with a tree, supported by dainty legs and carved with more feminine lines.

They left one room and entered another, a gallery of sorts, draped with flags and woven tapestries. One window above an ornate wall hanging had been shattered at some point, and glass crunched beneath their feet. The beam showed signs of dampness beneath the broken pane, but the tapestries had maintained their color, if somewhat dulled by dust.

They walked through the enormous kitchens, past the cold hearths and dangling fire irons and pots and pans. Only dirt marred the surfaces. Everything was in order, as if great preparation had been made for an extended absence. From the kitchens, Sasha led the way into a garden filled with plants that needed tending and rose bushes that were thorny and cross, their bite exceeding their unkempt beauty. Lining the garden were rows of trees laden with fruit of every kind, the rotted carcasses of the fallen apples, peaches, and pears giving the space an over-ripe stench that reminded Kjell of perfumed lords at a stifling soiree.

"There was no one here to eat the fruit or tend my trees," Sasha mourned.

Kjell plucked an apple from a branch above his head and found it covered with holes. He pitched it over the pale rock wall and reached for another that was without blemish. He bit into it and savored the burst of flavor against his tongue, but when he went to take another bite, he saw the remains of half a worm. His stomach turned, and he tossed the second apple the way of the first.

"Which fruit is forbidden?" he asked.

Sasha shook her head, not understanding. "None of them."

"Did King Aren plant this garden for his young queen?" he asked. "Or was that simply a story? I seem to remember a forbidden tree and a devious snake in that tale."

"You are angry," she said, perplexed.

"I am afraid," he admitted. "Your stories have all proven to be real."

She turned in a circle as if she couldn't quite match her memories with the neglect and didn't deny his claim.

"It is different than I remember. The landscape is overgrown, the castle abandoned. There aren't even any bones," she whispered.

There were animal bones here and there. But there were no Volgar or human bones. Kjell had noticed as well.

They joined the others in the courtyard, noting the listless travelers and the tired guard. The sailors were already talking about returning to the ship. Captain Lortimer wanted to turn back the following day.

"There is nothing here, Captain," he complained. "Our ship waits in the harbor. It will be close quarters, but there are sufficient supplies—especially considering what we found in Dendar Bay. Everyone wants to go home."

Padrig returned to the courtyard, Jerick and Isak trailing him, and caught the tail end of Lortimer's speech.

"We cannot leave. Not yet," Padrig cried. "I know where they are. I know what has happened. They are there." He pointed to the groves that hugged the four castle walls and peered down at them, the oddest collection of trees to ever grow side by side, few of them the same variety, none of them uniform in height or spacing.

Lortimer laughed and a few sailors joined him. But Sasha didn't laugh.

"Like Grandfather Tree?" she asked, horror tinging her voice. The story of Grandfather Tree was one she hadn't shared.

"No." Padrig shook his head, adamant. "No. Grandfather went to the forest to pass from this life to the next. The Spinners of Caarn didn't go to die. They went to hide."

"And they're still hiding?" Kjell pressed.

"Why?" Sasha cried.

"I don't know, Majesty," Padrig answered, and this time his voice rang true.

"We saw how well you communicate with the trees, Star Maker," Lortimer mocked, slumped against the stairs leading up to the castle doors.

"I know they are there!" Padrig insisted. "We have come all this way. Surely you can give me a few days to see what can be done."

Jerick and Isak shifted nervously, and Kjell raised his brow. Jerick moved beside him and spoke in hushed tones, his eyes on the Spinner. "The trees around the castle aren't like the ones blocking the road, Captain. The Spinner talked to them. He pled with them. But the leaves didn't even shiver."

Sasha turned toward Kjell, her eyes pleading. He knew what she was going to say before the words left her mouth.

"The trees at the border moved for you, Captain. Perhaps . . . these trees will listen to you as well."

"Tomorrow, Saoirse," Padrig interceded. "One more day won't matter. We will eat, and we will rest. Then we will see about the trees."

Sasha didn't argue, and Kjell let Padrig shuffle the weary travelers inside, promising them all would be well. When night fell, Kjell would slip out among the trees and see for himself if they could simply be asked to spin or if Padrig was in denial.

The Volgar nested like most birds, pulling bits of hair, rope, cloth, straw and mud into mounds to fall into. In the castle, the mattresses were destroyed—gutted and scored—but that was all. The Volgar were beasts, and beasts didn't sit in chairs or toast their success. They hunted. They grazed. They slept. And when there was no blood to drink or flesh to eat, they quickly moved on.

There had been nothing to eat in the castle. Nothing to eat in all of Caarn, besides other animals. The Volgar had cleared Caarn of her livestock and wildlife and quickly moved on to richer pickings.

A consensus was drawn that they would camp together in the Great Hall for the time being, and they cleared the soaring gallery of dirt and debris, beating the rugs and restoring order to the space. There were linens in the closets and brooms and rags stored neatly in the huge palace washroom. Kjell eyed the iron basins with longing. He wanted to be clean. The kitchen and washroom both boasted odd spigots that rose like great hooks with long handles and drew the water from deep in the ground. Sasha demonstrated the spigot in the kitchen to the awestruck gathering, pumping the odd handle determinedly until water gurgled forth, filling one bucket after another, to be heated later in the huge cauldrons on the row of hearths.

"The last three cauldrons are always kept full, the water hot, so that a bath can be easily drawn. There are hearths and cauldrons in the castle laundry as well, and the servants usually bathe there."

The sun was setting and fires were started, the travelers eager for warm baths and hot food. Fruit was plucked from the engorged trees and sliced and folded into dough prepared by the cook with flour and oil from Dendar Bay. There was no fresh meat, but there would be pies. The torches—still waiting in sconces on every wall of the castle—were lit, enlivening the spirits of the group. It wasn't until hours later, after appetites were sated and tubs were filled, emptied, and filled again, washing the miles from the bodies of almost four dozen travelers, that Sasha emerged from the room where the women had bathed, her hair still damp, her dress rumpled but clean. After his own bath, Kjell had waited outside her door, unwilling to let down his guard, even under the lulling glow of heat and warmth, of tired voices and rock walls. The other women had come and gone, hardly noticing him they were so accustomed to his watchful presence.

"Come with me," Sasha murmured, extending her hand to him. "There is something I must show you." The night was deepening and everyone but the assigned watch had retired to their pallets in the Great Hall to find sleep and a bit of solitude behind closed lids. Kjell took a torch from the foyer and followed Sasha up the shadowy staircase, keeping her hand in his and his eyes peeled to the darkness of the upper floor. No one had bothered to light the upstairs.

They walked down the corridors, lighting sconces as they did, chasing the darkness and the gloom as they passed elaborate tapestries and enormous portraits. A painting, rimmed in gold and adorned in cobwebs caught his eye. Sasha, her eyes wide and dark and her brilliant hair dulled by dust, had been captured against a backdrop of green. Kjell slowed, wanting to stare, but Sasha urged him forward, unimpressed by the beauty of her portrait.

She didn't look twice at the row of blond kings, but continued on until she stood beneath a picture of a royal family wearing crowns of gold branches and gilded leaves, gazing out of the painting in contented unity.

"Is that . . . Padrig?" Kjell asked, pointing to the bearded, blond man beside the king. The painting was dated four decades earlier, but Padrig hadn't changed very much. He looked old even then.

"Yes. He is Aren's uncle. Padrig was King Gideon's younger brother. That is Briona, Gideon's queen and Aren's mother." Sasha indicated the couple seated in the center of the portrait.

King Gideon and Queen Briona were stately, attractive people, painted with steady gazes and elevated chins.

"That is Aren," Sasha pointed at the tall youth in the painting. He looked about fifteen or sixteen summers, his hair golden, his eyes blue, his features sharp, and he stood next to a girl maybe two or three summers older. The girl was also fair with pale blue eyes and a solemn expression. There was something defiant and almost familiar about the set of her jaw and her unsmiling mouth. Sasha pointed at her. "That is Aren's older sister."

"Why are you showing me this painting, Sasha?" Kjell asked, trying to be patient and failing, as usual.

"Because . . . her name was Koorah," Sasha said softly.

Kjell froze, arrested by the painted face of the girl with the same name as his mother. Sasha reached for his hand again, anchoring him, but she continued, her voice adopting the sing-song quality she used whenever she told stories.

"No one talked about Koorah when I came to Caarn. She had been gone a long time." Sasha took a deep breath, steadying herself, and he glanced down at her, noting the flush on her cheeks and the trembling of her lips. She was as stricken as he. "She would have been queen, Kjell. In Caarn, the throne passes to the oldest child, not the oldest son. She never married, but Aren says she was well-loved. There were suitors, of course, but no one turned her head or won her heart. When she was twenty-eight summers, she disappeared. Aren believed she'd fallen in love with someone unfit to be king. She boarded a ship in the

Bay of Dendar, and no one ever saw her again. King Gideon and Queen Briona convinced themselves she was lost at sea. It was easier to believe her dead than to worry about her wellbeing. And everyone knew there were terrible creatures in the Jeruvian Sea," Sasha added on a whisper.

"Koorah was my mother's name," Kjell murmured, his throat too constricted for greater sound.

"I know," she answered, her voice as hushed as his. "You told me once. But I didn't even remember my own name then. Today, when you told the trees to move and they obeyed, Padrig asked you where your mother was from."

"And you remembered her name," he supposed.

"Yes." She nodded. For a moment they were quiet, contemplative. Kjell's mind pulsed with possibilities he discarded almost as quickly as they came. But Sasha wasn't finished.

"I remembered your mother's name, and I remembered the story of Koorah, the Healer, who would have been queen," she said.

"The Healer?"

"Yes, Captain, a Healer." Sasha lifted her eyes to his, and he could only gaze back, suddenly seeing another slave woman in a foreign land. He'd never known what his mother looked like. He still didn't, but he gave her blue eyes and golden hair like the portrait on the wall. He gave her a stubborn jaw and a mouth that looked like his.

"Koorah is not a common name," Sasha murmured.

"No," he agreed.

"The trees obeyed you," Sasha reminded.

"Yes." There was no denying it.

"She was a Healer. You are a Healer."

He nodded again.

"If you are Lady Koorah of Caarn's son, then . . . *you* are the King of Caarn."

He began shaking his head, adamant and disbelieving. This is where they would not agree. "It could never be proven. And I don't have any desire to be king."

"Kell means *prince* in Dendar," Sasha whispered.

"I was named after the Kjell Owl! The midwife named me," Kjell argued.

"Is it possible . . . Koorah . . . named you?" Sasha asked.

"I know only what I was told," he whispered, and turned away from the painting. "It makes no sense. My father—Zoltev —would have married her if she was heir to a throne. It would have been an advantageous match."

"Maybe she never told him . . . maybe, like you, she had no desire to be queen, and maybe Zoltev was not the man she followed to Jeru."

"Or maybe she simply loved . . . badly, and realized too late," he acquiesced, and his eyes found Sasha's. "We will never know."

"No. Not for certain. But I had to show you. It would have been wrong to keep it from you."

"Keep what from me? Her name was Koorah. It means nothing to me! *She* means nothing to me. There is no one here, Sasha. We are surrounded by trees and little else." He ground his palms into his eyes. He was tired, overwrought, and the words that he uttered next were not words he was proud of. "Come back to Jeru. Come back with me, Sasha. Please."

She bowed her head, and he felt her agony even as he cursed his own weakness. He clenched his fists and looked for something to break.

"I cannot turn my back on these people," she said.

"What people? They are all gone!" he roared. "The king, the villagers. They are all bloody trees in a damned forest. It's been four years, Sasha. You tell me I might be the King of Caarn? King of an empty castle and endless trees? I am a king of trees?"

He was so frustrated he couldn't spit the words out fast enough, and snatched the portrait of the family from the wall and heaved it down the hall, watching it cartwheel before it skidded to a halt at the top of the stairs, completely intact. Sasha did not protest or try to calm him, but watched him the way she always did, like she couldn't listen hard enough, like she couldn't possibly love him more than she already did, and that made him even angrier, because her feelings were as futile as his own.

"There is only one thing in this whole, godforsaken world that would make me want to be bloody King of Caarn. One. Thing." He raised a finger and jabbed it toward her. "You! I would be the court jester and wear striped hose and paint on my face if it meant I could be near you. But if I am King of Caarn, then you wouldn't be queen. You would simply be the wife of my *uncle*. Now that is funny! Maybe I *should* play the fool. This whole, bungled situation is just rich with hilarity."

He slammed his palms against the empty space where the portrait had hung and pulled at the cloak he wore around his shoulders, a cloak that suddenly felt like an anvil around his neck. Sasha's touch was light against his back, and he turned on her with a groan and wrapped his arms around her, lifting her off her feet. He buried his face in her hair, pressing his lips to the soft skin of her throat before finding her mouth and taking what he could before it was too late. He kissed her, imprinting the shape of her lips on his mouth, tasted her, committing her flavor to his tongue, and swallowed her sighs, taking the heat of her response into the coldest corners of his heart.

But the kiss did not douse his fury or quiet the flame of frustration in his gut. It simply accentuated the hopelessness of his desire. He pulled away slightly, and for a moment breathed her in, his eyes closed, his resolve hardening. Sasha would not turn her back on Caarn, and she would not deny him. But his need was hurting her. His presence was hurting her. Uncertainty was hurting them both. And it had to end.

Releasing her, he grabbed the torch from the sconce on the wall and strode from the corridor, not waiting to see if she followed, trusting she would. He resisted the urge to burn the picture resting precariously against the bannister, but let it be, if only for the young woman named Koorah who observed him with painted eyes.

Down the broad staircase, across the echoing foyer and through the iron doors he flew, determined to be done with it all, to end the torment of hope.

"Healer!" Padrig shouted, coming out of the darkness like a phantom. "Where are you going?"

"I'm going to set fire to the forest, Spinner," he mocked, not slowing. He'd alerted the watch, and it wouldn't be long until the whole castle was stirring. He quickened his pace, desperate to begin without onlookers. Sasha was running behind him, her breaths harsh. He was scaring her. The thought brought him up short.

"Which one, Padrig. Which one is the king?" he asked, moderating his tone.

"Why?" Padrig gasped, his eyes glued to the flame.

"You want me to heal them. That is why I'm here. That is why you helped me. You knew this is what we would find."

"I . . . suspected," Padrig confessed.

"How?" Sasha asked. "How did you know, Padrig?

"Your memories, Saoirse. When I showed Lady Firi your memories, I didn't tell you everything we saw." Padrig turned toward Kjell, beseeching even as he raised a hand to ward Kjell off. "We saw you touching the trees, Healer. And we saw the trees becoming . . . people. Ariel of Firi didn't understand. But I did." He placed a trembling hand over his heart. "I did."

"When you gave me back my memories, that one was gone," Sasha whispered, anger and realization making her eyes glow in the dancing torchlight.

"Yes," Padrig replied, not denying it.

"But you didn't tell me," Sasha said.

"You love him, Majesty. He loves you. If there was nothing to come back to in Caarn . . . I didn't believe you would . . . come back," Padrig offered timidly.

Instead of Padrig's confession making him angry, it gave Kjell an odd reassurance. Padrig was a manipulator. Even the trees judged him harshly, but Kjell couldn't see how knowing Caarn slept would have changed anything.

"Sasha. If Padrig would have told you, you would still have come. And I would have followed." Sasha's eyes clung to his, defeated and despairing, clearly torn between her duty and her desire to shield him. That also had not changed.

"I knew something had gone wrong. They were trees too long, Healer. They couldn't—they can't—spin back," Padrig rushed to expound, obviously relieved by Kjell's pardon. Kjell pushed the torch into the Spinner's hands and approached the nearest tree.

"How do we know whether the tree is a Spinner or simply a tree of Caarn?" Kjell asked.

Padrig inclined his head toward the trunk. "Touch it."

Kjell pressed his hands to the bark and immediately withdrew them. This tree was different from the trees blocking the road into the valley. The sensation was like standing on the deck of the ship again, swaying on stormy seas, his stomach tossing to and fro.

"You feel it!" Padrig crowed, jubilant. "It is not simply a tree. It is a Spinner."

"Yes." Kjell nodded, but he immediately stepped away. He didn't want to touch the tree. "But I am not."

"You are a Healer. They need healing. And you have proven you can talk to the trees." Padrig's eyes were bright with knowing, and Kjell wondered if his loss of temper in the gallery had been overheard by the inquisitive Star Maker.

Kjell approached the tree again, addressing it with flattened palms and a clear command. The sensation traveled up his arms, filling Kjell with nausea, but unlike the trees on the road to Caarn, the trunk didn't quake or shift, the roots didn't unfurl, and the leaves were silent. It didn't seem to hear him at all. He tried again, adjusting his message, but all he got for his efforts was a whirling head and a churning belly.

"Talking to them is not enough," he said, dropping his hands and stepping away. He breathed deeply, attempting to calm his stomach and quiet his nerves.

"You have to try to *heal* them, Captain," Padrig pled. "These are not simply trees of Caarn. They are *people*. Some of them were children so young they've been trees longer than they were babes. They were hiding, and they don't know how to stop."

Kjell placed his hands on a different tree, one of the smallest in the grove, its bark pale and thin and remarkably smooth. The swaying sensation welled immediately, and Kjell planted his feet to keep from falling. If the smallest tree in the wood made him feel this way, he had no hope of success.

"I will help you," Sasha said, and took one of his hands, pulling it from the trunk, just like she'd done in the unforgiving village of Solemn. She laid her other palm against the tree next to his, pressing her fingers into the smooth bark. Her eyes clung to his face, brimming with tears that began to streak her cheeks and drip from her chin.

"I need you to help me find compassion, Sasha," he murmured. "You loved these people once."

"I love them still. But I love you more," she wept. "May Caarn forgive me, I love you more."

For a moment they were silent, hands clasped, hearts heavy, trying to find the will to do what must be done.

"I believe this tree was a child," Padrig offered, stepping beside them with the torch. "If you look closely, you can see her face."

They peered, grateful for the distraction, for the opportunity to forget themselves and forge ahead.

"It is a child, a little girl. There are flowers in her hair. See?" Sasha whispered, tracing the eyes and the nose, barely visible in the orange glow of the torch and the shadows on the bark.

"I see," Kjell rasped. "But if I wake her, will she be afraid? Let us heal the parents first and let them help us wake the children."

They moved to the next tree, an umbrella tree that sheltered the smaller tree beneath its boughs.

"I know who this is," Sasha breathed, her eyes on the hollows that created a hint of a profile. "She is Yetta, the castle chef —so dour and dramatic. She was always convinced her next meal would disappoint, and worked tirelessly to make sure that it didn't. She knew how much I loved her tarts and would find me, wherever I was in the castle, and make me swear each batch was better than the last."

"Yetta had a granddaughter," Padrig said. "Let us see if we can't wake her, and then we'll wake the child."

It was not like healing a human or even a horse. The tossing in Kjell's stomach continued to intensify, as if he drew the fear that made the Spinners of Caarn hide into himself. The sound he heard was not a song but a wail, and he didn't try to duplicate it. He absorbed it, sinking beneath the layers of bark until the wailing became a whimper and a heartbeat emerged. He willed his heart to match the rhythm until he became the tree, and the tree became a tall woman, reed thin and clothed in a dress covered with a long apron. Her arms hung at her sides, and her eyes were closed like she slept upright.

Slowly her eyes opened, and she regarded Kjell in confusion before her gaze settled on the queen.

"M-majesty?" she stuttered, her voice raspy with disuse. "Queen Saoirse? Are the Volgar gone?"

Kjell dropped his hands, turned, and lost the contents of his stomach before bracing himself against the smaller tree and immediately starting again, Sasha at his side.

Not every tree was a Spinner, not every Spinner was a tree. Some were crouching bushes and shrubs; a climbing vine of roses was a woman by the same name. Some were easier to wake than others, and some refused to be roused. When he spent too long on one tree, Sasha forced him to move on. When he became too weak, she made him rest. But he slept in the groves, not even stumbling to the castle for reprieve, saving his strength for waking the forest. When he awoke, Sasha was always there, waiting. He made sure she ate when he ate, rested when he rested, and he commanded Jerick to watch her when he couldn't.

As Kjell continued to heal and awaken, the wailing abated and the heartbeats beneath the trunks and hidden in bristled branches became more like the melodies of human healing and less like terrified screams. Each healing was accomplished with less sickness and more song, as if the Spinners of Caarn had heard their loved ones reemerge and had begun to reemerge themselves. But the numbers were great and the press of the healed and the waiting became more trying than the healing itself.

"Healer—this is my son," a hovering mother said, patting a white sapling.

"Healer, will you help my child?" a father begged, standing beside a flowering lilac tree.

"Healer, will you wake my husband next?" the woman named Rose implored.

His guard formed a ring around him, asking the people to stand back, to be patient, but they obeyed only when Sasha commanded them to wait beside their loved ones, in whatever form they may be. Padrig began compiling a list of citizens, and slowly, families were reunited and sent home. One by one, the copses thinned and the village of Caarn grew around them.

There were so many. One day become another. And another. And another, until only one tree remained.

"He would have wanted to be last. He would have wanted to wait until everyone else was seen to," Padrig whispered. His eyes were bright and his compassion evident, and Kjell knew the time had come. He hadn't rested in many hours, but he would finish before he rested again.

"This is King Aren. He is good. And kind. He loves his people." Sasha's voice caught and her fingers clenched, and Kjell could only hold her hand, press his palm to the tree, and let her sorrow and his resistance roll over him.

"When I was just a girl, afraid of the things I saw, hidden away in a foreign land, he was my friend. I know what it costs you to call to him . . . but he is worthy of healing."

Kjell's heart began to tremble and quake, making a song of its own. Groaning and deep, a healing melody rose from his chest and rippled down his arms. The sound escaped through his lips, bellowing and great, like the rumble of the skies or the falling of the rocks, and just as before, he felt the moment when the tree awoke, when the old fell away and the flesh became new. Unlike the Changers when they shifted, the Spinners were fully clothed, their apparel becoming bark and leaves, branches and blossoms.

The trunk didn't dissolve or slip away, it simply morphed, becoming man. The leaves curled and condensed, the bark became bone and sinew, and the king, his hair white and his beard full, stood before them. He was as tall as Kjell but leaner and more angular, every plane of his body and feature of his face severe and squared, his sharp cheekbones and his beaked nose giving him the chiseled look of a man carved from wood.

Kjell fell to his knees, his strength gone, and King Aren gripped his arms, wrapping his large hands around Kjell's shoulders to bear him up.

"Saoirse said you'd come. She said one day a Healer would come to Caarn. She didn't know your name, but she saw your face."

Kjell lifted his heavy head, the weight making it loll to the side, but his eyes found Sasha's. She wept openly, as if she'd betrayed him, as if she'd traded his life for her kingdom.

"Forgive me, Captain. Forgive me," she begged.

"There is nothing to forgive," Kjell said. His vision narrowed, and he rested his head upon the ground, bent as if in prayer, and let the darkness sweep him away, releasing him.

EIGHTEEN

He was spared from watching Sasha greet her husband. Spared from their reunion. When consciousness found him once more, he was in a chamber, stretched across the wide bed, his boots removed, his weapons placed carefully aside. He wondered briefly how many men it had taken to carry him from the woods and marveled that he hadn't been left to recover under the trees. He felt bruised in layers—his skin was even sore to the touch—the ache deep, dark and multi-colored. The last time he'd healed a multitude, he'd slept for several days and awakened with his head in Sasha's lap. This time he awoke alone, sore and soul-weary.

His beard was back, but she was gone.

He eased himself up, knowing movement would be the surest way to loosen his stiff muscles. A jug of wine and a heavy goblet sat atop the small table near his head. He didn't bother with the goblet but took the jug with two hands and tipped it back, washing away the desert in his throat and the cobwebs in his head. It had a mild blackberry flavor with notes of cedar and pine, but like the wine in Quondoon, it was weak, a wine for slaking one's thirst rather than escaping one's reality. He could have used a little of both at the moment.

A pitcher of water and a shallow basin adorned the narrow chest along the opposite wall, placed directly beneath an oval mirror that reflected the light from the rear-facing window. He rose gingerly, walking to the glass and confronting his blood-shot eyes and shaggy hair. He was a man of thirty summers, and the hair at his temples was newly shot with white. He didn't worry that his efforts had aged him, but they had clearly taken their toll. He wore the gaunt mien of a battle-weary warrior, the growth on his jaw doing little to disguise the hollows in his cheeks or the circles beneath his pale gaze.

His blade had been sharpened and a wedge of soap—cedar and pine again—was placed on a neatly folded cloth. Beside it lay a brush for his teeth, another for his hair. It was all very considerate and impersonal. He shrugged off his tunic, grimacing a little at his weakened state. Every muscle and ridge on his upper body was starkly defined, carved out by complete physical depletion. He'd scrubbed the sleep from his eyes and the film from his teeth and had begun to loosen his drawers when a soft rap sounded on his door.

A head peeped inside, not waiting for him to grant entry, eyes trained to the bed, clearly expecting him to still be sleeping. She was blond, her hair woven neatly in a braided circle around her head. He remembered her vaguely from the forest—she'd been a peach tree, heavy with fruit. She gaped at his naked chest, and her jaw dropped slightly, but she didn't retreat.

"You're awake, Captain!" she chirruped. "We're bringing water for a bath. All your clothing has been washed and dried. You'll find it in the chest there. I'll fetch your supper. The queen said you'd be very hungry when you finally woke."

The queen had thought of everything. He wondered if this girl had been instructed to follow him around and see to his every need the way Sasha had once tried to do. An image of Sasha in Enoch, clothed only in moonlight, flashed through his head and made him flinch.

"Are you all right, Captain?" the blond inquired hesitantly.

"Fine," he answered, and picked up his blade, preparing to scrape away his beard.

"I can do that, sir," she offered.

"Did the queen demand it?"

She blushed. "No, Captain."

He dismissed her, certain that she would find a listening ear and report on the boorishness of the Healer from Jeru. When the water and the large tub were brought into his quarters, he made use of them before he ate everything on the heaping platter delivered and placed beside the empty jug of wine. It had been refilled. A pang of guilt pierced his chest. So much of the limited supply had been allotted him—there were now several hundred people to feed within the environs of the castle—but he ate with gratitude and gusto, promising himself he wouldn't take more than his share again.

He detected the sounds of a castle reawakened, the murmur of voices, the patter of shoes against stone, the clang and racket of industry. When he could find no reason to tarry, he left his chamber, resolving to find his men and move his things back into the garrison. He would not be waited on by the queen's handmaidens.

The floors gleamed and the wood glowed. The dust was gone, the tapestries beaten into brilliance, and the spiders made homeless. Every corner and crevice had been cleaned and scrubbed; even the air boasted a fresh scent and soft laughter. The healed had been busy.

Kjell trusted that Jerick had carried out his commands, keeping one of his men assigned to Sasha at all times. He found himself listening for her even as he avoided the places he thought she'd be—the wide halls and the great rooms, the kitchens and the library, the galleries and the porticos. But he hadn't thought to avoid the king.

Aren was surrounded by men—a steward who took endless notation as the king spoke, clearly compiling lists and taking direction, and several others who appeared to be listening intently and offering opinions when asked. They were surveying the outbuildings and had just exited the stables where the horses brought from Jeru were housed. Padrig huddled at the elbow of the king and was the first to draw attention to Kjell who had tried unsuccessfully to slink into the shadows.

The men began to bow in reverent gratitude, and the king, his crown sitting comfortably on his white hair, inclined his head as well.

"I trust your strength has been restored, Kjell of Jeru?"

Kjell nodded. "Yes. I took far more than my share. The supplies brought from Jeru won't last long with our numbers."

"They will be more than sufficient," the king answered graciously.

"The countryside has been stripped of livestock and wildlife. There is nothing to eat, Majesty," Kjell contended.

"We brought seeds, Captain," Padrig reminded him. "Fortunately, all the seeds were on Lortimer's ship. There will be plenty to eat."

"Seeds?" Kjell asked, incredulous. The people would be dead before seeds would be of any use.

"Ah. He doesn't understand," the king said slyly. "Come, Captain. You will enjoy this, I think. Today we plant."

Kjell trailed after the eager Spinners to the fields west of the castle, wishing he could see Jerick and inquire after the welfare of the queen. He shoved the thought away. *You will not be able to sleep outside my door.*

"Your Earth Mover was most helpful," the king said. "We have spent the morning clearing rocks, but we have many hands and he's saved us weeks of labor."

"My . . . Earth Mover?" Kjell asked.

"Jedah," Padrig supplied. "He turned the soil and prepared the ground for planting. In one day he accomplished the work of a team of laborers. He is in the southern fields today. Tomorrow he will travel to the east, the next day to the north. The growers will follow behind."

The king took a kernel of corn from his pocket and walked to a furrow. Bending his long back, he pushed the kernel into the dirt and covered it gently. Without explanation, he placed his hand against the freshly-churned soil, curling his fingers into the dark softness, his palm down and his fingers cupped. Slowly, as if he measured the height of a child from toe to crown, he coaxed a green shoot from the ground and made it climb, reaching for the sun, the stem plumping and the leaves unfurling. Around Kjell, other spinners began to do the same, the plants flowering and flourishing around him. They sowed the seeds only to cover them and immediately call them forth. Corn, carrots, and tomatoes so red and fat the vines couldn't hold them. They pulled bounty from the earth the way Padrig had pulled stars from the heavens.

Children poked the knotted roots of potatoes into mounds and patted them down. A woman walked behind them, placing her hands atop the rises. Green foliage would spill from the mounds, and she would move on to the next one. Several children followed behind her, digging into the earth she'd just touched, uncovering fully grown potatoes like they'd been there all along.

Ten spinners stood in a fallow field, and within the hour, had coaxed forth rows of waving wheat.

Kjell remembered the fruit trees in Sasha's garden—all the bounty and the variety. With the right seeds, Aren could have built it in a day. In a matter of hours.

There would be plenty to eat.

"Walk with me, Healer. You and I have much to discuss." When Padrig and the king's counselors fell in behind them, the king waved them off. "I wish to speak to the captain alone. Stay."

Kjell fell into step beside the king as they moved away from the growers, from the miracles spilling from their hands, and from the fields not yet sown. They climbed into the forest formed not of spinners, but of the towering trees of Caarn. Kjell could easily see the difference now.

"I am accustomed to looking down on men. You are even bigger than I am," the king commented, moving through the trees as though he belonged among them.

"My brother—King Tiras—is tall as well. We get our size from our father," Kjell answered, repeating what he'd always believed.

"As did I. We are a tall people. Maybe it is an outward manifestation of our gifts." The king stooped to pick up a sturdy, long stick and weighed it in his hands before he jabbed it into the ground, using it as a staff to climb the rise.

Kjell was silent, waiting for the king to say what he was bound to say. He had little doubt that much had been discussed and revealed while he slept. Sasha would not have withheld the entire story from King Aren. It was not her way.

"I am not a young man. I haven't been young for a long time. I was not young when Saoirse became my queen. Ours was a marriage designed to unite people and blend nations, but we were suited. And her gift was desirable to me. So many of us are Tree Spinners in Caarn. We have tried to bring in other gifts, but the gift to spin is a highly dominant trait. My father was a Tree

Spinner, and his father before him. Padrig has a unique gift. My sister had a unique gift as well. But she did not choose to stay in Caarn."

The king had stopped walking and faced Kjell, searching his eyes.

"Saoirse tells me your father, King Zoltev of Jeru, was a wicked man."

Kjell nodded, denying nothing. And still the king studied him.

"You may have gotten your size from your father. Your strength. But you are very like your mother," Aren said, his voice flat and heavy, as though declaring a royal edict.

Kjell stumbled back, the air whooshing from his lungs in surprise. That was not the accusation he had expected.

"She told me, Captain," Aren explained. "Saoirse told me who you are. I didn't want to believe it. But it is undeniable." Aren lowered his staff so it pointed at Kjell's chest. "So you took my queen and now you will take my kingdom?"

Kjell did not step back or lower his gaze.

"If I had taken your queen, Majesty, she would not be here. And if I'd wanted your kingdom, *you* would not be here," he said softly.

Aren's blue eyes were suddenly alight with mirth, and he threw back his head and laughed. Kjell did not join him. His feelings were too turbulent, his thoughts too troubled.

Aren lowered his stick and leaned against it, stroking his beard as his grin faded, his eyes thoughtful and his posture pensive.

"Why *did* you heal me, Captain?" he pressed. "You could have taken my place beside her."

"I don't want to take another man's place. I want only what belongs to me."

I belong to you now.

Kjell pushed her voice away.

"I could argue that the kingdom is rightfully yours," Aren said.

"If my mother was indeed Koorah of Caarn, then she walked away from her birthright. I did not come to reclaim it."

"Why *did* you come?" Aren asked.

"To make sure . . . the queen . . . is safe." He could not call her Sasha in the presence of the king. It was too familiar. But he couldn't call her Saoirse; it wasn't familiar enough. He decided not to say her name at all. It was easier that way.

As succinctly as he could, Kjell told the king about the Changer who had dogged their journey, about his fears, and about his certainty that the battle for power had not ended on the shores of Jeru.

Aren listened, his eyes widening at the tale. When Kjell finished, he was quiet for a long time, considering.

"Without you, the walls of Caarn would still be empty. Caarn needs a Healer," he said, finality in his voice. "I would be a fool to insist that you leave."

"I've healed the whole bloody village. I have nothing to offer anyone here. If someone grows ill or is gravely wounded, I will be useless."

"What do you mean?" the king gasped. "Saoirse said you healed an entire village in Quondoon. You healed a forest of Spinners. Surely you can heal again."

"A scratch. A minor wound. A small burn. Those things I can do, over and over again. But the kind of healing I've done here in Caarn? I won't be able to do it again. That kind of healing is a gift I can give only once."

"But the woman . . . the Changer. She doesn't know this?"

"No. And I believe that is what has protected the queen thus far. The changer doesn't know I can't simply heal her again."

"Are you sure she followed you to Dendar?" the king pressed.

"No. But if she is here, I led her here. I brought this to you. It is happening all over again, and I can't leave. Even if I wanted to. Even if it would be easier to go."

"Then we will wait. And we will watch." The king sighed.

"I will do what I promised. I will stay until the queen is safe. But you must guard her, Majesty," Kjell insisted.

"Saoirse is not helpless," Aren said.

"No. She is fearless, compassionate, and totally committed. But her visions are sporadic and incomplete. And she is not ruthless."

"This Lady Firi, this Changer—she is ruthless?"

"Yes."

"There are dreadful scars down Saoirse's back. How did she get them?" the king asked.

The rage swelled and bellowed in Kjell's chest, and he forced himself to look away, flexing his hands so he wouldn't ball them into fists. The Creator help him. He could not abide the thought of Sasha's pale skin bare to another man's eyes.

"That bothers you," the king whispered. "It bothers you that I have seen her scars. She is my wife, Healer."

"She is my heart," Kjell shot back, unable to hold his tongue.

The king cursed and Kjell braced himself for the king to swing his stick. He would take the punishment. He deserved it. But the blow did not come.

"It is a man's world, yet we are slaves to our women," King Aren whispered. "I do not blame you. I do not blame her. But you will keep your distance, Captain."

Kjell nodded, and without another word, retreated into the trees, unable to trust himself in the king's presence any longer.

Kjell was true to his promise, staying as far from the queen as possible. He had shared his suspicions and specific instructions with his men. If they didn't know what they were looking for, they couldn't possibly defend against it.

Lortimer and the sailors were more amenable to staying now that there was a village to reside in. They'd been well paid to take the voyage—the people in Caarn were friendly and welcoming, and a few months was not so much to ask when conditions were agreeable. The Gifted and the tradesmen who had made the journey had always intended to stay, and they went about making arrangements for themselves in the new community.

The King's Guard broached no complaint at the extended stay. Their lodgings were comfortable, their bellies full, and their devotion to Sasha evident. Jerick had begun calling them the Queen's Guard when he didn't think Kjell could hear. Kjell knew Tiras would worry when no one came back, but had no way to send him word. Hashim's messenger birds were not trained to fly across the sea.

Kjell moved his belongings from the castle and slept in the barracks with his men. He had found it worrisome that King Aren had no soldiers of his own. He had a court and counselors, cooks and seamstresses, stewards and grounds-men. There were artisans and weavers, growers and bakers, candle makers and gamekeepers—though there was little game anymore in Caarn. But there was no army.

A string of spindly guardsmen stood at attention by the entrances and on the castle parapets, but they did little more than bow and bellow the time, bugling the general welfare of Caarn like pesky roosters. Kjell wondered which of them had been the first to spin into a trembling tree when the Volgar attacked. The guardsmen worked in shifts and went home to their cottages when they weren't on duty. The barracks he and his men had commandeered were the least crowded corner of the entire keep.

Kjell took it upon himself to change that.

He kept a handful of guards assigned to the queen and enlisted the rest of his men to recruit and train a small army, and fortunately, there were men seeking work. King Aren had instructed the trees around the border to open, thinning them with a firm command. They had obeyed, ambling outward, creating a porous perimeter around the valley.

When Kjell had expressed concerns to Padrig and King Aren about the unprotected border, the king had nodded soberly, listening to his fears, but he had his own opinions.

"Caarn has always welcomed everyone. We only ask that if you come to Caarn, you contribute. If you want to eat, you will work. Everyone can do something. That has been our strength."

"That is noble. But there are monsters in the world. Your strength is also your weakness. Who will keep the monsters out?" Kjell asked.

"The Volgar are gone," Padrig protested, inspiring a growl from Kjell's throat. For a man who could harvest memories, Padrig's own memory was remarkably deficient.

"There are all types of monsters," Kjell shot back. "But don't be so hasty, Padrig. The people have returned. Maybe the Volgar will as well."

The king nodded slowly. "Then we will do our best to defend against them."

Kjell dedicated himself to doing just that. Empty cottages were filled, and the surrounding fields and streams continued to yield enough food to feed them. Making things grow was child's play for the Spinners of Caarn, but harvesting required the same toil and time as it did everywhere else. But those who didn't have a calling or a craft, a duty or a trade, were enlisted in the defense of Caarn.

With the opening of the forest wall along the border, wildlife began to trickle into the valley as well, and when Kjell wasn't creating an army he was hunting for the Changer. He didn't know what he thought he'd find, but he looked all the same, watching for signs and ciphers, for traces and tracks. If given the opportunity he would have to strike a killing blow. If he merely wounded her, she could change, and in changing, she would heal.

Each day, he mixed dirt with a bit of water from the carafe on his belt and darkened his skin. Then he wrapped himself in greenery and perched on a knoll beneath a sheltering tree, waiting faithfully. His size made it hard to hide, but his desire to escape the castle walls and avoid the castle's queen gave him patience and persistence. She was his reason to evade and his reason to endure.

Two weeks after waiting day after day, he was rewarded by the presence of a doe, picking her way through the foliage, her eyes on the castle just visible through the trees. The deer was sleek and brown, the same color as the wolf in the Corvar Mountains, and Kjell's heart leapt at the glimmer of possibility in the feminine line of her back and the deep brown of her eyes. The doe didn't strip the bark from the trees or nose the bushes, but stared at the castle as though it called to her.

Keeping his breath locked in his chest, Kjell drew his bow, notching the arrow, feeling the tension in his limbs and in the choice before him. He released his breath as he released the shaft. It flew true, slicing the air and piercing the soft pelt of the deer, burrowing deep behind her front leg. She crumpled, her head rising and falling, her only nod to resistance. He ran, hurtling rocks and skirting bushes, his eyes never leaving the downed animal.

There was little blood, but her gaze was fixed, and in death she remained exactly what she'd been in life.

A deer.

Kjell swore, sorry that he'd killed her and angry that he would do it again, and began the untidy work of removing her pelt. The meat would be welcome even if his efforts were fruitless.

A snapping in the undergrowth had him whirling with his knife raised. Jerick appeared, his own bow looped over his arm, his other hand outstretched, offering wine like he'd offered it once before.

"I will never drink from your bottle again," Kjell muttered.

"An unanticipated boon, I must say," Jerick retorted. "I prefer not to share."

"Report, Lieutenant," Kjell ordered.

"All is well, Captain."

"Nothing gets near her," Kjell insisted for the hundredth time.

"Not even a mouse," Jerick replied, his standard answer to Kjell's dogged demand.

"How is she?" It was the first time Kjell had asked. Jerick had managed to communicate her whereabouts and her wellbeing without elaborating, which had left Kjell both grateful and gutted.

Jerick regarded him with more compassion than he deserved.

"She is tireless."

"There is much to be done," Kjell said evenly.

"She is unhappy, Captain. She rises early, works without ceasing, and retires late. Every day she asks if you are well, and I tell her the same thing that I just told you. You are tireless. And you are miserable."

"Don't tell her that," Kjell snapped.

"All right. I will lie," Jerick agreed cheerfully.

"I do not want her to suffer," Kjell muttered.

Jerick nodded and immediately shifted subjects.

"There will be a celebration, Captain. Will you be there? There is talk you will be knighted."

"A hero of the realm." Kjell sighed, repeating the title that was to be bestowed on him.

"Yes. The people need a celebration. And you need to allow them to thank you."

"The king said the same thing. I promised I will be there," Kjell grumbled.

"He is a good king, Captain." Jerick said softly.

"Jerick? Why do you always say things I have no desire to hear?" Kjell asked, though his voice lacked its customary venom.

"Because I am the only one who dares," Jerick replied. "It's good for you, Captain."

"Yes. I am always healed by your presence and your words, Lieutenant," Kjell countered dryly.

Jerick snorted. "King Aren reminds me a little of you."

"Cease speaking, Lieutenant," Kjell sighed, knowing Jerick would never, ever cease speaking.

"It is something in his eyes," Jerick mused. "Though his are a brighter blue. And much warmer. Wiser. Maybe it is his mouth. Of course he smiles more." Jerick's grin was wicked as Kjell sought to sweep his feet out from under him. The lieutenant countered and danced away. Kjell let him scamper, crouching over the deer once more, too subdued to make chase, though he appreciated Jerick's company more than he would admit.

"She's a beauty. First one I've seen. The animals are coming back. The forest is coming alive. It's . . . comforting," Jerick mused, listening to the chirping of the birds and the chattering of the squirrels above them.

Kjell nodded, though he knew little comfort and even less peace. He considered again that Ariel of Firi had died in the depths of the sea. Or maybe she'd never left the Corvar Mountains or the Bay of Brisson at all. She was controlling him—his emotions, his time, his energy—with no effort at all.

"Don't drain the doe here. Yetta will want the blood. She will put it in her soup, and it will taste like the nectar of the gods." Jerick indicated the deer Kjell had just begun to skin.

"Then help me carry it back," Kjell said. They hoisted it upon their shoulders, walking in comfortable silence, the weight and warmth of the animal shared evenly between them.

"Captain, if Lady Firi followed you from the plains of Janda all the way to the mountains in Corvyn, she followed you here," Jerick offered as they neared the west castle gate. The newly-trained watchman saw their approach and called out a welcome and a query, just as he'd been taught.

"Are you sure you aren't Gifted, Lieutenant?" Kjell murmured, waiting for the gate to rise. "You have an uncanny way of reading my mind."

"No Captain. I am not Gifted," Jerick retorted. "I am just your friend."

NINETEEN

Kjell was summoned to the castle by the King's Council and asked to report on the "progress of the army and the readiness of the guard." The king's advisors were much like Tiras's council in Jeru—self-important, inquisitive, and full of suggestions that made them all feel productive but accomplished very little.

Still, they revered Kjell—everyone but the king, who treated him with respect but no awe—and that much was a new experience. He answered their questions, made a few requests for the building up of the castle's defense, and escaped as quickly as he could. He strode down the long corridor hung with the portraits of the Caarn royalty, refusing to cast his gaze at the woman named Koorah or the glowing picture of the young queen. He was down the stairs and through the expansive foyer when he heard her voice, echoing through the slightly-opened door of the Great Room just to the left of the entrance.

He paused and moved toward the sound, entranced, letting it flow over and through him like a caress. She was telling stories again, and he suddenly realized she was talking about him.

"The captain thrust his lance upward into the belly of Archi-teuthis," she said, injecting drama into every word.

"The giant squid!" a child interrupted.

"Yes, the giant squid. Mortally wounded, the squid retreat-ed, swimming back into the darkest parts of the sea, for that is where Architeuthis lives."

"Why is he so big?" a little voice inquired.

"Because he is lonely," Sasha replied, inexplicably.

"The captain is lonely?" the child asked.

"No." Sasha's voice hitched but she recovered quickly. "Ar-chiteuthis is lonely. He grows big to keep himself company. His tentacles are like friends. But sometimes he is so lonely, he tries to take the ships deep into the sea. But ships don't belong on the sea floor, and neither do men. So Architeuthis is destined to be alone."

"But why is the Healer so big?" the same child insisted, thoroughly confused.

"Because he is a warrior," Sasha was quick to answer.

"Not a Healer?" someone asked.

"I suppose he is both," Sasha said softly.

"Is he lonely too? My father says he isn't friendly," another child chimed in.

Kjell winced.

"Is that a true story about the giant squid?" a child pondered doubtfully. "How do you know he just doesn't want to gobble ships and eat people?"

Sasha quieted the children and before long only the soft sounds of independent study filtered through the window. Kjell turned away, the spell broken, his hands still in need of washing.

"You have found our school," Padrig said, startling him. "We're holding classes in the Great Hall until more permanent arrangements can be made."

"Is there no one else to teach them?" Kjell asked. Jerick said Sasha was tireless, but she could not do everything.

"There are a few others. But Queen Saoirse assists for a little while every day. She is the most educated among us."

"A slave from Quondoon," Kjell whispered.

"Yes," Padrig said, a pained expression crossing his face. "The children have struggled most in the transition. They have aged, just as they would have done had they been children instead of trees. They went to sleep one way and woke another. Bedwin was four when he began hiding. He is eight now. And he doesn't know how to read. Moira was eleven, still a child. Suddenly she is fifteen, with a woman's body and emotions, and she doesn't know how to act. She is too old for the school room yet too immature to be anywhere else. There are many like Bedwin and Moira. All their lives were interrupted, and they are all a little lost."

They weren't the only ones.

"We are looking for a permanent headmaster," Padrig continued. "The old head schoolmaster was one who did not come back."

"One of the trees?

"Yes." Padrig nodded.

"I remember. His heartbeat was faint." Kjell had felt no tossing or turbulence beneath the bark, and he'd almost moved on, believing the tree was simply that, a tree. It was the schoolmaster's wife who made him listen harder, insisting the elm was her husband who'd gone into hiding beside her. But the man could not be saved . . . or healed.

"The schoolmaster will become like Grandfather Tree."

"What does that mean, Spinner?" Kjell asked.

"He will die. But just like the stars in the sky, he will live on as long as his tree lives on. He has spun away and will never spin back."

"My brother Gideon, the king's father, died in his sleep. He did not know he was going to die. He did not take his place next to his father—Grandfather Tree—in the grove. Aren's mother, Briona, is there. But not Gideon. It is something that grieves the king terribly.

"When I die, I will not become a tree of Caarn either. I will simply become dust again." Padrig shrugged sadly. "But perhaps the Creator, in his mercy, will make me stardust."

The children suddenly burst out the doors as if being chased by Architeuthis himself, and Padrig threw up his hands, pretending he was being tossed about by a great wind.

"Slow down, children! You are in the palace!"

"Good day, Master Padrigus," they chorused, bobbing and bowing as they tumbled by him toward the castle kitchen. Three small boys of varying widths and heights came to a stumbling halt in front of Kjell and pulled at their forelocks dutifully.

"Good day, Healer," one stammered. Another didn't speak at all, but stared, wide-eyed. The third boy reminded him of Jerick, and the moment he opened his mouth, the resemblance was even more marked.

"Are you a Healer and a warrior like Queen Saoirse says? And are you terribly lonely like Architeuthis? I don't think he's lonely. He's mean. He's mean and nasty, and he likes to break bones and ships with his tentacles."

Kjell stared at the small boy, unsure of which question to answer first, if he should answer him at all. He had to agree that Architeuthis was not nearly as sympathetic a creature as Sasha had made it out to be.

"Run along, boys. We will have the captain come to our lessons one day. He can tell us about one of his adventures then," Sasha called from the door of the Great Hall. Kjell tried not to raise his eyes, knowing seeing her would hurt, but it was like holding his breath, futile and unavoidable. He filled his lungs as he met her gaze. Her cheekbones were flushed with two deep splotches of color, and Padrig sighed, bowing deeply as he excused himself.

"Where is your guard?" Kjell asked the queen softly.

"I am here, Captain," Isak spoke from behind her. The queen stepped aside and let him exit the Great Hall.

"Two men are outside the front entrance, two at every other entrance. One there," he pointed to the end of the long hall that extended from the foyer, "and one there." A guard named Chet moved from beneath the broad staircase and bowed his head, greeting the captain. Kjell hadn't even known he was present.

Kjell grunted in satisfaction. "Will the children return?" He asked Sasha.

"Not today. They were promised a sweet in the kitchens, but their studies are complete for the day."

"Much has been accomplished in a month," he said.

"Yes. And there is still much to do," she replied.

Their eyes locked, drinking each other in, their words falling off as their hungry observations interrupted their stilted exchange.

"There is white in your hair, Captain. At your temples," she breathed, and a radiant smile split her face. She reached a hand toward him before snapping it back, like she'd forgotten she wasn't supposed to touch him.

Kjell tugged at his hair the way the young boys had pulled at their own, minutes before.

"That makes you smile?" he asked.

"Yes," she whispered, and he heard emotion in her throat.

"Why?" he questioned, incredulous.

"I have not seen you this way," she replied.

She had not *seen* him this way. The memory of her fear in the alley in Brisson, of her dread that he would die in Dendar with a head of dark hair rose to his mind.

"I was not as pleased as you to note the change," he confessed.

"Vanity is for the weak," she teased, but her throat convulsed as if she swallowed back grateful tears, and he looked away, unable to abide her smile or her sweet relief without breaking his promises.

He turned to leave, but she stopped him.

"There is something you should see, Captain. Isak could . . . follow." Her sentence rose on the end like a question. Kjell nodded, making sure Isak heard the request.

"At your service, Majesty," Kjell said, inclining his head. Without further ado, she headed in the direction the children had gone, but instead of going to the kitchen she turned down the corridor that led beyond the huge galley. At the end of the wide hallway, she opened a door to a flight of stairs that disappeared into darkness after the first few steps.

"Isak? Light?" Kjell asked, pulling a torch from the sconce in the corridor. Isak obeyed and the sconce whooshed to life in Kjell's hand. Sasha immediately began to descend, her hand against the rock wall. Kjell stopped her, grabbing her arm, not liking the darkness or the unknown destination, and instructed Isak to move past them, leading the way with glowing hands and curious feet.

Once Kjell touched her, he couldn't let her go, and they stood for a heartbeat, his breath stirring her hair on the step above her before they began to descend behind Isak.

"There are twenty-eight steps to the bottom," Sasha said softly. "I discovered this place when I was just a girl and thought it a den of witches. I had forgotten about it. But King Aren reminded me yesterday that this was . . . Princess Koorah's . . . special chamber." She said Koorah's name carefully, as though she didn't want to explain her significance to Isak.

Kjell stiffened and knew Sasha felt his response.

"There are oil lamps on every surface, Isak," Sasha instructed as they neared the bottom. Isaac lit the lamps, one by one, and
as the wicks caught, the cavernous room brightened until the
shadows danced. Bottles and vials lined the shelves, and a dried
out inkwell and two leather-bound books, complete with draw-
ings and detailed descriptions, were open on a sturdy table as if
someone had been perusing them recently.

"Koorah was a Healer, but she wanted to be a physician too.
There are notes on everything—the tonics and ointments she created from the herbs of Caarn—and there are journals there,"
Sasha pointed at the far wall, "filled with accounts of healings
and sickness. Aren said that she believed the ability to heal
shouldn't be limited to the Gifted. She wanted to share her gift."

Kjell touched the bottles, noting the careful labeling—tonic
for fever, for snakebites, for coughing, for stomach ailments.

"These cures have to be older than I am," he whispered, and
immediately regretted his choice of phrasing. "They are liable to
poison anyone who partakes."

"But they could be replicated," Sasha urged.

"Sasha," he sighed. Then he flinched. He had promised himself he would not say her name, that he would remain removed
and politely appropriate. "Majesty, I am a warrior who has been
given the gift to heal. I am not a scholar or an alchemist. I can
barely read and would go mad in this room if left here more than
an hour. Surely, you know this." He cursed himself again. He did
not need to remind her of their familiarity.

She smiled at him, her lips curving in a way that was both
tender and tortured.

"Yes. I know this. I am going to seek out the gifts of my
people. If we do not know what we are capable of, what we each
have to offer, then we waste time and talent. We are not all Tree
Spinners. We are not all Growers. It is time we discover what
hidden abilities exist among us. These are Koorah's books. I only

wanted your permission and your approval if we find someone who could continue her work. Perhaps . . . you would like to take them to your chamber, to look through them first, before you allow someone else to study them?"

Kjell looked at Isak, who hung back, his expression carefully bland, his eyes neutral. Kjell was not fooled. He had little doubt his men had all heard the name Koorah by now, and that they had all discussed Kjell's possible link to the princess of Caarn in great detail. It was his own fault, he supposed. He had argued heatedly with the queen in the corridor where her picture was hung. Even so, his men were like gossiping hags, the whole lot of them. They all spent too much time together, cared too deeply about one another, and were endlessly curious about him. It had always been that way. The more he kept hidden, the harder they looked.

"Where would I begin?" he murmured, touching the page of the book that lay open on the table before him.

Sasha moved to the shelf that held the volumes. She pulled the first one down, ran her hand across it, wiping at more than three decades of dust.

"The best thing about books is that you can start wherever you like. The pages are in order, but no one will know if you read the last one first."

He took the heavy volume from her, enjoying the weight and the shape of it, the permanence and the possibility. If it had belonged to his mother, he would like to read it. Alone. With care.

His eyes skipped back to Isak and away again.

"I would like to begin immediately," Kjell said abruptly.

Sasha smiled, nodding, and he realized she misunderstood. He shook his head, correcting her assumption.

"The vials and potions can wait. The books as well. I want to know which gifts exist in Caarn."

He needed to find another Healer.

They began their query in the Great Hall, but quickly discovered the foolishness of the idea and retired to a clearing at the wood's edge. The Gifted were destructive. The edict had gone out—passing from mouth to mouth and ear to ear—that King Aren and Queen Saoirse were in search of rare gifts, and for an entire day the clearing was filled with both the curious and the brave. People were slow to come forward, afraid of laughter or scorn, but with a little reassurance from the king and kind pleading from the queen, the Gifted began to show themselves.

Kjell stood to the side, his hand on his sword, his eyes on the gathering, letting the king and queen conduct the quest. He kept close enough to observe and far enough away not to obstruct. The king was fascinated by the demonstrations and displays, laughing and clapping his hands in appreciation of every effort, big or small.

And some were very small.

A woman who had come to Caarn from another village in Dendar could make herself the size of a caterpillar. Her husband raised her proudly in the palm of his hand for them all to see before setting her back down so she could resume her size.

One of the young maids who had come from Jeru, a woman they called Tess, had a hidden gift as well. Sasha questioned her in surprise, asking her why she had not shared her ability sooner. Tess shrugged and worried her hands.

"It's a silly gift, Majesty," she said. She chewed her nail, caught herself, and shoved her hands into the deep pockets of her long apron.

"All gifts are welcome," Sasha urged.

"I can call water," she admitted.

"From the skies?" the king asked, surprised. Such a gift would be powerful indeed.

"Perhaps. I haven't tried very hard. There was never a need before. It is easier to call the water beneath my feet."

"Can you show us?" the king pressed.

Tess stepped out of her shoes and woolen socks and lifted her skirts to her knees. The assembly watched as the dirt around her bare toes became increasingly damp, growing in an ever-widening pool.

"My mother would slap me when I was small. She thought I . . . she thought I was wetting myself," she said in a rush. "I would think of water, and it would just . . . rise. I've gotten better at controlling it." The little maid turned red. "I know where to dig the wells, where the water is fresh, and where it will quickly run dry," she added. "Maybe that could be of use?"

"Such a gift would have been greatly appreciated in a place I once lived," Sasha said quietly. Her eyes found Kjell's before shifting away.

A man named Gaspar, who had come from outside of Caarn and sought work in the castle guard, stepped forward next. He was quiet and competent, always willing to do whatever was asked of him.

"I cannot change . . . but my eyes can," he said simply. With no further explanation, his eyes became elongated, the irises yellow, and the pupils tall and oddly-shaped, like those of a feline. "I can see in the dark. It makes me a good hunter, a good watchman." He looked expectantly at Kjell as he spoke, clearly eager to share his skill where it would be most appreciated.

"Tell Lieutenant Jerick. You will take the darkest shift," Kjell called out. The man nodded, pleased, and the demonstrations continued.

Emboldened by the cat-eyed watchman, a few others came forward, shyly displaying talons, tails, spikes, and gills. The changes exhibited were small, partial, and specific, and none of the people who stepped forward could change entirely. The queen nodded encouragingly.

"There were Changers like that in Quondoon. Surely there is a use for your gifts here in Caarn."

"I can change," a man spoke from the crowd. "But not on land."

"Completely?" the king pressed.

"Yes, Majesty. When I am in the water I can become any sea creature I wish."

"How much water do you need?" Kjell said, raising his voice above the murmuring of the excited spectators.

The man shrugged. "It depends on the size of the creature I become."

Kjell looked to Tess. "Can you make a pool for the Sea Changer?"

Tess stepped forward eagerly, hiking her skirts once more, and the water grew around her, a muddy patch that quickly became a large puddle.

The man asked the ladies to avert their eyes. None of them did. He shrugged, indifferent, and began to remove his clothes. The crowd gasped. Very few of them knew what Changing entailed.

"Have you ever seen a fish wearing a tunic?" the man asked with a smirk. "When I shift, my clothes fall off, and I'd rather not get them wet." A few of the gathered villagers turned their heads, mortified, but most watched as, with an audible plop, the man became a small orange fish, not much bigger than the palm of Kjell's hand. He swam in circles in the murky water before flopping on the ground beside the puddle and morphing back into a man. He calmly clothed his nakedness, a bit of mud smeared across his cheek.

A child of twelve or thirteen, a boy named Dev with green eyes and hair almost as red as Sasha's, made the wind gust around them, whipping at the queen's hair and parting the king's beard.

"That's a gift, isn't it Highness?" his mother asked, unsure. "He's a Tree Spinner too, but he spins like a storm. When he spins into a tree, he knocks the leaves off all the branches around him."

"It is indeed a gift," the king reassured as the boy sent a happy breeze through the uppermost boughs of the nearby trees.

A woman introduced her husband, Boom, claiming he was a special kind of Teller.

"I speak for him because his voice is so loud, it'll make your ears bleed," the woman explained. "That's why we call him Boom. Even when he whispers it's too much. He talks with his hands or writes on a slate to communicate most of the time."

The man had a chest cavity like a lion and ears like a mole, as though the sound of his voice made his own head ache. Boom walked into the trees, putting a hundred feet between the gathering and himself. When he opened his mouth and said "good day," the sound reverberated like a gong, and everyone assembled clapped their hands over their ears in pain.

The king asked Boom to walk to the borders of Caarn and try once more. He did so, his voice cutting across the distance clear and bold and decidedly less painful to endure. The king declared him the castle crier, charged with relaying royal messages throughout the valley, and the man found himself suddenly employed.

The gifts were odd and assorted, and more plentiful than Kjell had hoped. But as the day unfolded, no Healers revealed themselves. *The gift of the Healer is the easiest to deny.* He needed Gwyn of Jeru, the old Seer who could sense abilities in others, but he feared discovering a good diviner might be even harder than uncovering another Healer.

As the sun began to sink behind the trees of Caarn, the crowd thinned and the sharing of talents ebbed. The night watch began their rounds, the king and queen returned to the castle, and the gates to the keep were lowered. Kjell retired to his small quarters in the garrison and opened the book that belonged to another Healer of Caarn, a woman he'd never known. Painstakingly, he began to read, to peruse the pages, hoping to find answers to questions he'd never asked before.

Who were you?

Who am I?

How did you find the strength to leave?

TWENTY

The tables were laden with everything a man could grow, in a variety only a child could dream up. The meat was still scarce—a few wild turkeys, two geese, and one of the chickens brought from the Bay of Dendar—but two more deer had been felled since Kjell had slain the doe, and what was lacking in meat was more than made up for in everything else. Grain had been harvested and ground to flour to make breads of every kind. Bread stuffed with berries and wrapped around apples or studded with raisins and sprinkled with herbs, made the air smell of yeast and spice.

Stringed instruments and mellow drums made from the branches and trunks of fallen trees made warm music. No trees were cut down in Caarn. The tree had to die naturally before the wood was gathered. The people believed the trees gave freely of their branches and their leaves, their nuts and their needles in exchange for long life. Acorns were roasted, pine nuts were collected, sap siphoned, but only as much as the tree wanted to give. The trees had little use for any of the things they freely gave, and Kjell pondered whether the trees of Caarn had bleated like engorged milk cows, begging for relief, during the four long years no one had tended to them. Since the Spinners had been roused and the village enlivened, the forest floor had been harvested almost as thoroughly as the fields.

The celebration spilled out from the castle to the courtyard to accommodate the numbers, and the watch on the city walls was frequently changed, allowing Kjell's men and the new sentry to participate in the day-long festivities. The queen's guards were instructed carefully, but Kjell spent the hours of dancing, feasting, and celebration watching the corners and the lovely queen, fingering the blade beneath his sleeve and the sword swinging in its sheath.

Sasha wore the deep green of Jeru trimmed in the gold that suited her so well. The sleeves of her gown were wide, the edges trailing as long as her skirts, the bodice slim and the neck low, revealing the tops of her freckled breasts and the length of her slim throat. She wore her hair confined in dozens of braids coiled in dozens more, her golden crown resting in the wreath of her woven tresses.

Just before sundown the king instructed the trumpets to sound and the drums to rumble, announcing the court of honor to be conducted in the main courtyard, where the guard could stand at attention and the villagers could fill the lower bailey. Kjell played his part, bowing his head and dropping to one knee, allowing King Aren to pronounce him a defender of the realm. He kept his eyes on the king's boots as Aren laid his staff against Kjell's shoulders, one at a time, knighting him. The people rubbed their hands together in appreciation, creating a sound that mimicked the whisper of the leaves in the forests that surrounded them, crying his name and declaring him an honorary son of Caarn.

Kjell didn't know the custom but remained kneeling, his eyes level, trusting that he would be instructed to rise when the court of honor was complete. The king turned to his queen and extended his hand to bring her forward beside him.

Sasha curtsied deeply before Kjell, but when she placed the palm of her hand demurely on his bowed head, Kjell didn't look up. He was afraid his eyes would give him away, dishonor the queen, and insult a king who had done nothing to deserve the offense.

Her voice was strong when she began to speak, but he felt the tremor in her hand where it lay against his hair. He knew the words she spoke were part of the ritual, but they seared his soul, echoing love denied and oaths unraveled.

"You belong to us and we belong to you. Our roots will anchor you, our leaves cover you. From this day forward, there is a branch on the tree of Caarn that bears your name."

"Rise, Healer," the king said, projecting his voice. The queen's hand fell away and the people made their palms whisper once more.

"Let the feast begin!" The king bellowed, and the people cheered.

Kjell rose, keeping his eyes slightly averted, looking beyond the king and his queen, and he saw a flash of movement that chilled his blood. Perhaps it was the slope of her neck, her heavy black tresses, or the way she turned her head. But the glimpse was instantly gone, like his mind was playing tricks on him. He stared at the press of onlookers, at the dancing shadows created by the sinking sun and the newly-lit torches that encircled the courtyard. It was not yet dark, and the gloaming was pink and soft and mild, no brilliant colors and violent shades. Caarn was grey and green and deep brown—colors that spoke of earth and sky and things that grow. He separated himself from the celebration, slipping in and out of the spinning villagers and the dancing feet, searching.

Pale candlenuts as big as a child's palm would burn for hours, and everywhere Kjell looked, pyramids of the flammable seed on rock pedestals were being lit, permeating the castle and the grounds with their amber light and fragrant oil.

When Isak found him, his eyes wide and his cheeks flushed, Kjell knew he hadn't been imagining things.

"Captain, I saw her. The woman from the Jandarian plain. She is here," Isak gasped.

"Tell me."

"She was not a snake this time . . . not in animal form. She was on the edge of the crowd, dancing and drinking. She was clothed in silks and her hair was . . ." Isak tried to indicate with his hands, doing a poor job of description, and gave up. "It wasn't wild or snarled. It was coiled like a crown. She is beautiful . . ." he gulped. "I was near the queen, and didn't dare leave my post to follow the woman. She looked right at me, and she smiled."

Kjell cursed the press of people and the inability of his men to communicate effectively.

"You did well. You don't ever leave the queen to pursue the enemy."

Isak nodded but continued with his report. "The feast has begun. Jerick is guarding the queen. There are sentries at every door of the Great Hall and lining the walls. The king is asking for you, Captain. You are the guest of honor."

"I'll be there shortly. Spread the message. Tell the men the Changer is here."

"She can do little harm in human form, right Captain?" Isak asked, anxious.

"One would think," Kjell said. "But her confidence is concerning."

"Where did she come from? Where did she get the clothes . . . and the jewels?" Isak asked.

"I think I know," Kjell replied grimly. "Go Isak. Do as I said."

Kjell climbed the stairs with more haste than was seemly. He didn't want to draw attention, but he had no time for decorum. He strode down the long corridors to the wing of the castle where the royal chambers were located, the king's quarters on the left, the queen's on the right. Kjell hadn't slept outside Sasha's door, but he knew every inch of her room, every item within it, and every habit and practice of the queen. Sasha was tidy, prone to simplicity, and seldom took great pains or much time with her appearance. From the current state of the chamber, one would think someone else resided there.

The Changer had flown in. A small window, high on the wall, had been cracked to air the space, and a black feather, sooty and short, lay near an open chest of jewels. Kjell could picture Ariel of Firi perched there in the form of a crow, peering at all the shiny things before changing into a woman and helping herself to a few.

Sasha's tub had not been emptied after she'd bathed. A dirty footprint was outlined against the pale stone floor beside the huge iron basin. Lady Firi had washed herself in the queen's bathwater and upended the salts and oils when she was done, creating a perfumed cloud that made Kjell wheeze and retreat quickly.

Sasha's gowns were pulled from their hooks and scattered about the floor as well. A few of them were shredded and soiled, as if Firi had shifted into a beast and torn them apart for sport. Sasha was taller and slimmer than Ariel of Firi. The dresses would not have been a good fit. But clearly Lady Firi had found one and poured herself into it, dressing herself, fixing her hair, and donning her pilfered jewels. Then she'd walked from the chamber and down into the courtyard, joining the celebration of the people of Caarn who, for weeks, had been welcoming strangers into their midst. No one had stopped her. No one had sounded an alarm until she had safely slipped away.

The feasting had gone on much of the day, but in the banquet room long tables were arranged in a large rectangle for honored guests. The members of his council and their wives, as well as Padrig, Captain Lortimer, and a handful of respected villagers had all received invitations to dine with the king and queen. Kjell was seated as a guest of honor beside the king, eating food he couldn't taste, tasting food he didn't eat.

His men stood on high alert, necks craned and eyes peeled, but the night was one of the longest he'd ever spent. As the hours passed, the wine continued to flow, the villagers grew more and more merry, and King Aren regaled his audience with tales of Caarn from decades past, while Sasha, a storyteller who surpassed them all, sat stiff-backed and quiet beside him.

When she suddenly stood, her eyes black and her hands gripping her skirts, the king's voice trailed off and his eyes rose to her face.

"Saoirse?" the king asked, reaching a hand to steady her. She stared down at him blindly, her crown tipping over one ear, but she didn't right it or answer him. Kjell rose from his place beside the king and stepped toward her, unable to look away.

"They are drawn by our heartbeats. By the blood in our veins," she murmured.

"Who, Majesty?" Padrig asked from his seat on her left side.

"There were no bones," she continued, her voice hollow.

"Not here, Saoirse," the king warned, noting the attention she had begun to draw. "We will speak of this privately."

"No Volgar bones. Not in Caarn," Sasha said slowly, still lost in her vision.

The people within hearing distance exclaimed in fear, and the word trickled down the tables.

"The queen has seen the Volgar!"

"She is a Seer. The queen is a Seer and she says the Volgar will return."

"We will have to hide again!"

"We will have to leave Caarn."

The panic became a thrumming murmur as one person spoke to another, seeking comfort in conference, until the king stood, and with a booming voice, demanded quiet.

"The queen is weary. We are *all* weary, and sadly, we are still afraid. What the queen was speaking of is not a vision but a terrible memory. Sit. Eat. Be merry. We have much to celebrate. No one is in danger this eve."

The people nodded, some laughing at their own fear. Others looked unconvinced. Kjell didn't return to his seat but stood with his back to the wall, directly behind the queen's chair, standing guard. Sasha said no more, but bowed her head, lost in her own thoughts, and the temporary uproar was tamped down and smoothed more. But the mood had changed and soon the guests began to depart, blaming the late hour and the long day, their aching heads and their weary wives.

The king had lost his good humor as well, and sat woodenly beside the frozen queen, bidding adieu to bowing guests with a flutter of his hand and a tip of his head, until no one remained in the hall with him but the queen, Padrig, Kjell and the members of the guard still stationed at the doors.

"What did you see, Majesty?" Kjell asked quietly.

The king tossed his crown onto the table in front of him. It clattered heavily and Sasha flinched, but she answered Kjell.

"Wings. Talons. The eastern hills. Pounding hearts," she listed. Her voice was flat, cold even, but her eyes swam with distress.

"And what do you think it means?" Kjell pressed.

"The Volgar will be drawn back to Caarn. We are food. They smell our blood."

"There could be another explanation for your vision!" Padrig wailed. "We don't have to assume the worst."

"Padrig," the king warned wearily. "Don't be a fool. It is one thing to be optimistic. It is another to be blind."

"I can't leave Caarn again. I won't," Padrig said, shaking his head.

"And we cannot hide," the king agreed. "If I spin again, I won't be able to come back."

"Spinning is not meant to be permanent. It is one thing to change straw to gold. To change air to fire, to pull food from the soil. These things are not living. But when a man becomes something he is not, for any length of time, whether he be a beast or a tree, it dulls his spirit and represses his very self. We must use our gifts . . . but we can't hide behind them," Sasha said.

"So we will use what we have," Kjell said with finality.

"We cannot fight birdmen with leaves and roots, Healer!" Padrig cried.

"Maybe . . . we can," Kjell said. "If you can pull plants from the ground with the palm of your hands, King Aren, you can cause vines to grow. We will set snares. We will make traps."

Aren shook his head like he couldn't believe it was all happening again.

"We will fight back," Sasha urged. Her jaw was set and her color was high. She'd wanted to fight back once, and she'd been sent away.

Padrig moaned, but he didn't protest.

"When are they coming?" Kjell asked.

"When the leaves are vibrant on the hills," Sasha whispered.

The king and Padrig gasped, and Kjell's heart sank.

Summer was already waning. The leaves on the trees above Caarn were still green, but the light was shifting, the air smelled different, and the days weren't quite as long.

It seemed the village had been brought to life only to die a quick death.

The following morning, the gifted man with the bellowing voice stood on the highest tower in the castle keep, and with his head tipped toward the sky to avoid blasting the people below, he called the villagers to the castle keep. The people of Caarn trudged into the courtyard, bleary-eyed and yawning, drowsy from too much drink and drained from too much dancing. The celebration had barely ended, and the king was summoning them back.

In grave tones and sober words, King Aren told his people to prepare. There was shock and denial, anger and fear. Some asked why and how, others raged that fate was cruel. Many demanded answers and all demanded hope.

But no one wanted to hide.

The men were adamant. The women refused. The children trembled at the mere suggestion. Kjell began the work of drafting a battle plan based solely on Sasha's premonitions, calling on his guard and the Gifted to assist. The Spinners worked long hours, harvesting and storing, creating stock-piles for the cold months ahead, praying that Caarn would live to see them. The king spent his days among the growers, convinced that his gifts would be better used preparing for winter than preparing for war. He left that to Kjell and everything else to his queen. He wore the dejected air of a man defeated, and though he worked as hard as any man, his eyes strayed to the forests, and he listened with only half an ear when Kjell sought his counsel.

"In Jeru City the Volgar surprised us. In Caarn, we know they're coming."

"How did you defeat them?" a young recruit asked.

"Queen Lark made them fall from the sky," Kjell answered, remembering.

"How did she do that?" the Sea Changer marveled.

"With words. But we don't have words," Kjell mused.

"But we have wind," Dev's mother spoke up. "My son could make a great gust to knock them down."

"We have earth," Jedah added.

"We have sound," Boom bellowed, trying to whisper but making the glass in the windows shake instead.

"And we have vines," Jerick reminded.

"We will spread vines from the castle walls to the turrets. When we are finished, the Castle of Caarn will look like a giant tent, covered in green. And we will stand beneath, spears raised, waiting for the Volgar to fall into our pit. When they do, their wings will tangle in the vines, and we will kill them."

They would use everything they had, and Kjell would continue to pray that the Changer, who still lurked somewhere in the woods, would wait her turn to come against him, or give up altogether. Even Changers were not safe from Volgar bloodlust. The thought encouraged him.

Kjell was awakened by a shake to his shoulder and a reluctant voice in his ear. It was the cat-eyed Gaspar, and his irises gleamed above Kjell in the dark.

"Captain, there is someone at the gate who seeks entry."

Kjell was awake immediately, shooting up from his bed, images of the Changer pleading sweetly with the watchman playing through his head.

"He says he is King Tiras of Jeru. But he is . . . unclad. He insisted you would want to see him. D-do you want to see him, sir?" Gaspar sounded doubtful.

Kjell tumbled from his bed, pulling on his boots as his heart leapt with joy and disbelief. Tiras? In Caarn. God be praised. Tiras in Caarn.

His brother stood beyond the castle gates, his arms folded across his brown chest, his stance wide, his jaw defiant. It was the same way he stood when he was crowned and caped. And he was stark naked.

"Raise the gate," Kjell shouted, scrambling from the watchtower the way he'd scrambled up it.

Tiras strode into the courtyard as though the palace were his, and Kjell grabbed him up, laughing and shaking him, overjoyed and half convinced he'd finally broken under the strain of the last months.

"Where are your bloody clothes?"

"It is the burden of being a Changer, brother. You know this. I flew to Kilmorda, I swam to Dendar. Neither birds nor sea creatures have need of raiment."

Gaspar was gaping, and the garrison had begun to empty behind them, men streaming out and greeting their king. Jerick tossed Tiras a tunic and breeches, bowing as his smile split his face.

"Welcome to Caarn, King Tiras. I've never been so happy to see a naked man in my whole life."

"Lieutenant." Tiras grinned in greeting. "Count yourself among the blessed. Now where can an ill-clad king find some supper and some ale?"

"Come, brother," Kjell choked, too emotional to say more, and led Tiras to the west entrance to the castle kitchens, knowing Yetta would have something fit for a king in the larder. Isak ran ahead to light the lamps, a courtesy Kjell acknowledged even as he quickly dismissed his men. His composure was cracked, his emotions high, his heart full, and his mind swimming. He didn't want his men to see him weep.

He loaded a platter for his brother, watching as Tiras shoved food into his mouth and gulped at his ale, hungry in a way that gave testament to the miles he'd come.

"How did you find us?" Kjell choked, still struggling to compose himself.

"The roads in Dendar all lead to Caarn." Tiras swallowed and went back for more. "The Star Maker was quite proud of the fact. The bird's eye view is quite remarkable."

"You should not have left Queen Lark," Kjell murmured. "She would never forgive me if you didn't return."

"I could not stay away. You would have come for me."

Kjell could not deny that truth and nodded, overcome once more.

"You promised me you would return," Tiras chided. "What happened?"

Kjell hardly knew where to start. "There was no one here when we arrived. Not a soul," he began. He relayed the events of the last months, the wolf in the woods, the loss of the ship, and the empty bay. He told Tiras about the Spinners disguised as trees and the healing that had brought them all back. He told him how the forest had parted at his command and about the woman named Koorah who would have been queen. Finally, he expressed his fears that Lady Firi had followed him from Quondoon to Caarn.

Tiras listened with a lowered brow and thin lips, and by the time Kjell had finished his account, he had risen to his feet, his meal consumed and his third glass of ale forgotten.

"The Creator have mercy, brother. What a tale," he whispered. "What a tale."

"It is true. Every word. I thought I might not ever see you again."

Tiras faced him, and Kjell could see his own feelings mirrored in his brother's eyes.

"You are thin, Kjell," he observed.

"I am not," Kjell scoffed.

Tiras laughed and shook his head, relieving the emotional tension. "All right. You are not. But you *are* thinner. You look worn."

"Sasha is pleased with the grey in my hair," Kjell disputed, running a hand over his head.

"She is pleased with the hair on your arse, but don't let that convince you it's attractive," Tiras retorted. Kjell glowered and Tiras groaned.

"I'm sorry, brother. I mean no disrespect to Queen Saoirse. I fear for you. That is all. There is Volgar stench in the air."

"They are coming, Tiras. Sasha has seen it," Kjell said, realizing he had not told his brother everything.

"Damnation, Kjell!" Tiras cursed.

"You need to leave. You need to go back to Jeru, to Lark, and to your child," Kjell urged. "Rest tonight. Leave tomorrow."

"Is that what you would do, Kjell?" Tiras asked softly. "We've fought the Volgar together many times before."

"Please don't do that to me, Tiras. I cannot demand Sasha leave, and I cannot leave these people to face the Volgar alone. King Aren is not a warrior. They have no army. No weapons. No bloody defenses. But this is not your fight. This is not your kingdom. And it is not worth your life."

"I will stay until you can return with me," Tiras replied, adamant.

It was Kjell's turn to swear and sigh.

"We will fight them together, and you will come home," Tiras repeated, his voice brooking no argument.

Kjell nodded wearily, bending to Tiras's will as he had a dozen times before, but in his heart he knew he lied. When the battle was done, live or die, Kjell would not be returning to Jeru.

TWENTY-ONE

In the battle of Kilmorda, the stench of Volgar was ever-present. In Caarn, it grew, fluttering in on the breeze, warning of death and decay. Tiras, with his heightened animal senses, had been the first to detect it, but by dawn of the following day, he was not the only one. Kjell told King Aren to bring his people, every last one, inside the castle walls.

"Look at the hills, Captain," Jerick murmured. Kjell didn't have to. They were brilliant, the leaves vibrant in their death song.

The growers left their fields and began spinning vines, stretching them from the castle walls to the parapets, the long streamers of thorny green snagging on everything they touched. The plan was to create a net of sorts, crisscrossing the twisting vines over the castle, wrapping it in a web of green.

"How do you know the Volgar will attempt to tear through the vines?" King Aren worried as he coaxed the foliage to climb and crawl across the courtyard.

"Because we will be standing beneath them," Kjell said grimly. "And the birdmen want nothing more than to tear our flesh from our bones."

"They will not be able to help themselves," Jerick agreed.

"If we take away their ability to dive and fly, we can defeat them," Tiras reassured. King Aren had greeted the Jeruvian king with surprise and hope, but when he discovered Tiras was alone, without a delivering army in tow, he grew morose once more.

As the nets were strung, Kjell's men barred the castle windows so the Volgar could not break the glass and crawl inside. The children and a handful of women, along with Captain Lortimer and enough sailors to man a ship, would stay inside the hall. Provisions had been gathered, arrangements made, and food prepared. Once the Volgar arrived, the doors would remain bolted. Jedah, the Earth Mover, had created tunnels from the forest, beneath the walls, and up into the castle cellars and stores. If the King's Guard and the fledgling army of Caarn were defeated, Queen Saoirse would have a way to get everyone out of the castle and into the forest without ever crossing the yard or raising the gates. A ship still waited in Dendar Bay. Some of Caarn's children could be saved. It was the most Kjell could promise.

Everyone else who was willing to fight—women and men— would be armed with vertical spikes, swords, lances and spears, waiting beneath the canopy of vines, packed in tight formation, just as Kjell's men had done on the Jandarian plain. He would have preferred to protect all the women, to tuck them away with the very old and the very young inside the Great Hall and the endless rooms of the castle. But many of the women of Caarn had rejected that idea with flat eyes and sharp sticks. Queen Saoirse was among them.

What could not be done below with weapons and vines could be accomplished above with a hundred archers on the wall and a handful of Gifted in the turrets. It was not hot oil and catapults, but Kjell was optimistic that the unique skills would provide a measure of support. The Gifted in Jeru had turned the tide against Zoltev and his army of birdmen.

"Isak can light anything on fire. It's his gift, but it is also dangerous to those around him. We don't want the castle to burn down in the midst of battle," Kjell explained to the little maid who could draw water. Tess nodded, her eyes wide. "Keep your eyes on Isak. Don't let the fire spread," Kjell instructed.

"I cannot draw water from stone, Captain," Tess whispered, her eyes on the rock walls of the turret where she would stand.

"There is water in the air. You will have to call it from the skies." Tess bobbed her head reluctantly, but Kjell could see her fear. He could not calm it. There was every reason to fear. But if she was afraid for her life, she would be able to call her gift, he had no doubt. Dev, the boy who could spin like a storm, calling the wind and flinging gales, would be beside Tess in the tallest turret. Boom would be there as well, making the air quake and Volgar wings tremble with his voice.

The Sea Changer would battle with the rest of the men, armed with a spear and a stake. But Kjell had pulled him aside and quietly given him a mission of his own. If Caarn should fall, the Sea Changer was to leave through the tunnels and make the journey to Jeru City. Someone would have to tell Queen Lark what had occurred in Caarn.

When the vines were strung and the sun began to sink, they waited, ready and dreading, eating and sleeping in short shifts, eyes and ears to the east where the queen had seen the birdmen come. Sasha made constant rounds, soothing and speaking softly, making sure needs were met and every eventuality had been seen to. Aren moved among his people as well, reassuring and encouraging, claiming full confidence in Kjell's plan and the strength of Caarn, and Padrig padded behind him, wearing the dazed demeanor of a man who'd borne too much.

Tiras took direction from Kjell, playing the role of brother instead of king, but he missed nothing, absorbed everything, and his hands were never idle. Sharpened sticks, lances and blades were stacked like tinder in every corner, so he took to the skies, climbing the watchtower and winging out above the valley, determined to warn of a Volgar approach.

After two days of cramped quarters and bated breath, the nerves of every person in Castle Caarn were at a breaking point. Hope that no conflict would ever come, that the queen had lost her sight, infused the vigil, making the wait harder to endure. Even the stench had seemed to abate, though Kjell knew it was the direction of the wind and not a reversal of fortunes.

When the shadows deepened on the third day, Tiras returned from his eagle patrol with sweat-slicked skin and hooded eyes. The Volgar swarm had been spotted, and the numbers were great. Tiras donned his clothes, retrieved his sword, and without grief or regret, he descended to the bailey to wait with the rest.

The archers on the ramparts, tucked beneath the overhang and bent beneath shields, would wait for the Volgar to begin clawing through the vines before they took aim. The Gifted in the tower would wait for the second wave to come. The Volgar liked to swarm and fly, swarm and fly. Kjell prayed they would swarm and die. Swarm and die. Confident that his orders would be followed and that he'd done all he could, Kjell climbed down from the watchtower.

Sasha waited for him at the base of the winding stairs.

For a moment, in the shadowy alcove, they were alone. She watched him take the last few steps, her hands clasped in front of her. He stepped close, so close that the warmth of her body and the thrum of life beneath her skin painted him in her colors. He did not touch her, but he allowed himself to relish the sweetness of her and the memory of them. Her mouth was not his to kiss, her hands were not his to hold, and though her eyes still pledged forever, her lips could not. His face hovered above hers, close enough to feel her breath, to taste the hope that stirred from her breast as she spoke.

"We will not die today," she said fiercely. "Caarn will not die today."

Her words were infused with so much faith that he breathed them in, believing.

"Promise me," he whispered.

"I promise," she breathed.

With that assurance, Kjell stepped away, praying the Creator would honor her vow.

The young were herded into the Great Hall, the doors barred, prayers uttered, and the citizens of Caarn took up their arms, found their positions, and lifted their faces to the vines they stood beneath.

The sound of the Volgar was one Kjell refused to recall and couldn't forget. They screamed and cawed, their wings beating the air and their talons clicking. A collective shudder rippled through the villagers of Caarn as the distant cries became a roaring cacophony. The shudder became a shout when the first birds collided with the vines, and Kjell roared for every knee to bend and every weapon to brace. The people obeyed, gripping their weapons more firmly in their hands and willing the web of leaves and twine to hold.

A volley of arrows whistled from the ramparts into the writhing swarm, and the shrieking of the Volgar swelled to screams. One birdman partially broke through, then another, until two dozen of the Volgar dangled above the bailey, wings and talons caught in the vines, beaks snapping.

"Spears!" Kjell cried, and the members of his guard rose and threw their lances at the dangling horde. A few lances fell, but many more found their mark. The weight on the vines increased as the swarm doubled, then tripled, the living scratching and scrabbling through the dead, the scent of human flesh and pounding blood drawing the Volgar further into the swinging snare. Sticks and arrows bristled like quills from the bulging net and green blood began to drip from the vines and trickle into the upraised faces of the villagers, but the people held steady and followed Kjell's commands.

Then the vines began to snap and the birds began to fall like flies to the bailey below.

"Group!" Kjell roared as the birdmen broke free, and the people circled and stabbed, circled and stabbed, their spears out and their backs together, a dance of death and survival accompanied by Volgar shrieks. The living birdmen were skewered, and the tumbling dead were shoved aside as lances and spears were pulled free, only to be used again. Confidence soared among the three hundred makeshift warriors as the vines continued to tangle and trap, and the birdmen continued to plummet. Kjell didn't count the numbers, he didn't celebrate, and he didn't rejoice, but in the black of his belly and the back of his mind, he began to believe that Caarn would indeed live to see another day.

"Swarm!" Tiras bellowed, his eyes trained above them. Through the jagged holes in the vines, the sky grew dark with a hundred wings. Kjell's blood surged and his hopes plummeted as the Volgar began to dive. The netting would not hold another swarm so large.

Boom roared, the thunder from his chest creating ripples in the air, knocking the villagers from their feet and sending the birdmen cartwheeling through the sky as effectively as Lark's words had done in the fields of Kilmorda. As the villagers rose to their feet, the wind began to howl, and the screams of the birdmen were swept up in the gale. Lightning dashed and thunder clapped, and the winds were infused with rain.

The Gifted had come through.

Kjell screamed for the men and women to rise and hold their positions, spears raised, eyes lifted. The broken vines billowed and blew and the rain became a billowing mist, but the Volgar swarm did not return.

For a moment joyful tears mixed with the blood-tinged rain.

"Repair the vines, bury the Volgar—burn them if it's not too wet—and ready yourselves for another attack," Kjell demanded.

The people gasped, deflated and disbelieving, but instantly obeyed, retrieving arrows, gathering weapons, and piling the Volgar dead. Only one man was lost—an archer who fell from the ramparts. His body had been carried away by birdmen. Another man had a long slice down his forearm, and a badly-thrown lance had skewered a woman's thigh. Both the wounded were Spinners of Caarn, healed once before, and Kjell managed to partially close the cut on the man's arm, but couldn't heal the deep wound on the woman's leg. Kjell turned her over to a midwife who applied a poultice and assured her she would heal, albeit slowly.

They spent the night in restless waiting, falling asleep in snatches only to wake, gasping and flailing at winged beasts that hadn't yet returned. The vines above them created a curtain against the sky, obscuring the stars, giving them a sense of both security and confinement, thickening the air with dread and desperate hope.

The courtyard stunk of loose bowels and singed hair, like fear-soaked skin and tightly-packed bodies. Tess's rain had dampened the air and deterred the beasts, but the lingering wet made the night long and the tempers short, and when dawn poked prodding fingers at the nervous Caarns, most were ready for the battle to commence, if only to escape their discomfort.

As the sun rose with no sign of the Volgar horde, Kjell took his turn in the castle washroom, desperate to be clean but more than that, to find a reprieve from the faith the villagers had placed in him. He shrugged off his tunic and washed the Volgar stench and the tang of dread from his skin, the scent of soap and the cold water giving him even more comfort than the quiet.

King Aren found him there. He still wore his crown, as if he needed to continually remind himself of his responsibility. Kjell understood that. A crown could not be shelved when it wasn't convenient. It was the reason he'd yet to remove his sword or set aside the blade in his boot. The heft and rub of the weapons reminded him that soap could not wash away duty.

"Saoirse says the birdmen will not fall into the nets again," Aren said without preamble. Kjell's stomach twisted, wishing Sasha had come to him directly, and knowing why she didn't. He patted himself dry and pulled a clean tunic over his head, shoving the ends into his breeches and tightening his belt, his thoughts pinging like tired moths to a covered flame.

"She says some will dive but *most* will wait," Aren added. "She insisted I tell you."

"Where will they wait?" Kjell asked. Aren's shoulders slumped and his eyes closed briefly.

"On the ramparts," he said tiredly. "Where the archers are hiding."

"Most will wait," Kjell muttered, considering. Volgar were not men. But they could adapt. He had seen it before.

"Just once, I would like her to see something that gave me hope. Just once," the king sighed.

"Preparation is hope," Kjell replied quietly. "She gives us that."

Aren nodded once and turned to leave. "She is outside the door," he said abruptly. "Tell us what you want us to do. We will do it."

In the weighty silence of the king's exit, Kjell considered his options. Then, unable to focus on anything but the fact that Sasha lingered nearby, he left the washroom. Sasha stood in the corridor, straight-backed and hollow-eyed, waiting to deliver a message she knew would not be welcome. Kjell felt a flash of anger that she might have been chastised for the bad news she bore.

"Tell me," he said, halting in front of her, his voice gentle.

"I see them, perched and patient, so thick on the ramparts that the walls crawl with them. The archers will be picked off, and then they will wait," she said wearily.

"They cannot eat what is not there," he reasoned. "We will move the archers to the forest."

"Will that not simply draw the Volgar away as well?"

"Not if three hundred pounding hearts still stand beneath the vines. We know the vines will hold. We simply have to make the Volgar dive into them."

"And how will we do that?"

"We will make ourselves bleed," he said.

Sasha did not blanch or step back, but gazed back at him steadily, eyes inward, examining his plan.

"I need a blade," she murmured, thinking out loud.

"You do not need a blade, Majesty," he murmured.

"I may not need it today, but it will comfort me to have it. Please, Captain," she whispered, the plea so heartfelt and sweet he bowed to it immediately.

He reached for the knife in his boot, the hilt comfortable and smooth in his hand, an old friend. He pressed it into Sasha's palm and wrapped her fingers around it, showing her how to hold it.

"If you must use it, commit to it. Do not wield it to discourage your enemy. Wield it to kill."

She nodded, her eyes on his hand around hers.

"If you must use it, I have failed you," he muttered darkly, releasing her hand, relinquishing his blade. He watched her tuck it into her boot, copying his actions exactly.

"You have never failed me," she replied, straightening. "And I will not fail you."

The edge of the forest nearest the palace had been thinned and cleared as the Spinners were healed, leaving an empty ring of earth around the castle walls. Just beyond the sparse perimeter, the archers would wait —cloaked in greenery and shielded by the trees—for the Volgar to perch on the ramparts above the canopy. Jerick and King Aren would be among the archers in the forest, Kjell would direct the action beneath the vines, and Tiras would slip between, changing form as circumstances demanded, coordinating the effort between the forest and the castle.

"If there is nothing to eat on the ramparts, and the Volgar smell blood beneath the vines, they will try to break through," Kjell explained to those most fearful of the new plan. There was little argument but plenty of apprehension. New positions were staked out, new signals established, and a new round of fearful waiting embarked upon.

Near dusk on the third day, the cry finally went up.

"Volgar!" Tiras warned, shifting from eagle to man in a fluttering mix of feathers and flesh. The archers in the trees scrambled for cover and lifted their bows, shaking off the lethargy and the denial of the long wait. The throng beneath the nets braced their lances and clutched their blades, waiting for the sign to use them.

Just as Sasha had predicted, the birdmen shrieked and swarmed, circling the castle in the skies over Caarn until, one by one, they began dropping to the ramparts, peering down through the thick carpet of vines that partially obscured the villagers below. With the feathered haunches and wings of vultures and the torsos of human men, the Volgar were truly terrible to behold, especially when they rimmed the walls above the courtyard showing rare sentience and self-control, their eyes gleaming and their attention fixed.

"Bleed," Kjell ordered, his voice low, his gaze lifted. The word rumbled and spread through the armed crowd, and with shaking hands, the villagers of Caarn passed their blades and scored their palms, smearing the blood into their skin, hoping to draw the birdmen down into their snare once more.

The Volgar began to shift and scream, batting their wings and snapping their beaks, the scent of blood stealing their sense and luring them into a collective lean.

"Arrows!" Kjell yelled, and the villagers shielded their ears with bloodied palms, preparing for Boom to repeat the word.

"Arrows," Boom repeated, the word reverberating over the wall and down into the trees. The archers obeyed.

The eager screeching became desperate confusion as birdmen fell and others teetered, abandoning the exposure on the ramparts for the blood below. Bodies began to collide with the vines, and the people of Caarn began the coordinated slaughter of hundreds of Volgar birdmen.

"Lances—"

"Scatter!"

"Circle—"

"Attack!"

Kill and repeat. Jab and retreat. One by one, the Volgar fell beneath the onslaught, ensnared and skewered or trapped in the vines beneath the bodies of the dead and dying. The volley from the forest continued, urging the birdmen to drop from the wall into the nets below.

The Volgar were not the only ones to fall. A birdman broke through, his talons extended, and sunk his beak into the back of the Sea Changer before being brought down by a dozen lances.

Kjell dragged the man to a barrel of ale and stuffed him inside, commanding that he change. The wounded man became a silvery trout an instant before Kjell plucked him out again and tossed him to the ground. The Changer morphed immediately, dripping and naked, but completely healed. He donned his sopping clothes and took up his spear.

Each time the Volgar would break through, a skirmish ensued, circling villagers with upraised spears facing the talons and beaks of enraged birdmen, and more often than not, bringing them down.

When the net began to bulge and break, the edges snapping like frayed rigging in a hurricane, Kjell gave the warning to abandon the bailey.

"Gate!" Kjell shouted.

"Gate!" Boom repeated, and the villagers in the courtyard ran for the entrance, pressing themselves against the castle walls as they filed out beneath the hastily-raised gate.

"Burn it down, Isak," Kjell commanded, making sure the bailey was clear.

Isak began to pummel the air, his fire-filled fists swinging left and right, releasing flames that billowed upward, engulfing the center of the enormous net in fire.

The archers had heard the signal and were waiting to provide cover. As the people began to spill out the castle gate, the Volgar who'd resisted the lure of fresh blood and avoided the arrows of the archers in the trees, began to dive from the ramparts, desperate to snatch supper from the chaos. One woman was seconds from being swept up when suddenly she was the size of a small mouse. She scurried away, unscathed as the birdman above her collided with the ground and was instantly surrounded and impaled.

Some birdmen tried to fly, their wings on fire, only to tumble to the earth, unable to continue. But when the winds chased the fire, and the rain chased the flames, the remaining birdmen took to the sky, their numbers a tattered fraction of what they'd been before.

TWENTY-TWO

Kjell began to move through the villagers, closing the ooz-ing cuts across their palms, seeking out the wounded and the dead. The villagers clutched his hands in thanks, their eyes heavy with gratitude.

"Do you think they will return, Captain?" they asked, hope-ful and hesitant.

"If they do, we will destroy them," he reassured, and they nodded, believing him.

So many had been destroyed. The smoldering pile of Volgar remains tinged the air with a green haze. Bits of flotsam floated and flurried, causing the people of Caarn to cover their mouths and cough as they found each other amid the smoke. Tiras had changed and now circled the skies above Caarn, keeping watch in case of an unexpected return.

"Is everyone accounted for?" Kjell pressed, his eyes on the triumphant archers flooding the bailey from the woods, embrac-ing each other and recounting the battle from where they'd stood.

His question was met with blank stares and furrowed brows, as one man questioned another, unable to give him a response.

"Is everyone accounted for?" Kjell raised his voice above the din. "Where are your wounded?"

"The kitchen, Captain. The queen, the midwife, and Tess are providing aid, water, and bandages there," Jerick answered, pushing through the bailey toward him.

"And King Aren?"

"He was in the rear with me. We almost lost Gaspar, but His Majesty was able to briefly spin and give him cover. The bird-man got a beakful of green leaves before we took him down. The king was shaken but unharmed, and Gaspar has a broken arm. He might appreciate a Healer in the kitchen, although the queen might not."

Jerick grinned as if it had all been a marvelous adventure, as if he enjoyed irritated females and the smell of Volgar flesh. Kjell found himself grinning back. If Sasha's irritation was the worst he would suffer this day, he would count himself a lucky man. She had not been pleased when Kjell had ringed her with his men. She'd clutched her sharpened stick with annoyance and sliced her palm alongside the others, but she'd been shadowed and preempted with every parry and thrust. Kjell had known exactly where she was every second of the conflict.

He moved through the corridors to the kitchen, taking stock and counting heads as he went. When he saw her, the pressure in his chest and the ache in his belly eased. Her nose was smudged with soot and a few curls twined around her cheeks, but she was whole. Well. Busy. Kjell looked around for Gaspar and immediately located the watchman, curled in the corner. Gaspar's face was pale with suffering, his arm clutched against his abdomen, his cat-eyes glittering with pain. Kjell crouched in front of him and touched his thrumming heart, listening for the tone that would ease his suffering. Gaspar had come to Caarn after the border had opened. It would take no effort to heal him.

Gaspar's healing sound was more like a purr—cats were not famed for their song—and Kjell pulled the rattling vibrations into himself, setting the broken bone and quelling Gaspar's pain with an ease that had him stepping away and looking for someone else to assist.

"The king is still in the woods, Captain," Gaspar exhaled, his relief so great his words were slurred and his eyes fluttered closed. "He wanted a moment by himself, but you should see to him. He was . . . troubled."

The king was not hard to find. He stood propped against the gate that led to the western wood, his eyes on the queen's garden, a hand pressed to his heart as though lost in pleasant remembrance. It was a peaceful spot, and Kjell could not fault the man for needing a chance to collect himself.

"We've defeated them, Captain," Aren said as Kjell approached. He remained slumped, his eyes still clinging to his own thoughts.

"Yes. For now. Maybe forever. But some of the villagers were injured. Some were lost, Majesty," Kjell answered.

"Most were saved," Aren replied, and his gaze shifted from the queen's garden and rested on Kjell. He pushed himself away from the wall with the hand that had rested on his chest.

"You're wounded," Kjell gasped. The king's hand was slick and scarlet with blood. Kjell yanked the king's cloak aside, revealing a saturated tunic and Aren's arm tucked firmly against his body, attempting to stem the flow.

The king staggered, and Kjell took his weight, easing him to the ground.

"You are the son of Koorah, Captain. Of that I have no doubt. I can see her in you. Like you, she was convinced she had nothing to offer. She never wanted to be queen. But she would have been a good queen. And you will be a good king," Aren reassured.

"Cease speaking, Aren," Kjell bellowed, and pressed his hands to the king's side, searching for the source of the blood.

"Tiras!" Kjell shouted. "Sasha, help me!"

"You cannot heal me again, Captain," the king said, his voice strained but his face serene.

Kjell groaned, helpless, and bore down, pressing his hands to the king's sodden tunic, demanding submission from his gift. He would heal Aren's wounds, just like he'd healed the Volgar slashes on Sasha's back. He just needed time. He gritted his teeth and closed his eyes, refusing to meet the king's gaze, denying his inability to save him.

"There isn't time," the king said, reading Kjell's desperation. "I don't want to die here. Help me stand."

"I can heal you!"

"Help me stand, Captain!" the king bellowed, adamant. He pushed up to his knees and found his feet, swaying as he took a step. Kjell was there to brace him, and they began to stagger toward the trees, Kjell bearing much of Aren's weight, the king focused on the tallest of the wooded sentries bordering the rise behind the castle.

"Take me to the glade," the king urged. "There's a spot there for me."

Then they weren't alone. Villagers were streaming behind them, responding to Kjell's call. Gaspar and Sasha weren't far behind, Padrig on her heels. Tiras, bare-chested and shoeless but with his sword in hand, was just beyond them. King Aren ignored them all, pushing forward, his teeth gritted, his face set, determined to reach the grove.

"Here, Healer," he groaned as the woods opened up into a small clearing. "This is the place." Kjell tried to ease the king to the forest floor, but Aren insisted on standing, bracing himself on Kjell's shoulders.

"It is your birthright, Kjell of Caarn. Don't squander it," King Aren said, his face grey. With bloodied hands, he lifted the crown from his head and placed it on Kjell's.

Aren swayed, and Kjell braced his legs, keeping the king upright, ignoring the crown on his head as he continued to plead with his gift, magnifying the song that emanated from the king's spirit. But the melody did not mend, the blood did not abate, and the king was dying in his arms.

"Sasha," Kjell called out to her. "Help me heal him. Help me."

Sasha rushed to his side, but it was not Kjell's hand she took. With streaming eyes and trembling lips, she clasped Aren's large palm between both of hers and gave him the strength he needed to spin one last time. Forever.

"I'll be close to Grandfather Tree. Just as I planned," the king said, his eyes on hers. "Be happy, Saoirse," he whispered. Clinging to her hand, he closed his eyes.

The king's beard changed first. Then the hair on his head became writhing leaves, green and glossy, carrying the scent of earth and rain. The ground began to tremble, and the boots Aren wore became burrowing roots, snaking through the dirt and sinking deep beneath their feet. Sasha stepped back as the king let go, lifting his arms to the heavens, branches sprouting from his fingertips, thickening even as they extended and spread. Aren's body, supported by Kjell's arms, became the trunk of a towering oak, shooting upward beneath burgeoning branches and multiplying leaves. Then it was done, the change complete, and Kjell stepped back, his arms empty, his heart heavy. Around him, the grove was sacred and silent, as if the spirit of the passing king whispered through the wood.

Kjell knew if he pressed his hands to the bark, he would not feel the breathless fear of the hidden or the repellant push of a false veneer. This tree did not camouflage a Spinner with a beating heart, waiting to be reawakened. It was not a man, but a memorial. A monument of resurrection and remembrance.

"Farewell King Aren, son of Gideon," Padrig called, his voice shaking, his eyes wet, and he knelt at the base of the tree, bowing his head, folding his old bones to pay homage.

The villagers began to kneel too, their glowing triumph at the Volgar defeat becoming tearful lamentations. Where their tears fell, a flower grew, springing up on the forest floor, tiny petals and green shoots, dedicated to the man they mourned. Kjell withdrew his sword, a sign of his own fealty, and with a roar, stabbed it into the soft ground. He could not make flowers grow, but he could honor a good man.

Tiras did not kneel and he did not bow. He gripped the hilt of his sword, gaping at the scaled bark and the pointed leaves, at the lofty heights and sturdy roots, his shoulders squared and his legs braced, absorbing the wonder of what he'd seen. Astonishment lined his features and hardened his jaw, and when his eyes met Kjell's he bowed his head slowly, never lowering his gaze.

"Hail King Kjell, son of Jeru," he roared, and jabbed his sword into the air.

Padrig was the first to raise his head and join his voice with Tiras's.

"Long live King Kjell, son of Koorah," Padrig cried, still kneeling, still weeping.

The people had seen their king place his crown on Kjell's head. They'd watched Aren leave one life for another, becoming reborn, taking his place beside his grandfather's tree in the grove of his ancestors. But Padrig's words stunned them, and Koorah's name fell from their lips in wonder and awe as they realized what it all meant. One by one, they lifted their voices with Padrig's, recognizing the loss of one king and heralding the ascension of another.

"Long live King Kjell, son of Koorah," they cried, and the leaves shimmered and shook above their heads, raining softly upon the kneeling assembly.

Kjell wanted to reject them.

He wanted to hurl the crown into the trees and leave the glade.

But he could not.

The crown resting on his brow belonged to him, and he could not renounce it any more than he could deny the gift that flowed from his hands, his allegiance to his brother, or his love for the queen. The assurance rested on him like light, the knowledge pulsed in his blood, and in that moment he accepted the call, for that is what it was, and he could not forsake it.

Slowly, as if her legs became numb in stages, Sasha sank to her knees, her back bowing, her hands curling into the dirt, her hair caressing the new roots that forked the earth and anchored Aren's tree. One at a time, the villagers approached and bowed with her, pressing themselves to her side in sympathy and commiseration before rising and letting another take their place. After each one rose, they approached Kjell and kissed his palms before leaving the clearing and the prostrate queen. Kjell didn't recognize the ritual or his role in it, but he remained beside her, beside the tree, a new crown on his head, a new burden on his shoulders.

When the last villager left the clearing, Padrig rose as well, staggering as though his legs had lost all feeling. Tiras stepped forward and took his arm, steadying him. Together they moved toward Kjell.

"We must leave her now, Healer," Padrig instructed.

"I can't," Kjell refused.

"She will mourn here in silence for three days."

"Then I will mourn with her," Kjell said.

"There is much to do, Majesty."

The title caused his heart to turn and his stomach to knot, but he accepted that too, his fists balled and his eyes on the Star Maker's grief-stricken face.

"Then see that it is done, Spinner. I won't leave the queen."

"The people will expect you to sit on the throne, to tell them what to do now that the battle is done," Padrig said.

"I am not that kind of king." He was not Aren. He was not Tiras. But he would do the best he could.

"No, you are not," Padrig whispered, still stricken.

"Send Jerick to me. Take instruction from him, take advice from Tiras, and let the King's Council continue as Aren would have wished. Let the villagers put the castle and the countryside to rights. When the three days have passed, I will sit on the bloody throne if I must. But I will stay with the queen." His jaw was so tight his teeth radiated with pain, and he waited for an argument from the old man.

None came. Padrig bowed gingerly and began to make his way from the clearing back toward the wall around a kingdom that would never be the same.

"I will wait for you, brother," Tiras assured. "And Caarn will wait."

Sasha ate only dry bread and sipped water from the carafe Jerick brought each morning. She didn't speak, and she didn't raise her eyes to Kjell.

It rained but the trees bowed above them, sheltering them, and they remained dry. The nights were cold but Isak built a fire of candlenuts that never ceased burning. Two of Kjell's guard stood watch in the darkest hours, giving Kjell a brief reprieve from Sasha's silence and her downcast eyes. But he always woke with her hand in his. She rose only to relieve herself and slept only when she could not stay awake. She didn't weep, but he wished she would. Her silence was part of the ritual, but her dry eyes were not.

When the three days had passed, she stood but could not walk, and he swept her up in his arms and walked for her, entering the castle for the first time as its king.

In Jeru, death was marked by processions and bells that rang at intervals of seven, marking the period of Penthos—mourning. Monuments were built on the hill behind the palace, pale sepulchers of fallen kings. But in Caarn, many of the monuments were trees, and many villagers had witnessed the royal shifting. In one fell swoop, a king had passed and another took his place. Kjell's coronation and Aren's transformation had occurred simultaneously, and the whole village walked in a stupefied reverence superseded only by Kjell's own shock and awe.

He was king. Against his will and despite his reservations, Kjell of Jeru had become Kjell of Caarn, King of Dendar, saddled with a land and a kingdom he didn't understand and a people he barely knew.

He had been given a kingdom, but the queen was another matter entirely.

For a week after her vigil ended, Sasha never left her chamber. She was attended by Tess and the blond maid who had once offered to shave Kjell's beard. The blond was afraid of him and could never look him in the eyes, and Tess kept insisting that Sasha was well, though she clearly was not. Kjell stewed and couldn't sleep, burdened by her behavior, by his new responsibilities, and by the continual dread that the danger in Caarn had not ended. Tiras stayed by his side, a constant in the chaos, helping Kjell to navigate a position he'd never wanted or aspired to. But it was not until Tiras prepared to leave for Jeru City that Kjell broke down and begged his brother for advice.

"Tell me what to do, Tiras," Kjell pled, his confusion and concern teetering on the edge of anger. He needed Sasha, and she was suffering alone.

Tiras, perusing the kingdom's holdings and various ventures —none of which Kjell cared about at the moment—looked up at Kjell thoughtfully. He closed the ledgers and rolled the maps on the steward's desk in silence, clearly stewing over the advice he was about to dispense.

"Have you ever watched a sconce as it is lit? For a moment the torch and the wick both flare, as if spreading the flame makes each stronger. That is what happens when you and Queen Saoirse are together. I see it. King Aren saw it. All of Caarn sees it," Tiras said.

Kjell stared at his brother balefully, waiting for him to continue.

"You have been released, Kjell. She has not," Tiras said slowly, enunciating every word, and Kjell immediately lost his temper.

"I have been *released*?" Kjell repeated, incredulous. "I have not been released. I have been crowned! I wear this bloody wreath of gold and am expected to sleep in the king's chambers listening to the queen cry when she thinks no one can hear."

"The king is gone, and you can love his queen without constraints," Tiras insisted. "You are freed, but she is not. She cannot simply run into your arms, brother. Guilt makes grief unbearable."

Kjell groaned and rubbed his eyes wearily. He didn't want Sasha to grieve for Aren. It was an awful truth, but a truth all the same.

"Suddenly she can have what her heart desires most. *You.* But getting what we want at the expense of someone else taints the fulfilment of even our fondest dreams," Tiras said, his frank assessment making Kjell hiss in frustration.

"She is blameless. She didn't cause Aren's death or seek it," Kjell said.

"It doesn't matter. She loves you, he died, and the whole kingdom is watching," Tiras contended.

"It is a never-ending round!" Kjell raged. "One thing after another. I love her. And I cannot have her."

Kjell surged to his feet and strode around the perimeter of the library, along the rows of books he had no intention of ever reading, and ended back in front of his younger brother, dejected and deflated.

"She is yours, Kjell. Heart and soul," Tiras said, his compassion evident. "It is obvious. She was yours from the moment you met. But you must let her mourn."

"I cannot be King of Caarn if she is not by my side, Tiras," Kjell whispered. "I cannot do it."

"Time, brother, and patience," Tiras urged. "It is something you can give her. It is something you can give yourself. When I see you again, she will be your queen and these ledgers won't be so outdated. I have no doubt."

And so Kjell gave Sasha patience the way he'd given her his body and his gift, the way he'd surrendered his heart and his life. Freely. Completely. He kept a guard at her door and two in the ramparts facing her window. He gave her time, and he prayed for the strength to wait.

TWENTY-THREE

Kjell's meager belongings had been moved from the garrison to the king's chambers shortly after his unexpected ascension. He'd quietly allowed it, knowing he could not remain where he was, bunking with his men while managing a kingdom. And he had wanted to be closer to Sasha.

King Aren's possessions were whisked away, his rooms stripped of his presence, and the heavy furniture repositioned to make the space feel new. Kjell had never been in the king's chamber before Aren died, and the furnishings didn't matter to him. Still, the echo of the old king in the quarters made him feel like a usurper, and he never remained in the chamber for long.

One night, a week after Tiras's departure, feeling over-tired and under-appreciated, Kjell walked through the queen's gardens, staring up at Sasha's rooms and feeling like a love-sick fool. The fruit had been harvested, the trees pruned, and the chill of fall permeated the moonlit air. He didn't want to return to the castle or sleep in Aren's rooms, so he tossed his cloak upon the ground and stretched out beneath an apple tree, his eyes on the flickering light from Sasha's window and the silent sentries on the ramparts. Jerick was on the queen's watch tonight, his bow in his arms, his shoulders straight, facing her window like he'd been instructed to do, and Kjell let his eyes drift closed, weary but reassured that all was as well as it could be.

He dreamed of Sasha and their marriage announcement in Jeru, of her gold dress and her fiery tresses, of her happiness and her soft touch. He awoke to hands on his skin and lips on his mouth, and kept his eyes closed, believing he still dreamed. But the hands that roamed his body were aggressive, the lips dry and abrasive, and the breath that fluttered against his mouth tasted of blood. When he lifted his bleary lids, it was not Sasha's face above him.

Lady Firi's hair still wreathed her head in a coil, evidence of her preparations and her blatant trespasses the night of the celebration, but that had been more than a fortnight before, and Kjell wondered if she'd spent the last weeks as an animal, never changing into human form. Her plaited hair only accentuated her nakedness, making Kjell long for the matted curls and wild length, if only to shield her from his eyes.

She scampered back, putting space between them, and licked her lips as though she too had noticed their texture. Kjell sat up slowly, cataloging the weight of the new blade in his boot, the speed at which he would have to move, and the odds of bringing her down with a well-thrown dagger. She increased the distance, sensing his intent.

"There was a time when you welcomed my presence and my touch, Kjell of Jeru," she purred. "You will welcome it again."

"There was a time when you wore clothes, Ariel. There was a time when you smelled sweet and kissed softly. A time when I didn't know who you really are. That time has passed," he replied.

"No, Kjell. The time has finally come. This kingdom is yours now. These people are yours. They will bow down to your every wish."

"And to you?" he asked.

"Yes. I will be your queen."

"No," he said. "You will not."

She pouted playfully. "So serious. So stubborn. So foolish. I can be whatever I wish, Kjell of Jeru. King Kjell of Caarn," she mocked. "I was the little brown mare you purchased in Enoch. I was the gull who stirred the Volgar. I was the black adder in the grass, the wolf in the Corvar Mountains, the squid in the sea." Her eyes flashed with temper. "I didn't want *you* to die, but you almost killed me. I could have tossed you *all* into the sea."

"Why didn't you?" he asked, easing to his feet. She stepped back again, and moonlight pooled around her.

"I didn't want you to die. I wanted you to be afraid," she said. "You are afraid of me, Kjell. And fear is even better than love."

"And you will make Caarn fear you as well?"

"If I must. I have been following you for a long time, Kjell. Years. Waiting for the things the Star Maker showed me to come to pass. Then you found *her*. And I realized that she was the Seer who'd seen visions of you becoming a king.

"I tried to toss her over the cliffs so you could not heal her, to strike her in her sleep so you didn't know she lay dying, to attack when she was alone. But she is never alone. You've kept her so close and you care so deeply. Do I mean nothing to you?"

He was silent, and her eyes narrowed with irritation.

"I have been made an outcast in my own country. But in Dendar . . . I can have everything I want. Even you. Imagine my surprise when there was no one here." She laughed, incredulous. "What good is a kingdom if there is no one to bow down before you? If there is no one to rule?"

"So you've continued to wait."

"Daughter, daughter, Jeru's daughter, wait for him, his heart is true," she sang, parroting the old tune. "You've brought them all back for me. You've defeated the Volgar. And I don't have to wait any longer."

An arrow, straight and long, pierced the air and sank into her shoulder, knocking her forward. Kjell lunged, drawing his blade as he closed the distance between them. An angry scream tore from her throat and became the shriek of a falcon, flapping and rising into the sky. The arrow fell as she climbed, insulted but uninjured, and Kjell could only watch her go with a frustrated bellow, his knife in his hand, the Changer shrouded by the night.

Jerick joined him a moment later, breathless, clutching his bow. "I missed, Captain. I'm sorry. She stepped back, and I had a clean shot."

"You didn't miss, Lieutenant." Kjell swore. "She is simply hard to kill." Fear billowed in his chest, and his legs quaked, a delayed reaction to the Changer's presence. His eyes found the light of Sasha's window, needing to reassure himself she was unharmed. He realized suddenly that no one stood watch on the ramparts.

"I need to see the queen," he clipped.

Jerick nodded, not questioning Kjell's request, but he gave a report as they walked. "Isak is on duty outside her chamber. Her window is closed, Kjell. The Changer did not enter. All is well."

They pounded up the broad stairs and through the corridors, but Isak was not at the queen's door. Instead, he stood outside Aren's old chamber, watching them approach with dawning confusion.

"Captain?" he queried. He looked at the heavy door at his back as if it had beguiled him. He rapped on it sharply.

"Majesty?" he called.

"Why are you standing guard over the king's chamber, Isak?" Jerick asked, his voice uncharacteristically sharp.

"The queen went inside and closed the door, Majesty," Isak explained. "I've stood guard here since."

Kjell pushed into the room. The door was unbarred and the chamber beyond was empty. He rushed to the bathing chamber, to the wardrobe, to the narrow staircase that led to the king's private wine cellar. Kjell stared at the steps with growing horror.

"She never left this room, and no one went in," Isak insisted behind him.

"Kjell, there is a man at every entrance. Everyone is accounted for," Jerick reasoned.

"Everyone but the queen," Kjell said, trying desperately not to shout. "Did you ever leave the door, Isak?"

"No. I was here the entire time. I thought she was with you, Captain. I . . . was . . ." Isak stuttered. "I was trying to . . . respect your . . . privacy."

"She went through the tunnels in the cellar. She left the castle through the tunnels Jedah made before the battle," Kjell breathed, fisting his hands in his hair.

"Why would she do that, Captain?" Isak cried, incredulous.

"Isak," Jerick moaned. "You know why."

Sasha, who never let Kjell's men take him for granted, who threw herself over him to shield him from Volgar talons, who conspired to drug him and leave him in Brisson to protect him, who worried about the cost of his gift and her inability to spare him from suffering. Sasha would walk into the forest calling Lady Firi's name if she thought she could save him. Of that he had no doubt.

"How long? How long has it been since anyone saw her?" Kjell whispered, angrier at himself than the trembling guard. Kjell had stayed away to give her clarity, to give her time, to shield her from his impatience and his longing. And she'd slipped away.

"An hour, Captain," Isak answered, his lips tight, his eyes pleading for forgiveness.

"Find her," Kjell begged.

Isak descended the wine cellar stairs to enter the tunnels, his hands glowing and his feet quick, but Kjell did not follow. He knew where the tunnels led, and crawling through them on his hands and knees would take too long. Kjell ran from the castle keep, Jerick and a dozen of his men at his heels, but they separated at the edge of the woods, his men fanning out into the forest. Kjell hesitated, knowing he could not run in blind terror and hope to find her. He breathed, closing his eyes and pressing his hands to the bark of the watchful trees, petitioning them for their guidance and their direction. For a heartbeat his legs buckled and his head bowed.

"I am Kjell of Koorah. I carry the blood of Caarn. Please . . . help me find the queen."

The tree beneath his hands trembled, or maybe it simply moved with him, shuddering in dread and fear, but a long thin branch lowered and stretched, a skeletal finger pointing deeper into the grove. Kjell ran, not questioning the wisdom or instruction of the woods, and after several steps, he realized where he was.

Maybe Sasha had simply gone to sit beneath the bows of Aren's tree, making peace with what had passed. But the hour was late, and Kjell's instincts screamed that solace and silence among the trees was not the queen's design; Sasha had not slipped into the wood to kneel in remembrance in a sacred grove.

A twig snapped and a soft wind stirred, and for a moment he was certain he had found her, the gossamer spill of her dress like silver moth wings, dancing in and out of the light. He breathed her name, quickening his pace, but something made him hold his tongue.

It was Sasha's dress, but it wasn't Sasha.

Ariel of Firi darted through the grove, clothed in the queen's raiment, as if his words in the garden had pricked her vanity and her humanity. The gown pulled at her breasts and dragged through the underbrush, collecting bits of leaves and sticks that tore at the pale garment. The trees warned silence, but his heart could not comply. It thundered in his ears and sent his blood roaring through his veins as he crept forward, following the Changer.

Then the curious moon stepped out from behind the clouds and illuminated the clearing where Aren had crowned him king. Sasha waited there, bathed in moonlight, her bearing both regal and resigned, her unbound hair melding against the deep red of her dress, and her hands hanging loosely to her sides. She didn't hitch her skirts to flee, look to the trees for a place to hide, or call his name for rescue. She simply stood in the center of the grove, watching as Lady Firi approached, wearing her dress, as if she'd been expecting her all along.

Kjell drew up, struck by the terrible beauty of the scene, of the vicious serenity of the woman he loved quietly facing the woman he feared above all else.

He didn't know whether to charge through the trees, upsetting the hushed balance of life and death that permeated the grove, or to hold back, drawing his bow, and trusting in his ability to make the shot.

"It is time for you to go, Changer," Sasha said, her voice calm and oddly kind.

"It is time for you to die, Saoirse," Lady Firi crooned. The glee dripped from her words like the Volgar blood had seeped through the vines. She circled Sasha with scorn and confidence, smoothing her borrowed dress and prancing as though her feet were clothed in bejeweled slippers and not caked in the soil of Caarn.

Then the gown puddled and pooled, abandoned like snake scales, as Lady Firi grew claws and her face became feline. Silken black fur rippled over crouching limbs and a curling tail. She scampered up the wide base of Grandfather Tree and skulked along the widest bough, positioning herself above the queen.

It was the form she had taken during the battle for Jeru City. Kjell had seen her perched on the parapets, watching havoc unfold around her. She'd left her mark on Queen Lark but had been denied the kill, interrupted by an archer's arrow and Zoltev's wrath. She had shifted from shape to shape, purging the arrow in her side before reassuming the panther's grace, stalking along the ramparts the way she now padded along a low-hanging limb.

Sasha took three steps back as if bracing herself for battle. Then she lifted her chin to the Changer, an unmistakable challenge that evoked a bellow from Kjell's lungs, a denial that rang through the trees as he began to run, too far to save her, too close to deny the events unfolding before his eyes.

The panther leaped, a black slash against the pale light, her teeth barred, claws protracted, and Sasha raised her arms— almost as though she meant to embrace the beast —and was knocked to the ground. The cat roured, the sound like a thousand swords unsheathing in unison, and covered the queen, swallowing Sasha beneath its superior size.

Kjell hurtled through the trees, releasing one arrow after the other, screaming as the whistling shafts flew wide and long, missing his target. He flung his bow as he threw himself at the Changer, wrapping his arms around the body of the huge cat, rolling as he heaved the weight from atop the queen.

There was no resistance, no yowling flex of muscle or slashing teeth and claws. Kjell released the Changer and scrambled free, his eyes on the inert beast, shock and disbelief replacing the horror in his chest.

His blade, the blade he'd pressed into Sasha's hand before the second Volgar attack, protruded from the panther's chest, skewering its heart. He crawled to Sasha's side, running his hands over her body, begging the Creator for mercy and assistance.

She was gasping for breath, her eyes black and bottomless, her lips parted and panting, and Kjell moaned her name, the palms of his hands stained in blood and trembling with denial.

"Sasha," he begged. "Sasha, Sasha, Sasha."

Her breath shuddered and caught, then caught again, and her eyes fluttered closed in relief.

"She stole my breath, Captain. That is all," she whispered, her voice hitching on every word. "I am unharmed."

He caught her up, embracing her, feeling the warmth and the wet of spilled blood between them, a reminder of near death and deliverance. He began to shake, and she held him, pressing her lips to his neck, wrapping her arms around him, reassuring him.

But he needed distance between his beloved and the beast.

He half-crawled, half-staggered, dragging Sasha with him, moving so his back was braced against Aren's tree, Sasha across his lap. They watched as the inky black of the panther's fur became the pale skin of limbs and legs, the rise of a feminine hip and the fall of a narrow waist. Ariel of Firi, wrapped in the length of her matted hair, lay unmasked in death and stripped of her gift. The knife did not fall from her breast, expunged by the change, but remained buried deep, the hilt glittering and wet.

"All is well, Captain. It is done," Sasha soothed.

"You *saw* this. You knew this day would come," he cried, the knowledge flooding him as his heart quieted.

"I knew there would be a battle," she confessed. "And she would not protect her heart."

He started to laugh, incredulous relief robbing him of breath and sense, and then his laughter became a rasping moan, and he felt the heat and slide of tears down his cheeks, washing the blood from his skin and the fear from his heart.

"You are weeping, Captain," she whispered, and he heard the tremor in her voice as she clutched him to her.

"I am healing, Sasha," he said, and her mouth found his, administering her own cure, tasting the salt of past sorrow, relieving the weight of old wounds. For several moments he returned her kiss, gratitude falling from their tangled tongues and urgent lips, hushed whispers and professions of love moving between their mouths.

He rose, drawing her up with him, wanting to be free of the grove where his queen had faced the Changer and kings went to die. But Sasha held back, stepping from his arms and turning back to the dead woman with the same compassion she approached everything else.

"We cannot leave her here," Sasha protested. "Not like that. This is a sacred place."

"I will send Isak to turn her body to ash. He has suffered this night. He will be relieved to see it end."

"I think we should ask the trees," she said, turning to the largest oak in the grove. With complete confidence, she pressed her palms to the bark, speaking with the firm authority of a monarch.

"I am Queen Saoirse of Caarn. I carry the blood of Caarn. I ask that you return the body of the woman who lies dead beneath your boughs to the earth from whence she came."

Like the day on the road to Caarn, a day that felt like a lifetime ago, the ground quaked beneath their feet, and the biddable tree exhumed its roots. Enormous fingers shook off the soil and curled around the body of the Changer, dragging her into the earth and swallowing her whole. The ground trembled again, the leaves sighed, and Ariel of Firi was no more, freeing him at last. Even the furrows were softly filled, the loose dirt sliding back into place as the roots retreated with their dead.

Sasha moved to his side, slipping her hand into his.

"You carry the blood of Caarn?" Kjell asked, not understanding.

"I am carrying the blood of Caarn," she said, her eyes rising to his.

He drew back, gazing down at her, still flummoxed.

"Your child—a child of Caarn—grows within me," she explained gently.

"My child . . . grows . . . within you," he stammered.

"Yes, Captain."

He staggered, and Sasha steadied him, wrapping her arms around his waist. He pressed his lips to her hair, to her cheeks, dropping to his knees so he could press his hands to the slight swell between her hips. Then he pulled her toward him, replacing his hands with his mouth, reverent and reeling. For a moment he could only pray to the god of fortune and the creator of all things. He didn't pray with words but with the overflowing of his spirit, his lips pressed to the womb of the woman who stood before him.

"I have not forgiven you for coming out here alone," he whispered against her body.

"You will," she said, stroking his hair.

He swept her up, needing to be as close to her as he could, and began walking back to the castle, weaving through the forest, her body clutched to his chest.

"I can walk, Captain," she murmured, her head tucked beneath his chin, her lips touching his heart.

"I want to hold you a little longer," he said. And she did not deny him.

The sentry above the rear castle gate cried out in alarm as he saw Kjell approach through the trees, the queen in his arms.

"Majesty!"

"Open the gate. All is well," Kjell called.

"You should let me walk, Captain," Sasha pressed. "You will frighten everyone."

"I don't care. I will do as I wish. For once, I will do as I bloody wish."

Sasha was right. She often was. The guard poured from the castle and the grounds, their search for the queen ending back where it began. They rushed to Kjell's side, distressed, peppering him with questions that Sasha fielded with calm reassurance.

Padrig, his long robes streaming after him, was not far behind.

"Is she injured?" he asked, trembling, his eyes clinging to the blood darkening the red of Sasha's gown.

"No. But we are in need of your services, Spinner," Kjell said.

"Anything, Majesty," Padrig said, nodding eagerly.

"I wish to marry the queen."

Padrig gaped and Jerick snorted.

"N-now?" Padrig stuttered.

"Now."

"Can we change our clothes, Highness?" Sasha asked, her voice mild but her eyes dancing.

He hesitated, unwilling to let something as inconsequential as clothing detain them. He would not wait any longer.

"I will not make vows covered in Ariel of Firi's blood," Sasha insisted softly. "And I will not marry the King of Caarn in the dead of night, as if I am ashamed to be his queen. We will welcome all of Caarn—all of Dendar—to witness the marriage."

Kjell sighed, still not releasing her. "Soon?" he grumbled.

"Soon," she reassured.

"If we can prepare for a battle in two days, we can prepare for a celebration in the same amount of time," he insisted. Padrig opened his mouth to argue, but Kjell silenced him with a look. "The day after tomorrow, I will marry the queen, Star Maker. Let it be written. Let it be done."

"Kjell of Jeru, son of Koorah, King of Caarn, will wed Queen Saoirse of Caarn, daughter of the late Lord Pierce and the late Lady Sareca of Kilmorda. May the God of Words and Creation seal their union for the good of Caarn," Boom announced from the watchtower, shouting the words to the quaking trees, the impatient king, and to all the people of Caarn.

Kjell worried the people would not come, that the queen would be ashamed, and the celebration shunned. He wouldn't allow it, wouldn't abide it, and had already drawn up his first royal edict to make sure it didn't happen.

But all of Caarn came. They came bearing flowers and well-wishes, food and song, and when Padrig raised his arms to the heavens, declaring the couple man and wife, the people wept. The King's Guard wept too, baptizing the moment their captain bowed his head and kissed his queen, reaching the end of one journey and eager to start another.

The festivities interrupted by the queen's warning less than a month before were cheerfully resumed, long life and true love were toasted without reservation, and faith in the future of Caarn was joyfully reestablished. But when the villagers departed and the castle was cloaked in slumber, the king held his queen in the soft light of the closest stars, repeating the promises he'd made beneath the cliffs of Quondoon, when he'd been lonely and she'd been lost, and the future had not yet been fulfilled.

Kjell whispered in Sasha's ear, sing-song and coaxing, "Can you hear me, woman? Come sing with me."

"Come to me, and I will try to heal you. I will try to heal you, if you but come back," Sasha sang softly, the melody sweet, the lyrics heartfelt, and it fell from her lips in a husky plea.

"Come to me, and I will give you shelter, I will give you shelter, if you but come back," he added, picking up where she left off. His lips brushed the lobe of her ear, and he felt the shudder that swept from the crown of her head to the tips of her toes. Her heart galloped, her skin grew damp beneath his, and he continued to chant, making the promise all over again.

"Come to me, and I will try to love you. I will try to love you, if you but come back."

He heard a single, solitary tolling that grew between them, around them and within them, deep and demanding, and Kjell lifted his voice, grasping the pitch and pulling the tone from her pounding heart. It grew and grew, and still he hummed until her pulse resonated in his skin, in his skull, behind his eyes, and deep in his belly. He was euphoric, vibrating with sound and triumph, his hands smoothing back crimson hair from speckled cheeks and staring down into eyes so dark they appeared infinite. Their gazes locked, and for a moment, there was only reverberation between them.

"I saw you," she whispered, her body quaking and her fingers caressing his face. Kjell leaned in, filling his hands with her hair and his mouth with her kiss.

"I saw you," he said against her lips. "And I never looked away."

EPILOGUE

Light glanced off of the empty throne and streaked across the wide room, peeking around corners and climbing the walls. Silence was the only occupant. Something fluttered overhead, breaking the stillness. Vines with leaves so emerald they appeared black in the shadows, wrapped their way around the rocks and past the windows, filtering the light and casting the interior in a wash of green. The castle was holding her breath. She'd been holding her breath for so long.

Then, through the stillness, a cry rang out, lusty and strong, and the castle released her breath on a long sigh. The child had arrived. A girl. The first daughter of King Kjell and Queen Saoirse, a new daughter of Caarn. Her mother had longed for her, her father rejoiced when she was placed in his arms, and her brothers—all four of them—gazed down at her with varying degrees of adoration and distrust. Princess Koorah had finally arrived.

The staff had been busy in anticipation of her birth. The happiness of the day clung and quivered, breathing welcome and promise to all who entered there. The wood shone, the tapestries glowed, and in the corridor, the portraits of the kings had been carefully dusted. The row of painted royals looked down on passersby, pale-haired and softly smiling. Except for the last. His hair was dark, his eyes fierce, and his mouth turned down. He wore his crown of gold as though it were a crown of thorns, sharp and uncomfortable against his brow. The woman beside him in the picture—her own crown as natural to her as the golden flecks on her skin—gazed up at him with soft eyes and curved lips, his hand clutched in hers. She rarely let go.

Some speculated that young Kjell, the oldest prince of Caarn, was actually the son of the late king. He was born six months after Aren died and the Healer made vows to the Seer. But as he grew, few had doubts as to his sire. He was big for his age and had the same pale eyes and dark hair as his father. When people saw him, they always knew.

His mother had caught him with his head tipped, listening to things she couldn't hear, mimicking a melody she hadn't taught him. His father had shown him how to press gentle fingers to the breast of a dying bird, and together they'd watched it fly away, whole.

Twin boys—Gibbous and Peter in honor of the men who'd lost their lives on the Jyraen Sea—were born two years after their older brother. Their red hair and vivid eyes gave them the look of mischievous elves, and Grandfather Tree recognized their small hands and their climbing feet, widening his boughs and spreading his branches to catch them should they fall. The walls of their nursery were constantly flowering, and the castle staff had found a stalk of corn growing in Peter's chest of drawers.

When King Kjell declared his fourth son Lucian Maximus, everyone commented on the fine name and never knew it was chosen to honor a beloved horse and a patient dog. Lucian Maximus longed to run and fly and swim, not unlike his namesakes, and the first time he changed he was only three years old. Queen Saoirse found a small bear in her young son's cradle and got her first grey hair.

Caarn had grown. Dendar had flourished. People had returned, and the Volgar had not. Animals roamed the hills and the surrounding fields. Grazing cattle and galloping horses dotted the countryside. Dogs barked, lazy cats sunned themselves on the rock walls, and the chickens clucked and strutted, chastising the pigs in their pens.

The forests had grown too, welcoming the Spinners of Caarn when their days grew numbered, watching over the valley that thrived and spread. The trees were not aware of the passing of days or the turn of the seasons. They simply grew, keeping their patient vigil, graciously sharing their gifts. Sometimes the Healer, a son of Caarn, would walk among them with reverent hands, greeting them and whispering thanks, and the trees would nod their leafy heads, thanking him in return.

OTHER TITLES

Young Adult and Paranormal Romance

Slow Dance in Purgatory

Prom Night in Purgatory

Inspirational Romance

A Different Blue

Running Barefoot

Making Faces

Infinity + One

The Law of Moses

The Song of David

Historical Fiction

From Sand and Ash

Romantic Fantasy

The Bird and The Sword

ACKNOWLEDGMENTS

To my husband and my children, thank you. At the end of a project I'm always tired, overwrought, and irritable. But you all still love me. Every time.

To my assistant, Tamara, thank you for making time for me in your life, for keeping me organized and efficient, for filling in ever-growing gaps. Your friendship over these last years has been one of the best parts of my writing success.

To Nicole Karlson, your effusive praise and late night messages gave me so much encouragement on this project. You love this book, and because you love it, I was able to love it more.

To my publishers around the world, to my readers in every corner, to the bloggers and tweeters, book groups and book-grammers, thank you for spreading the love for my books. I am indebted to you.

To Jane Dystel and Lauren Abramo, thank you for your support and for taking care of me. I am always reassured that I am working with the best literary agents in the world.

To Karey White, you are such a blessing. Thank you for editing for me, for knowing your stuff, and for keeping it real, always.

ABOUT THE AUTHOR

Amy Harmon is a *Wall Street Journal, USA Today*, and *New York Times* Bestselling author. Amy knew at an early age that writing was something she wanted to do, and she divided her time between writing songs and stories as she grew. Having grown up in the middle of wheat fields without a television, with only her books and her siblings to entertain her, she developed a strong sense of what made a good story. Her books are now being published in fifteen different languages, truly a dream come true for a little country girl from Levan, Utah.

Amy Harmon has written eleven novels — the *USA Today* Bestsellers, The Bird and The Sword, Making Faces and Running Barefoot, as well as From Sand and Ash, The Law of Moses, The Song of David, Infinity + One, and the *New York Times*

Bestseller, A Different Blue. Her recent release, The Bird and the Sword, is a Goodreads Best Fantasy of 2016 finalist.

Website:
http://www.authoramyharmon.com/

Facebook:
https://www.facebook.com/authoramyharmon

Twitter:
https://twitter.com/aharmon_author

Instagram:
https://www.instagram.com/amy.harmon2/

Newsletter:
http://eepurl.com/46ciz

Goodreads:
www.goodreads.com/author/show/5829056.Amy_Harmon

Pinterest:
https://pinterest.com/authoramyharmon/

BookBub:
https://www.bookbub.com/authors/amy-harmon

Made in the USA
Lexington, KY
28 May 2017